The
SARA
CRAVEN
Collection

TITLES IN THIS SERIES

JUNE 1987
Carole Mortimer   BURNING OBSESSION
ELUSIVE LOVER

AUGUST 1987
Janet Dailey   THAT CAROLINA SUMMER
WITH A LITTLE LUCK

OCTOBER 1987
Charlotte Lamb   STRANGER IN THE NIGHT
A WILD AFFAIR

DECEMBER 1987
Penny Jordan   FORGOTTEN PASSION
PHANTOM MARRIAGE

FEBRUARY 1988
Sara Craven   COUNTERFEIT BRIDE
PAGAN ADVERSARY

APRIL 1988
Penny Jordan   CAMPAIGN FOR LOVING
THE DARKER SIDE OF DESIRE

COUNTERFEIT BRIDE

COUNTERFEIT BRIDE

BY

SARA CRAVEN

MILLS & BOON LIMITED
Eton House, 18–24 Paradise Road
Richmond, Surrey TW9 1SR

First published in Great Britain 1982
by Mills & Boon Limited

© Sara Craven 1982

Australian copyright 1982
Philippine copyright 1982
Reprinted 1982
This edition 1988

ISBN 0 263 76069 3

Set in Monophoto Times 10 on 10½ pt
19–0288–59205

Printed and bound in Great Britain by
Cox & Wyman Ltd, Reading

CHAPTER ONE

'You know something?' Elaine Fairmont announced. 'I'm really going to miss Mexico.'

Nicola looked up from the files she was packing into a carton, her lips curving in amusement.

'What's prompted this sudden, if belated, change of heart?' she enquired. 'I thought nothing in Mexico City could possibly compare with Los Angeles?'

'Well, I've been giving the matter some thought, and I've decided that actually they have quite a lot in common,' Elaine said solemnly. She began to count off on her fingers. 'There's the traffic and the smog—and the possibility of earthquakes—we mustn't forget those. Of course L.A. isn't actually sinking into a lake as far as I know, but the San Andreas fault could change all that.'

'It could indeed,' Nicola agreed, her eyes dancing. 'I suppose there's no chance that you'll change your mind a step further and come with me on my sightseeing trip?'

Elaine shook her head. 'No, honey. To me a ruin is a ruin, and who needs them? I'm no tourist, and besides, I've read about those Aztecs, and they had some pretty creepy habits. I'm not going back to L.A. with nightmares.' She paused. 'I suppose you haven't changed your mind either?'

'About returning to California with Trans-Chem?' It was Nicola's turn to shake her head. 'No, I've thoroughly enjoyed working for them, but this contract was really just a means to an end—a way of letting me see Mexico.' And a way of getting me as far away from Zurich and from Ewan as possible, she thought with a pang.

'So, sign another contract and see the U.S.A.,' Elaine

suggested amiably. 'Martin's all set to fix you up with a work permit the moment you say the word, and all my folks are dying to meet you.'

Nicola smiled. 'It's very tempting, I admit. But I'm not sure where I want to work next time. I think it will almost certainly be Europe again.'

'Then why not Spain?' Elaine asked. 'Your Spanish is terrific, thanks to Teresita's coaching. It would be a great chance to make use of it.'

'Perhaps.' Nicola gave a slight grimace. 'Actually I'd planned on finding somewhere a little more liberated next time.'

Elaine laughed. 'Don't tell me you've gotten tired of all this *guera preciosa* as you walk down the street?'

'I hate it.' There was a sudden intensity in Nicola's tone which made Elaine glance curiously at her before she returned to her task of feeding unwanted documents into the shredder. 'It's insulting. I haven't any illusions about my attractions, such as they are, and I don't need my ego boosted by meaningless compliments from total strangers. "Precious light-haired one" indeed! It's not even a particularly valid description,' she added, tugging at a strand of her tawny sun-streaked hair. 'Surely you of all people can't go along with this incessant reduction of women to mere sex objects?'

Elaine lifted a negligent shoulder. 'It doesn't really bother me. It's harmless as long as you don't take it seriously, or respond in any way, and I quite like being admired. The Women's Lib movement isn't the whole answer, you know. I've seen what it's done to people—to my own sister, in fact. She was happily married, or she sure seemed to be until someone started raising her consciousness. Now she's divorced, the kids cry all the time, and there's endless hassle with lawyers about alimony, and who gets the car and the ice-box.'

Nicola closed the carton and fastened it with sealing tape.

'That's rather going to extremes,' she said. 'What I

can't get used to is the attitude here that a woman is just—an adjunct to a man. Industrially, Mexico is making giant strides, but there are some things still which haven't changed from the days of the conquistadores—and that's what I find so hard to take. Well, look at Teresita, for instance.'

'I'm looking,' Elaine agreed. 'What's her problem?'

'Everything.' Nicola spread her hands helplessly. 'There's this guardian of hers. She's been sharing our apartment for three months now, and she still hasn't told him. He thinks she's living in that convent hostel, and from things she's said, I gather even that was a concession.'

Nicola's tone became heated, and Elaine smiled.

'Calm down,' she advised. 'If there was ever anyone who doesn't need our sympathy, then it's Teresita.'

'You mean because she's actually going to escape from the trap?' Nicola reached for another carton. 'I suppose you're right.'

'No, that wasn't what I meant,' Elaine said drily. 'Nor am I too sure she is going to escape, as you put it.'

Nicola put down the files she was holding, and stared at the other girl with growing concern.

'But of course she will, when she marries Cliff. He won't keep her chained up. Or are you saying you don't think they will get married?' When Elaine nodded, she burst out, 'But that's ridiculous! You've said yourself you've never seen two people so much in love. Why, she's living for him to get back from Chicago, you know she is.'

'Sure,' Elaine said. 'Teresita and Cliff are the year's most heartwarming sight—but marriage?' She shook her head. 'I don't think so. Do you imagine that guardian of hers is going to allow her to throw herself away on a mere chemical engineer?'

'Perhaps he won't care,' said Nicola. 'After all, he doesn't take a great deal of interest in her. He never comes to see her—which is just as well under the circumstances—and his letters are few and far between.'

'True, but that doesn't mean he won't get good and interested if she plans to marry someone he doesn't approve of.'

'But why shouldn't he approve of Cliff? Apart from being one of the nicest guys you could wish to meet, he's well qualified, has a good job, and is more than able to support a wife.'

Elaine shrugged. 'I have a feeling that he'll need a lot more than that to be acceptable as husband material for Teresita. Just consider—since we've known her, how many paying jobs has she had?'

'Only one,' Nicola acknowledged. 'The couple of weeks she spent here as receptionist.'

'Right,' said Elaine. 'And were we surprised that other offers didn't come her way—considering that as a receptionist she was a walking, talking disaster area?'

Nicola grinned, remembering the mislaid messages, misunderstandings, and interrupted telephone calls which had distinguished Teresita's brief sojourn at the reception desk. No one had the least idea how she had ever got the job while the regular girl was on holiday, or how she had lasted in it for longer than five minutes, although Elaine had commented that the management had probably been too dazed by the whole experience to fire her.

'No, we weren't in the least surprised,' she said, and hesitated. 'But she does work.'

'Social work—with the nuns—unpaid,' Elaine pointed out. 'And very estimable too. So, where does she get the money to pay her share of the rent, and buy all those gorgeous clothes that she has—all those little numbers from the boutiques in the Zona Rosa? Not to mention her jewellery.'

'What about her jewellery? It's rather flamboyant, but . . .'

'It's entitled to be flamboyant. It's also real,' Elaine said drily.

There was a small, shaken silence then Nicola said, 'You must be joking.'

'I promise I'm not. I have an uncle who's a jeweller in Santa Barbara, and I spent some of my formative years learning to pick the fake from the real stuff. I'm not making any mistake.'

'My God!' Nicola put her hands to her face. 'She lent me—she actually lent me her pearls that time we all went out to dinner.'

'I remember,' Elaine nodded. 'They looked good on you.'

'That isn't the point,' Nicola almost wailed. 'Suppose I'd lost them—or they'd been stolen?'

'You didn't, and they weren't, and they'll be insured anyway,' Elaine said reasonably. 'But we're getting away from the subject here. What I'm saying is that Teresita isn't just a nice girl we met, who shares our apartment and cooks up the greatest *enchiladas* in Mexico. She's also a rich lady, and if this guardian of hers knows what he's doing, he'll want to marry her money to more money, because that's the way things are, so Cliff and she may have some problems. That's all.'

It was enough, Nicola thought unhappily. She said, 'Teresita's of age, so there's nothing to stop her getting married, if she wants to, and she does want to.'

'Don't sound so fierce! Okay, so she and Cliff are Romeo and Juliet all over again, and she is a very sweet gentle girl. No one would argue. But she's led a very sheltered life. She was practically brought up by nuns, after all, and she'd still be living in that hostel if we hadn't invited her to move in with us. I'm amazed that she ever agreed anyway, and she still trails round to the convent to see if there's any mail for her each day because she's scared her guardian may find out that she's left—because basically she knows in her heart that if he cracks the whip she'll jump, whether she's of age or not.' She paused, giving Nicola a quizzical look. 'And if she dare not tell him she's sharing an apartment in a good part of town with a couple of *gringas*, then just how is she going to break the news that she's engaged to a *norteamericano*?'

'It's rather different,' Nicola argued. 'If he'd forbidden her to leave the hostel, she'd have been unhappy perhaps, but it wouldn't have been the end of the world. But if he makes any objection to her marrying Cliff, then it will break her heart. She might have yielded to pressure over the apartment issue, but not over Cliff. I'm sure of it.'

'Well, you have a touching faith in her will power which I don't share.' Elaine turned back to her paper-shredding. 'I guess we'd better get on with the packing. The place already looks as if we'd moved out.'

'Yes,' said Nicola with a little sigh.

She hadn't expected to enjoy her stay with Trans-Chem. She knew very little about the technicalities of chemical plants and their construction and was happy in her ignorance. She'd just been desperate for some kind of contract which would take her away from Zurich, and ensure that she wasn't there to see Ewan marry the stolid blonde daughter of his company chairman.

Nor had she really expected to get the job, although she knew that the fact that she already spoke Spanish, garnered from an intensive course at the Polytechnic where she'd undergone her secretarial training, would stand her in good stead. Trans-Chem were after all an American company, and most of their personnel were recruited in the States, as Elaine had been.

But the job was offered to her, and she accepted with a growing excitement which helped to alleviate some of the pain and humiliation Ewan had made her suffer. She had fallen so deeply in love with him that it seemed impossible for him not to share her feelings. In fact, he did share them. He admitted as much, but it made no difference to his plans. Ewan intended to marry well, and a mere secretary earning her own living didn't fill the bill as a potential bride at all. Although he did have other plans for her, as Nicola had shamingly discovered when finally he had been forced to tell her that his marriage to Greta was imminent.

She'd sat in the circle of his arms, feeling as if she'd been turned to stone, while part of her mind registered incredulously that he was telling her that his marriage needn't make any difference, that it could even be an advantage. When the promotion which his future father-in-law had promised as a certainty finally materialised, then he would have Nicola transferred to his office as his own secretary. There would be business trips which they would make together, he'd said, and he would help her to find a bigger flat where they could be together as often as possible.

She sat there in silence, listening to his voice, to the confidence in it as he made his sordid plans, and wondered why he should have thought she would ever agree to any such thing, when they had never even been lovers in the generally accepted sense. She had often asked herself what had held her back from that ultimate commitment, and could find no answer except perhaps that there had always been a deep, barely acknowledged instinct which she had obeyed, warning her not to trust too blindly, or to give herself without that trust.

When she was able to think more rationally about what had happened, she knew she ought to feel relief that she hadn't that particular bitterness to add to her disillusionment, but it had seemed cold comfort then, and still did.

She had come to Mexico determined not to make a fool of herself again, and her bitterness had been her shield, not merely against the Mexican men whose persistent attempts to flirt with her had at first annoyed and later amused her, but also against the mainly male American staff of Trans-Chem, many of whom would have shown more than a passing interest in her, if she had allowed them to.

Sometimes she wished she could be more like Elaine, who uninhibitedly enjoyed a series of casual relationships, and wept no tears when they were over. Nicola was aware that some of the men had privately dubbed her 'Snow Queen', and although it had stung a little at the time, she had come to welcome the nickname as a form of protection.

What she hadn't realised was that some men, observing the curve of tawny hair falling to her shoulders, the green eyes with their long fringe of lashes, the small straight nose, and the wilful line of the mouth, would still be sufficiently attracted to find her determined coolness a turn-on, forcing her to an open cruelty which she wouldn't have been capable of before Ewan came into her life.

'My God,' Elaine said once. 'You don't fool around when you're giving someone the brush-off! Poor Craig has gone back to the States convinced he has terminal halitosis.'

Nicola flushed. 'I can't help it. I try to make it clear that I'm not interested, and then they get persistent, so what can I do?'

'You could try saying yes for once.' Elaine gave her a measuring look. 'Whatever went wrong in Zurich, sooner or later some guy's going to come along and make you forget all about it, only you have to give him a chance.'

'Perhaps,' Nicola said woodenly. 'But I can promise you that it's no one I've met so far.'

Probably there never would be anyone, she thought. She was on her guard now. Indeed, she had sometimes wondered if she would have fallen for Ewan quite so hard if she hadn't been confused and lonely, away from home for the first time.

Travelling, seeing the world, had always been her own idea ever since childhood, and her parents, recognising the wanderlust they did not share, had given her the loving encouragement she needed. Her undoubted gift for languages had been the original spur, and she was fluent in French and German before she had left school.

Nicola wondered sometimes where the urge to travel had come from. Her parents were so serenely content on their farm at Barton Abbas in Somerset. It was their world, and they needed nothing better, no matter how much they might enjoy her letters and photographs and stories of faraway places. And Robert, her younger brother, was the same. One day the farm would be his, and that would be enough for him too. But not for her. Never for her.

Now, she wasn't altogether sure what she wanted. Working for Trans-Chem had been more enjoyable than she could ever have anticipated. The company expected high standards of efficiency, but at the same time treated her with a friendly informality which she had never experienced in any previous job, and certainly not in Zurich. And they had been keen, as their contract to assist in a consultative capacity with the building of a new plant in Mexico's expanding chemical industry began to wind up, for her to work for them in the States on a temporary basis at least.

Nicola didn't really know why she'd refused. Certainly she had nothing better in mind, and there would have been no problem in fitting in her longed-for and saved-for sightseeing tour first. Yet refuse she did, and for no better reason than that she felt oddly restless.

Perhaps it was the anticipation of her holiday which was making her feel this way. The last months had been hectic, and the past few weeks of clearing out the office and packing up especially so.

She would miss Elaine, she thought. She'd been a little taken aback when she first arrived in Mexico City to find that she had a readymade flatmate waiting for her. How did she know that she and this tall redhaired Californian were ever going to get along well enough to share a home? And yet from the very first day, they'd had no real problems. And then, later, Teresita had made three . . .

Nicola smiled to herself. Had there ever been a more oddly assorted trio? she wondered. Elaine with her cool laconic humour, and relaxed enjoyment of life, Teresita the wealthy orphan, shy and gentle and almost morbidly in awe of the guardian she never saw—and Nicola herself, a mass of hang-ups, as Elaine had once not unkindly remarked.

In some way, Nicola almost envied Teresita. At least she had few doubts about the world and her place in it. Her upbringing in the seclusion of the convent school had been geared to readying her for marriage, and a subservient role in a male-dominated society. The purpose of her life was to be someone's wife and the mother of his children, and she seemed to accept that as a matter of course.

Even her one small act of rebellion against her strictly ordered existence, her decision to move into the apartment with Nicola and Elaine, had contributed towards her chosen destiny, because without it, it was unlikely that her relationship with Cliff Arnold could have prospered.

They had met during Teresita's brief but eventful spell at the Trans-Chem reception desk. Cliff had been one of many finding himself suddenly cut off in the middle of an important call, and he had erupted into the reception area looking for someone to murder, then stopped, as someone remarked later, as if he'd been poleaxed, as he looked down into Teresita's heart-shaped face, and listened to her huskily voiced apologies. His complaints forgotten, he had spent the next half hour, and many more after that, showing her how to operate the switchboard.

As Elaine had caustically commented, it had improved nothing, but at least they'd had a good time.

Cliff had been a constant visitor at the apartment after Teresita moved in. He had adapted without apparent difficulty to the demands of an old-fashioned courtship, bringing gifts—bottles of wine, bunches of flowers, and once even a singing bird in a cage. Teresita sang too, all round the apartment, small happy songs betokening the inner radiance which showed in her shining eyes and flushed cheeks.

That was how love should be, Nicola thought, bringing its own certainty and security, imposing its welcome obligations. Perhaps it was the constant exposure to Teresita's transparent happiness which was making her so restless. Not that there'd been much radiance about lately, she reminded herself drily. Cliff had been sent to Chicago for a few weeks and in his absence Teresita had drooped like a neglected flower. But he was due to return during the next few days, and Nicola was sure they would be announcing their engagement at the very least as soon as he came back.

That was if Teresita managed to break the news to her guardian, the remote and austere Don Luis Alvarado de Montalba. She seemed very much in awe of him, reluctant even to mention his name, but Nicola had still gleaned a certain amount of information about him.

He was wealthy and powerful, that went without saying. At one time, his family had owned vast cattle estates in the north, but later they had begun to diversify, to invest in industry and in fruit and coffee plantations, apparently foreseeing the time when the huge ranches would be broken up into smaller units and the landowners' monopolies broken.

Not that any government-inspired reforms seemed to have made a great deal of difference to the Montalbas, she thought. They still owned the ranch, although its size had been reduced, as well as a town house in Monterrey where much of their industrial interest was concentrated, and a luxurious villa near Acapulco. Nicola gathered that Teresita's father had been a business colleague of Don Luis, and this was why she had been assigned to his guardianship after her parents had been tragically drowned in a flash-flood some years before.

Clearly, his guardianship operated more on a financial and business level than a personal one. Teresita had admitted candidly that it was over a year since he had visited her, and she seemed more relieved than otherwise at this state of affairs.

Clearly he was the type of aloof and imposing grandee who would be incapable of putting a young girl at her ease, Nicola thought. Teresita always behaved as if even to talk about him was a form of *lèse-majeste*.

Nicola could just picture him—elderly with heavy moustaches, perhaps even a beard, probably overweight, pompous and arrogant. She hoped fervently that Elaine was wrong and he wouldn't make an attempt to interfere in Teresita's happiness. There was no reason why he should, she thought. Cliff was no fortune-hunter, even if he didn't have the sort of wealth that the Montalba family had at its disposal.

She fastened the last carton, sealed and labelled it, then sat back on her heels with a sigh.

'So that's done. I could murder a cup of coffee. Do you think the machine's still working?'

'If so it's the only thing in the building that is, apart from us,' said Elaine. 'In my next life, I'm coming back as a boss. You finish up here, and I'll go see about this coffee.'

She was gone for some time, and Nicola guessed that the machine, never enthusiastic about its function at the best of times, had finally given up the ghost and that Elaine had called to buy coffee at the small restaurant a few doors away.

She wandered over to the window and stood looking down into the square. The noise of the traffic seemed muted in the midday heat and from the street below she could hear the plaintive strains of a barrel-organ. The organ-grinder was there most days, and she knew his repertoire almost by heart, but today the jangling notes seemed to hold an extra poignancy, and she felt unbidden tears start to her eyes.

She was being a fool she told herself. What had she got to cry about? She'd had a marvellous time in Mexico City, and within a few days she would be embarking on the holiday of a lifetime. Unlike Elaine she had always been fascinated by the history of the New World, and her tour had been carefully planned to take in as many of the great archeological sites as possible. She found herself saying some of the names under her breath—Palenque, Uxmal, Chichen Itza. Great pyramids, towering temples, ancient pagan gods—she'd dreamed of such things, and soon, very soon, all her dreams would come true. So why in hell was she standing here snivelling? She heard the outer door open and slam in the corridor, and turned hastily, smearing the tears from her face with clumsy fingers, hoping that Elaine would not notice or be too tactful to comment.

As the office door crashed open, she made herself smile.

'You've been long enough,' she began teasingly. 'Did you have to pick the beans personally or . . .'

She stopped short, her eyes widening in disbelief as she studied the dishevelled, woebegone figure in front of her.

'Teresita!' she gasped. '*Querida*, what is it? Has something happened? Are you ill?' Her heart sank as she saw Teresita's brimming eyes. 'Cliff—oh, my God, has something happened to Cliff?'

'No,' Teresita said. 'He is well—he is fine—and I shall never see him again.' And she burst into hysterical tears.

Nicola had got her into a chair and was trying to calm her when Elaine returned with two paper cups of coffee.

'I guess I should have brought something stronger,'

she remarked as she put the cups down on the nearest desk. 'What's wrong?'

'I wish I knew.' Nicola scrabbled through drawers until she came across a box of tissues in the last one. 'All she keeps saying is that she wants to die, and begging our Lady of Guadeloupe to take her.'

Elaine raised her brows. 'Clearly, she means business. Talk to her in Spanish, Nicky. She may make more sense that way.'

Nicola mustered her thoughts and said crisply 'Stop crying, Teresita. If we can help you we will, but first we must understand why you're so distressed.'

Teresita was still sobbing, but she was making an effort to control herself. When she spoke, Nicola could just make out the whispered words, 'I am to be married.'

'Yes, we know that.' Nicola passed her another tissue. 'To Cliff, just as soon as it can be arranged—so what is there to cry about?'

Teresita shook her head. 'It is not so.' Her voice was steadying, becoming more coherent. 'Today I visited the convent to pray in the chapel for Cliff's safe return. The Reverend Mother, she tells me there is a letter for me, and I see at once it is from my guardian, Don Luis. I read the letter. *Madre de Dios*, I read it and I wish only to die!'

'You mean he's forbidden you to marry Cliff?' Nicola asked sharply.

'He does not yet know that Cliff exists,' Teresita said bleakly. 'Always I have waited for the right time to tell him, because I feared his anger.'

'Will someone please fill me in on what's going on?' Elaine demanded plaintively.

'I wish I knew myself,' said Nicola, hurriedly outlining the gist of the conversation so far.

'It's obviously this letter,' Elaine said. She crouched beside Teresita's chair, taking her hands in hers. 'Hey, honey, what was in the letter? Does the mighty Don Luis want you to marry someone else? Is that it?'

Choking back a sob, Teresita nodded, and Elaine darted Nicola a sober glance which said 'I told you so' more clearly and loudly than any words could have done.

'Tomorrow,' Teresita said. 'Tomorrow I must leave Mexico City and travel to Monterrey with Ramón. Later we shall be married.'

'You and this Ramón? Just like that?' Nicola demanded, horrified.

Teresita's eyes widened. 'Not Ramón, no. He is just the cousin of Don Luis. I met him once when I was a child.'

'For heaven's sake,' Elaine muttered, and Nicola said hastily, 'I'm sorry, darling, we're trying to understand. But if Ramón isn't the bridegroom then who . . .?'

'It is Don Luis.' Teresita's voice was flat.

Nicola muttered 'My God!' and Elaine's lips pursed in a silent whistle.

'Nice one, Don Luis,' she approved. 'Nothing like keeping the cash where it belongs—in the family.'

'It is what my father intended. I have always known this,' Teresita said tonelessly. 'But, as time passed, and he said nothing, I began to hope that it would never happen. A man so much older than myself, a man who has known so many women.' For a moment, a world of knowledge that the good sisters had never instilled showed on the heart-shaped face. 'I—I allowed myself to hope that perhaps he would choose elsewhere— perhaps even marry Carlota Garcia.'

'Just who is that?' Elaine asked.

Teresita gave a slight shrug. 'A—a friend of his. Her husband was a politician. She has been a widow now for several years, and their names have been coupled together many times. A girl—one of the boarders at the convent—told me it was known that she was his— *amiga*. She said it was impossible that he would marry me because I was too much of a child for him, accustomed as he is to women of the world.'

Disgust rose bitterly in Nicola. Not just elderly and arrogant, but mercenary and a womaniser into the bargain.

She said hotly, 'You can't marry him, Teresita. Write to him. Tell him it's all off. He can't make you.'

Teresita almost cowered in her chair. 'I cannot disobey.' Her voice shook. 'Tomorrow I must leave for Monterrey in Ramón's charge. You do not know Don Luis—his anger—how he would be if I wrote him such a letter.'

'But he must know that you don't love him—that you're even frightened of him,' Nicola argued stubbornly.

Teresita sighed. 'My mother would have said that it is a good thing to respect the man that one must marry—and that love can follow marriage,' she added doubtfully.

'When you already love Cliff?'

Teresita's mouth quivered. 'That was craziness, a dream. I must forget him now that Don Luis has spoken at last.'

'Oh, no, you mustn't,' Nicola said forcefully. 'Teresita, you can't let yourself be pushed around like this. Your father may have intended you to marry Don Luis at one time, but if he was here now, and knew Cliff, and realised how you felt about him, I know he'd change his mind.' She looked across at Elaine, who gave a silent shrug. She tried again. 'Why don't you and Cliff elope?'

For a moment, a hopeful light shone in Teresita's eyes, then she crumpled again.

'He is in Chicago.'

'Well, I know that, but we could cable him, tell him it's an emergency and he has to get back right away,' said Nicola.

Teresita shook her head. 'I must leave tomorrow. There is no time for him to return.'

'Then he'll just have to follow you to Monterrey and make Don Luis see reason.'

'It would be no use. Don Luis would not receive him, or allow me to see him.' Teresita spread her hands helplessly. 'Nicky, you do not understand.'

'On the contrary, I understand only too well,' Nicola told her grimly. 'You're not prepared to stand up to this guardian of yours.'

Teresita seemed to shrink. 'Nicky, it is not possible to stand up, as you say. He follows his own will at all times, and always he is obeyed.'

'Oh, is he, indeed?' Nicola said wrathfully. 'I just wish I could meet this lordly gentleman. I'd do anything to stop him getting his own way for once in his life!'

'Then why don't you?' said Elaine.

'Why don't I what?'

'Stop him.' Elaine gave a shrug. 'Correct me if I'm wrong, Teresita, but you're not very well acquainted with this Ramón, are you?'

'No.' Teresita gave a puzzled frown. 'As I said, he is Don Luis' cousin, and many years ago I met him at La Mariposa and . . .'

'Right,' Elaine interrupted. 'And all he knows is that tomorrow he has to collect you someplace—the convent, I guess—and escort you to Monterrey. Well, Nicky can go in your place.'

There was a shaken silence, then Nicola said, 'That's the silliest idea I've ever heard.'

'It's not so silly,' Elaine said calmly. 'Stop and think. You speak Spanish like a native, and if we fitted you out with a brunette wig, some dark glasses and a heavier make-up, you could pass for Teresita—especially with a guy who saw her once when she was a kid, for God's sake.'

Nicola gasped, 'But I'd never get away with it! Just supposing I could fool this unfortunate man—which is by no means certain—what would happen when I got

to Monterrey? I couldn't hope for the same luck with
Don Luis.'

'You wouldn't need it. You take your big leather
shoulder bag in which you have one of your own dresses,
and your papers and vacation tickets. When you get to
Monterrey, you make some excuse to stop off somewhere—a store or a restaurant, and you go to the
powder room, where you take off the wig and dump it,
change your dress—and—*voilà*. Goodbye, Teresita
Dominguez and hello, Nicola Tarrant, leaving Don Luis
with egg on his face because his *novia* has run away.
Oh, he'll be looking for her, but he won't be equating
her with any blonde English chick, and he won't be
searching in Mexico City, where she'll be marrying Cliff,
with me as chief bridesmaid. When she's ready, she can
write and tell him she's already married, and let him
figure out how she did it.'

Nicola was about to tell Elaine that this time she had
finally flipped, when she saw Teresita looking at her,
with the dawning of a wild hope in her eyes.

She said, 'Teresita, no—I couldn't! It's crazy. It's
impossible. It wouldn't work.'

Teresita's hands were clasped tightly in front of her
as if she were praying. 'But we could make it work,
Nicky, in a wig, as Elaine said, and some of my clothes.
It will take two days, maybe even three to drive to
Monterrey, because there are business calls which Ramón
must make on the way for my guardian. Then when
you reach Monterrey, there could be at least one more
day while Don Luis searches there . . .' She turned
eagerly to Elaine, who nodded.

'We'll cable Cliff right away,' she said. 'Maybe Nicky
could play for time in other ways on the trip—pretend
to be sick or something.'

'I wouldn't have to pretend,' Nicola said desperately.
'Stop it, the pair of you. You're mad!'

Elaine gave her a steady look. 'You said you'd do
anything to stop this happening. What Teresita chiefly

needs is time—time for Cliff to get back here and marry her himself—and this you could give her.'

'Yes,' Teresita said with a little sob. 'Oh, yes, Nicky. If I go to Monterrey, then I shall never see Cliff again. I know it.'

'But I really don't think I could get away with it,' Nicola said, trying to hold on to her sanity. 'Oh, I know people congratulate me on my fluency and my accent, but all it would need would be one small mistake and I'd be finished. And I can hardly drive hundreds of miles in stony silence.'

'But why not? Ramon would not expect me, the *novia* of his cousin, to talk and chatter to him. It would be *indecoroso*. And if you pretended that the motion of the car was making you ill, then he would not expect you to speak at all. He is much younger than Don Luis, and when I was a child, he was kind to me.' She was silent for a moment, then she said pleadingly, 'Nicky, I beg you to do this thing for me. I could not love Don Luis, and he does not love me. He marries me only because it is time he was married, and because he wishes for a son to inherit this new—empire that he has made. Would you, in your heart, wish to be married for such a reason?'

Nicola was very still. As if it was yesterday, she saw Ewan smiling at her, and heard his voice. 'Of course I'm not in love with her, darling. It's you I care about. But Greta knows what the score is. She understands these things. Once I've married her, there's no reason why you and I shouldn't be together as much as we want, as long as we're discreet.'

She suppressed a little shudder, remembering how, even through the agony of the moment, there had been a flash of pity for Ewan's wife, who would never possess the certainty of his love and loyalty. A marriage of convenience, she had thought bitterly. Very convenient for the man—but heartbreak for the woman.

Teresita didn't deserve such a fate.

She said, 'All right, I'll do it.'

CHAPTER TWO

NICOLA stood nervously in the shadow of the portico and stared down the quiet and empty street. Ramón was late, and at any moment the door behind could open and one of the nuns emerge, and ask what she was doing there.

For the umpteenth time she had to resist the impulse to adjust the wig. It was a loathsome thing, totally realistic, but hot and itchy. Orchid pink silky dress, strapped sandals with high heels in a matching kid, and two of Teresita's expensive cases as window dressing. The only thing out of place was the bulky leather bag on her shoulder, but it would just have to look incongruous. It was her lifeline.

She glanced at her watch, biting her lip nervously, thinking how funny it would be if it was all for nothing and Don Luis had changed his mind—and then she saw the car and her stomach lurched in panic.

It was too late now to run for it. She could only cross her fingers that the wig and cosmetics and the large pair of dark glasses would be sufficiently convincing. Swallowing, she adopted an air of faint hauteur as Teresita had suggested and stared in front of her as the car came to a halt in front of the convent steps.

There was a uniformed chauffeur at the wheel, but Nicola barely registered the fact. She was too busy looking at the man who had just emerged from the front passenger seat and was standing by the car watching her.

Young, Teresita had said, or at least younger than Don Luis. Well, he was at least in his mid-thirties, so that figured, but what she hadn't mentioned, either because she'd forgotten or had been too young to notice, was that Ramon was a disturbingly, even devastatingly, attractive man. Tall—unusually so—with black hair, and eyes darker than sin. Golden bronze skin over a classic bone structure that went beyond conventional good looks. A high-bridged aristocratic nose, a firm-lipped mouth, the purity of its lines betrayed only by a distinctly unchaste curve to his lower lip, and a proudly uncompromising strength of chin.

'Ye gods,' Nicola thought, 'and this is only the poor relation! What the Mark II model is like makes the mind reel.' Somehow the image of the plump, pompous gran-dee didn't seem quite so valid any more.

He walked forward, strong shoulders, lean hips and long legs encased in a lightweight but very expensive suit. His black silk shirt was open at the throat, allowing a glimpse of smooth brown chest.

He was smiling faintly, and Nicola thought, her hackles rising, that he was clearly under no illusion about his effect on women.

'Señorita.' He stood at the foot of the steps and looked up at her rather enquiringly.

'I am Teresita Dominguez, señor,' she said coldly. 'And you are late.'

Now that the words were uttered, and the charade begun, it was somehow easier.

If Don Luis had informed his cousin that his future wife was a submissive doormat of a girl who would speak when spoken to, then Don Ramón de Costanza had just had the shock of his life, she thought with satisfaction. She was pleased to see that he did look taken aback.

'My apologies, Señorita Dominguez. I was detained. And of course I could not know—I was not warned what a vision of loveliness awaited me.'

No one warned me about you either, she thought silently. And Don Luis must be off his head to let you out of your cage to prowl round the girl he's going to marry, cousin or no cousin.

She primmed her mouth disapprovingly as he came up the steps to her side. 'Don Ramón, must I remind you who I am?'

'Indeed no, *señorita*. You are the *novia* of Don Luis Alvarado de Montalba, the most fortunate man in Mexico. Welcome to our family, Teresita—if I may call you that?' He lifted her hand as if to kiss it lightly, then at the last moment turned it over, and brushed his mouth swiftly and sensuously across the palm instead.

'*Señor.*' Nicola snatched her hand away, aware that she did not have to pretend the note of shock in her voice. Her flesh tingled as if it had been in contact with a live electric current. 'I hope I do not have to inform Don Luis of your behaviour.'

'Forgive me.' He didn't sound particularly repentant. 'I forgot myself. You will have nothing further to complain of in my conduct, I swear. Will you allow me to put your cases in the car?'

She assented with a cool nod, and followed him down the steps, her heart still thumping.

'And your bag?'

She swallowed, shaking her head and taking a firm hold on the strap.

'I prefer to keep it with me.'

He surveyed the bag in silence for a moment. 'It lacks the charm and elegance of the rest of your appearance.'

'It has sentimental value,' she said shortly.

'I'm glad it has something,' he said smoothly. The chauffeur was holding the rear door open, and she climbed in, taking pains to do so without displaying too much leg. The door was shut and she saw her travelling companion detain the man with a hand on his arm and tell him something which clearly caused the chauffeur some surprise before he nodded and turned away.

The next minute Ramón came round and also got in the back of the car beside her. She saw the chauffeur watching covertly in the mirror, his face deliberately stolid and expressionless.

. Keep your eyes on that mirror, *amigo*, she addressed him silently, and if he puts a hand on me anywhere, call in the army.

She leaned back in her seat, forcing herself to relax, reminding herself that she was occupying a very spacious, luxurious air-conditioned vehicle, and the fact that it felt crowded was purely imaginary.

The car began to move, and she felt tiny beads of perspiration break out on her top lip. They were on their way. So far so good, she thought, then stole a glance at her travelling companion and realised that there was absolutely no room for complacency on this journey. And she had promised Teresita that she would use delaying tactics, and make it last as long as possible. She swallowed, and turned her attention as resolutely as possible to the scenery outside the car.

They had been travelling for over half an hour when he said, 'You are very quiet.'

It was her chance. She produced a lace-trimmed handkerchief from her bag, and dabbed her lips with it.

'I am not a good traveller, Don Ramón. You must excuse me.'

She hiccuped realistically, and settled further into her corner of the seat, relishing the slightly alarmed expression on his face. She closed her eyes and pretended to doze, and eventually pretence was overtaken by reality, and, lulled by the smooth motion of the car, she slept.

She awoke with a start some time later. Her eyes flew open and she saw that he was watching her, the dark face curiously hard and speculative. As she looked at him uncertainly, the expression faded, and there was nothing but that former charm.

'Welcome back, *señorita*. Are you feeling better?'

She said, 'A little,' and sat up, her hands automatically smoothing some of the creases out of the skirt of her dress. His eyes followed her movements, observing the rounded shape of her thighs beneath the clinging material, and she flushed slightly, thankful that her bag was on the seat between them, an actual physical barricade.

'Where are we?' They seemed to be passing through a town. He mentioned a name, but it meant nothing.

'I had intended to stop here for lunch,' he said, after a pause. 'But as you are unwell, perhaps it would be unwise.'

Nicola groaned inwardly. She could hardly confess the truth, that she was starving. Tension seemed to be giving her an appetite.

'Please don't let my indisposition interfere with your plans, Don Ramón,' she said meekly. 'While you eat, I can always go for a walk. The—the fresh air might do me good.'

Again she was conscious of the speculative stare, then he said, 'As you wish, *señorita*.'

The chauffeur, whose name was Lopez, parked in a small square behind the church.

Ramón helped her out. 'Are you sure you will be all right?' He paused. 'It is only a small place, you can hardly get lost.'

'I'll be fine,' she assured him, reaching for the strap of her bag.

'You don't wish to take that heavy thing with you. Leave it in the car,' he suggested.

Rather at a loss, she said, 'I'm used to carrying it. It—it doesn't worry me.'

'Clearly you are not as frail as you seem,' he murmured.

She waited to see what direction he took with Lopez, and made sure she went the other way. In one of the streets off the square a small market was in full swing, and there were food stalls, she saw thankfully. Black bean soup, she decided with relish, and *sopes* to follow. She had learned to love the little corn dough boats filled with chili and topped with cheese and vegetables and spiced sausage which were to be found cooking on griddles at so many roadside foodstalls. She ate every scrap, and licked her fingers.

She felt far more relaxed, and in a much better temper as she sauntered back to the car. Ramón de Costanza was standing outside the car, looking at his watch and tapping his foot with impatience as she approached.

'I wondered if I would have to come and find you,' he said silkily. 'Did you enjoy your stroll?'

'*Gracias, señor*. Did you enjoy your lunch?'

'It was delicious.' He looked faintly amused as he surveyed her and Nicola wondered uneasily whether she had left any traces of black bean soup round her mouth.

As he took his seat beside her in the car, Ramon said, 'I have a business call to make a few kilometres ahead, and then we will find somewhere to stay for the night.'

'Already?' she asked with a frown.

He looked surprised. 'It will soon be the time for *siesta*. You don't want to continue our journey through the full heat of the day, or ask Lopez to do so.'

'No, of course not,' she said, feeling a fool. 'I—I wasn't thinking.' That had to count as a slip, she thought. Surely by now she should be used to the way life in Mexico slowed to a crawl in the late afternoon. She was taking too much for granted, losing her edge, and it couldn't happen again, or he might begin to suspect.

They eventually arrived at a motel, a large rambling white building surrounded by lush gardens, fountains and even a swimming pool. Nicola stared at it longingly, and then banished even the thought regretfully. Ladies wearing wigs stayed on dry land. Besides, her bikinis were all in her own cases on the way to Merida by now, and that was just as well, because the prospect of appearing before Ramón de Costanza so scantily clad was an alarming one.

Every time she had as much as glanced in his direction, he had been watching her, she thought broodingly.

And that was putting it mildly. What he had actually been doing was undressing her with his eyes, and in her role as Teresita she couldn't even make a protest, because the innocent Teresita wouldn't have known for one moment what he was doing.

But I know, she thought, grinding her teeth, and longing to embed the delicate heel of her sandal in his shin.

The cabin to which she was shown was spotlessly clean and comfortable, with a tiny tiled bathroom opening off the bedroom. She turned to close the door and found Ramón on her heels. He gave the room an appraising look, which also encompassed the wide bed under its cream coverlet. Then he turned to her, taking her hand and lifting it up to his lips.

'A pleasant *siesta*. You have everything you need?' He looked straight into her eyes, and with a sudden rush of painful and unwelcome excitement she realised she had only to make the slightest sign and the door would be locked, closing them in together.

She snatched her hand away, seeing the mockery in his eyes.

'Everything, thank you, *señor*,' she said in a stiff little voice.

'Can I hope for the pleasure of your company later at dinner?'

She gave him a cool smile and said that it would be very nice. When he had gone, she turned the key in the lock herself. She wanted to collapse limply across the bed, but first she took off the orchid pink dress, and the wig. She saw herself in the mirror across the room. Except for the slightly heavier make-up, she was herself again. She ran her fingers through her sticky hair and moved towards the bathroom. As she did so, she had to pass the bed, and just for a moment she let the tight rein she kept on herself slacken a little and wondered what would have happened if she had given him the signal he wanted—a smile would have been enough, she thought, or even the faintest pressure of her fingers in his.

And just for a moment her imagination ran wild, and he was there in the bed waiting for her, his golden skin dramatically dark against the pale sheets, his eyes caressing her as she moved towards him.

She stopped the pictures unrolling in her mind right there with an immense effort of will.

Then she said, 'Hell,' quite viciously, and went to have her shower.

She had managed to recover her composure by the time she was due to join him in the dining room. She was wearing a simple dark red dress with black high-heeled court shoes, and a small evening bag. Her precious leather holdall was safely stowed in the closet.

The verandah bar outside the motel restaurant was crowded with people, many of them tourists, but she saw him at once. He was sitting at a table near the verandah rail, with a glass in his hand, and he was frowning. Nicola noticed wryly that a party of American women at the next table couldn't take their eyes off him.

She threaded her way through the other tables, and joined him. *'Buenas tardes, señor.'* She meant to sound cool, but only succeeded in being shy. He rose immediately, holding a chair for her to sit down and summoning a waiter with a swift imperious flick of his fingers. She asked for a *tamarindo* and it came at once.

She sipped, relishing the coolness of the drink and its faintly bitter flavour.

'Tell me,' he said, 'those dark glasses—surely you don't need them in the evening. I hope there is nothing the matter with your eyes.'

'Oh, no,' she said calmly. 'I've just been advised to wear them all the time for a short while.' And that, she thought with satisfaction, was nothing less than the truth.

'A pity,' he said. 'One can learn so much about a woman from her eyes.'

She said sweetly, 'And about a man, *señor*.'

His mouth quivered slightly. 'As you say,' he agreed.

It was pleasant, looking out into the darkness with the scent of the flowers wafting to them on the night air, and hearing the distant splash of water from the fountains interspersed with the bursts of laughter and conversation all around them. Nicola had to suppress a little sigh. She would have other memories to take with her, apart from ancient pagan artefacts, when she came to leave Mexico. She was conscious of a feeling of recklessness, and decided it would be wiser to stick to fruit juice for the remainder of the evening.

She tried to remember everything Teresita had told her about Ramón. There wasn't a great deal. He lived at the *hacienda* La Mariposa and ran the cattle ranch for his cousin. His mother, Doña Isabella, and his sister Pilar lived there too, and Teresita had said he was 'kind.' Nicola had got the impression that Teresita would not have applied the same epithet to his mother and sister, however, even though there had only been that one meeting all those years ago.

She had asked Teresita why the *hacienda* was called La Mariposa—the Butterfly, but Teresita had simply shrugged vaguely and said it was just a name.

Anyway, what did it matter? Nicola told herself. She wasn't going to the *hacienda*, but to Monterrey, and none of the Montalba residences would be available for her inspection.

She wondered what Ramón would say when he realised how he had been fooled, and whether Don Luis would be very angry with him. She stole a glance at him. The arrogant set of his jaw indicated that he might have quite a temper himself.

It was a delicious meal. He had ordered chicken for them cooked in a sauce made with green peppers and a variety of other tantalising flavours she didn't have time to analyse. And, in spite of her protests, there was wine, one of the regional varieties, cool and heady.

And she sat across the table from him, hiding behind her dark glasses, and weaving silent fantasies where she was no longer playing a part, but was herself, Nicola Tarrant, free to talk, to smile, to laugh and enjoy herself in his company.

Because in spite of her instinctive wariness of him, in spite of the strain of having to maintain a conversation not in her own language, she was enjoying herself. It was a pleasant sensation to encounter covertly envying glances from other women, to notice the deferential service they received from the staff. Some tourists at a nearby table were sampling tequila for the first time, getting in a muddle over the salt and lemon juice amid peals of laughter, and Nicola smiled too as she watched, her fingers toying with the stem of her wineglass. She looked at her companion and saw that he shared her amusement, and the moment seemed to enclose them in a bubble of intimacy. His hand was very near hers. If he moved it as much as an inch, their fingers would brush. Nicola took a deep breath and moved, picking up her glass and pretending to drink.

She was playing a dangerous game with this crazy charade she had embarked upon, but in a way it might prove to be her salvation. As Nicola Tarrant, she could be fatally tempted to respond to any further advances he might make. As Teresita, she could not be.

All the same, she found his attitude a puzzling one. Teresita had given her the impression that Ramón was Don Luis' trusted and highly regarded employee as well as cousin. She would have supposed that under those circumstances he would have treated his cousin's future wife with the greatest respect. Perhaps he was a man who could not resist a flirtation with any attractive woman who crossed his path, she thought, conscious of a vague feeling of disappointment. Or maybe there was some deeper, darker motive for his behaviour. Perhaps he secretly hated Don Luis, or out of loyalty to him was testing his *novia*'s virtue to make sure she was a worthy bride for a Montalba.

She wondered wryly how the shy, unworldly Teresita herself would have made out on this journey. Would she have even recognised the kind boy she remembered from her childhood? Or would the predator in him have been defeated by her gentleness? After all, Cliff had not been a model of rectitude before he began to associate with Teresita, but now he was tenderly protective towards her.

Some musicians had appeared and were moving among the tables, playing guitars and singing. Nicola recognised the tune they were playing. It was a love song, which had been popular in Mexico City only a few weeks earlier, and she began to hum it softly under her breath. The musicians were approaching their table. They had clearly noticed her enjoyment and were coming to continue the serenade just for her. The leader was smiling broadly and looking at her companion, then Nicola noticed his expression change. She sent a swift glance at Ramón and saw that his face had become a dark mask. His fingers made a swift imperious movement, and the *mariachi* band turned away, and serenaded someone else.

She drank her wine, trying to hide her disappointment. A private flirtation conducted in the car was one thing, and a public serenade quite another, apparently.

Pushing back her chair, she said coolly, 'The journey has tired me. I think I will go to my room. Goodnight, *señor.*'

There was faint mockery in his eyes as he rose courteously. 'Of course, *Buenas noches*, Teresita.' There was a brief hesitation before he used her name, as if to emphasise his rejection of her own formality.

She walked away, wondering in spite of herself why he had not offered to see her to her cabin. Perhaps he had decided that it was wiser to call a halt after all, to treat her with appropriate reserve. Probably that was why he had sent away the *mariachi* musicians.

She undressed slowly, and lay for a long time in the dark, tired, but unable to sleep. It was a relief to know that she had to disappear when they reached Monterrey. It was also a warning not to relax, or forget even for a moment what she was doing on this journey. Playing a part, she thought, and playing for time. Nothing else. And it's just as well that I'm committed to vanish completely in a couple of days.

She breakfasted in her room early the following morning, enjoying the sweet rolls and strongly flavoured coffee a maid brought her. Then she dressed and made up with care and went to find Ramón. She found him in the main reception area, just coming out of one of the private telephone booths.

He said coolly, 'Thank you for being so punctual. We have a long and tedious drive ahead of us. I hope you will not be too bored. Was it explained to you that I had business calls to make on the way?'

'Yes.' She was puzzled by this sudden aloofness.

He gave her a swift sideways glance. 'I have been speaking to my cousin. I have a message for you from Don Luis.'

Her heart gave a little panicky jerk. She said, 'Is that so?'

'Don't you want to hear it?'

'No,' she said, 'I do not. If your cousin has anything to say to me, then it can be said when we meet, and not relayed through a third person.'

He said evenly, 'As you wish, *señorita*,' but she saw a muscle flicker in his cheek, and guessed he was annoyed.

This time the journey was very different from that of the previous day. He sat in the back beside her, but there was a briefcase with him and his attention seemed riveted on the papers it contained. There was a distance between them that wasn't purely physical, and today she didn't even need to use her shoulder bag as a barricade.

She sat and stared out of the window at the purple and grey shades of the *sierras* in the distance. This was a region of Mexico she hadn't expected to see, and normally she would have been fascinated by the changing scenery, the unrolling fertile farmlands they were passing through, but she was unable to summon much interest at all.

Nicola bit her lip. She was altogether too distracted by the presence of her fellow-passenger, and while that might have been forgivable the day before when he had apparently been deliberately making her aware of him, there was no excuse at all today when he was doing quite the opposite.

Clearly the conversation with Don Luis had reminded him of his obligations and responsibilities, she thought.

They made several stops on the way. Nicola wondered whether she was expected to remain obediently in the car on each occasion, but the first time Ramón glanced at his watch and said briefly, 'I shall be not longer than twenty minutes,' which seemed to indicate that she was to be left to her own devices.

And yet that was not altogether true, as she discovered when she left the car and stretched her cramped limbs. Ramón had disappeared inside some large official-looking building, and the car was parked between this and a large ornate church.

Nicola strolled towards it and found Lopez behind her. She gave him a cool smile and said that he could remain in the car.

'This is a very small town,' she added ironically. 'I shall not get lost.'

But Lopez was civil yet determined. It was the Señor's wish that he should accompany her, he said, and his tone made it clear that that was that. She was a little disconcerted, to say the least. No watchdog had been considered necessary yesterday, so why today? She visited the church, first tying a scarf over her head as she guessed Teresita would do, then wandered round the streets, examining pottery and fabrics on roadside stalls, and looking in shop windows full of leather goods, but conscious all the time of Lopez' silent presence at her shoulder.

And when the twenty minutes were up, he reminded her politely that they were keeping the Señor waiting.

That, she found to her annoyance, was to be the pattern of the day. The swift and silent drive along the highway, while Ramón read documents and made notes on them, then the brief stopover and the saunter round the neighbouring streets.

At last, exasperated, she said to Ramón, as the car moved off once again, 'Is it on Don Luis' instructions that I'm being taken round the streets like a prisoner under guard?'

He glanced at her. 'I thought you were not interested in his instructions.'

'Am I expected to be?' she demanded. 'For months on end he behaves as if I don't exist, and then on his command I must go here and there, do this and that. What else can he expect but my hostility—and resentment?' she added for good measure, sowing the seeds to provide an explanation for her disappearance in Monterrey.

For a moment he was silent, then his mouth slanted cynically. 'I think you will find that he expects a great deal more than either of those.'

'Then he's going to be be bitterly disappointed,' Nicola snapped. 'Now please call off your sentry!'

She wasn't just acting. She meant it. Having Lopez following her everywhere was going to cause endless difficulties when she eventually made her bid for freedom.

'Don Luis wishes you to be adequately protected,' the even voice said.

'Does he?' she asked bitterly. 'Then perhaps he should

be informed that I'm in far less danger wandering round the towns than I am in this car, Don Ramón!'

He looked at her with open mockery. 'Then why don't you tell him so when you meet him? I am sure he would be fascinated.'

She hunched a shoulder irritably, and turned to stare out of the window, hearing him laugh softly.

'I am glad your travel sickness has not troubled you today,' he said after a pause. 'Perhaps before the trip is over I may also be able to persuade you to remove your glasses.'

Still with her back turned, she said calmly, 'That is quite impossible.'

'We shall see,' he said softly, and she turned and looked at him sharply, only to find he was once more immersed in his papers.

They ate lunch in a hilltop restaurant overlooking a lake. Nicola ate fish, probably caught from the same lake, she thought, and incredibly fresh and delicately flavoured. Ramón ate little, but he drank wine, staring broodingly into the depths of his glass.

She had expected that he would instruct Lopez to stop at a motel again before the siesta hour, but he did not do so. Instead the car sped on through the heat-shimmered landscape, and eventually, lulled by the motion, Nicola dozed.

She awoke eventually with a slight start, aware that she had been dreaming, but not sure what the dreams were about. Until she turned her head slightly, and then she remembered.

In his corner of the car, he was asleep, his lean body totally relaxed. Nicola felt herself draw a deep shaken breath as the memory of her dreams whispered enticingly to her mind. He had discarded his jacket, and his brown shirt was half unbuttoned, showing the dark shadow of hair on his bronzed body. The shirt fitted closely, revealing not an ounce of spare flesh round his midriff or flat stomach.

Nicola moistened dry lips with the tip of her tongue, conscious of a pang of self-disgust. She had never stared obsessively at a man like this, not even Ewan whom she had loved. Still loved, she thought.

She looked back at him slowly, reluctantly. He wasn't her idea of a rancher, she thought. His shoulders were broad, but his body seemed too finely boned. Her eyes drifted downwards over the long legs and strongly muscled thighs—the result, she supposed, of long days in the saddle. Yet his hands were a mystery, not calloused and rough as she would have imagined, but square-palmed with long sensitive fingers.

She caught back a sigh, as her eyes returned to his face, then gasped huskily as she realised too late that he was awake and watching her.

She sat motionless, thanking heavens for the dark glasses which masked any betrayal there might be in her eyes, but her breathing was flurried, and she saw his eyes slide down her body to her breasts, tautly outlined inside her dress, the nipples hard and swollen against the softly clinging fabric. She saw the dark eyes narrow as they assimilated this shaming evidence of her arousal.

He said softly, 'You overwhelm me, *querida*. Shall I tell Lopez to drive further into the hills and lose himself for an hour or two?'

She felt the hot rush of colour into her face. She wanted to die.

She said icily, 'You are insulting, *señor*.'

'I thought I was being practical.'

'Your vile suggestions are an outrage!' she accused, her voice shaking.

'Of course.' He smiled slightly. 'What a lot you will have to tell Don Luis—when you meet him.'

'You can even think of him?'

'I have been thinking of him a great deal,' he said coolly. 'And always with you, naked and more than willing in his arms, *querida*. A disturbing vision, believe me.'

Her lips parted, then closed again helplessly. Nicola couldn't think of a single word to say, but she knew she had to say something, for Teresita's sake. Although there was no way Teresita would have ever got into this situation, she realised despairingly. She couldn't really believe that she herself had done such a thing.

She said haughtily, 'Please do not speak to me again, Don Ramón.'

It was weak, but it was the best she could manage. She turned her back on him resolutely and stared out of the window, totally unseeing, praying that the blush which seemed to be eating her alive would soon subside.

She couldn't think what was wrong with her. She wasn't completely unsophisticated. He'd made a verbal pass, that was all. It wasn't the end of the world. It had happened to her before, and she'd demolished the perpetrator without a second thought. She was Nicola Tarrant, the Snow Queen, who could cut a too ardent male down with a scornful look. She had never fluttered or flustered in her life, and especially not over the past year. And it wasn't enough to tell herself that her outrage was assumed, part of the role she was playing. She was shaken to the core, and she knew it.

When the car finally stopped, she almost stumbled out of it, barely aware that they were at yet another motel, but smaller this time and far less luxurious. She knew that Lopez was watching her curiously, and tried desperately to pull herself together and act normally.

Ramón came to her side. 'Will you have dinner with me?' His voice sounded constrained.

She avoided his gaze. 'No—I have a headache. I'll ask for some food to be sent to my room.'

'As you please.' He made no attempt to detain her, and she fled. Safe in her room, she made no attempt to order any food, knowing that she wouldn't be able to swallow as much as a morsel. She undressed and showered and lay down on top of the bed, staring into the gathering darkness, her whirling thoughts refusing to cohere into any recognisable pattern.

There was one rock to hang on to in her sea of confusion—that tomorrow they would be in Monterrey, and this whole stupid, dangerous masquerade would be over. She should never have embarked on it in the first place, she knew, and she could only pray that she would emerge from it relatively unscathed.

Just let me get through tomorrow, she thought, and then it will be all right. I'll be able to take up the rest of my life, and forget this madness. I'll be free.

She kept repeating the word 'free' as if it was a soothing mantra, and eventually it had the effect she wanted and the darkness of night and the shadows of sleep settled on her almost simultaneously.

CHAPTER THREE

IT was a maid knocking on the door which woke her eventually. She sat up, pushing her hair back from her face, to find to her horror that it was broad daylight.

'*Señorita*, your car is waiting,' she was reminded, and heard the woman move away.

She glanced at her watch and groaned. She had over-slept badly. She dressed rapidly, and almost crammed the loathsome wig on to her hair. She smothered a curse as she adjusted it. She had wanted to meet Ramón in the clear light of day, looking well-groomed and in con-trol of the situation, and instead she was going to appear late, harassed and looking like something the cat had dragged in.

She grabbed her bag and left precipitately, aware that a porter was waiting in the corridor to fetch her cases.

As she emerged from the reception area into the sun-shine, she made herself slow down and take deep, steadying breaths, as she saw the waiting car. Lopez was standing beside it, looking anxiously towards the entrance, but when he saw her he smiled in relief and opened the back door.

Nicola, steeling herself, climbed in. But the other seat was unoccupied. She twisted round, looking out of the rear window, but she could only see Lopez supervising the bestowal of her luggage in the boot. When he took his place in the driving seat, she leaned forward.

'Where is Don Ramón?'

He turned. 'I am to give you this, *señorita*.' He handed her an envelope, then closed the glass partition between them.

Nicola opened the envelope and extracted the single sheet it contained.

'I regret that urgent business commitments take me from your side,' the writing, marching arrogantly across the page, informed her. 'I wish you a safe journey, and a pleasant reunion with your *novio*.' It was signed with an unintelligible squiggle.

Nicola read it several times, relief warring with an odd disappointment. So she would never see him again. On the other hand, it meant she only had Lopez to shake off when they reached Monterrey, and that had to be welcome news.

She read the terse words once again, then folded the note and stowed it in her bag, biting her lip.

Later, making sure that Lopez' whole attention was concentrated on the road ahead, she reached into her bag and drew out the itinerary for her trip. There was an airport at Monterrey, and she would have to find out whether there were direct flights from there to Merida. There had been no time to finalise every detail before she left Mexico City. Teresita had seen to it that she had enough money for any eventuality, firmly cutting across her protests.

'You are doing this for my sake, Nicky. It must cost you nothing,' she had said.

In retrospect her words seemed ironic to Nicola now, but she dismissed that trend of thought from her mind, and began reading the brochures for her trip, trying to recapture her earlier excitement at the prospect. But it wasn't easy. The names, the jungle temples no longer seemed to work the same potent magic with her as they had done. Nicola sighed and replaced them in her bag, arranging the crush-proof blue sundress she was going to change into on top of the papers.

She yawned, feeling earlier tensions beginning to seep away. Her little adventure was almost over, and she could begin to relax. Her sleep last night had been fitful, which probably explained her failure to wake this morning. She put her feet up on the seat, and relaxed. Next stop Monterrey, she thought.

It was the car slowing which woke her at last. She struggled to sit upright, putting an apprehensive hand up to touch the wig. She was stiff, and her mouth was dry, as if she had slept for several hours, but surely it couldn't be true.

She expected to see suburbs at least, and signs of an industrial complex, but there wasn't the least indication they were approaching a city. On the contrary, it seemed as if they were in the middle of nowhere. There were vestiges of habitation—a few shacks, and a tin-roofed *cantina*. And the road had altered too. They were no longer on a broad public highway but on a single track dirt road.

There were petrol pumps beside the *cantina* and this was clearly why Lopez was stopping. But where were they?

Lopez came to her door and opened it. 'Do you wish for coffee, *señorita*? I did not wake you for a meal because I thought you would be glad to reach your destination at last.'

'I would be glad of coffee.' She got out of the car. 'When do we reach Monterrey, Lopez? Is this a short-cut?'

The stolid face expressed the nearest thing to amazement it was probably capable of. 'Monterrey, *señorita*? But surely you know—we no longer go to Monterrey. It is Don Luis' order that we should go directly to La Mariposa instead.'

Nicola's lips parted in a soundless gasp. For a moment, she thought she was going to faint, and caught at the edge of the car door to steady herself. She saw Lopez look alarmed, and pretended she had turned her ankle slightly on Teresita's high heels.

She managed to say, 'No—I didn't know.' This must have been the message Ramón had tried to give her, she thought frantically. 'When—when shall we arrive at the *hacienda*?'

'In less than two hours, *señorita*.' He spoke as if expecting to be congratulated. 'You will be pleased, I think, to reach your journey's end.'

Journey's end, Nicola thought as she negotiated with some difficulty the patch of dry and barren ground which separated the *cantina* from the road. Journeys end in lovers' meetings—wasn't that what they said? But there was no lover waiting for her—just a formidable and justly enraged man whose path she had dared to cross.

Inside the *cantina*, a girl was frantically wiping off a table and chairs, and Nicola sank down on to one of them, trying to control her whirling frantic thoughts.

What was she going to do? She knew from Teresita that the Montalba *hacienda* was miles from anywhere, with no nearby stores where she could unobtrusively perform her transformation, or crowded streets for her to fade into. And there was nowhere to hide, or means of escape here. This looked like the kind of place where there might be one bus a week to the nearest town.

The girl brought coffee, black, hot and freshly brewed. Nicola gulped hers. It didn't quench her thirst, but at least helped to revive her a little.

She had been mad to let herself fall asleep again, she reproached herself. If she'd been awake, she would have seen they were turning off the highway, and asked why. She might even have put some kind of a spoke in Don Luis' plans, although it was difficult to know what.

Lopez had come in, and was drinking his coffee at an adjacent table. Moistening her lips, Nicola asked him a little falteringly if he knew why Don Luis had changed his mind about their destination.

'The *Señor* did not honour me with his reasons,' Lopez said a little repressively, then his face relaxed a little. 'But I think, *señorita*, it is because of the chapel. There is a beautiful chapel at La Mariposa and no doubt Don Luis wishes to be married there. It is a family tradition.'

'A family tradition,' Nicola echoed weakly. All

Teresita's forebodings had been right, it seemed. If she had taken this journey in person, there was no way Cliff could ever have traced her. She tried to feel glad for them both, but inwardly her stomach was churning with fright.

She stole a glance at Lopez, wondering what he would do if she threw herself on his mercy and confessed everything. She had money, perhaps she could bribe him to drive her to Monterrey. Then she remembered the note of respect in his voice when he had spoken of Don Luis—the way he had said, '*It is a family tradition*', and knew there was no hope there. He would take her straight to his employer, and a search for Teresita would be mounted immediately. And if by some mischance she and Cliff were still unmarried, then it would all have been for nothing.

She got up abruptly from the table, and asked the girl who had brought the coffee to show her the lavatory which was housed in a rough-and-ready corrugated iron shack across the yard at the rear of the building, where a few scrawny chickens pecked in a desultory manner among the dirt and stones.

The flushing apparatus didn't work, and the tiny handbasin yielded only a trickle of rusty water. Nicola took off her dark glasses and stared at herself in the piece of cracked mirror hanging above the basin. Her eyes looked enormous, and deeply shadowed, and she felt as taut as a bowstring.

It had all gone hopelessly, disastrously wrong, and she had not the faintest idea how to begin to put it right. All she could do, she supposed, was go with the tide, and see where it took her. And if that was to the feet of a furious Mexican grandee, then she had only herself to blame for having got involved in the first place.

As she crossed back to the *cantina*, she noticed a battered blue truck standing in the yard. The driver was standing talking to an older man, probably the *cantina's* owner. Nicola looked longingly at the truck as she passed. She'd asked for a way out of here, and now one was being presented, dangled in front of her, in fact.

But could she take it? The driver had stopped presumably for petrol and a drink, which meant that the truck would be left unattended at some point. But would the driver be obliging enough to leave the keys in the ignition? And how far would she get anyway in a strange vehicle, when only yards away there was a powerful car with a driver who knew the terrain, and would overtake her quite effortlessly because it was his duty to do so?

As she looked away with an inward sigh, she encountered the driver's smiling eyes.

'*Bonita rosita*,' he called, his glance devouring her shamelessly. She saw the *cantina* owner put a hand on his arm, and say something in a low voice. It was obviously some kind of warning, and she heard the word 'Montalba.' The truck driver sobered immediately, his expression becoming almost sheepish, and he turned away shrugging, and moving his hands defensively.

Nicola shivered a little. What kind of man was Don Luis that the mention of his name could have such an instant effect?

On her way back to the table, she saw a telephone booth in the corner. If it hadn't been so totally public and within earshot of anyone who cared to listen, she would have been tempted to try and get through to Mexico City and say to Elaine a loud and unequivocal, 'Help—get me out of here!'

Not that she could blame Elaine for her present predicament, she reminded herself wryly. No one had forced her into this masquerade. She had said herself that it was a crazy idea. She could have and should have stuck to her guns, and refused to have any part in it.

She sat down at the table and drank the rest of her coffee. It was cool now, and left a bitter taste, and she had to repress a shudder. Lopez had vanished, but Nicola could hear voices and a giggle emanating from behind a curtained doorway on the other side of the bar, and guessed he had taken advantage of her absence to further his acquaintance with the pretty waitress. His cap and gloves lay on the table, awaiting his return. And—Nicola took a shaky breath—so did the keys to the car. Almost before she knew what she was doing, she leaned across and took them, dropping them into her bag. The die was cast, it seemed.

Biting her lip, she got up and crossed to the back door again. There was on one in sight. The truck basked in the heat of the afternoon. Nicola looked round, her heart thudding uncomfortably, then crossed and looked into the driver's cab. The keys were there, she registered incredulously. But then why shouldn't they be? This was a remote corner of nowhere, not a busy urban street. The door squealed rustily as she opened it, and she froze for a moment, expecting the sound of running feet, raised voices, but there was nothing.

She climbed up into the cab, wincing as the heat from the torn and shabby upholstery penetrated her thin dress. She drew a deep breath and made herself sit calmly for a moment while she briefly studied the controls. She needed to make a clean getaway, not fumbling and stalling. Nor would she take the road they'd just come on. She would head across country for the distant *sierras*, and hope that somewhere she would encounter the highway or at least a town of reasonable size.

With a silent prayer on her lips, she turned on the ignition. The engine didn't fire at the first attempt, but it did at the second, and she eased down the clutch, swallowing nervously. Bumping and lurching over the rough ground, the rickety vehicle took off with a speed which belied its battered exterior.

Behind her, Nicola heard a shout, and then another. She risked a look over her shoulder. The truck driver was standing with Lopez, like a frozen tableau depicting horror, then they both moved, running forward in a futile effort to catch the truck before it was too late. Nicola smiled grimly, and put her foot down hard. A glance in the mirror showed that Lopez had thrown his cap down and was jumping on it, and a giggle of sheer hysteria welled up inside her. She didn't look back again. This was practically desert she was driving over, and she needed all her wits about her.

She drove for over an hour, and then stopped the truck in the shade of a large rock and took stock of her position. So far she hadn't seen as much as a sign of a road, and although she knew she was bound to come across one sooner or later, there was a niggle of anxiety deep in the pit of her stomach. She remembered hearing that drivers were not advised to turn off main roads in the northern regions without qualified guides. Tourists had been known to be lost, and worse. She wasn't a tourist, of course, she was a fugitive, and that made it no better.

There were no maps in the truck, she discovered, after a perfunctory search. There was a service manual for some other vehicle entirely, a dilapidated torch, and a few tools, as well as an oil-stained jacket. No food or drink—not even as much as a slab of chocolate.

Nicola took off the wig and ran her hands luxuriously through her hair. Never again, she thought, and pitched it through the open window. Some desert bird was welcome to use it as a nest. She unzipped her bag and took out the long-suffering blue dress, giving it a critical shake, then found the simple leather sandals she wore with it. When she had changed, she rolled the orchid pink dress and the elegant shoes into a bundle and left them under the rock.

As she re-started the engine, she thought thankfully, 'It's over.'

Another two hours had passed, and Nicola had just realised that she was hopelessly lost, when the truck ran out of fuel. Alerted by the sputtering of the reluctant engine, she searched among the dials on the dashboard for the petrol gauge, and realised with a sinking heart that the needle was vacillating nervously in the red section.

She groaned aloud, wishing that she'd checked more carefully on the fuel situation ages before, although it would have made very little difference. She'd seen no village, filling station, or any other sign of human habitation since she'd embarked on her headlong flight. Plenty of cattle, the odd *burro*, but no people. At first she had been reassured by this, because it also meant no sign of pursuit, but gradually that niggle of anxiety had begun to increase, and now, with the approach of nightfall, anxiety was giving way to fear.

She had no idea where she was. The distant hills seemed no nearer, although that might be some trick of the light, but somehow she didn't think so. She had so constantly had to adapt her route to terrain the truck could cope with that she had begun to suspect she could be driving in a large circle.

The cab had been bakingly hot all afternoon, but now that the sun had set, Nicola knew that it would soon become chilly, and her thin dress would not be adequate protection.

As the truck wheezed to its final stop, she could have burst into tears, but that would solve nothing, she told herself. She had to think. As a stopping place, this was far from ideal. She was in a shallow depression, surrounded by rock and scrub, and it was all too easy to imagine that there were unseen eyes looking down at her.

No more of that, she adjured herself firmly. Positive thinking, my girl, and another more thorough search of the truck. This time she discovered a jerrycan in the back, but it was empty, and she threw it down with a disappointed groan. Under the seat, she came across a couple of lurid girlie magazines which indicated that the truck driver had his own priorities.

She had hoped for a lighter, or at least some matches so she could build a fire. There was enough dry brush around, certainly, but it seemed that the driver didn't include smoking among his vices.

She picked up his jacket and regarded it with disfavour. It was far from clean, but this was no time to fuss about inessentials. Any kind of warmth, however unsavoury, was better than none at all.

She had a long and hungry night ahead of her, and she didn't dare think what the following day would bring, on foot under the blistering sun. She could hardly stay here in this hollow and hope to be found. Even when the inevitable search was mounted, the surrounding rocks would hide her. She tried to think about what she knew of this part of Mexico. It was pitifully little. All her interests had been concentrated on the areas where Aztec and Mayan remains were to be found, yet she could remember one of the men at Trans-Chem talking about a particularly deadly white scorpion which was to be found in the Durango area. Was she anywhere near there? she wondered frantically. And even if not, might there not be other scorpions in various colours it would be wiser to avoid? And mountain lions—she felt certain someone else had mentioned them. Bears too . . .

Oh, stop it, she thought biting her lip. All the same, she wished she had paid slightly more attention to the flora and fauna of this wild country. She'd read somewhere—or had she seen it in a film—that you could keep alive by taking moisture from cactus. But which variety? She'd seen so many. There were others, she knew, which were prized by the Indians for their mind-blowing side effects. That might be the answer, she thought. I could get so high, I'd just float out of here. She chuckled weakly.

It was getting dark very rapidly now, and after only a momentary hesitation she switched on the truck's headlights. Without fuel, there was little point in conserving the battery, and perhaps there was a chance that the lights would be seen, perhaps by a passing aircraft, and investigated. That was a more rational explanation for her action than admitting she was afraid to be alone in the dark, or that if there were wild animals in the vicinity, the lights might keep them at bay.

She picked up the jacket and huddled it round her shoulders with a shiver. Tomorrow, as soon as it dawned, she would set off towards the east again, and see how far she could get before finding some shelter against the fierce heat of the day.

But now she needed to rest. The next day was going to take as much energy as she possessed. She curled up on the seat, her cheek resting on her hand like a child's. Sleep came more easily than she could have hoped, worn out as she was by the tensions of the past few days and the long struggle with an unfamiliar and often recalcitrant vehicle. She dreamed of Barton Abbas and her childhood, lying in a cornfield and watching a hawk turn in a long slow circle in the blue sky above her. It was peaceful and reassuring, and Nicola's lips curved contentedly as she slept. It was good to be a child again, to let the worries and pressures of adult life slide away. Good to be in a sunlit landscape and watch the hovering hawk—until suddenly the dream tilted sideways into nightmare, where the hawk was swooping, and she was the prey, transfixed and helpless, unable to run or defend herself.

She sat up with a little cry, staring round her. The air in the cab was chill, but she was drenched with sweat, and shaking. What had woken her? she wondered dazedly. The dream—or something else? Some sound?

She reached for the torch and slid across the seat to the door. She climbed down from the cab slowly and gingerly and stood rigidly, her head bent, listening.

Yes, there was a sound. A chinking, scraping sound. She shrank nearer to the bulk of the truck, gripping the torch, and peering into the pool of light still cast by the headlights. The torch was hardly ideal for the function it had been designed for, but it was all she had as a weapon.

Hooves, she thought, still listening intently, her nerves screwed up to screaming point. More cattle? Another burro?

There was a shadow now on the edge of the circle of light, a big dense shadow which moved, and she heard the unmistakable creak of harness, and a soft whinny.

She called out, '*Quien es*?'

The shadow moved forward into the light. Dark horse, dark rider. A man, dressed in black, with a broad-brimmed hat shadowing his face. Her hand tightened round the torch.

He said, '*Que pasa*?'

Her body went rigid. Those two laconic syllables had been delivered in a voice which was only too familiar. But it couldn't be true, she argued desperately with herself. Ramón was miles away on his cousin's business. He couldn't be here. Surely fate couldn't play her a trick like that. It was her own nervousness, the fact that she'd just woken up from a bad dream that was making her imagine that it was no one but him confronting her from the back of the tall black gelding.

Almost dizzily she waited for his accusation, and then realisation dawned. He didn't recognise her. How could he? When he'd seen her, she'd been a vivid brunette dressed in pink, speaking Spanish—whereas now . . .

She said slowly and haltingly with no accent at all, '*Señor—me he perdida*.'

'So you are lost,' he said in English. 'It is hardly surprising. This is not good country to drive in. There is a good road ten kilometres to the south. Why didn't you use that?'

She hesitated. 'I was heading that way—but the truck ran out of fuel.'

'Would it not have been wise to have filled up the tank before starting on your journey?'

'I—I left in rather a hurry,' she said, her heart beating so loudly it seemed impossible that he shouldn't hear it. 'I—I'm also very hungry and thirsty.'

He nodded. 'No gasolene, no food and drink and——' he looked her over—'no adequate clothing. Even for a crazy *turista*, you seem singularly badly equipped. Where did you get the truck?'

His tone was hardly sympathetic, but the abruptness of the final question threw her. It would be just her luck if he recognised the damned thing. She would have to be careful.

She said, 'That's a little difficult to explain, *señor*.'

'Try.' It was a command, not an invitation.

'I—I needed a lift, and the truck was going in the right direction—only the driver—misunderstood.'

'I think the misunderstanding was yours, *señorita*. You are even crazier than I thought, to have accepted such a favour from a stranger.'

'It wasn't a favour,' she protested. 'I was going to pay. I have money.'

'But not the currency he wanted, plainly.' For the first time, he sounded amused. 'And may I ask the fate of this man?'

'He—he got out of the truck—to relieve himself. I drove away and left him,' she improvised wildly.

'You are truly resourceful, *señorita*,' he drawled. 'I will bid you *adios*. No one with wit as as keen, or so strong a sense of self-preservation, can possibly be in need of my poor assistance.'

His hand went up to his hat brim in a mocking salute, and he turned the horse's head.

My God, Nicola thought, he's going! She ran forward.

'*Señor*—please! You—you can't just leave me here like this!'

Her movement startled the horse. It threw up its head

and began to sidestep, only to be brought effortlessly back under control by its rider.

He said coolly, 'I have told you where the road is, *señorita*. To walk that distance should not be beyond your powers. You seem young and healthy.'

Nicola stared up at him, wondering how on earth she had ever found him attractive. His face was dark and forbidding under the shadow of his hat, his mouth harsh and uncompromising.

She hated him more than she had ever dreamed it was possible to hate anyone, but she made her voice pleading. 'I'm tired, and hungry—and very frightened, *señor*. There must be some shelter of some kind that you know of.' She paused, and then said flatly, 'I'll pay you to take me there!'

'Aren't you afraid I might ask the same price as the truck driver? You wouldn't rid yourself of me quite so easily.'

Nicola swallowed. 'That's a chance I shall have to take. I—I don't want to spend the night alone in that truck.'

'I think you already take too many chances, *señorita*.' His tone was soft and chilling.

Nicola shivered inside the jacket. This was a side of Ramón she had not seen before. No sign now of the charm, or the sensual teasing which had so embarrassed and disturbed her.

Her hands gripped together. She said in a low voice, 'Please help me.'

There was a silence, then he shrugged slightly. 'Very well. Tonight we will find some shelter, and in the morning we will see what is best to be done. Are you travelling quite alone?'

'No,' she said hastily. 'I'm joining friends. In Monterrey. That's where I was heading for.'

'Then you are well off the track, *señorita*.' Again that faint amusement. 'At the moment you are on your way to La Mariposa, the hacienda of Don Luis Alvarado de Montalba. You have perhaps heard of him?'

She forced herself to say casually, 'I think I've heard the name—yes. Is this his land?'

'It is. And he would be desolated to know that he was harbouring unsuspected so charming a guest. Perhaps I should take you to the *hacienda*.'

'No.' She hoped he hadn't picked up that note of panic. She tried to laugh. 'Please, *señor*, I'm not really in any fit state to meet any great Spanish landowner. I've behaved like a complete fool, and I know it. If you could just guide me to where I can get transport for Monterrey, I'd be eternally grateful, but I don't want to meet this Don Luis.'

'Very well,' he said evenly. 'What luggage have you?'

'Just a bag.'

'Then I suggest you fetch it, so that we can be off.'

She was pulling it out of the truck when the thought struck her that if nothing else he might recognise the bag. But she could hardly pretend that she had lost it, and there must be a million similar bags in the world, she told herself, slinging it over her shoulder like a satchel. If the worst came to the worst, she would brazen it out.

But he never gave it a second glance. 'The horse has good manners. You need not be frightened.'

I wish I could say the same for his owner, Nicola thought as she unwillingly prepared to accept his assistance. She'd expected the use of a stirrup and perhaps a helping hand into the saddle, but instead he bent towards her, his arm going round her waist and lifting her as if she was a featherweight. And she was to sit in front of him, she discovered to her dismay.

She ventured on a protest. 'I know how to ride, *señor*.'

'I have already commented on your resourcefulness, *señorita*. Unlike the unhappy driver of the truck, I prefer to keep you where I can see you. And I should warn you that Malagueno accepts you on his back because I am here, but you should make no attempt to ride him alone.'

Nicola stared straight in front of her, glad that he could not read her expression. Her paramount wish was that she had pushed jeans instead of a dress into her bag, although the skirt was full enough to allow her to ride astride without too much difficulty. But it still revealed more of her slender legs than she could have wished under the circumstances, and this made her feel nervous and vulnerable and acutely conscious of her femininity. But then that was how she had been feeling from the moment she had met him, she thought in self-accusation.

'Relax, *señorita*.' His voice was mocking. 'I am told that rape on horseback is not merely dangerous but impossible, so you need have no fears.'

She didn't deign to answer, but instead caught hold of the edge of the saddle to steady herself, while gripping a handful of Malagueno's mane with the other hand.

She was held in the circle of his arms, but casually. He made no attempt to hold her more intimately, and she was thankful, because she was finding their present proximity, the warmth of his breath on her neck and ear quite disturbing enough. The truck seemed suddenly a much safer bet, but she could hardly say at this stage that she had changed her mind.

A weird inhuman sound broke the stillness of the night air, and she shuddered, tightening her fingers in Malagueno's mane. 'What was that?'

'A coyote,' he said. 'Or did you think they existed only in movies?'

That settled it. The truck would stay where it was, unattended, although she would have to make arrangements of some kind for its recovery in Monterrey. But what, she couldn't even begin to think.

All she could in fact think about was the strange workings of fate which had brought Ramón back into her life when she had been sure she would never see him again. In fact, she'd counted on it. His dark and dangerous attraction had roused feelings and emotions in her which she wanted no part of. And if some foresight could have warned her that she would be spending the night in his company, even if it was on horseback, then she would never have embarked on her flight in the first place. It would have been preferable to have allowed Lopez to convey her to La Mariposa and the wrath of Don Luis, she thought. She stifled a little sigh, and looked up at the dark velvet of the sky with its spangling of stars.

'No moon,' she commented, half to herself.

'Alas, no. Nor a balcony, nor a *mariachi* band.' The mockery was open now, and she scowled, remembering that moment in the restaurant when he had sent the musicians away.

'It was just a remark,' she said, glad that the darkness hid the sudden colour in her cheeks.

'And the sigh?'

Was there a trick he didn't miss? she wondered.

'Let's just say I've had a bad day and leave it at that.' She paused. 'Malagueno's a beautiful horse—very sure-footed.'

'He suits me very well,' he said laconically. 'He bears his name because his sire came from Malaga.'

Another silence. She hastened to fill it with words. 'You said that all this was Montalba land. It must be a vast estate.'

'It was once. Now much of it belongs to the *ejidatarios*, peasants who are given free grants of land by the government. Here in the north much land which was once pasture for cattle is now being turned into small farms.'

'You don't agree with government policy?'

'All men must live,' he said after a pause. 'And the Montalbas could well spare the land. Some of the *ejidatarios* work hard on their holdings, but others do not. They find the life too hard, and prefer to remain peasants, selling their labour as they can.'

'As you do yours?' Nicola asked slyly.

'As I do mine,' he agreed.

She was disconcerted. She had expected at this point that he would tell her that he was Ramón de Costanza, cousin of the great Don Luis. She could see no point in his keeping it a secret. The thought that perhaps he was not communicating his identity because she was not of sufficient importance was a riling one.

Meanwhile this ride through the darkness was playing havoc with her unaccustomed muscles, and she moved restlessly.

'Is it much further—wherever we're going?'

There was a smile in his voice. 'I thought you were used to horses, *chica*. But no, you will not have to suffer for much longer.'

'Where are we going?'

'So many questions.' He sounded faintly exasperated. 'We are going to a nearby *ejido*.'

Nicola's spirits rose slightly. It sounded hopeful. A house, however primitive, occupied by a farmer and possibly his wife and family too. Food and warmth, and somewhere to lay her head. But most of all, other people, she thought with sudden unease.

She began to peer forward into the darkness, looking for a lighted window, but there was only the night, which made it all the more surprising when her companion said, 'Your ordeal is over, *señorita*. We have arrived at our destination.'

Malagueno had stopped, and lowered his head to crop at unseen grass. Nicola found she was being lowered to the ground beside him, and she ran her fingers caressingly down the satiny neck. '*Gracias*, Malagueno,' she said under her breath.

Dismounting, her companion looped the horse's reins over the branch of a nearby tree.

'Where is this place?' She stared round her helplessly.

'You don't believe it exists?' His hand closed round

her arm, and she was urged gently but firmly forward. Had she been alone, she could well have blundered into it, she realised. It was only a shape, slightly darker and more solid than the darkness around it. No lights, no dogs barking, or friendly welcome of any kind. In fact it looked—deserted.

She said sharply, 'Where is everyone?'

'There is no one but ourselves,' he said coolly. 'Believe me, *chica*, when you see the size of the cabin, you will be grateful.'

Nicola felt anything but grateful. She hung back as he opened the door, which creaked eerily.

'Frightened?' He was laughing at her again. 'Wait here, then, while I light a lamp, and dislodge any intruders which may have taken up residence in Miguel's absence.'

'There's no need for that,' Nicola protested. 'Other people are just as entitled to a night's shelter and . . .'

'I was not thinking of people,' he said gently, and a shudder went through her, as she suddenly imagined unnamed horrors waiting there in the dark. Rats, she thought. Ugh—or scorpions—or even—snakes.

She heard the rasp of a match and saw a glimmer of light which gradually swelled into a steady flame. A moment later, and another appeared in a corner of the room. Nicola stepped gingerly across the threshold and looked around her. It was not a prepossessing sight which met her eyes. There was a blackened fireplace built into one wall, with a rusty-looking cooking pot suspended from a hook in the chimney, and in the opposite wall was a deep alcove with a wooden bedstead actually built into it. A frayed curtain hung from a rough pole above the alcove, and could be drawn for privacy, Nicola supposed. The first lamp her companion had lit hung from the ceiling. The second stood on a square wooden table in the corner. Two stools and a lumpy mattress on the bed seemed to supply the rest of the furnishings.

Something of her feelings must have shown on her face, because her companion gave a low laugh. 'What did you expect, Señorita Turista? A room at the Continental in Mexico City?'

She looked at him, her eyes widening involuntarily. He had discarded his hat and the poncho-like garment he had been wearing during the ride. The elegant urban suit had gone too, and he was wearing close fitting dark pants and superbly made riding boots. Another of those expensive dark-coloured silk shirts moulded his shoulders and chest. He looked the business man no longer, but very much the man of action, and Nicola realised suddenly that in this guise he was even more formidable. She felt the force of his attraction before, but now she had no charade to hide behind, no outraged grandee's *novia* to play. She was herself alone, and she realised with alarm that he was watching her in that same speculative way as at their first meeting, as if he was both amused and intrigued.

For a moment their eyes held in silent challenge, then he gave a slight shrug and turned away.

He said, 'I'll get a fire started. There's some food in my saddle bag. Perhaps you would get us a meal while I attend to Malagueno.'

Again she rushed into speech. 'Where did you learn to speak such good English?'

'Here and there. Where I could.'

She said, 'You're not very communicative.' She forced a laugh. 'Have you got something to hide?'

'No, *chica*,' he said softly. 'Have you?'

He disappeared through a door at the back of the cabin, leaving her gasping. When he returned he was carrying a bundle of firewood which he arranged deftly in the fireplace, and coaxed into flame with his matches.

'You certainly know how to make yourself at home,' Nicola commented, recovering a little. 'You mentioned Miguel. Does he own this place, and is he a friend of yours?'

'He did, and he was.' He stood up dusting his hands together.

'He's dead. I—I'm sorry.'

He shook his head. 'Miguel is very much alive. I'll go and get that food.'

Nicola sat down on one of the stools and stretched her legs out in front of her. There was no real warmth from the fire yet, but the flicker of the flames was in itself a comfort. And comfort was what she needed, because her unease was deepening with every moment that passed.

Ramón had changed, and not just in exterior details like his clothes. His manner had changed too. It was cooler and more incisive. On the journey at times he had seemed a charming playboy, but there was no trace of that any more. Now, he was no one's second in command. He behaved like a man who was used to giving orders and having them obeyed.

She thought, 'But of course he runs the ranch, and he's back on his own territory. That explains it.'

But her explanation lacked conviction, and she knew it. There was something deeply wrong, something which was eluding her.

'*Que pasa?*' She started violently and turned to find him watching her from the doorway, frowning. 'You are very pale. Are you ill?'

Nicola shook her head. 'Reaction, I suppose.' She tried a weak laugh. 'It's been quite a day.'

And could turn out to be quite a night too. She had tried to avoid looking at the bed in the alcove. Even with the curtain drawn, it was far from being a sanctuary.

With an effort she turned to the articles he had just placed on the table—a can of some kind of stew, with an opener, a packet of coffee, and a tin mug and plate.

He met her gaze, and the corner of his mouth lifted in a sardonic smile. 'I regret there are no tortillas. I apologise too that there is only one set of dishes.'

That, she assured him silently, doesn't worry me half as much as the fact that there's only one bed.

'There is a well in the yard at the rear.' He pointed to another door at the back of the cabin. 'I'll fetch you some water. There is also a hut there—for your convenience.'

'Thank you,' Nicola muttered, and he laughed.

'The word is 'gracias,'' he said. 'Perhaps after we have eaten I will give you a lesson in Spanish. You can hardly hope to traverse my country on the two phrases you have used so far.'

'No,' she said weakly. She had pushed her leather bag under the table hoping it would be less obtrusive there, and she saw him look at it as he turned to leave, but he said nothing and she breathed again. She debated whether or not to take off the truck driver's jacket and decided against it. In one pocket, her fingers encountered the torch which she had completely forgotten about, and its solid presence idiotically cheered her.

There was a sink in one corner of the room, consisting of a tin bowl with an attached waste pipe. Nicola decided that one priority was to give the cooking pot even a rudimentary wash. There was an enamel coffee pot, battered but usable, standing under the sink, and Nicola shook her head as she looked at it. The preparation of this meal was going to be a challenge, and surviving it could well be a miracle.

Yet, in the event, it proved simpler than she had imagined, and when the spicy savoury smell of the stew began to fill the cabin, Nicola forgot her qualms and allowed herself to realise how hungry she was.

She knew he was watching her. They were watching each other, taking each other's measure like adversaries who know battle is about to begin. She'd seen him bring in a blanket roll and toss it on to the bed, and had bent towards her cooking, glad that the heat from the fire gave her an excuse for the sudden flare of colour in her face.

She tried to remind herself of all the times she had been alone with Ewan. When she had been close in his arms, kissed and caressed by him as he tried to persuade her to let him make love to her. Yet even then she had always felt she was ultimately in control of the situation.

But not with this man, she thought. This man who was a law unto himself.

He came back into the cabin, humming softly to himself. She recognised the tune. It was the one the *mariachi* band had been playing at the hotel restaurant, and her face went blank as she listened.

'Is the food ready?' he broke off the tune to ask, and she jumped.

'Er—yes, but I don't know how we're going to manage . . .'

'I found a fork and spoon in my saddlebag. You can have the spoon.'

Her hands were shaking as she tried to ladle the stew on to the plate, but eventually she managed and placed it on the table between them. She picked up the spoon and made herself eat, forcing each mouthful down her reluctant throat, while her mind ran feverishly like a tiny animal on a wheel.

His choice of tune had been purely fortuitous, she tried to reassure herself. He hadn't recognised her. To him, she was just a silly tourist who'd got herself into a difficult situation and wanted to be rescued.

'You are very quiet.' He was watching her. 'Have you run out of questions, *chica*?'

All, except for the sixty-four-thousand-dollar one, she thought shakily, and I don't think I want to know the answer to that.

She tried to smile. 'Tell me some more about Miguel.'

He shrugged. 'He was a friend, and the son of a friend. While he was at university, he became imbued with political ideals about equality. He saw it as his duty to work with the *ejiditarios*, and fight for their rights. He even tried to become one of them—not with any great success, as you see.'

'And you disagreed with him?'

'No. I respected his view, his ideals. But then the government's measures on land reform were not sufficient for him. They did not move fast enough. He began to say that landowners who were unwilling to surrender their estates should be dispossessed—by force if necessary. And he did not stop at talking. He led a group of *peons* to an estate north of here. They had guns, shots were fired, and an overseer injured. Miguel has placed himself outside the law.'

Nicola asked huskily, 'What happened? Did the landowner agree to their demands, and give up his land?'

'*Si.*' His mouth curled. 'The spineless fool.'

Her heart missed a beat. 'You wouldn't do so?'

'No,' he said softly. His eyes met hers across the table, as hard as obsidian. 'What I give, I give, but I allow nothing to be taken from me against my will.'

She went on looking at him, trying to tell herself she had imagined that note of menace in his voice.

He said, 'You appear nervous, *chica*. Are you?'

'No,' she denied too hastily.

'Don't lie to me. I can see fear in your eyes. I told you once how much you can learn from a woman's eyes. I am glad that you have taken off your glasses at last, Señorita Tarrant.'

Her throat seemed to close with fright. She said, 'How—how do you know my name?'

'You still wish to play games?' He shrugged. 'While you were asleep that first day I looked in your bag and found your passport. I had to know, you see, who was masquerading as Teresita Dominguez.'

'But how did you know?' Nicola said huskily. 'You haven't seen Teresita since she was a child.'

He shook his head. 'Wrong, *señorita*. You see, I have also been playing a game with you. It is my cousin Ramón who is a stranger to Teresita. I know her well.'

Nicola had a weird sensation that the cabin walls were closing in on her. She pushed the stool back so violently that it fell with a clatter, and stood up.

She said, 'Who are you?'

He rose too. He seemed to tower over her. 'I, *señorita*? As I am sure you have guessed already, I am Luis Alvarado de Montalba.'

She heard herself gasp, saw the barely controlled anger in the dark face, the glitter in his eyes, and saw his hands curving like talons as he reached for her. She remembered the hawk plunging on its prey out of the clear sky, and cried out as she too plunged into swirling darkness.

CHAPTER FOUR

CONSCIOUSNESS returned slowly. Nicola was aware of a feeling of nausea and oppression, and then a cup placed at her lips. She was told succinctly, 'Drink,' and liquid like fire trickled into her mouth and down her throat. She moaned faintly and moved her head from side to side, trying to escape, but the arm which held her was implacable, and she was incapable, anyway, of any real resistance.

Eventually she opened her eyes. She was lying on the bed in the alcove, which explained the sense of oppression. She turned her head warily and surveyed the rest of the cabin. The lamp on the table had been turned low, and this, with the firelight, provided the only illumination.

He was there, her captor, her enemy, sitting beside the fireplace, staring into the flames. Then, as if aware that she had stirred, he turned and looked at her.

Nicola made as if to sit up and realised just in time that her blue dress was lying across the foot of the bed, and that her only covering was her lacy half-cup bra and tiny briefs. She snatched at the blanket and wrapped it around herself quickly, then realised what a fool she was being. There was only one person who could have removed her dress, so what use was there in trying to conceal herself from him? He could already have looked his fill while she was unconscious, she thought, shamed to her bones.

Something else she noticed too. Her bag had been emptied and her money, tickets and passport stood in forlorn heaps on the table.

Luis Alvarado de Montalba rose from his stool and walked across the room. Nicola turned her head away

and closed her eyes to block out the sight of him.
Unbidden, a tear squeezed out from beneath her lashes
and trickled down the curve of her cheek.

'Weeping, *chica*?' he mocked. 'What for? Your past
sins, or their future retribution?'

She said in a low voice, 'I can explain.'

'I am sure you can,' he said drily. 'I am sure your
fertile imagination can probably conjure up at least a
dozen explanations, but this time I want the truth.
Where is Teresita Dominguez?'

'Safe from you by this time, I hope,' she said wearily.

'You speak as if I pose some threat to Teresita,' he
remarked.

'Don't you?' Her voice was bitter. 'I suppose an ego
like yours can only imagine that a proposal of marriage
from you would flatter and overwhelm any woman. It
would never occur to you that Teresita would find the
prospect of marrying you utterly repulsive.'

'You speak as if I planned to drag her to the altar by
her hair.' The dark eyes glinted as he looked down at
her. 'I promise that I had no such intention. I believed
that she was as—resigned to the idea of our marriage as
myself.' He paused. 'But I had not allowed for the influ-
ences which would be brought to bear on her once she
had left the convent.'

Nicola gasped. 'Then—you knew about that?'

'Naturally I knew,' he returned impatiently. 'She was
my ward, therefore it was my business to know when
she left the shelter of the accommodation I had provided
for her. However, I was assured by the general manager
of Trans-Chem that you and the other girl were respect-
able, and that Teresita would only benefit from your
company. How wrong he was!'

'Then you also knew we'd met Teresita at Trans-
Chem?' Nicola sank back on the mattress, utterly chagrined.

'Of course. I arranged for her to work there on a
temporary basis at one time, because she was insistent

that she wished to have a job like other girls.' A wintry smile touched the corners of his mouth. 'I imagine you know how that worked out. She was given the job as a favour to me because I was on the board of the company for which Trans-Chem were acting as consultants. I imagine it was only out of respect for me that she was not ignominiously sacked on the first day.'

'How well informed you are,' Nicola said bitterly. 'It was lucky for Teresita that your informant slipped up over Cliff.'

'If you refer to Clifford Arnold, I knew about his visits from the beginning, but I did not take them seriously.' His mouth twisted cynically. 'I did not grudge the child a flirtation. Knowing her, I was sure it would go no further than that.'

'Then you're wrong.' Nicola lifted her chin defiantly. 'Cliff is Teresita's husband by now.'

'I would not be too sure of that,' he said coolly. 'There are lengthy formalities before any marriage can take place between a Mexican national and a foreigner.'

She heard him with dismay. The legal aspect of the situation had not really occurred to her. She'd heard so much about the ease of divorce and marriage in Mexico that she had not realised there could be any snags where the bridal couple were of mixed nationalities.

So it had all been for nothing, she thought miserably, and a little sob escaped her.

'Don't think you will escape the penalties of your actions by such abject behaviour,' he said crushingly. 'What happened to the spirit you showed over the past two days?'

'I'm not crying for myself,' she choked, 'but for Teresita.'

'Then I would save your tears,' he said caustically. 'She seems in little need of them.'

'No?' She stared up at him accusingly. 'When you're going to go to Mexico City, and drag her away from the man she loves? When you're going to ruin her life?'

He shrugged. 'Teresita has taken her future into her own hands. Whether or not her life is ruined would seem to depend on herself and this man she has chosen. However, she is of age, so legally no concern of mine. I shall not interfere.'

Nicola digested this in some bewilderment. 'But don't you even care?'

'Oh yes, *chica*,' he said silkily. 'I care that I have been made a fool of. I care that Teresita allowed the arrangements for our marriage to go ahead without informing me that she no longer wished to become my wife. I care that a stranger has forced her way into my life, throwing my plans into chaos.'

'But what does that matter? You never really wanted Teresita. You can't have done!'

'The match was made between our families,' he said bleakly. 'Perhaps neither of us was overjoyed at the prospect, but we could have expected to be reasonably happy—eventually. It is time I was married. I have a number of houses, but no real home. I need a son to whom I can pass on the inheritance I have built for him. I need some grace and serenity in my life. I felt Teresita could give me these things.'

Nicola's eyes flashed. 'It sounds a very one-sided bargain to me. What would Teresita be getting in return for bearing your children and surrounding you with 'grace and serenity'? The sort of joyless, loveless relationship which your family has specialised in probably for generations?'

His mouth curled. 'You will not speak of my family in that way, *señorita*. Your tongue will be your downfall.'

'Don't you like to hear the truth?'

His hands descended on her shoulders, jerking her into a sitting position.

'And what do you know of truth?' he said harshly. 'You—who have acted a lie since the moment I saw you. What do you know of love? You talk a great deal, *chica*, but your eyes tell me that you are as untutored in passion as Teresita herself.'

His words were like a lash across an open wound.

'That isn't true,' she cried in protest. 'I've been in love—deeply and passionately in love. I love him still. That's why I decided to help Teresita to be happy. Because I knew that she deserved better than the pallid, cold-blooded arrangement which was all you were offering.'

His smile was grim. 'So you think me cold-blooded, *amiga*? I promise that Teresita would not have found me so. And neither will you.'

He pulled her towards him, and his mouth descended mercilessly on hers. She was unable to breathe or even think coherently. Panic rose in her, and she beat with clenched fists on his shoulders, but neither his hold nor his brutal assault on the softness of her lips slackened even for a moment. Her half-covered breasts were crushed achingly against the muscular wall of his chest, and a whimper rose in her throat as his hand twisted in her tangled hair, dragging her head back, so that his mouth could travel bruisingly down the length of her throat.

When she could speak, she said pleadingly, 'No—please!'

He lifted his head and stared down at her, his eyes glittering with mockery, and something else that she was frightened to interpret.

'Who is speaking now, *chica*? The experienced woman of the world in your imagination, or the frightened virgin of reality? I want the truth!'

Her throat closed, making speech impossible. She could only shake her head, staring up at him with eyes that begged wordlessly for understanding, even for mercy.

Almost gently, he lowered her back on to the mattress. Then he sat up, his eyes travelling slowly and broodingly down the slender length of her body. Nicola felt humiliated under the intensity of his gaze, but she made no effort to drag the blanket around her, or even shield herself with her hands. She deserved to feel this shame, she thought, just as she deserved every harsh word he had thrown at her, and more. Whatever her private opinion of his motives or morals, she'd had no right to interfere. He was entitled to be angry, even to exact some kind of retribution, but not—in that way. Dear God, not that.

His hand cupped her chin, forcing her to look up at him, and one finger stroked softly and sensuously across the swollen outline of her mouth.

He said very quietly, 'You have done me a great wrong, *amiga*. You have insulted me, and robbed me, and made me lose face. Are you prepared to make amends?'

'If I can.' She tried to sound brave, but in spite of her efforts there was a quiver in her voice.

'Oh, you can,' he said softly. 'I need a wife, as I told you. Thanks to you, the girl I had chosen is lost to me. The least you can do is take her place.'

For a moment she lay staring up at him, her mind trying to make sense of what he had just said. She began to shake her head slowly.

'No, you can't—I couldn't! You're not serious.'

'No?' he asked mockingly. 'Perhaps another display of my ardour will convince you.' He bent towards her, and her hands came up, pushing against him.

'No!' Her voice cracked in panic, and he laughed.

'Then say you will marry me, and I will wait like a gentleman until you are legally mine.'

'But you don't want to marry me. You can't want to. We don't know each other. You don't like me . . .' The words tumbled over each other. She knew she wasn't making any sense, but then what was in this whole crazy situation?

'You have made me very angry, I admit,' he said. 'But you inspire other emotions in me, *amiga*, which make fair recompense for any amount of anger. Why do you imagine I did not unmask you immediately? Why did I allow you to think I was Ramón? Because you intrigued me, *chica*. Because you stirred my blood. My decision to escort Teresita north myself was a last-minute one, prompted by a sense of duty.' His mouth twisted ruefully. 'I felt I owed it to the child—and myself—to spend some time with her, to get to know her—perhaps, if she seemed willing, to woo her.'

'How kind of you,' said Nicola on a little flare of bitterness. 'I'm sure she would have been overwhelmed.'

'You flatter me, *chica*,' he said mockingly.

But in a moment of self-revelation, she knew that wasn't the case. He was a practised seducer. If he had employed the same wiles with Teresita as he had with her, she would have been eating out of his hand by the time they reached La Mariposa. She remembered with shame her own reactions. And she knew without looking at him that he was remembering too.

After a pause, he said, 'But I must confess, I wasn't looking forward to the journey, until the car stopped outside the convent and I saw you waiting for me, *chica*. For a moment I was not even sure what was happening, and then you spoke and I realised that it was all a trick to fool my unfortunate cousin. The impulse to turn the tables on you was irresistible.'

She shook her head. 'But—weren't you worried about Teresita—that she might have been harmed in some way?'

'If it was that, there would have been a ransom note waiting, not a girl in disguise. No, I guessed at once that you were one of the girls with whom she was sharing an apartment, and that you were the English girl, because I knew the American spoke little Spanish. Yours is excellent. I must congratulate you.'

Nicola swallowed. 'But why did you let it—go on like that?'

'Because I was bored. I decided that you might alleviate that boredom, provide me with some amusement on the trip. Which you did, *amiga*,' he added cynically. 'Although only by day, to my regret. I had not envisaged that I would be spending my nights alone, but then it had not occurred to me that a girl who could lend herself to such an adventure could possibly be as innocent as you were.'

His eyes met hers, and she felt a shock run through her entire body. 'I want you, Nicola, and I intend to have you—with the bonds of matrimony or without them. The choice is yours.'

'And if I say I won't marry you?'

He gave a slight shrug. 'Then instead of La Mariposa, we'll go somewhere else. To my house near Acapulco, perhaps. At night, the bedroom is full of the sound of the ocean.'

'Fascinating,' she said, conscious that her heart was beating wildly. 'I'm sure that all your lady loves find that a terrific turn-on. Only I won't be joining them. Isn't there any other choice beside the two you've mentioned?'

'Oh yes. There is the little matter of the stolen truck. We still operate the Napoleonic code in Mexico, *querida*. You would have to prove your innocence of the theft. Our jails are not comfortable places, as you would have a long time to find out. On the other hand, the truck could be retrieved, and the driver handsomely compensated for the trouble and inconvenience you have caused him. I could probably persuade him to bring no charges against you—or I could wash my hands of the whole affair and allow justice to take its course with you.'

Dry-mouthed, she protested, 'But I didn't steal it! I— I only borrowed it. I was going to let the driver know where I'd left it and . . .'

'How?' he said unanswerably.

There was a long silence, then Nicola said huskily,

'But—your family. What will they say? They know you intended to marry Teresita.'

'*Si*,' he agreed. 'There was a small sensation earlier today when I informed them that I had changed my plans. My aunt was overjoyed, taking it as a sign that I am about to gratify her by proposing to my cousin Pilar.' His mouth twisted. 'But I am not. I therefore blighted her hopes yet again by requesting her to have a room prepared for you. It was not long afterwards that I received an agitated phone call from Lopez.'

'Oh,' she said guiltily.

'Oh, indeed, *chica*,' he agreed rather grimly. 'I still do not understand how he can have been such a fool, especially after I had warned him to be vigilant. The tickets and itinerary in your bag made your intentions perfectly clear.'

She bit her lip. 'But you've told your family about me. And about me running away?'

'Some of it,' he said. 'Not the whole story.'

She spread her hands. 'Then you must see how impossible it is. They would never accept me as—as a suitable wife for you.'

He lifted a cynical shoulder. 'Tia Isabella would never accept any woman I chose, but you needn't fear her, or any of them. Only Lopez and my cousin Ramón know of the deception that you attempted to practise. And it will never be referred to again by anyone if I make it known that is my wish.'

'How nice to have such power over people,' Nicola said bitterly. 'But don't expect it to work with me. I hate and despise you and all you stand for, and I always shall. Do you really want to be married to a woman who finds you—repugnant?'

'No, and I might hesitate if I thought that it was true. But I don't believe you, Nicola.' His hand smoothed her bare shoulder, then slid down to the curve of her breast where it swelled above the lacy confine of her bra. Nicola felt her breathing thicken uncontrollably

and a spasm of sensation clench in her body, so exquisitely intense that she could have cried out, as his fingers
pushed the lace aside and circled the throbbing rosy
peak. He looked down at her, the dark face taut, its
planes and angles suddenly sharply accentuated. 'Deny
it now,' he said hoarsely. 'Deny that I can make you
want me—if you dare.'

She didn't dare. Huskily she said, 'Please—stop.'

'Then promise me that you will marry me.' His fingers
still moved on her, creating their own delicious agony.
'Promise me—before I finish what I began with your
dress, and take you here and now.'

Her hands dug into the mattress as she had to fight
to stop her body arching towards him in mute and helpless invitation. She whispered, 'Yes, I'll marry you—
only—no more, please.'

For a moment he remained very still, then, with a
faint groan, he pushed himself away from her and drew
up the blanket to cover her body.

'You spoke only just in time, *querida*,' he said
unevenly. '*Dios*, Nicola, fight me all you wish in the
day, but at night, in my arms, you will do what I want—
be what I want.'

Nicola said nothing. Her eyes closed, and she turned
her head away, trying to hide the dull, hot colour which
had invaded her face. She wanted to die of shame—
shame at the ease of her capitulation—shame because
of the wild aching excitement he had so easily roused in
her. For over a year she had worn her Snow Queen
image like invisible armour, yet all the defences which
hurt and disillusion had built round her had vanished
like thistledown in the wind as soon as he had touched
her. And even before that, she thought, lashing herself
as she remembered her body's helpless arousal in the
car the previous day.

And if she had responded then, accepted his insolent
invitation? Well, she would belong to him—would be
on her way with him to the villa near Acapulco or some

other suitable love nest for a few weeks, or perhaps even months.

Not that marriage would really change anything, she made herself realise. It would only bring more hurt, more disillusionment eventually. Because it couldn't work. Once his frankly expressed desire for her body was sated, there would be nothing left.

She would live at La Mariposa, or one of his other houses, and bring up his children, and try not to wonder where he was when the bed beside her remained empty. It was the sort of existence she had pityingly envisaged for Teresita—that was why she was here—but not for herself. Never for herself.

She heard Luis moving round the room, and opened her eyes a little. He was raking down the fire, and the lamp on the table was already out. As she watched, he stood up and came back to the alcove. He sat down on the edge of the bed and started to pull his boots off.

She said, 'What are you doing?'

'Preparing for bed,' he said briefly. 'It is time we got some sleep.' He glanced at her and grinned when he saw the all too evident apprehension on her face. 'Don't alarm yourself, *querida*. My boots are all I intend to remove—unless you insist, of course,' he added mockingly.

She moistened dry lips. 'You promised . . .'

'And I shall keep my word.' He swung himself fully on to the bed beside her. 'However, I do not intend to spend what remains of the night on the floor, and this way I can sleep in reasonable comfort, and also make sure that you keep your promise too. You are too fond of running away, *chica*, and if I lie with my arm round you—so—I can make sure that you will still be here in the morning.'

He slept eventually, the unhurried regularity of his breathing told Nicola that, but she could not. She lay in the darkness, staring ahead of her, trying to come to terms with the fate that her rashness had apparently proved. Luis' arm was heavy across her, and she hated the promise of possession that it implied, but she was afraid to push it away lest she woke him.

When the first light came through the window, she turned her head slightly and watched him, wondering how she could ever have been such a fool as to mistake him for anyone else. But he was far removed from the plump middle-aged grandee of her imagination, or the ogre who haunted Teresita. Relaxed in sleep, a hint of stubble along his jaw, and long eyelashes curving on his cheek, he looked even younger than his years.

If Teresita had ever seen him like this, she thought wryly, then things might have been very different. As it was, she had only seen the power, the sexual charisma, and felt crushed by it.

Nicola could understand her fears only too well. She remembered the strength of the arms which had taken her prisoner so easily, and shivered. He had told her she could fight him by day, but he meant with words. Physically, he would always be the master, yet she could oppose him with her mind, and she would.

He might take, she thought fiercely, but she would never give. He would possess her body, but she would never surrender her spirit. She dared not, because the eventual desolation when his passion dwindled into in-difference would be too much to bear.

Eventually she must have slept, because the next thing she remembered was Luis shaking her shoulder gently.

She sat up with a gasp as the events of the past night came flooding back.

'It is time we were on our way,' he said.

Her eyes were enormous as she looked at him. He had stripped to the waist, presumably to wash, and she wasn't proof against the potent masculine attraction of his lean golden-brown body. She made herself look away, wondering as she did so how many other women had lain in bed and watched him dress with the same hungry excitement leaping inside them.

She asked huskily, 'Is—is there any water?'

'I have warmed some for you, *querida*. I used cold. Have your wash while I saddle Malagueno.' He pulled on his shirt and began to fasten it as he walked to the door.

Nicola was thankful she didn't have to leave the shelter of the blanket in front of him. Her scraps of underwear were altogether too revealing, and the fact that he would soon have the right to see her without even that elementary covering made no difference at all.

She rinsed her face and hands swiftly, and dragged on her dress, jerking at the zip in her haste. The table was bare, and her shoulder bag, as she lifted it, empty except for cosmetics. Money, tickets, passport, everything had presumably passed into Luis' keeping. No possible avenue of retreat was being left open, she realised. She draped the folded blanket over her arm and went to the door. It was still early morning, and the sun hung low in the sky, a huge orange ball. The air was cool, and she breathed it gratefully.

Luis appeared leading Malagueno. '*Vamos, querida*. We can be at La Mariposa in time for breakfast.'

She gasped, 'So soon? But it must be miles away!'

'It is closer than you think,' he said drily. 'Your tracks were easier to follow than your route, which seemed to go in circles. Have you got all your things?'

'Those that have been left to me, yes,' she said coldly, then remembered. 'Oh—the driver's jacket. I can't leave that.'

When she reappeared, Luis took it from her.

'I was going to wear it,' Nicola protested.

His mouth hardened. 'You do not wear a garment belonging to another man. If you feel cold, take this.' He handed her the poncho he had been wearing the night before, and reluctantly she slipped it on.

As he lifted her into the saddle in front of him as he had done the previous night, she wondered if he would kiss her, hold her closely as they rode together. But he did not. In fact they might have been strangers.

But that's what we are, she thought, shivering in spite of the enveloping folds of the poncho. I'm going to marry a man I hardly know—someone I've only spent a few hours with.

It was a frightening thought, but on its heels came the even more disturbing realisation that if she had the chance to escape again, she was not sure that she would take it. And the implications of that kept her thoughtful all the way to the *hacienda*.

There was inevitably a reception committee waiting in the entrance hall of the *hacienda*. Nicola was deeply conscious of Luis' hand under her arm, urging her forward. On the fringe were several servants, all trying to be unobtrusive, but clearly eager to catch a glimpse of the girl who was to marry the *dueno*.

She drew a deep and shaky breath as she assimilated precisely who was waiting to receive her. She could hear Luis performing introductions, his tone cool and composed as if this was a perfectly conventional meeting.

'May I present my aunt, Doña Isabella de Costanza, my cousin Pilar, and her brother Ramón.'

She was aware of hostility in two pairs of dark feminine eyes, knew that the murmured welcome was words alone. But Ramón was altogether different. He stepped forward beaming.

'*Señorita*, may I welcome you to this house which is your home.'

His English was hesitant and deeply accented. Luis shot him a caustic look.

'Don't struggle, *amigo*. She speaks our language fluently.'

Doña Isabella stepped forward. Her bearing was regal, and her face stony as she looked at Nicola.

'No doubt you will wish to go to your room, *señorita*. I have assigned Maria to wait on you. When you are ready she will bring you to the *comedor* for breakfast.'

As she walked towards the stairs, following the pretty girl who had shyly come forward at Doña Isabella's imperious nod, Nicola tried to take in something of her surroundings.

The *hacienda* itself, she had thought as they approached, was more like a fortress, a rambling low building protected by a high wall. The family living quarters, it seemed were built in a large square round an interior courtyard, with separate wings for guests, and for the staff. Inside, the *hacienda* was incredibly spacious and cool, the fierceness of the sun being kept at bay by shutters on the windows. The floors were tiled, and such furniture as Nicola had glimpsed was clearly very old, opulently carved in dark wood.

She followed Maria along a wide corridor to a pair of double doors at the end. The girl pushed them open and stood back to allow Nicola to precede her into the room.

Nicola paused to look around her, her lips parting in sheer delight. It was a large room, and its charm lay in its utter simplicity, she thought. The walls were washed in a pale cream shade, and the highly polished furniture had probably made the journey to the New World from Spain in the sixteenth century. The bed was enormous, with four carved posts, and a cream silk counterpane embroidered lavishly with butterflies in green, pink, gold and silver. Hanging at the back of the bed was a huge embroidered panel in the shape of a butterfly, using the same colours as the bedcover.

Nicola thought, 'La Mariposa—of course!'

Maria smoothed the counterpane with an almost proprietorial air.

'This was the room of Doña Micaela, the mother of Don Luis, *señorita*,' she volunteered in a hushed tone. 'And before her, may God grant her peace, it was the room of his grandmother. Always the mistress of the *hacienda* has slept in this room.'

And the master? Nicola wanted to ask. Where does he sleep? She looked across at the wide bed, imagining generations of Spanish-born brides lying there, waiting and wondering if the door would open to admit their husbands.

And soon she too would lie waiting in the shadow of the butterfly.

'The bathroom, *señorita*,' Maria announced proudly, and Nicola turned away, thankful to have another focus for her attention. It was a charming bathroom, probably converted originally from a dressing room, tiled in jade and ivory, and including a shower cabinet among its luxurious appointments. Nicola noticed toiletries ranged on the shelves, all brand new, the seals on the flasks and jars unbroken, most of them made by names which a girl earning her own living had only heard of. It was a room dedicated to beauty, and to the art of making oneself beautiful for the appreciation of a man, and it made Nicola feel slightly sick. A little cage, she thought, where the bird can sit and preen herself all day.

But the thought of the shower was an irresistible temptation. Her hair was like tow, and she needed a change of clothes. She groaned inwardly as she remembered that the only luggage available to her was Teresita's. The Mexican girl had hastily filled a couple of cases from her vast wardrobe, in spite of Nicola's protests.

'You must have luggage with you, Nicky, or it will seem suspicious,' she had said. 'And all these are things I no longer need, so that you may leave them behind you when you run away.'

All the clothes now hanging in the cupboards and filling the drawers were elegant and expensive, but few of the styles or the colours were what she would have chosen for herself, and the thought of having to present herself downstairs in another girl's dress to the scornful looks of Doña Isabella and Pilar was unpleasant.

The next shock was that Maria clearly considered it

her duty to assist Nicola with her shower. Nicola spent several minutes firmly disabusing the girl of this notion, and dismissed her, promising that she would ring if she needed anything.

The shower was delicious and she revelled in it, letting the warm water stream through her hair and down her body. She wrapped herself in a fluffy bath sheet, tucking it round her body like a sarong as she came back into the room. No doubt somewhere there would be some means of drying her hair, but she was reluctant to ring for Maria again. She needed to be on her own for a while.

She sat down on the stool in front of the dressing chest and stared at herself. Could this really be happening? It seemed impossible. Tomorrow or the next day she should have been in Merida, preparing to start her holiday, and instead she was here in this beautiful room, a virtual prisoner.

And somewhere in this house was the man who had made her his prisoner. The man she had promised to marry. She swallowed, fighting back the bubble of hysteria rising in her throat. It was all a monstrous joke—it had to be. She was no demure Spanish dove accepting the gilded cage provided for her, and offering in return her duty and obedience to a comparative stranger.

Not love, she thought, but compliance, surrendering herself to her master's will, but making no demands of her own. Asking no questions.

Men like Luis de Montalba—men like Ewan—expected the wives they had married for convenience to look discreetly the other way while they amused themselves. She wondered whether Greta had learned her lesson yet, and whether it had been a painful one for her. Yet perhaps she simply regarded it as part of the price she had paid for Ewan. Because she wanted him, and always had.

Nicola had seen the hungry way in which the rather blank blue eyes had fastened on him from the first. She had even laughed about it with Ewan, secure in the knowledge that it was herself he wanted to be alone with, to hold in his arms. The possibility that that was all he might want had never entered her head, although it should have done, because she had recognised from the first that he was ambitious, and had even applauded it.

Well, at least Teresita was going to spared that kind of misery, Nicola thought. She had Cliff, and they loved each other, and although nothing was certain in this uncertain world, they had the chance to be happy together. Teresita wouldn't have to spend her life dutifully bearing children and being moved from one expensive prison to another.

She shivered convulsively, pressing her clenched fist against her mouth.

Was this the fate she had brought upon herself when she had unthinkingly embarked on her masquerade?

She reached for her hairbrush and pushing back the stool went towards the window. She unfastened the shutter and stepped out on to a balcony running, she saw, the whole length of the first floor. The heat of the sun was like a blow, and she closed her eyes against its fierceness, moving her shoulders in sensuous pleasure as she pulled the brush through her hair, lifting the soft strands to dry them.

She heard a sound below her and looking down saw that Ramón was standing in the courtyard beneath, his expression a mixture of admiration and embarrassment.

'I did not mean to disturb you,' he said. 'I was on my way to the stables.' He gestured towards a gated archway in the corner of the courtyard.

'You're not disturbing me at all,' she said lightly. 'I've been washing my hair.'

'As I can see. It's very beautiful.' He smiled at her, and Nicola found herself warming to him. He had an attraction all his own, she thought. He was shorter than Luis, and swarthier, and his features were less aquiline, but he possessed an open friendly charm, and Nicola knew that a journey of several days in a car with him would have been pleasant without posing any problems at all.

As if reading her thoughts, he said ruefully 'Luis has the luck of the devil himself.'

She felt herself flushing. 'Then you know—everything?'

He spread his hands, shrugging. 'Luis telephoned me from the first stop he made. He wished me to check on Teresita on his behalf. He could hardly do so without telling me what had happened, although . . .' He stopped suddenly.

'Although you never expected that he would bring me here,' Nicola supplied drily.

It was his turn to flush. 'Well—perhaps not. But I am delighted, I assure you. It is time he was married. He has been lonely, I think.'

Nicola lifted her eyebrows. 'That's not the word I would have chosen.'

'Señorita Tarrant!' He looked more flustered than ever. 'He is only a man after all, not a saint. And besides . . .'

'Besides, I shouldn't know such things,' she finished for him, making herself smile. 'And please call me Nicola.'

He smiled too, delighted and plainly relieved at the shift in the conversation. 'I shall be pleased to do so. I hope we can be friends.'

'I hope so too.' She looked around. 'This courtyard is charming.'

There was a well in the centre, with a stone seat around it, and above it a parched-looking tree providing shade. Nicola wondered whether the well held water, but looking at the brazen sky she was inclined to think it was purely decorative.

'I am glad you like it,' said Ramón. 'It is cool here in the evenings, which makes it a pleasant place to sit. And when there are parties, the servants hang lanterns in the tree, and around the gallery.'

'Are there many such parties?'

'Not for some time, but all that will change now.'

He meant there would be celebrations in honour of Don Luis' marriage, she thought. Well, as far as she was concerned, the lanterns would remain in storage for the foreseeable future. Yet, she could imagine how the courtyard would look when it was lit by the lights from the house, and the tree, instead of the glare of the sun, and when perhaps a golden moon swung above it in the night sky. There would be exotic foods laid out on white-clothed tables, and the enticing smell of meat grilling over charcoal. And above the murmur of voices and laughter, the swish of silks and the flutter of fans, would rise the sound of a *mariachi* band.

It was all so real that for a moment Nicola felt dazed, as if she had suffered a time-slip—as if the *hacienda* was speaking to her in some strange way.

What nonsense, she told herself forcibly. She was merely suffering from the combined effects of emotional stress, a bad night, and an empty stomach.

She watched Ramón cross the courtyard and disappear under the arch, then turned back into her room, running her fingers through her hair to test its dampness as she did so.

She came face to face with Luis who was standing, hands on hips, waiting for her, his face set in grim lines.

He said coldly, 'My aunt is waiting to order breakfast to be served. I came to see what had detained you.'

She said, 'I'm sorry, I washed my hair. I went outside to dry it.'

'And to talk to my cousin Ramón.' He paused. 'Perhaps in future you would wait to converse with him until you are fully dressed.'

Nicola glanced down at herself, then looked at him incredulously. She was fully covered from the top of her breasts down to her feet.

She said heatedly, 'I'm perfectly decent. I'm wearing a damned sight more now than I was last night!'

His voice became icier than ever. 'What you wear, or do not wear, for my eyes only is a different matter. You will please remember that. Now Tia Isabella is waiting.' He turned on his heel and left the room, leaving Nicola staring after him, torn between anger and amusement.

Anger won. 'Who the hell does he think he is?' she raged inwardly, snatching a handful of filmy underwear from a drawer and dragging a dress from a hanger.

But the answer was already formulating in her mind. He was her captor, her jailer, the man with the key to her prison, the man who made his wishes known and was quite capable of enforcing them.

She swallowed, and her hands clenched, her nails digging into the soft flesh of her palms.

She thought, 'Dear God, I've got to escape from here before it's too late.'

CHAPTER FIVE

NICOLA's face was set and mutinous as she sat in the shade of the gallery. A chair and a footstool had been set for her there by Carlos, the grizzled-haired martinet who appeared to be the household's major-domo, and a table bearing a tray with a jug of iced fresh fruit juice and a glass was to hand, but she ignored it.

Breakfast had been a horrendous meal from beginning to end. Entering the *comedor* in Carlos' wake had been like walking headlong into a brick wall of hostility.

Luis' eyes had looked her over coolly and swiftly, assimilating the ill-fitting bodice and loose skirt of the dress she was wearing, and she saw his mouth tighten in exasperation.

He said, 'Tia Isabella, Nicola needs a new wardrobe. Perhaps you would arrange for your dressmaker to be sent for.'

'I have plenty of clothes of my own,' Nicola protested. 'They're just—elsewhere.'

He shrugged. 'And there they can remain. In any event they would hardly make a suitable trousseau.'

Nicola sank down into the chair he was holding for her, hearing Doña Isabella draw in a swift breath like the hiss of a snake.

She said, 'Luis, you cannot expect . . .'

'But I do expect,' he said softly. 'I thought I had made that clear.'

There was a silence like knives, and Nicola stared down at the polished surface of the table. She glanced up and encountered an inimical glance from Pilar which brought the colour into her cheeks. She was a pretty girl, but the sullen expression, which seemed habitual, spoiled her looks.

'My nephew informs me that his marriage to you will take place as soon as the arrangements can be made,' Doña Isabella broke the silence at last, her gaze resting pointedly on Nicola's waistline. 'It will naturally be a very quiet wedding.'

'On the contrary,' Luis said coolly. 'Invitations will be sent to the entire family, and to our friends.'

Doña Isabella gasped, her back becoming, if possible, more rigid than ever. 'But under the circumstances—the very doubtful circumstances . . .' She floundered to a halt with a suddenly martyred air. 'As you wish, Luis, of course.'

'Thank you, Tia Isabella,' he bowed. He glanced at Nicola. 'Your own family, *querida*. Can they be persuaded to make the journey, do you think?'

She moved her shoulders helplessly. 'My father is a farmer. This is a busy time for him—and my mother certainly wouldn't come without him. I just don't know.'

'But when you write to them, you will offer the invitation.' It wasn't a question, it was a command, she knew. Her mind closed completely when she tried to imagine how she was going to break the news to her family—what she could say.

'So you are a farmer's daughter?' Pilar spoke for the first time, her tone openly insolent. 'How sad that Luis spends so little time at the *hacienda*. You would feel quite at home among the cattle and horses.'

Nicola smiled lightly. 'And pigs,' she said. 'I feel quite at home with them too.'

There was a startled hush as Pilar digested this, then an angry flush mounted in her face and she gave Nicola a venomous look. Another sharp silence descended, and a look stolen under her lashes told Nicola that Luis' face was icy with displeasure at the interchange.

Carlos came into the room followed by a uniformed maid. Coffee was placed on the table, and warm rolls, and then an enormous dish of scrambled eggs mixed

with finely minced onion, tomato and chili appeared.
Nicola was hungry, but she had to force each forkful
down her throat. As she ate, she allowed herself gradually to look round the room, and take in her surroundings. It had a somewhat repressive atmosphere, the dark
heavy furniture giving a feeling of solidity and stability,
as if reminding the onlooker that this house, this land
had been wrested from the wilderness centuries before,
and that the Montalbas had set their hand and seal over
it. This impression was deepened by the family portraits
which hung in gloomy splendour round the walls.

It was inbred in them all, and had been from the beginning, she thought, that look of cool arrogance. Dark
patrician faces looked down in command from every
canvas, proclaiming their lordship of this New World
they had made their own. And the women were cast in
the same mould, she thought ruefully. They sat staring
rigidly into space, their hands disposed to show their
beautiful rings, their rich lace mantillas decorously
draped over high combs, expressionless, guarded and
without visible emotion.

All except one, and Nicola found her gaze returning
to this particular portrait over and over again, fascinated by the wilful expression in the dark eyes, and the
faint smile playing about the full lips which seemed to
deny the studied decorum of the pose. She was obviously
much younger than most of the other women depicted,
and while none of them looked as if they had ever given
their respective husbands even a moment's anxiety, this
girl seemed as if she might have been quite a handful
for any strait-laced grandee.

Instead of the conventional head-covering, she wore
a silver butterfly gleaming against her dark tresses, and
in one hand she held a dark red rose which provided a
dramatic contrast against the silvery brocade of her
gown.

Nicola would have liked to have asked about her, but
it was unlikely that Doña Isabella or Pilar would wish

to enlighten her, and Luis was frowningly examining a pile of mail which Carlos had just presented to him and clearly preoccupied.

When the meal was over, he excused himself abruptly and left the room, and after a moment Doña Isabella rose too, followed by Pilar, leaving Nicola sitting alone at the big rectangular table.

She bit her lip as the door closed behind them, but reminded herself that she could have expected little else. She was unwelcome here, an interloper, and if it was any consolation Teresita would probably have fared little better.

Eventually Carlos had found her loitering rather uncertainly in the hall, and had installed her with a certain amount of ceremony on the shaded terrace which encircled the courtyard.

But I can't sit here for ever, she thought. There must be something I can do.

She looked across to the archway. The stables were through there somewhere, and she supposed there would be no real objection to her visiting them, exploring a little on her own account. She rose, and moved slowly and languidly along the terrace to the archway. It was as she had thought. She could see other buildings, rather less impressive than the *hacienda* itself, and in the distance she could hear a vague hum of voices, and an occasional shrill laugh. She thought she could also hear the faint strum of a guitar, but perhaps that was her imagination.

She pushed open the gate and walked through, half expecting to be intercepted and sent back where she belonged, but if anyone had observed her arrival they gave no sign, and she wandered on without interference.

The kitchens seemed to be a separate wing altogether, she thought, her nose wrinkling appreciatively at the appetising aromas drifting towards her. Everyone would be far too busy preparing the massive midday meal to worry about her.

She crossed another courtyard and turned a corner, her eyes widening as she came upon what seemed to be a small village street lined with single-storey cabins. Washing dried in the sun, and a group of small children played in the dust—some complicated and absorbing game with flat stones she noted as she passed.

She smiled, and said, '*Buenos dias*,' but they gaped at her in silence, clearly disconcerted by her appearance among them.

Nicola walked on slowly. Two separate communities, she thought, occupying the same limited space, and totally interdependent. Don Luis appeared to look after his workers well, she admitted grudgingly. The cabins were well built and properly maintained and there was a feeling of tranquillity pervading the entire street.

When she reached the end, she paused, uncertain which way to take next. A dog, lying in the shadow of a wall, lifted its head and barked with the air of an animal prepared to go through the motions, and no more.

Nicola grinned to herself. 'Love and peace, man,' she said half under her breath. She paused and looked around her, shading her eyes with her hand. Over to the right, she could see cultivated land, streaked with irrigation channels, and men working there, so she turned left instead, and found herself in yet another courtyard surrounded by stable buildings. Ramón was there, talking to a small squat man in a broad-brimmed hat. He broke off as he caught sight of her and came across immediately.

'Señorita—Nicola. What are you doing here? Is Luis not with you?'

'I decided to take a look round,' she said, evading the question. 'Isn't it permitted.'

He smiled. 'Of course—this is your home. Perhaps if we can persuade you to like it, then Luis would spend more time here.'

She said drily, 'Please don't overestimate my influence with your cousin.'

Ramón laughed. 'How could I?' He paused, sobering a little. 'Perhaps I should explain. Luis loves La Mariposa and always has done, but in recent years he has spent less and less time here—and not altogether because of his business commitments.' He hesitated. 'It is difficult for me to say this, but Madrecita—my mother and Luis have not always—agreed as I would wish. He is good to her, of course. For years she has been the mistress here, but now that he is to marry all that will change.' He grimaced slightly. 'If—if there was anything—lacking in her welcome, perhaps you can understand. And also she had certain plans of her own . . .'

'She wanted Luis to marry Pilar,' Nicola translated, and he looked embarrassed.

'She did. It was nonsense, of course. Luis had never given any indication—and Pilar herself would never have thought—except . . .'

He paused again, and Nicola prompted, 'Except?'

Ramón sighed. 'Why should you not know? My sister is young and impressionable. A year ago she formed—an attachment for a man, but it was unsuitable, and she was told to think no more of him. At the same time, my mother began to suggest . . .' He shrugged. 'I am sure I need say no more.'

Nicola said ruefully, 'I see.' Poor Pilar, she thought. A double loser. No wonder she had sensed that white-hot resentment!

'Do you think she was—in love with Luis?' she asked.

'I doubt it,' he said. 'He never gave her the least encouragement. I think she was—prepared to be in love with love, for the sake of being mistress of—all this.' He spread his arms wide. 'Not that this is all of it, by any means, as you must know.'

'I know very little,' Nicola confessed. 'Only what Teresita told me.'

'Ah yes. From what Luis told me, I understand you shared an apartment with her.' He smiled reminiscently. 'A sweet child.'

'She spoke well of you too.'

'She did?' He seemed pleased. 'And yet she can have little reason to remember this place or any of us with much pleasure. Her visit was a disaster. She was frightened of horses, and Luis, thinking to please her, took her up on his saddle. *Ay de mi* !' He gave a groan. 'First she cried and screamed, then she was sick.'

'How clever of her,' Nicola said acidly. 'I wish I'd tried the same thing myself.'

Ramón gave her a puzzled look. 'You too are afraid of horses? That is sad—Luis is an expert horseman.'

'I've ridden since childhood.'

He beamed at her. 'Then that will please him greatly.'

Nicola bit her lip. 'Pleasing your cousin is not the sole object of my life.'

His smile vanished altogether. 'But as his wife . . .'

'We're not married yet,' Nicola said tautly.

'But you will be. Luis is a man of his word.'

'And that's all that matters? Don't my wishes come into this?'

'I had assumed that in this your wishes would coincide with his.' Ramón looked embarrassed. 'You must consider, Nicola, the circumstances of your meeting—all that has happened since.' He paused. 'When Luis telephoned me to say that you had taken Teresita's place, it was clear he had—certain intentions towards you.'

She felt slow colour rising in her face. She strove to make her voice casual. 'But not marriage?'

'No—not then. But something clearly has happened to change his mind and . . .'

'Nothing has happened,' she interrupted. 'For heaven's sake, it isn't a question of honour—his, mine or anyone else's. You must believe me.'

'It is not my affair,' he said flatly. 'I should not have spoken at all. Forgive me. You came to see the horses. Will you permit me to show them to you? There is, alas, only one suitable for a woman to ride and that belongs to my sister Pilar.' He added without any real conviction, 'I am sure she would be happy to lend her to you if you wished.'

Nicola took pity on him. 'If I want to go riding, then I'll ask her. What I'd really like is to have a look around the *hacienda*. It's so old that I'm sure it must have a fascinating history.'

'Oh, it has.' Ramón cheered up perceptibly. 'I would be happy to escort you—perhaps later, after luncheon?'

She smiled and nodded before turning away. For a moment it had occurred to her that it might be possible to enlist Ramón's support in getting away from here, but she had already thought better of that idea. Ramón was his cousin's man to the last degree. It had been apparent in every word, every inflection in his voice. There was no help for her there—or anywhere else, for that matter.

Ramón obviously thought she was a very fortunate lady, she told herself wryly as she made her way slowly back to the house. He thought Luis had seduced her either on the way here or the previous night, and was making honourable amends. She remembered Doña Isabella's gimlet stare and grimaced.

Maria was hovering on the terrace when she returned. 'The Señor Don Luis has instructed me to make alterations in some of your dresses, *señorita*. If you would come upstairs and show me those you wish me to begin on.'

The girl sounded a little subdued, and Nicola wondered with a pang whether she had been told off for not taking better care of her new mistress. She could hardly explain that she just wasn't used to having a maid. But it was a fact that she could use Maria's services. She was no hand with a needle, and never had been, and it was no fun walking round in clothes which patently didn't fit her even as a gesture of defiance.

Going through Teresita's dresses and choosing those that could be adapted to her needs filled in the time before lunch quite adequately. Maria bloomed with new importance. She sighed with admiration over the colour of Nicola's hair, but shook her head at its condition. She also hinted that Nicola was too thin. Perhaps the Señor Don Luis' taste ran to plumper women, Nicola deduced with exasperation from the girl's demure smile.

She told herself that it was a matter of indifference to her what his tastes in that direction might be, but believing it was a different matter. Unwillingly she remembered that first evening at the motel—the way those women tourists had watched him—the odd pang she had felt . . .

Resolutely, Nicola closed her mind against that. All she needed to recall now was that he was the man who was forcing her into an unwanted loveless marriage to satisfy his injured pride. Not that that was the sole satisfaction he required, she thought, suddenly dry-mouthed as she remembered the searing effect of his lips and hands, the little shaken storm of desire he had so effortlessly aroused in her.

And Maria had her orders, she thought, to make sure that the bride was desirable at all times because the *dueno*'s will was paramount.

She had no wish at all to go down to lunch, but nor did she wish to face the inevitable questions, probably from Don Luis himself, if she remained in her room. Her blue dress had been returned, freshly laundered and pressed, and she changed into it with a feeling of relief.

When she entered the *comedor*, an instant silence fell, forcing her to the conclusion that she had been the subject under discussion, and she checked for a moment, flushing a little, until Ramón's friendly smile welcomed her.

Luis wasn't there, she discovered, looking round her.

'My cousin apologises for his tardiness,' Ramón told her in an undertone. 'He is interviewing one Pablo who drives a truck.' He gave her a conspiratorial side-glance.

'A truck driver?' Pilar's ears were as sharp as her voice

apparently. 'Why doesn't Juan Hernandez speak to such people?'

Ramón shrugged, clearly wishing he had said nothing. 'Because this is a matter which Luis prefers to deal with himself.'

Pilar subsided, but there was a speculative look in her eyes.

Thoroughly embarrassed, Nicola looked round her, and saw the portrait which had so intrigued her earlier. Surely it wasn't just a trick of the light that put such an expression of dancing mischief in the dark eyes as she surveyed her descendants.

'You are admiring Doña Manuela, little cousin?' Ramón leaned forward.

'Ramón!' his mother snapped. 'Please remember that there is as yet no established relationship between our family and—Señorita Tarrant.'

Ramón jerked a shoulder unabashed. 'The relationship will be established soon enough,' he said with an ill-concealed grin. 'If I were in Luis' shoes I would wait no longer than it takes for Father Gonzago to get here from the mission.'

'Well, you are not in his shoes, and never will be,' Doña Isabella's voice was even snappier. 'I must apologise for my son, *señorita*. His manners have apparently deserted him.'

'On the contrary,' Nicola said sweetly, 'Don Ramón has been all that is kind ever since I arrived here.'

Doña Isabella's frankly fulminating glance indicated that Don Ramón was an idiot, but she said nothing.

The door swung open and Luis strode in. 'My regrets for having kept you waiting. You should have told Carlos to begin serving.'

'It was of no importance,' Doña Isabella assured him with an acid smile.

'Why have you been talking to a truck driver?' Pilar demanded.

Luis lifted a shoulder in a cool shrug. 'I found myself

in his debt, and preferred to repay him in person. I am grateful to you, Pilar, for this concern in my affairs,' he added silkily. 'But perhaps we can now consider the matter closed.'

Pilar's eyes flashed mutinously, but she said nothing as the door opened to admit Carlos bearing a large silver tureen of soup.

It was a delicious meal from the soup itself, full of spicy meatballs and aromatic with herbs, to the pork cooked with chili and vegetables and served on a heaped bed of rice, and ending with *cocada*—a concoction of syrupy, sherry-flavoured coconut.

Many more meals like that, and all Maria's wishes about her figure would be fulfilled, Nicola thought wryly as she put down her napkin.

'You like Mexican cooking, Señorita Tarrant?' Pilar leaned forward, smiling with patent insincerity. 'I thought our food would have been too warm, too highly spiced for pallid Anglo-Saxon tastes.'

If food were all that she was talking about, Nicola thought with sudden anger. She said, 'But you forget that I've been in Mexico for more than a year. I've had plenty of time to accustom myself.' She turned to Ramón, smiling at him. 'Please don't forget you promised to show me the *hacienda*.'

'Certainly.' Ramón rose gallantly. He looked at Luis, leaning back in his chair at the head of the table, his dark face enigmatic. 'You permit, Luis?'

'You are the expert on the house, *amigo*.' His tone sounded bored, but Nicola sensed that he was not pleased, and found it oddly exciting.

As they crossed the hall, Ramón said with a trace of awkwardness, 'You may think it strange that my mother did not offer to act as your guide, but . . .'

'I don't find it strange at all,' she returned drily. 'I'm sure that she and your sister would much prefer to continue their listing of all the ways in which I fall short of being a suitable bride for your cousin.'

He sighed. 'So they make it so obvious? Nicola, I am truly sorry. In truth, my mother has become so accustomed to being the mistress here that she will find it hard to take second place to another woman—to any woman. It is not a personal thing, believe me.'

Nicola wasn't so sure, but she smiled at him. 'Thank you for the reassurance.' They were in the *salón*, and she glanced around, wanting to turn the conversation from the personal to the general for Ramón's sake as much as anything. He couldn't be blamed for his mother and sister's behaviour.

'What a beautiful room this is.' She made her words deliberately conventional. 'The furniture is very old, I suppose.'

'Most of it was brought from Spain on sailing ships and then hauled here on waggons drawn by mules.' He grimaced comically. 'What a journey! What an undertaking! It makes one feel ill to contemplate it even in these modern times.' He smiled. 'Doña Manuela must have had a singularly persuasive way with her.'

Nicola remembered that he had referred to the portrait she had admired earlier as Doña Manuela.

'Then it was all her doing?' She gestured round her.

'To a great extent,' Ramón nodded in confirmation. 'It is a romantic story. I am surprised that Luis himself did not wish to tell it to you. She was a great beauty and an heiress, but she fell in love with a soldier who had little but his own courage, so her family forbade her to think of him. She could have married anyone, it was said. She was used to court life, crowded gatherings, balls and festivals. She was a wonderful dancer, so light on her feet that she was called La Mariposa, the Butterfly.'

'Then the *hacienda* was named after her?'

'*Si*. Her lover became a *conquistador* and made himself a fortune. This time when he sought her hand, her family did not refuse, although they begged her not to come to this wild and primitive land—not to leave

Spain. And she laughed, and said that she would take a little of Spain with her.'

'She certainly did that.' Nicola's fingers moved appreciatively over the ancient, heavily carved wood. She wondered if the *hacienda* had altered very much from those days. It had developed, and become more luxurious with succeeding generations, but if Doña Manuela were here at this moment, walking beside them with her silk skirts rustling, it would probably still be familiar to her.

What could she have thought, coming from her pampered and cossetted background in Spain to this wilderness! Compared to a castle in Spain, the *hacienda* would have seemed primitive indeed to the *conquistador*'s bride. Had she still smiled as she rode in her waggon with her servants and outriders to protect her from the hostile Indians, or had even her lively spirit quailed as she contemplated what lay in front of her?

She asked, 'Was she happy here—after all that?'

Ramón shrugged. 'She did not have long to enjoy her happiness. She died in childbirth about a year after the portrait of her was completed, and her husband nearly went mad with grief. It was only the son she had borne him that saved his sanity.'

Nicola shivered. 'You said it was a romantic story. I think it's a sad one.'

He looked faintly surprised. 'Cannot it be both? To love and be beloved in return—isn't that what every woman secretly desires, no matter how short such happiness may be?'

Nicola said shortly, 'I wouldn't know. Shall we go on with the tour?'

There were numerous rooms on the ground floor, all graciously sized and quite sufficient to give any of the *hacienda*'s inhabitants as much privacy as any of them might desire. In fact Nicola couldn't imagine what half of them were used for, but Ramón seemed to take the opulence of his surroundings totally for granted.

The room she liked least was Luis's study. No concessions to luxury had been made there. It was a starkly masculine room, equipped with a workmanlike desk, and lined with books.

'This is Luis's sanctuary when he is here,' Ramón commented. 'It is a rule that no one interrupts him when that door is shut, but of course it will not apply to you, little cousin.'

'I can't imagine any exception being made in my case,' she said. The severe simplicity of it surprised her. She had expected something rather more hedonistic for the master. 'You don't share it with him?'

'*Dios*, no,' Ramón laughed. 'I have my own office. I don't intrude on Luis' privacy. I am not so brave.' He glanced at her quickly. 'But I think his solitude will not be so precious to him now.'

Solitude? Nicola questioned inwardly. Luis Alvarado de Montalba was the last person in the world who needed to be alone.

She turned to leave the room, and started violently as she saw him leaning in the doorway watching them. Ramón looked taken aback too.

'I'm sorry, Luis.' He spread his hands swiftly. 'But I thought you would wish Nicola to see everything—even here.'

'Of course.' He did not move. 'But it might be more appropriate if Carmela were to show her the kitchen quarters—and the bedrooms. Juan Hernandez is looking for you.'

'I'll go at once,' said Ramón. He disappeared before Nicola was even able to thank him.

Luis strolled past her to the desk and took a thin black cigar from a box there. He lit it unhurriedly, still watching her.

'Do you like my house, *querida*?'

She noticed he did not say 'home'.

'No one could help liking it,' she said, a little helplessly. She paused. 'Ramón told me about Doña

Manuela—La Mariposa. I wondered about her, when I saw the butterfly in her hair.'

'It is said he had it made for her,' he said. 'From silver mined near Santo Tomás.'

'Does it still exist?'

He shook his head. 'I believe it was buried with her.' His hand moved towards one of the telephones on the desk—the house phone, she guessed. 'Shall I summon Carmela to show you the rest of the place?'

'Not—not for a moment.' She swallowed. 'I must talk to you.'

Luis blew a reflective cloud of smoke. 'I am at your service, *amiga*.'

Nicola took a deep breath. 'It's hopeless—you must see that. Keeping me here—marrying me—just won't work. Your family will never accept me as your wife. It would be better—much easier for everyone if you—let me go.'

'Easier for you perhaps,' he said drily. 'But I have no intention of letting you go. However, you need not fear. Tia Isabella will mellow to you in time. She has too much to lose if she does not,' he added cynically.

She stared at him. 'I don't understand.'

'It is simple enough. Her husband had money, but he was a gambler, a speculator in minerals. He invested heavily in mines which yielded nothing, and lost everything. Fortunately the shock killed him before Tia Isabella had a chance to do so. As Ramón's passion had always been ranching, and not ill-starred investments, it seemed sensible to offer him La Mariposa as his home and allow him to run it for me. But Tia Isabella is my guest here, and only my guest, as I was forced to remind her.'

She moistened her lips. 'You told Ramón the truth—about how we met, and other things—but what did you tell your aunt and your cousin?'

His mouth twisted. 'Not the truth, *chica*, but a story to fit the circumstances. Does it matter?'

'I suppose not,' she said defeatedly.

He took her chin in his hand, forcing her to look up at him. 'A word of warning. Do not make my cousin Ramón fall in love with you. I should not find it amusing.'

'I don't find any of this particularly amusing,' she snapped, pulling away from him. 'But you don't have to worry. With an unwanted bridegroom in my life, I'm not likely to start encouraging anyone else!'

She turned to leave, but he gripped her arm, pulling her round to face him.

'So you don't want me,' he said softly. 'What a little hypocrite you are, *amiga*.'

He bent his head and found her lips with his. This time there was no savagery, no coercion. His mouth moved slowly and persuasively on hers, coaxing her lips apart in a sensually teasing caress which sent her blood hammering through her veins. All her good resolutions about remaining aloof and unbending died a swift death as he drew her closer against the hardness of his body, his own urgency firing a response she was helpless to control.

She thought, 'I never knew it could be like this. God help me, I never knew . . .' Then all thinking processes were suspended as her awareness yielded totally to these new sensations he was evoking in her. Her hands linked behind her neck, her fingers curling into his thick dark hair, and eyes closed, she swayed against him, blind and deaf to everything but the clamour of her body as his kiss deepened endlessly.

Pilar said from the doorway, 'Luis, is your telephone switched off? There is a call for you . . . Oh!'

Without any great haste, he lifted his head and looked at her.

'*Gracias*, Pilar. Perhaps you would be good enough to find Carmela and tell her that my *novia* is anxious to be shown the rest of the house.'

Pilar gave a little sniff and turned on her heel to leave,

sending, as she did so, a look at Nicola which combined the usual hostility with a kind of shocked curiosity.

Nicola's face burned as she stepped back, her hands going up to smooth her dishevelled hair.

When she was sure Pilar was no longer within earshot, she said unsteadily, 'I hate you.'

He smiled. 'Perhaps, *querida*, but at least you are not indifferent to me.'

'I'll be working on it,' she whispered, staring at him.

He shrugged slightly, his amused gaze roaming over her flushed face, and the swift rise and fall of her breasts under the tight fitting bodice. 'What a waste of energy, *querida*, that might be employed in more—agreeable ways. And now, if you will excuse me . . .' He reached for the telephone.

Nicola longed to slam the door as she left the room, but it was too heavy and solid, resisting her efforts to close it even, so that she had ample time to hear his soft-voiced, '*Si*? Carlota, how is it with you?'

She stood in the corridor outside, staring at the heavy timbers which prevented her hearing any more, and knowing a childish desire to beat on them with her convulsively clenched fists.

The unknown caller had to be Carlota Garcia, the woman Teresita had mentioned. She had assumed the affair was in the past, but it seemed she was mistaken. Luis had not the slightest intention of allowing a little thing like marriage to interfere with his chosen pleasures. The sudden ache in her throat made her feel as if she was swallowing past knives, and yet what had she really expected?

She began to run down the corridor. In the hall, she encountered Carmela, a stout woman with greying hair whose ready smile faded to puzzlement and sympathy as Nicola explained that she had a headache and would not be seeing any more of the *hacienda* that day. She refused all offers of cool drinks and medication, and fled upstairs to her room.

But even there, there was no sanctuary. She lay on the wide bed and looked up at the butterfly, its delicate embroidered wings shimmering in the sunlight. Her emblem was everywhere—this girl who had travelled half across the world to find her love.

Nicola thought, 'I've travelled as far—but what is there here for me? No love, certainly.'

There were tears on her face, but she welcomed them, knowing that, without love, she would one day know a bitterness too deep for tears, and wondering, with a kind of despair, why she should suddenly be so sure of this.

By the time Maria arrived to help her to dress for dinner, she had regained some measure of control. Maria had brought with her the dress she had been altering, a simple black sheath, with a deep square neckline and elbow-length sleeves. Dressed in it, Nicola felt prepared to face the world, if not enjoy it. She had finished doing her face under Maria's approving scrutiny and was applying some gloss to her lips, when there was a knock at the door.

Maria went to answer it, and stood aside giggling as Luis walked in. Then, before Nicola could stop her, she vanished, leaving them alone together.

She sat staring into the mirror, watching him approach. He came and stood behind her.

He said, 'I regret, *querida*, that I shall not be here for dinner. I have to go to Santo Tomás quite unexpectedly.'

Nicola replaced the cap on the tube of glosser and put it down. She was pleased to see how steady her hands were.

'Have you nothing to say?' His eyes watched hers in the mirror.

'What do you want me to say?'

He shrugged. 'Just a word that you are sorry—that you might even miss me.'

She said without a trace of expression, 'I'm sorry. I shall miss you,' and saw his mouth tighten.

He said, 'I had intended to give you this later, but I thought perhaps you might wish to wear it at dinner—as a reminder of me,' he added cynically.

He put a flat velvet case on the dressing table in front of her. For a moment she didn't move, and he said with a trace of impatience, 'Open it, *amiga*.'

It was a pendant, a single lustrous pearl on a long golden chain. Nicola had never seen anything so lovely. As she stared at it, she felt as if she could scarcely breathe.

He leaned over her shoulder and lifted it out of its satin bed. He put the chain round her neck, and the pearl slid coolly into the hidden shadowed valley between her breasts. Luis bent and put his lips to the curve of her shoulder.

If she had been calm before, then she was trembling now, her pulses hammering at the slightest brush of his mouth on her body.

He said softly, 'It matches your skin, *querida*.' His hands moved on her shoulders, sliding the dress away from her.

Nicola said, 'No,' hoarsely, and her hands came up, snatching at the material to cover her breasts.

He frowned a little. 'Don't be frightened, *amada*. I only want to look at you—not touch—or kiss. I shall keep my word. But when you are my wife, and perhaps less shy of me, then you can wear it as I wish—with nothing to hide either the pearl—or you—from me.'

Slowly, almost mockingly he readjusted her dress. He said, 'Aren't you going to thank me?'

Nicola said coolly, '*Gracias, señor*. It's very lovely. I'm sure Teresita would have been delighted with it too.'

The dark face hardened, and he straightened abruptly. She expected some stinging retort, and closed her eyes as if to shield herself from his anger. But none came, and when she ventured to look, he was alone.

Her legs were shaking as she got up from the stool at

last. She got downstairs somehow, and into the *salón* where they were waiting for her.

She said, 'I'm sorry if I'm late.'

Ramón came forward drawing a deep breath. 'If you are late, little cousin, then you are more than worth waiting for, believe me. May I get you a drink?'

She said with mock plaintiveness, 'Would you think me rude, Don Ramón, if I said I would rather have my dinner? I'm very hungry.'

Doña Isabella rose with a snakelike rustle of skirts. 'Then by all means let us go into dinner. It has been delayed long enough. Come, Pilar.'

She swept past Nicola, without a second glance, followed by her daughter.

Ramón said hurriedly, 'Nicola, I am truly sorry that Luis cannot be here tonight.'

She raised her eyebrows calmly. 'Why?'

'Well——' he spread his hands defensively, 'it is your first evening—your first dinner in your home. An auspicious occasion. You have every reason to complain about his absence.'

Nicola said, 'Don Luis' absences are something I shall have to get accustomed to. I may as well begin at once.' She had managed to say it without wincing, she thought, but she couldn't suppress the bitterness totally. 'Besides, I suppose there's something to admire in such—loyalty to an old friend.'

She had expected Ramón to faint with embarrassment and shock, but he registered nothing but surprise and dawning approbation.

He said, 'So you know—and you understand?'

'It seems I have little choice,' she said in a brittle voice. 'Now shall we go into dinner?'

And all through that interminable meal, she sat with Luis's pearl like a frozen tear between her breasts.

CHAPTER SIX

As her wedding day drew inexorably nearer, Nicola found the days were taking on a strangely dreamlike quality. She was very conscious that she was no longer in control of her own destiny, and as a consequence reality seemed to withdraw to a distance. But afterwards, certain incidents seemed to her to stand out with startling clarity.

She had spent quite some time writing letters—to her parents, to Elaine and to Teresita. The first had been incredibly difficult, because she had to leave so much unsaid. For instance, she could hardly write to two people who loved her, 'He makes me burst into flames if he so much as takes my hand, but he has a mistress in Santo Tomás a few miles away and he visits her several times a week, and will probably continue to do so after the wedding.' So instead she told them that she was very happy and that if they thought they could come to the wedding, Luis would send the air tickets immediately.

The letters to Elaine and Teresita were much easier, because she confined herself to a bald statement of the facts without explanation or expansion. Her sole concession was a 'Please don't worry about me' scrawled at the end of each.

Doña Isabella did not mellow as Luis had predicted, but her attitude gradually became more resigned as the wedding approached. Nicola suspected she derived a great deal of secret enjoyment from the arrangements in spite of her constant complaints. Certainly she made the most of playing the gracious hostess when visitors began arriving to meet Don Luis' *novia*. There were luncheon parties and supper parties, with guests from all over the state and beyond, some of them even arriving in their own private planes and helicopters on the landing strip at the rear of the *hacienda*. Nicola had discovered that Luis himself possessed a pilot's licence, and frequently took the controls at his own light aircraft which he kept at Monterrey airport.

Nicola found the frequent parties an ordeal, even when Luis was there at her side, and far worse when he was not. And he was not always there by any means. She was beginning to realise the extent of his wealth and responsibilities, and understand why he was often away at meetings, sometimes for days at a time.

She always felt uneasy when he was away from the *hacienda*. Not because she missed him, she assured herself swiftly, but because without his presence and protection she was always more aware of his family's hostility and disapproval.

Not Ramón, of course. If he had misgivings about his cousin's choice of bride, he concealed them well, and was always friendly and considerate, but he wasn't always there either, and it was then that his mother and sister began to plant their barbs, holding long conversations from which Nicola was excluded because she knew nothing of the people they were mentioning, or the incidents to which they referred. She knew they were deliberately showing her that she did not belong to their leisured world, and she wanted to say, 'Don't worry—it wasn't my idea. But the alternatives were pretty appalling too.'

She had sometimes wondered if she could appeal to Doña Isabella for help. The border with the United States couldn't be all that far away, but she guessed that if Doña Isabella had to weigh ridding herself of Nicola against deliberately arousing Luis' wrath, there would be no assistance there. Besides, Luis still had her passport, and during his absences, the door to his study was kept locked.

But her life wasn't just a constant stream of visitors

and social events. Señora Mendez, the dressmaker, was now installed at the *hacienda*, a small stout woman with flashing eyes and an imperious manner, trailing a downtrodden daughter carrying pattern books and fabric samples in her wake. Nicola was aware that the Señora was there to make her wedding dress, but she was frankly taken aback at the extent of the trousseau which was to be provided, particularly in view of the fact that there was to be no honeymoon trip as such. Luis had informed her abruptly that his business commitments were too pressing, but that he would arrange something later in the year.

'But if we're not going away, then I don't need all these clothes,' Nicola protested.

He lifted a brow, sending her a sardonic grin. 'I agree, *chica*, but we must not scandalise Tia Isabella.'

She had turned away, flushing, half in anger, and half with the forbidden excitement which always uncurled deep inside her when he looked at her like that. And it happened too often for comfort. Sometimes as she sat at the dining table, or on the terrace, or walked in the courtyard she would look up and see him watching her, a deep sensual hunger in his eyes which he made no effort to conceal.

In a way, although her mind rejected all the conventional connotations of a honeymoon, she felt it might have made things easier for her if they had gone away somewhere, if only for a few days. She would find it embarrassing in the extreme to have to face the small enclosed world of the *hacienda* each day as Luis's bride. But at the same time, it was impossible to confess her misgivings to Luis, to tell him frankly that she would prefer her transition from girlhood to womanhood to be observed by no other eyes but his.

Because that wasn't strictly true either. Each day, the implications of what she was about to do pressed more heavily upon her, filling her with a kind of panic. She might feel that she no longer had any real will of her own, that some unknown current was sweeping her away, and she could no longer swim against it, but the fact remained that the ultimate intimate submission still lay ahead of her, and she was terrified.

It was not just the thought of being alone with him which intimidated her, or of having to accede to demands which were still, in spite of any amount of theoretical enlightenment, very much a mystery. He had enough expertise, enough experience, she knew helplessly, to make it easy for her, to gentle her into acceptance of him—if he chose.

But instead he might simply choose to give free rein to the tightly leashed passion she sensed every time he came anywhere near her. After all, he had made no guarantees of consideration, or tenderness. He had said that he wanted her, and warned her not to fight him. And, worst of all, he knew that he could make her want him.

She had never dreamed it was possible to be so deeply, physically aware of another human being. And yet each time he returned to the *hacienda* from one of his trips, it was as if she was warned by some secret, invisible antennae. Long before she heard his voice, or recognised his long lithe stride, she knew when he was near her.

This was what frightened her—the prospect of total physical enslavement, the subjugation of her personality to his. If she was honest, it could already have taken place if he had made the slightest attempt to woo her, or even be alone with her. But he never did, and never had since that evening in her room when he had given her the pearl.

She had not worn the pearl since, although she had worn other jewellery he had given her—family heirlooms, most of them in exquisite if old-fashioned mountings.

And the best gift of all had been no heirloom, but barely more than a trinket, which he had handed to her quite casually one evening when they were all gathered in the *salón* before dinner. Inside the tissue wrappings of the small package, Nicola had found a butterfly, its body silver and its wings mother-of-pearl, to fasten in her hair. She had exclaimed in delight, turning to him with shining eyes as she tried to thank him, knowing that if only—if only they had been alone she would have cast restraint to the winds and kissed him. But she didn't dare, not as much as a swift peck on the cheek. He had shrugged, turning away. '*De nada*, Nicola. You seemed so intrigued with La Mariposa, I thought it might be appropriate.' Even a muttered comment from Pilar about 'cheap rubbish' had not dimmed her pleasure.

Although she had made a positive effort to establish some kind of relationship with Pilar, this had borne no fruit at all. The other girl avoided her whenever possible, and was inimical when they were in each other's company. Nicola was not convinced her behaviour was prompted by thwarted love for Luis either. She used no arts to allure him, to show him what he was missing. Her attitude wavered between bare civility and smouldering resentment, and in his turn Luis treated her with a guarded patience bordering on exasperation. Only the blind maternal love of someone like Doña Isabella could ever have linked them as a couple, Nicola decided ruefully.

As the days passed, the fact that she wasn't dreaming or that this whole situation was not some vast hideous joke being perpetrated on her in revenge began to come home to her fully. There were legal details to be settled, and papers to be signed, and she found herself obeying like an automaton, knowing as she did so that there was no turning back.

But did she even want to? If by some alchemy it was possible to wipe out the past weeks, to transform her into the girl she had been in Mexico City with nothing ahead of her but a sightseeing trip, would she do so?

I don't know, she thought. I just don't know. And

that, strangely, was the most disturbing thing of all.

From the niche above the altar, the painted eyes of the Virgin looked down. Nicola found her own gaze returning to the image time and time again as the ceremony which made her Luis' wife proceeded according to the time-honoured ritual. It was not so very different from the service which would have been held at home in England in the village church, as Father Gonzago had explained during one of his visits in the past week to instruct her briefly in the Catholic faith.

But the church was very different—almost alien with its carving and gilding and the smell of incense heavy in the air, and the statue of the Mother of God was the most alien of all, in her heavy gold brocade robes stitched with precious stones, and the high gold coronet on her head. She was nothing like any of the smiling blue-robed Madonnas in English churches, Nicola thought. An honoured Christian symbol she might be, but at the same time there was something essentially pagan about the gorgeous robes, and the fixed almost inhuman smile, reminding Nicola, if she needed reminding, that the land they stood on had had Christianity imposed upon it, but that older, darker gods, worshipped in blood, still lingered in the memory of its people.

How many Montalba brides had those painted eyes watched? she wondered, as her voice obediently repeated the vows after Father Gonzago. None of it seemed real, least of all herself in this dress—yard upon yard of billowing ivory silk—and the exquisite antique lace mantilla which Luis had asked her to wear. He did not explain, and she didn't ask, but there was something in the way he touched it as he handed it to her which told her it had been his mother's.

She wondered what her own mother would have thought if she had seen her like this. Her parents had wanted to come, but there was too much to do on the farm, so they had promised a visit later. 'When you're settled, darling,' her mother had written, and Nicola's lips had twisted ruefully at the homely phrase. It bore no relationship to any life she might expect to have with Luis.

But she had been surprised to learn that Luis had also written to them. He had never mentioned any such intention to her, and she had been pleased and a little touched by the gesture.

In the absence of her father, she had wondered who would give her away, until Luis's godfather had informed her during one of his visits that it would be his privilege to do so. He was a correct man, inclining towards stoutness, with a neat grey beard, and he was so like the mental image that Nicola had once harboured of Luis himself that she had had to fight to conceal a smile when she had first been introduced.

But he had been amazingly kind to her as he took her down the aisle on his arm, patting her hand reassuringly, and telling her that she was as beautiful as an angel.

Nicola didn't believe him, but she had been satisfied as she took a final look in her mirror. Señora Mendez was a genius, and her dress was wonderful, fairytale, dreamlike. And it would bring her good fortune, the Señora had smilingly assured her. Had she not sewn good luck tokens into the hem with her own hands?

'And there is also this.' With a droll look, she had slipped a flat tissue-wrapped parcel into Nicola's hands. 'Always for my brides I do this. One gown for the day, and another for the night.' She sighed sentimentally, gave Nicola's skirt one last professional twitch, and departed.

Nicola undid the white ribbon and unfolded the tissue, knowing what she would find. It was a nightdress, white as a cloud in chiffon, falling from the tiniest of bodices in handmade lace. Nicola stared at it, feeling panic rising in her throat again.

'Ah, how beautiful!' Maria who was hovering nearby,

darted forward. 'Let me take it, *señorita*. See?' She allowed the material to drift across her hand and arm so that Nicola could see just how sheer and transparent the wretched garment was.

Maria sent her an arch look, began to say something, then thought better of it.

Nicola wrenched her thoughts back to the present, aware of a frozen feeling in her throat, as Luis' ring slid into place on her finger. She was married—married twice, in fact, because earlier in the cool of the morning they had driven to Santo Tomás for a brief civil ceremony.

The evening before, she had chosen a moment when she knew Luis was in his study and alone and had gone to him there.

He had risen as soon as she appeared hesitantly in the doorway, his brows lifting in surprise.

'You honour me, *querida*. I had imagined you busied with a thousand last-minute details.'

'No,' she said. 'There's nothing. Your aunt is very efficient. Everything is ready—except . . .' She hesitated.

'Except?' he prompted.

'Except myself,' she said wretchedly. 'Luis, it still isn't too late. You could let me go.'

He came round the desk to her side, his eyes narrowed, and the dark brows drawn together in a swift frown.

'What nonsense is this?'

'It isn't nonsense,' she protested. 'You can't marry me—you know you can't. Why don't you just—allow me to leave? There might be talk at first, but Doña Isabella would soon convince everyone you'd had a lucky escape.'

He shook his head. 'There will be no talk, because you are not leaving. How could you, anyway, without this?' He reached behind him and picked up her passport which had been lying on the desk. He opened the cover and looked down at it. 'I see I am required to allow the

bearer to pass freely, and without "let or hindrance." '
He smiled faintly. 'Much as I respect your Queen, I have
no intention of obeying this request.' He slipped the
passport into his pocket. 'This stays with me, *amiga*,
and so do you.'

She went on looking at him. 'Oh God, why are you
doing this?' she asked raggedly. 'What do you want from
me?'

His voice was silky 'I want a wife, Nicola. And I want
a son. You will give me both. You forced your way into
my life. Now you will remain there—always.'

She said tonelessly, 'For the last time, Luis—please
let me go.'

Mockingly he shook his head. '*Jamas, amante.*
Never.'

She left him without another word, and went straight
to her room. That morning in the car on the way to
Santo Tomás they had sat like strangers, without a
word. In fact she wasn't sure if he'd even looked at her
properly until much later, as she came into the chapel
on his godfather's arm. All the way to the altar, he had
watched her with arrogant possession in his eyes.

Now Father Gonzago was pronouncing a final blessing, and Luis was helping her up from her knees. His
eyes were enigmatic as they met hers, and her own
glance slid nervously away.

People were smiling and bowing to her as she moved
with her bridegroom towards the open doors and the
sunlight. Many of them were now familiar faces from
previous visits to the *hacienda*, and Nicola forced herself
to respond to the greetings, pretend to be the happy
bride they all expected.

Yet there was one face that was not in the slightest
degree familiar. Nicola noticed it at once, because she
knew she would not have forgotten if she had ever met
such an outstandingly beautiful woman. Her jet black
hair was drawn severely back into a chignon, and she
was exquisitely dressed and made up, her heavy lidded

eyes and full-lipped mouth being particularly accentuated.

Then they were outside in the late sunlight, and there were others crowding round, the *peons* who worked in the fields, the *vaqueros* who rode with the cattle, the servants, all offering their congratulations.

The religious ceremony had been held after the hour of siesta, because it would be followed by a party. Soon there would be music in the courtyard, as she had once imagined, and dancing and the inevitable fireworks. All the hallmarks of a celebration, and she, who was the centre of all these festivities, felt as if she was dying inside.

Presently she would be expected to dance, and to dance with Luis. Everyone, she supposed, would want to dance with the bride, but he was her husband, so it was his right. She didn't want to think about those other rights which he would demand later, much later, when the music had stopped. Perhaps she could bribe the musicians, she thought, to play and play all that night, and through the following day and the one after that . . . She caught at herself as a little bubble of sheer hysteria rose within her.

Inside the house Carlos, all smiles, was opening wine—imported vintage champagne. Nicola took the glass she was offered and sipped, still with that mechanical smile on her lips.

Doña Isabella and Pilar came and embraced her, their cheeks brushing hers swiftly and formally before they stepped away, their duty done. Ramón kissed her hand and whispered, 'Luis is the most fortunate of men.'

She went on smiling until she thought her face would crack into a thousand little pieces as the guests filed past to utter their congratulations. So much good will, so many good wishes, and yet she could believe in none of it. It was all still part of the charade she had begun back in Mexico City. She was like a puppet, dressed in garments which didn't belong to her, and manipulated by strangers. But all too soon there was coming a time when the doll would change into a woman. She might have come to this place as a counterfeit bride, but tonight Luis would exact full recompense from her in a currency which was only too real.

Suddenly she knew she had to escape from the smiles, the torrent of words, and the knowing looks.

She turned to Luis. 'The mantilla is making my head ache. May I remove it before the dancing?'

'Of course.' He studied her pale face frowningly. 'Shall I send Maria to you?'

'Oh, no, I can manage,' she said hastily.

The quiet room upstairs was no longer hers alone. The bed had been re-made, she saw at once, with lace-edged sheets and extra pillows, and Señora Mendez' nightgown was laid across the foot of it like a cloud of foam.

Nicola removed the pins which held the mantilla, working carefully to avoid tearing the delicate lace, then started violently as a knock came at the door.

It was Carmela, smiling broadly. 'This letter came for you, *señora*. Señor Don Luis said I should give it to you at once.'

Nicola took it wonderingly, her brow clearing as she recognised her mother's handwriting. It was just a note, brief but full of love, to tell her that they would all be thinking of her, and sending affectionate messages to Luis that she would never dare pass on, because it was her fault that they believed that this was a conventional marriage, and that they were getting a son-in-law who would value such sentiments.

There was also a postscript. 'I'm enclosing this letter which came for you the other day from Switzerland. I think it's probably from Tess. Did you manage to keep in touch with her?'

The short answer to that was no, Nicola thought wryly. She had avoided writing to any of her Zurich friends in case they inadvertently included news of Ewan which she didn't want to hear, although most of them knew what had happened.

She glanced at the other envelope, then slipped it into a drawer. She would read it later.

It was getting darker outside, and out in the courtyard she could hear the sound of musicians tuning up. The dancing couldn't start without her, so it was time she went down.

Luis advanced to meet her, an elegant stranger in his black suit, its short jacket embroidered in silver. Nicola let him take her cold hand in his, and put his arm round her waist. She had been frightened that she might go to pieces altogether when he touched her, but his clasp was too light and formal for that. At any other time, she might have enjoyed moving with him in a swift waltz round the circle of smiling faces, while they applauded and showered them with flower petals. Her dress billowed out as he swung her round, and then it was over, and someone else was eagerly claiming her hand, and she was whirled away. She caught a glimpse of him over her new partner's shoulder, and saw that he was smiling faintly. He could afford to smile, she thought, because he knew however many men she might dance with, in the end she would be alone with him. Wherever she went and whoever she danced with, his glance seemed to find her. He was the hawk of her nightmare, she thought, hovering, knowing his prey is there for the taking.

She ate food she did not want, replied to questions she barely heard, and eventually turned to a touch on her arm to find Pilar confronting her.

'Nicola.' Her smile was sugary. 'There is someone here who so much wishes to meet you. May I present the Señora Doña Carlota Garcia?'

It was the woman she had noticed in the chapel. In close-up she was even more striking, Nicola thought numbly, and her dark red dress was exquisitely cut to draw attention to her slim waist and full voluptuous breasts.

Her voice was low and charming. 'It is a pleasure to meet you, Doña Nicola. I would have called before, but since my husband's death I have myself become deeply involved in politics, and I travel a good deal. But I would not miss the wedding of such an old friend as Luis for anything in the world.'

A number of replies occurred to Nicola, but a glance at the spiteful triumph in Pilar's face kept her silent.

She said at last, slowly, 'It is a—pleasure for me also, *señora*. I have heard a great deal about you.'

Señora Garcia laughed, displaying perfect teeth. 'Not from Luis, I hope! We know each other so well that he is hardly a reliable informant. He flatters me too much.'

Nicola raised her eyebrows coolly. 'I don't think Luis has ever mentioned you to me. No, it was someone else who spoke of you.'

Señora Garcia looked slightly disconcerted, she was pleased to note. 'I—see. Well, I hope we can be friends.' She gave Nicola another smile and walked away, followed by Pilar.

And I, Nicola silently addressed her departing back, hope we never meet again. She was surprised how angry the unexpected encounter had made her, but told herself defensively that it was not the fact that Luis had a mistress—for all she knew he had half a dozen—but that he had had the unmitigated gall to invite her to his wedding. But then he had no reason to believe that his bride even suspected her existence, she thought.

'You look cross, little cousin. Has some clumsy fool stamped on your foot?' Ramón had suddenly materialised at her side, and beyond him she could see Luis advancing through the crowd.

She smiled swiftly. 'It's nothing. Dance with me, Ramón.'

He looked taken aback. 'But Luis . . .'

'Oh, he won't lack for partners, and you've hardly

been near me all evening,' she protested with almost a pout. She put out a hand and traced some of the embroidery on his sleeve. 'I shall begin to think you dislike me as much as your mother and sister do.'

Nombre de Dios,' Ramón muttered, looking suddenly anguished. 'They do not—I do not—I—oh, very well, let us dance.'

Luois had stopped and was watching them, she knew, and quite deliberately she allowed her hand to slide from Ramón's shoulder towards his collar, smiling radiantly into his face as she did so.

He looked as if he was about to have a heart attack. 'Nicola, I beg of you! Is this some game? I warn you, it is a dangerous one. Luis is my cousin and my friend, but his anger can be formidable.'

'But you're a wonderful dancer, Ramón.' She looked at him through her lashes. 'I am sure my—husband wouldn't grudge me these few minutes of pleasure at my own party.'

'If you think that, then you do not know him at all,' Ramón said bluntly. 'Let me take you to him, Nicola. Please do not provoke him further.'

'Spoilsport!' She pulled a face at him. 'Very well, if you're so frightened of him.'

'I am more frightened for you than for myself. Do you wish to begin your married life with a beating at his hands?'

'He wouldn't dare,' she said defiantly.

He gave her a despairing look. 'If you believe that, then you are—forgive me—a fool. Anyway, the dancing will end soon. It is nearly time for the firework display, and when that starts it is the custom in our family for the bride to—to retire.'

'I've no intention of doing anything of the sort. I want to see the fireworks. This is supposed to be my party, and I shall enjoy every last minute of it,' Nicola said coolly. 'Customs like that belong to history, not the present day, anyway.'

Ramón's pleasant mouth set in a line which indicated that he would not be averse to starting off the prescribed beating with a box on the ears on his own account.

In a carefully neutral tone, he said, 'That is an argument which should more properly be directed to your husband, my cousin, *señora*. I will take you to him.'

Luis was lounging against one of the pillars of the terrace, glass in hand, as they approached. He straightened and smiled, but the smile did not reach his eyes.

Ramón said, 'I have brought you your errant bride, *amigo*. It seems she does not care for some of our customs.' He took Nicola's hand from his arm and placed it firmly in that of Luis before moving off.

Luis raised her hand to his lips. To a casual onlooker it would have been a charming, gallant gesture, but then a casual onlooker would not have seen the cold rage in his eyes.

He said, 'And which of our conventions do you wish to flout now, *chica*?'

Her heart thudding painfully, Nicola said, 'Ramón told me that I would be expected to leave before the fireworks display. He said it was a family custom—but I don't see why I should do so.'

He shrugged. 'Stay, then. It was designed originally to spare the blushes of the bride, I believe, but no one who has witnessed your conduct tonight, clinging round my cousin's neck like a *puta*, would believe you had any blushes to spare.'

He let her hand fall and walked away, leaving her standing there, the colour fading from her cheeks. Out of the corner of her eye she could see curious glances being cast at her, some of them slightly censorious, and, what was worse, Doña Isabella bearing down on her, bristling with self-righteousness. Nicola took a deep breath, picked up her skirts and fled through the laughing, chattering groups, along the terrace and into the house.

Maria was waiting in her room. Nicola allowed her

to unhook the wedding dress and take it away, and then to the girl's obvious chagrin told her that she could go.

From the noise of explosions, the flashes of light and colour, she guessed the fireworks had begun. She could hear laughter and applause as she sat in her long waist slip and scrap of a bra and looked at herself defeatedly. Luis didn't need to beat her, she thought. He could take the skin from her by his tone of voice alone. And she had stood there like a fool. Why hadn't she accused him in turn?

Furiously she blinked back the tears which for some unaccountable reason were pricking at her eyelids. Soon, when the display was over, those guests who were not being accommodated overnight in the guest wing would be leaving. Luis would say goodbye to them as a courteous host, and then, angry or not, he would come to her room. She didn't want to be found skulking at the dressing table in her undies.

Quickly she undressed and showered, then reluctantly donned the exquisite nightdress waiting for her. She brushed her hair, then on an impulse looked in her jewellery case and pinned the silver butterfly among the tawny silk strands.

She was just going to close the drawer when she saw the letter her mother had sent on. She wasn't in the mood for Tess's usual brand of cheerful chat, but on the other hand she didn't want to sit here, waiting for Luis and becoming twitchier by the moment, so she tore open the envelope and extracted the thin sheet of paper inside. The envelope had been typewritten, but she knew the writing on the letter as soon as she saw it. It was Ewan's.

She felt sick suddenly. Ewan writing to her? It couldn't be possible! She unfolded the paper and began to read, her heart thumping slowly and painfully.

'My dearest Nicola,' she read, 'I expect I'm the last person you ever thought to hear from again. After the things we said before we parted, I'm amazed I have the guts to write to you at all, but I can't stop thinking about you, and all we meant to each other once.

'You probably don't know that I've been a widower for over six months. Greta was killed in a road accident. Her car skidded on some ice and went out of control on a bend. It was a shock, naturally, but I won't pretend it was the end of the world for me. Frankly, our marriage wasn't working out, and we'd discussed separation just before she had the accident. You know how fast she always used to drive. I always thought it was out of character, as she was quite a stick-in-the-mud in other ways.

'I was a fool to let you go—I've known that for a long time. I'm beginning to get my life together again now, and I want you back in it. I know I treated you badly, darling. Forgive me, and tell me that we can start again. Don't let one mistake ruin both our lives a second time. The way you used to feel about me, there must be something left in spite of all the hurt. Write to me, Nicky. Tell me you love me still. I need you. All my love, darling, Ewan.'

Nicola sat stunned, the words dancing crazily in front of her eyes. Ewan—Greta—could it be true? Breathing shakily, she read the letter again, then crumpled it into a ball and thrust it back into the drawer which she slammed shut.

She looked at her white-faced image in the mirror. Ewan, she thought incredulously. Ewan was free and wanted her. And life had played her its cruellest trick of all by allowing her to know this tonight of all nights. Her stifled laugh sounded like a sob, and she lifted her hands to her head, trying to get her thoughts into some kind of coherent order.

But Ewan—Zurich—everything that had happened there between them seemed light years away, like a half-remembered dream.

Ewan, she thought. Ewan, whom she loved, and who had hurt her so that she would never love again.

Desperately she tried to conjure his face up in her mind. Brown hair, curling slightly, blue eyes always smiling, a deep cleft in his chin, she thought feverishly. But that wasn't the image that she saw. The man in her imagination was as dark as night itself, the planes and angles of his face, harshly carved, with strength and pride in its lines. And his eyes did not smile, but looked at her with bitter scorn.

Oh God! She got up from the dressing stool and began to walk round the room, her hands pressed to suddenly heated cheeks. What did it all mean? Ewan had been her love, her only love. He had broken her heart. How could she have forgotten so soon?

The answer was a sombre one. Because Luis had made her forget. From the moment she had met him, he had occupied her thoughts to the exclusion of everything else. Each time he had kissed her, and God knew they had been few enough, each caress had been indelibly printed on her memory, making her ache with longing. Ewan hadn't been able to awaken half the dormant passion which the first brush of Luis' mouth on hers had brought searingly to life.

Her appalling behaviour downstairs, turning her back on him to dance with his cousin, hadn't been because she fancied Ramón even for a moment, or because she wanted to establish herself as an independent spirit, untrammelled by outworn conventions, but because she had been so blazingly jealous of Carlota Garcia.

All the time she had been dancing with Ramón, driving him near to a nervous breakdown with her come-hither looks, she had been seeing Luis with Carlota, imagining them making love, and the pain had been almost more than she could bear.

She had wanted to hurt Luis, and she had only succeeded in hurting herself, because he didn't care. He wanted her—he had never made any secret of it. He wanted her to give him children, and he would expect conduct from her befitting his wife, but nothing else.

And tonight when he touched her at last, and she turned to starlight and flame in his arms, he would know beyond doubt what she herself had only just come to realise—that she loved him.

She shivered, wrapping her arms round her body. It had been there in her mind for so long, unacknowledged, that it was almost a relief to admit it at last. She had fought it from the beginning, labelling it as a sheer physical attraction, but she had lost.

Now she could confess to herself how empty her life had seemed every time Luis had gone away, and how eagerly she had waited for his return. She had never shown it, of course, and she still could not, because nothing had changed.

He was marrying because he desired her, and that was all. If she hadn't appealed to him sexually, then she would probably be in jail at this moment. As it was, he had decided on some whim to create his own intimate prison for her.

And this room was to be her cell. She lifted her head and stared round her. It was quiet now, the sounds of revelry fading from the courtyard beneath. She would not be alone for very much longer. Did she have the strength to pretend the indifference she had threatened? Could she endure to have Luis only as her lover when the truth was that she wanted him as her love?

She stood, pressing one fist against her lips like a bewildered child, wondering what to do. There was nowhere to run, nowhere to hide, not even from herself.

But in spite of her inner agony, she was becoming slowly aware of something else. Not far away, there was music, softly played on guitars, and someone singing in a warm baritone. She went over to the window and peeped round the shutter. They stood in a semi-circle in the courtyard below, looking up towards the window, a group of *mariachi* serenaders, probably from Santo Tomás. Hidden by the shutter, she stood and listened, a wistful smile touching the corner of her mouth. Once he had sent them away, but they were here tonight probably because it was yet another custom.

Nicola wasn't sure when she first realised that she was no longer alone in the bedroom, but she didn't turn immediately because she could use the song as an excuse.

Finally it ended, and the guitars took up another melody, sweet and sensuous, and slowly she turned and looked at him. He was standing only a few feet away from her, wearing a dressing gown in some dark silk, and nothing else, she was certain, because the robe was open to the waist and his legs were bare.

He was looking at her as if the sight of her had turned him to stone, and with a sudden surge of shyness she realised what he was seeing—the gleam of her body through the film of chiffon, her small high breasts cupped but not concealed by the tiny lace bodice. She wanted to speak, but no words would come.

He said huskily, 'Skin like ivory, and hair like gold. *Alma de mi vida,* do you know how beautiful you are?'

The sensual hunger in his eyes was a devastation, and every fibre in her responded to it in a great blaze of yearning. More than life itself she wanted to take the few steps into his arms. But if she did, she would be betrayed utterly, and she panicked, stepping backwards, lifting her hands as if to ward him off.

Yet he had not moved—and nor did he, for one long moment. She saw that fierce desire fading from his face, to be replaced fleetingly by incredulity, and then an immense weariness as he turned away and walked towards the bed, untying the belt of his robe as he went.

Realising that she was right about his nakedness, Nicola averted her gaze hastily. When she did venture to look towards the bed, Luis was in it, safely covered by the sheet, staring up at the ceiling with his arms folded behind his head.

He said at last on a note of polite interest, 'Do you intend to stand there all night?'

'Yes—no—I don't know,' she stammered feeling more of a fool and worse than a fool with every second that passed.

'Then I advise you to make up your mind,' he said. There was a pause, then he added expressionlessly, 'Unless you wish me to make the decision for you by raping you?'

Appalled, she gasped, 'No!'

He turned his head on the pillow and looked at her coolly. 'It is what you seem to expect. A moment ago you looked at me with terror in your eyes. I did not enjoy the experience, which is a new one to me, I confess.'

'I'm—sorry,' she said inadequately. 'But—but you're not making this very easy for me.'

'Perhaps because I do not fully understand the difficulty. You have shared a bed with me before, or had you forgotten?'

'No.' She shook her head. 'But that was different.'

'How so?' He sounded faintly bored.

Nicola hesitated. To say 'Well, for one thing you had your clothes on,' was going to sound ludicrously prim and schoolgirlish, and besides that, hadn't she secretly speculated a dozen times or more on what he would look like without them?

Instead she said, 'I—I wasn't your wife then,' which was hardly any better.

His voice was cold. 'Nor are you now, either in body, or in your stubborn little mind, *amiga*. A few words said over us does not make a marriage. Or did you think that after all I would be content to admire you at a distance?'

'No,' she shook her head again, feeling totally ridiculous. 'You made it clear you wanted—children.'

He turned on to his side, supporting himself on an elbow, a brief crooked smile touching his mouth. 'Eventually, yes. But you are deluding yourself if you think I want you here in my arms simply to make you pregnant. You do not really believe that?'

Huskily, she said, 'No.'

'Muy bien.' He reached over and threw back the sheet on the other side of the bed. 'Then join me, *querida, por favor,*' he added mockingly.

Nicola walked across the room as slowly as she dared, and slid under the turned-back sheet, lying rigidly on the very edge of the bed. There was a click and the big lamp beside the bed was extinguished, plunging the room into darkness.

Nicola scarcely breathed, waiting tensely for—what? A kiss, a touch, the removal of her nightgown, all or any of them.

'You see?' Luis said silkily. 'It was not as impssible as you thought. Sleep well, *querida.* I am glad for your sake that the bed is so wide. A metre or so less and there might have been a chance of my brushing against you accidentally in the night. As it is, you can cower there with your virginal fears in perfect safety. *Buenas noches.'*

Endless seconds spun themselves into an eternity of minutes as Nicola lay, staring into the darkness. Her heart thudding she said at last, 'Luis . . .' her voice low and tentative.

'Si?' His tone was not encouraging, and he actually sounded drowsy, she thought incredulously.

Taking her courage by the scruff of the neck, she ventured, 'If you want me . . .'

'You do me too much honour, *amiga,* but no. I have as little taste for rape as yourself. And don't forget you made me very angry earlier. Be grateful for your re-prieve, and go to sleep.'

The humiliation of it made her shrink, while the space between them yawned as wide and unfathomable as an ocean.

But how could she explain to him—ever—that it was not the act of love she feared, but the unwanted emotions she might betray while she was in his arms?

Meanwhile her body ached for fulfilment, and she turned her head miserably, seeking a cool place on the pillow. Luis wanted her: she knew it. Perhaps he was waiting for her to make the next move. What if she turned towards him, touched him, let her hand slide from his shoulder down his arm to his hip . . .

And what if he told her to go to sleep again? she asked herself bitterly. Could she face another bleak rejection?

She was still debating the point when exhaustion finally dragged her into a fitful and troubled sleep.

CHAPTER SEVEN

IT was late when she awoke. Maria was standing beside the bed, holding a breakfast tray, and smiling selfconsciously.

'Buenos dias, señora.' As Nicola sat up dazedly, she seized her pillows and plumped them up for her to lean against before placing the tray across her lap. 'It is a beautiful morning, *señora*.'

Nicola gave a wry glance at the bright sunlight spilling across the floor. 'I think it's more like afternoon, Maria.'

'Perhaps,' Maria shrugged. 'What does it matter? The Señor Don Luis gave orders that we were not to disturb you earlier.' She giggled. 'Also he sends you this,' she added triumphantly, pointing to a single red rose in a small crystal vase in the centre of the tray.

Nicola stared at it, completely at a loss. 'How kind of him,' she remarked at last.

Maria gasped. 'Kind? Ah, no, *señora*. You do not understand. It is a local custom.'

'Another of them,' Nicola muttered, but Maria went chattering on.

'Here, when the wedding night is over, the husband sends his wife a flower as a token of how she has pleased him. And the Señor Don Luis sends you a red rose, *señora*, the flower of love itself.' She giggled again. 'He must be a happy man this morning!'

The Señor Don Luis, Nicola thought savagely, was a cynical, sarcastic bastard. She pushed the tray away.

'I'm not hungry, Maria. I want to get dressed.'

'But, *señora*,' Maria's eyes nearly popped out of her head, 'should you not—remain where you are?'

Nicola felt a slight flush rise in her cheeks. She said, 'No, Maria. Run me a bath, please, and I'll wear the green dress.'

'*Ay de mi!*' Maria lamented. She did as she was told, but her expression said plainly that any woman fortunate to be sent a red rose after a night of passion with Don Luis should lie back and wait for further goodies to come her way.

She looked reasonable, Nicola thought, as she gave herself a last critical look in the mirror. A little shadowy under the eyes, but that would be expected, she thought ironically.

She was on her way to the door when Maria's shocked voice halted her. '*Señora*—your flower!' She was holding out the rose.

Nicola stared at it. 'What am I supposed to do with it?' she asked flatly.

Maria gestured almost despairingly. 'Wear it in your hair, *señora*. Or carry it, or pin it to your dress against your heart.'

'I'll carry it,' Nicola decided with ill grace, but she was beginning to wonder whether the rose had been presented to her with quite the irony she had at first thought. She hadn't realised it was a token she would be expected to exhibit publicly, but now she could see that in its way, the flower was a chivalrous gesture on Luis' part. After last night's fiasco, he could have sent nothing at all, or the Mexican equivalent of bindweed, and given the whole household something to whisper about in corners. Whereas now, everyone would think that the *dueño* was well pleased with his bride.

She looked down at the rose with sudden tears in her eyes. And it could have been true, she thought fiercely, if only she hadn't been such a fool.

As she walked slowly towards the stairs, nerving herself for the ordeal by curiosity ahead, she wondered wistfully how differently the day might have begun for her if Luis and she had been lovers. She might have been kissed awake in his arms instead of finding herself alone, she thought, and sighed.

As she reached the foot of the stairs, Pilar came into the hall from the *salón* and stood staring at her.

'*Buenos dias.*' Her lips curled unpleasantly. '*Pobrecita*, I suppose you are searching for your bridegroom. How sad for you that his ardour cooled so quickly, and what a pity for him that he didn't come to his senses sooner.'

'I can't think what you mean,' Nicola said coolly.

'No? When the whole world knows how early he left your room this morning, driven away by your English coldness, no doubt.'

Nicola suppressed a wince, then deliberately she lifted the rose which had been hidden by the folds of her skirt and brushed it almost casually across her lips.

Pilar's eyes widened incredulously, then, with a noise like a kitten which has just received an unexpected boot in the midriff, she flounced away.

Nicola was still standing rather hesitantly at the foot of the stairs when Carlos appeared carrying a tray of glasses. He gave her a respectful bow and a smile, and was disappearing towards the *comedor* when she called him back.

'Carlos, do you know where—my husband is?'

'I think Don Luis is at the stables, *señora*. Shall I have a message sent to him?'

'Oh no,' she said quickly. 'I'll go and find him myself.'

'As you wish, Doña Nicola.'

Luis was standing talking to Juan Hernandez as she approached, and they both turned and looked at her. Luis smiled, but his eyes were hooded and enigmatic, and she felt herself blush faintly.

He said, 'I was about to request you to join me, *mi amada*. I have something to show you.'

In some bewilderment she followed him to one of the stalls. Juan Hernandez whisked inside and Nicola heard him murmuring caressingly in his own language and clicking his tongue. When he reappeared he was leading one of the prettiest mares Nicola had ever seen, chestnut with a star on her forehead. She gasped in delight.

'Oh, she's beautiful!'

'I am glad she pleases you, *querida*.' Luis' voice was laconic. 'She only arrived earlier this morning, so she will need a day or two to get used to her new home—and for Juan to make sure she has no hidden vices. Although it seems unlikely,' he added, running his hand down the satin neck.

Nicola made herself meet his eyes. 'You mean—she's for me?'

'For no one else,' he drawled. 'Her name is Estrella.'

Juan Hernandez had tactfully vanished. Nicola said, 'I—I don't know how to thank you.'

'Don't you, *amiga*?' His smile slanted mockingly. 'Perhaps we had better postpone any discussion of that to another occasion.'

Her flush deepened hectically, but before she could think of a reply, he had turned away and was putting Estrella back in her stall.

As Luis rejoined her, she said quickly, 'I also have to thank you for this.' She held out the rose.

He gave it a casual look and shrugged. '*De nada*. I suppose Maria told you its significance.'

'Yes, she did.' Nicola bit her lip. 'It was—kind of you.' She gave a little uneven laugh. 'It's already saved me from some unpleasant remarks from your cousin Pilar.'

His mouth tightened. 'That girl needs a good hiding—or something to do with her time. I blame myself. At one time she was keen to go to university, but her mother set up such scenes, such weeping and lamentations at the idea that I allowed myself to be persuaded against it.'

'But why?'

He gave her a dry look. 'Tia Isabella belongs to a school of thought which believes that women should be trained solely in the domestic virtues. She sees education as the cause of all the ills in our world. And she believed that if she kept Pilar at La Mariposa and thrust her at me continually, I would eventually ask her to be my wife. She has fixed but mistaken views on the value of proximity,' he added drily.

'But you could have overridden your aunt, surely.'

'Yes—but I had my own doubts about Pilar's wish to go to university. At the time she was very much under an influence which I found undesirable.'

Nicola stared at the ground. 'It might have solved a lot of problems if you'd married her. Why didn't you?'

'You have a poor memory, *querida*. Only yesterday I married you.'

'Yes—but when you decided to marry me, it was because you wanted a wife, not me particularly. I mean, you were prepared to marry Teresita whom you hardly knew, because your families wanted it—so why not Pilar?'

He said, 'The only time I have been tempted to lay a hand on my cousin Pilar is when I have also been holding my riding whip. Teresita was at least well-mannered and docile. After marriage she would probably have wearied me with her devotion, but she would have created no problems.'

Wearied me with her devotion. The words were like a knife in Nicola's heart.

'You were really going to marry her,' she said slowly. 'And yet losing her hasn't cost you a single sleepless night.'

'Why waste a sleepless night on a woman who is absent?' he asked mockingly. 'And I must correct you, *chica*. If I'd wanted any wife, I could have married a dozen times over. I married you because I wanted you, Nicola. I was angry at the trick you attempted to play on my family, but at the same time I could not help admiring your audacity and being amused by it. As our journey together proceeded, I began to realise that some

of the assumptions I had made about you were untrue.
Your reactions to me showed plainly that you were still
a virgin, which I had not expected. It was then that I
decided to make you my wife instead of my mistress.'

'So really the choice you offered was no choice at all.'
She paused. 'What if I'd stuck to my guns and refused
to marry you?'

He laughed. 'Then I would have spent a long and
enjoyable night persuading you to change your mind.'

She said in a low voice, 'Then what makes—that night
so different from last night?'

The amusement died sharply from his face. He said,
'Because at the *ejido*, although you were apprehensive,
you did not look at me as if I were your executioner.'

Nicola flushed painfully. 'I'm sorry,' she said in a
constricted tone.

'And so am I,' Luis said wryly. 'I am not accustomed
to being regarded by a woman as if I was a monster,
nor having her cringe away from me in sheer terror. But
as for the sake of appearances, at least, we should
continue to share a room for a few weeks, it is something
I must learn to live with.'

Her heart began to thud slowly and uncomfortably.
She did not look at him.

'You mean—you're not going to . . .'

'That is precisely what I mean. I have never forced
myself on an unwilling woman in my life, and I do not
intend to begin with you. Don't look so troubled, *querida*,' he added harshly. 'I shall come to your room after
you are asleep, and leave before you wake. You will be
disturbed as little as possible.'

She moved her shoulders helplessly. 'I don't understand—one minute you say you want me—and now . . .'

'Oh, I still want you, *querida*, make no mistake about
that. But I shall not take you. Or did you imagine my
lust was so great that I would be prepared to pursue my
own gratification while you lay there—and thought of
England, as I believe your saying is? *Muchas gracias,*

señora. I prefer to wait in the hope that some time you will come to me willingly.' He paused. 'In the past you've used words like "hatred" and "repulsion" to me. I told myself you did not mean them, but after what I saw in your face last night, I am no longer sure.'

But I didn't mean them, she thought in agony, and if you said one word of love to me, I'd throw myself at your feet.'

Aloud she said woodenly, 'You are very generous, *señor*. Shall—shall I see you at lunch?'

'Of course. As far as the household is concerned, we shall lead a normal life together—and we still have guests.' He gave her a long cool look. 'It would be wiser to give them no more cause for gossip.'

She said, 'Yes, I understand,' and left him.

She was halfway back to the house before she noticed the blood on her hand. She unclenched her fist, and found one last unsuspected thorn left on her rose. As she stood in the sunlight, she felt tears on her face.

She felt limp with exhaustion by the time of the *siesta*. Playing the part of the happy bride was not easy when she felt as if she was cracking apart, and matters were not improved by Luis' effortless assumption of the role of devoted and attentive groom. Under the approving gaze of everyone at the *hacienda*, with the notable exceptions of his aunt and Pilar, he hardly stirred from her side, his arm curving possessively round her slim waist, brushing his mouth gently against her cheek or the lobe of her ear, or holding her hand and pressing lingering kisses to each finger in turn.

Nicola burned, and not solely from embarrassment. She was thankful that she was able to look shyly away, and not meet the mockery in his eyes.

Safe at last in her room, she leaned against the panels of the door for a moment, drawing a deep breath, hardly able to believe that she had escaped at last from the indulgent smiles downstairs that said without words that all the world loved a lover.

If they only knew, she thought drearily. She shed her clothes and had a long, relaxing shower before wrapping herself in her thinnest robe and coming back to the bedroom to collapse on the bed in the shuttered half-light.

The opening door was the last thing she expected, and she sat up, propping herself on her elbow and staring in open alarm as Luis came in carrying a bottle of wine and two glasses.

She stammered, 'You—what are you doing here?'

Her evident apprehension made him smile cynically. 'Don't worry, *querida*. I am simply fulfilling the expectations of our well-wishers by spending the *siesta* in the arms of my loving wife. Or that's what they are supposed to think. The truth will remain our secret. Would you like some wine?'

'No.'

'As you wish.' Deftly he opened the bottle and poured some into his own glass. 'Now, shall we remain here in silence and contemplate what might have been, or shall we talk?' There was a chaise-longue near the window, and he stretched out on that.

Nicola said reluctantly, 'Talk, I suppose.'

'A wise choice,' he said drily. 'Will you choose the topic?'

'Very well.' Her heart began to thump. 'Why don't we discuss—politics?'

Luis looked at her in amazement. 'Are you interested in politics?'

'I'm sure I could be,' she said. 'After all, you find them fascinating, don't you?'

'Do I, *amiga*? What has given you that idea, I wonder?'

She backtracked hurriedly. 'Well, a lot of your friends are politicians.'

'I have friends in a great many walks of life. I wasn't aware of a bias towards politics.'

She wanted to face him, to say bluntly, 'What about

Carlota Garcia?' But she couldn't bring herself to frame the words. She felt too vulnerable. And besides, questions of that nature might lead him to deduce that she was jealous, with everything that implied. It was better, she thought unhappily, to leave well alone.

She said like a polite child, 'I'm sorry, I must have made a mistake.'

'You seem to make a great many.' There was an edge to his voice. 'But while we are on the subject, my godfather has informed me that there has been further agitation over land reform to the east of here, so you will oblige me, when Estrella is ready for you, by not riding anywhere alone. If Juan Hernandez is not free to accompany you, then one of the grooms must do so. Do I make myself clear?'

'Perfectly clear.' She paused. 'Is—your friend—the man you used to know involved in this?'

'Not directly, perhaps.' Luis said briefly. 'But like many idealists he is now finding it is much easier to begin something than to control it once it is under way. Compared with some of his disciples, he is now almost a moderate. An irony, certainly.'

'Where is he?' asked Nicola.

He shrugged, drinking some of his wine. 'In hiding somewhere.' He sent her a sardonic look. 'You seem to be taking a close interest in him, *querida*. Does the thought of an outlaw's life appeal to the romance in your soul?'

No, she thought. You appeal to me—physically, mentally, in every way there is. You and you alone.

She traced some of the embroidery on the coverlet with her finger. 'Perhaps.'

'Then at least you and my cousin Pilar have something in common,' Luis said, and rose abruptly, and began to unfasten his shirt. 'You'd better close your virginal eyes, *amiga*. I'm going to take a shower.'

Nicola lay listening to the sound of running water in the bathroom, and wondering what he had meant about

Pilar. Was it possible that this Miguel was the man she had fallen in love with and been forbidden to associate with? If it was true, then some of her bitterness at least was understandable. She remembered what Luis had said about Pilar's wish to go to university. Perhaps he had feared she might be drawn into the radical elements there too. It wouldn't be easy, but she was going to try and be nicer to Pilar, she resolved.

She realised the sound of the shower had stopped, and, turning her head, realised Luis had come back into the bedroom. His sole concession to modesty a towel draped round his hips, he was pouring himself another glass of wine. Nicola watched him, feeling suddenly uneasy as he strolled back across the room and stood beside the bed, looking down at her.

The robe she was wearing was not transparent like her nightdress, but it clung revealingly, and she regretted bitterly that she was lying on top of the bed instead of seeking the concealment of the coverlet.

Luis lifted the glass to her in a mocking toast, drank some of the wine, then set the glass down very slowly and deliberately, his eyes never leaving hers. Then he sat down on the bed beside her, leaning over her and resting his hands on the bed on each side of her body so that she was virtually imprisoned.

She said helplessly, 'You—promised . . .'

'I promised I wouldn't force you,' he said softly. 'I said nothing about a little gentle persuasion.' He bent and kissed her throat, his mouth finding its unerring way to the erratic pulse there. When he lifted his head, there were little devils dancing at the back of his eyes. He murmured, 'You're trembling, *mi amada*. Is it just panic, or could there be another reason? I think—I really think I shall have to find out.'

His mouth caressed hers warmly and sensuously, without haste or urgency, then moved lower, pushing the impeding robe aside as his tongue explored the hollow at the base of her throat. He lowered his whole weight on to the bed, and slid his hand into the neckline of the robe, his thumb stroking softly along her shoulder.

His lips followed the same caressing path, and his hand moved downwards, cupping her rounded breast in his palm while his fingers stroked gently across her swollen nipple.

Nicola stifled a gasp, and her body tensed.

'Relax, *mi querida*,' Luis said huskily against her skin. 'I am not going to hurt you, or make demands of you. I just want to share a little pleasure with you . . .'

A little pleasure. His words seemed to quiver along her nerve-endings. She was half mad for him already. It was torture to deny the response she yearned to give. It was misery to lie unyielding, when what she wanted was to twine herself around him, giving him kiss for kiss and so much more.

He was kissing her breasts now, his mouth touching the soft flesh with lazy sensuality, the flicker of his tongue re-creating the pleasure his questing fingers had begun.

Nicola thought desperately, 'I have to stop him—now, or it will be too late.'

His wickedly experienced hands were travelling again, stroking down her body in total mastery, and she said hoarsely, 'Luis—please . . .'

His mouth smiled against her body. 'Willingly, *amada*. Anything you desire.' His hand slid from her hip down the smooth curved length of her thigh, and back, easing aside the folds of her robe as he did so.

The breath caught in her throat. 'You mustn't . . .'

'I must,' he contradicted softly. 'Ah, *querida*, you know that I must . . .'

Her eyes widened endlessly, looking up into his. The caressing, exploring hands were opening up new dimensions of sensation she had never dreamed existed, and she heard herself groan softly.

The dark eyes were intensely brilliant as they watched

her. He whispered, 'Do I please you, *querida*? Tell me that I do.'

There was an odd note in his voice. Something like diffidence, the corner of her mind that was still working, registered incredulously, as if he was some callow boy with his first love instead—instead of a practised seducer for whom a woman's body and a woman's responses held few mysteries.

And for a moment she saw Carlota Garcia so clearly that she might actually have been physically present in the warm shaded room, the serenely beautiful face contorted with passionate pleasure as she responded totally to the same caresses, from the same man.

She heard herself moan, 'No—oh, no . . .' and then she twisted away from him, striking his hands away from her body, levering herself desperately across the bed and burying her flushed unhappy face in the pillow.

Luis said her name on a shaken breath, and his hands came down on her shoulders to lift her back into his embrace, and she almost wailed, 'Don't touch me! I—I can't bear it!'

There was a long silence, then he said, 'What hypocrisy is this? You want me, or did you imagine that I would not know?'

'Oh, yes,' she said dully, still keeping her face averted. 'But I expect you could make a stone statue want you. God knows you've had enough experience.'

'Jealous, *mi amada*?' He actually sounded amused.

'No,' she said. 'Just—not interested. How could I be when—when I already love someone?'

'Indeed?' he drawled, the grip on her shoulders tightening painfully. 'And who is he?'

She said, 'I'll make a bargain with you, *señor*. I won't enquire too closely into your private life, and you can leave me mine.'

The cruel grip fell away from her shoulders. She lay very still and heard him leave the bed, the rustle of his clothes as he dressed, and then the slam of the door.

She was alone, which was what she had aimed for, but it was a sterile victory, because it had left her lonely also, and afraid.

There was a nightmare quality about the days which followed. The guests departed, and Nicola found herself living at the *hacienda* in the old hostile atmosphere. Only Luis was no longer her sheild against it. For one thing, he was rarely there, at least during the daytime. When he was around, he treated her civilly when other people were present, and as if she did not exist when they were alone.

She had not expected he would return to her room, but he slept there each night he was at the *hacienda*. Or she supposed he slept. His breathing was even, and he never moved, or spoke to her or touched her. Nicola herself found sleep elusive, and when it came it brought wild disturbing dreams, so that she often awoke with tears on her face. And one recurring dream was the worst of all.

It seemed to happen on the nights when Luis was away, and it always began in the same way, with her riding in Luis' arms on Malagueno, safe and warm and secure, the queen of the world. It was so real that she could feel the warmth of his body, the brush of his lips on her hair, but as she turned to smile at him, to offer him her lips, everything changed. The face under the wide-brimmed hat was blank, without recognisable features, and the arms which held her were a choking prison. She usually woke up at this point gasping for breath, but then one night the dream went on and the face of the man who held her began to take shape, and with a cry of protest she realised it was Ewan, smiling triumphantly at her. Still protesting, she began to struggle against him, but his hold was too strong, he was shaking her, and she moaned his name, turning her head wildly from side to side in rejection.

Then, suddenly, her eyes snapped open and she saw

the shimmering wings of the butterfly spread like a beneficent canopy above her. And she saw too that Luis was there, leaning over her, holding her wrists, his shoulders and chest bronze in the lamplight. For a moment she thought she was dreaming still. He had not been expected back that night, and she had fallen asleep alone in the big bed.

She said with a little gasp, 'I was dreaming.'

'Not for the first time.' He released her wrists, and moved away from her. Nicola wanted to say, 'Don't leave me. Please hold me,' because she was still shaking, but it was already too late. He pushed the covers aside and got out of bed, standing naked for a moment while he retrieved his robe.

He said, 'I'll ring for Maria. She can make you a *tisana* to calm you. And I will spend the rest of the night in my own room.'

Nicola watched helplessly as the door closed behind him. There was a kind of finality about it, as if he had decided that it was time to put an end to this pretence of normality about their marriage.

She didn't want the *tisana* which Maria brought her, but she drank it anyway, and whatever it contained worked like a charm, because when she eventually opened her eyes, it was almost the middle of the day.

She dressed hurriedly and went downstairs, to find a furious row raging. Luis, it seemed, had gone early into Santo Tomás, returned sooner than expected and summoned Pilar to the study where they could be heard shouting at each other. As Nicola hesitated in the hall, wondering rather helplessly whether she should intervene, and what on earth she could say or do if she did, the study door opened and Pilar erupted like a small fury, and ran up the stairs, clearly in floods of tears.

She did not appear at the midday meal, or at dinner that evening, and Luis, in a fouler mood than Nicola had ever seen him, would have gratified his family by absenting himself as well. After he had systematically

bitten everyone's head off in turn, Dona Isabella rose to
her feet, quivering with outrage, and announced maj-
estically that she was withdrawing to the *salón* as her
appetite had been destroyed by her nephew's lack of
consideration.

'I regret that married life has not improved your
temper,' she added acidly, giving Nicola a scathing look
as she swept from the room.

Nicola stared down at her half-finished plate, her face
burning. As she looked up, she encountered a look of
commiseration from Ramón, and she gave him a
wavering smile in return.

'Perhaps you would prefer to be alone together,' Luis
said silkily from the head of the table. 'Do not hesitate
to tell me if you find my presence an inhibition.' His
eyes glittered dangerously as he stared at them.

Ramón cast his eyes to the ceiling, pushed back his
chair, and left the room in silence, leaving husband and
wife confronting each other from either end of the long
and shining table.

Nicola thought it would be pleasant to pick up every
plate, glass and piece of cutlery on the table and throw
them at Luis' head, screaming very loudly all the while,
but she decided that the soft answer which was supposed
to turn away wrath might be a better bet in the circumstances.

She said, 'I don't know what Pilar has done to anger
you, Luis, but if I can help in any way . . .'

'So you actually wish to be of some use, do you?' he
said harshly. 'Perhaps if you had taken the trouble to be
friendly to Pilar, to attempt to win her over and be a
companion to her, then this whole situation might have
been avoided.'

The injustice of it made her blink. Over the past
miserable three weeks she had done everything possible
to try and win Pilar over, but the girl's hostility to her
was inexorable. She spent long hours in her room,
reading parcels of books sent to her from Mexico City.

Nicola would have liked to have borrowed some of them, but a tentative suggestion had resulted in such a chilly negative that she had never dared ask again.

She had asked Pilar more than once if they couldn't ride together, but had met with a curt refusal. And she knew perfectly well that Pilar had scorned Luis' direct orders, and invariably rode out alone, being missing sometimes for several hours. And yet the only time Nicola had tried to escape on her own from the atmosphere at the *hacienda*, she had encountered Ramón, who had spoken to her quite severely about taking unnecessary risks before he escorted her back to the stables, and the the unspoken but no less potent criticism of Juan Hernandez. Perhaps that was why Pilar got away with her solitary rides so easily, she thought wearily. Juan Hernandez was far too busy keeping an eye on her to perform the same service for his master's young cousin.

'Pilar hates me,' she protested. 'I have tried. Really I have . . .'

'Of course you have, *amiga*,' Luis interrupted derisively. 'No half measures in your efforts to achieve harmony with us all. Who should know that better than myself?'

Her lip trembled. 'That isn't fair! I—I didn't ask you to leave my room last night.'

'No, that was a decision I managed to make for myself,' he said grimly. 'And you should be grateful for it, *querida*, because if and when I return to your bed it will be to end this—half-marriage of ours, whether you are willing or not.'

She said faintly, 'I don't understand.'

'No? Then allow me to explain, my charming, chaste little fraud. I have no wish to lie beside you night after night, suffering the agonies of the damned, only to hear you call out another man's name in your dreams.' She gasped, and he said, 'Exactly, *amiga*. Next time you speak a man's name in my bed, it will be my name, and in circumstances I leave to your imagination.'

She began, 'But, Luis . . .'

'Oh, I am sure you have some perfectly reasonable explanation, my lovely cheat. Who is this—Ewan? The great passionate love you once mentioned to me—the one that still holds your heart?'

'It isn't as you think——' Nicola began desperately, trying to push out of her mind that it was exactly what she had intended him to think.

'But then what is? Meanwhile, *querida*, here is a thought for you to take upstairs with you. One of these nights I shall come to you, and I swear that this time no—simulated terror, no cowering in corners, no dreams of other men are going to hold me away.' He pushed his chair back and left the room.

Nicola leaned limply back in her chair. Unwillingly her eyes lifted to meet the painted gaze of Doña Manuela, which seemed in her imagination to twinkle with amused sympathy.

'It was all right for you,' Nicola addressed the long-deceased beauty in her thoughts. 'Your husband loved you so much that he carved out his own empire for you to rule over.' Her glance went to the red rose Doña Manuela held in her hand, and she sighed. 'And when he gave you that, he probably meant every petal of it.'

She prepared for bed that night feeling miserably apprehensive, aware that Maria was sending her puzzled glances. She lay awake half the night, waiting for the door to open, but Luis did not appear, and she didn't know whether to be glad or sorry.

But when she went down to breakfast the following day and heard that he had left for Sonora and would probably be away for several days, she knew that she was sorry.

Doña Isabella was at breakfast, heaving martyred sighs, but Pilar was not, and when she had finished her meal, Nicola decided to take her courage in both hands and seek the girl out.

It was with something of an effort that she knocked on her bedroom door. After a short pause, the door was flung open and Pilar confronted her.

Nicola smiled, feeling awkward. 'I wondered if you would care to go riding with me today.'

'No, I should not.' Pilar's eyes flashed. 'Has Luis set you to spy on me?'

'No, of course not. Why should he?' Nicola suppressed a sigh. 'It's just that—I think he would like us to be—better friends.'

Pilar gave her a contemptuous look. 'I do not wish to be your friend. Have I not made it plain? I do not need your company—or your patronage, Señora de Montalba,' she added with heavy irony. 'Who are you to marry into our family? A nobody without background or breeding. An *Inglesa*, with hair like straw—thin, without breasts or hips. A girl whom my cousin saw and fell in love with. *Dios*, he must have been mad! But his madness has not lasted. The whole world knows he has tired of you, and no longer sleeps in your bed.'

Nicola could not restrain her indrawn breath. But what else could she have expected? she thought miserably. In a small enclosed society like this, everyone's actions were under a microscope.

She tried again. 'Pilar, when people are unhappy they often say and do things they don't mean, so I'm going to pretend you didn't say that. I want to help—really I do.'

'Then help yourself, *señora*,' Pilar said maliciously. 'What a fool you are! Why did Luis have to marry you? Why did he not just keep you in an apartment in Monterrey as he has his other women?' She giggled suddenly. 'And today he has not gone to Sonora alone. Carlota Garcia has gone with him. I heard him arrange it yesterday, so . . .'

Nicola lifted her hand and quite deliberately slapped Pilar's cheek hard.

'*Puta!*' The Mexican girl's eyes blazed at her. 'I will

make you sorry that you were ever born!' She slammed the heavy door in Nicola's face.

Nicola stepped back involuntarily, and collided with Ramón, who was just emerging from his own room on the other side of the corridor.

'What has happened?' He sounded alarmed as he steadied her.

'A little feminine squabble,' Nicola said slowly and evenly.

Ramón groaned. 'Is she still jealous of you? The good God only knows why she should be. She never wanted Luis until Madrecita put it into her head that she should—but I suppose her disappointment over Miguel . . .' He shrugged.

'Luis mentioned that to me once,' Nicola said slowly. 'At least, he didn't tell me the man's name, but I guessed.'

Ramón grimaced. 'It is not hard to guess. In many ways they were well matched. Miguel is a firebrand and Pilar was swept off her feet by him. There was no reason why she should not be. He and Luis had attended university together, and been friends since childhood. He was a constant visitor here, so it was a tragedy when his political activities led him into trouble with the authorities.' He sighed again. 'He had a good law practice too, until he decided it was more moral to become a *peon*. He was given a small grant of our land, and built a cabin there, but he did not work the land—it was harder labour than he had imagined, I think—and even the cabin is now derelict.'

'Not quite derelict,' said Nicola, flushing slightly as he gave her a questioning look. 'Luis and I once—spent the night there.'

'So that was where.' Ramón digested this for a moment or two. 'Obviously we knew that you had been somewhere together, but Luis said nothing—and one does not ask him what he does not volunteer.'

She said in a low voice, 'Ramón, what did he tell

your mother about how—we met? Can you remember?'

He groaned. 'Can I ever forget? Madrecita was in a fury, swearing that Luis insulted her by installing one of his—ladies under her roof, and Luis gave her one of his cold looks and said that you were his future wife. Madrecita screamed and said, "A stranger—a creature you have only just met!" And Luis said, "I fell in love with her the moment I saw her." '

Nicola was silent, remembering how she had asked Luis what story he had told them, and he had said, *'Not the truth, but a story to fit . . .'*

Ramón glanced at her. 'You are very pale, Nicola. What is it? Not this silly quarrel with Pilar?'

It was hardly that, Nicola thought. There had been an almost frightening venom in the other girl.

'Perhaps,' she said. She forced a smile. 'I need some air, I'll go for a ride, I think.'

'But not alone,' he said anxiously. 'Do not even attempt it. There are all kinds of rumours, and Luis has ordered constant patrols.' He paused. 'It is why he was so angry with Pilar. Miguel Jurado is said to be somewhere in the locality again. One of the *peons* was bribed to bring Pilar a note asking her to meet him in Santo Tomás, only the man brought it to Luis instead. As she has been forbidden to have any communication with Miguel, you can understand why Luis reacted as he did.'

And she could also understand Pilar's reactions, Nicola thought a little sadly as she made her way to her room to change into her jeans and boots. She had insisted on wearing the close-fitting denims she would have worn in England for riding, and several pairs had been brought from Santo Tomás for her, even though Doña Isabella heartily disapproved of the way in which they outlined her slim hips and legs. The older woman considered a divided skirt more suitable attire for the wife of Don Luis.

When she had changed, and picked up her hat and

gloves, Nicola paused for a moment, looking at herself in the mirror. Pilar had a point, she conceded reluctantly. She had no reason to intervene in anyone else's personal affairs when her own were in such a mess.

As it was, her unthinking attempt to salvage some dregs of self-respect had simply exposed her to a bitter reckoning that could happen at any time.

And the bitterest part of all was that even if she were to tell Luis the whole truth—that she loved him to the point of despair—he would not believe her.

CHAPTER EIGHT

NICOLA sat with her back against a sun-drenched rock, wondering what to do for the best. Three days had passed since her quarrel with Pilar and relations between them hadn't improved one iota since then, she thought ruefully. Luis was expected back the following day, and he was sure to sense the atmosphere, and would probably blame her, which would make their reunion even less joyous than it already promised to be.

She made a little sound halfway between a sigh and a groan. Was she the only one at the *hacienda* who saw what was going on, and drew conclusions from it? Ramón, of course, was too busy, leaving the *hacienda* after an early breakfast, and often not returning until late in the day. But didn't Doña Isabella ever wonder where her daughter got to?

Each day since Luis' departure, Pilar had taken her horse and vanished for several hours at a time. Nicola had tried to follow more than once, but each time she had lost the trail, even though she suspected she now knew where Pilar headed each time.

Nor had it been easy, getting rid of her own assiduous escort, but she had managed it by saying mendaciously that she was going to meet Don Ramón. There had been some raised eyebrows and subdued mutterings in the stables, but she had been allowed to take Estrella and ride off unhindered. What would happen if Juan Hernandez ever checked out her story with Ramón, she chose not to think about.

She supposed she was a fool even to consider trying to help Pilar after everything that had passed between them, but she was doing it for Luis' sake, she thought, and that changed everything. He would be angry if he ever thought she had stood idly by and watched his young cousin ruin her life, as she seemed likely to do.

Nicola had little doubt that Pilar went every day to meet Miguel Jurado, and that although the letter Luis had intercepted had mentioned Santo Tomás as a rendezvous, they actually met at the *ejido*. That was the direction Pilar had taken each day, even though she had always slightly varied her route. Nicola knew this because she had taken the trouble to check a map of the estate which was kept in Ramón's office, but she had never dared ride that far herself.

She had wanted to several times, but on each occasion in the past something had held her back, reminding her how many memories that she might now find painful were attached to the place.

Nevertheless today she was quite determined. She was going to ride to the *ejido* and confront Pilar, and Miguel Jurado, if necessary. She was going to try and convince the girl that there was no future with a man who was having to live virtually in hiding, but if she failed—if Pilar refused to listen, as was more than likely, then she would just have to tell Luis the whole messy story when he returned from Sonora. That was something she could use to make Pilar see sense, she thought. The girl might rail against his autocracy, but she seemed to have a real respect for his anger.

She had not attempted to follow Pilar this time. She had ridden out ahead of her, and was waiting in the shelter of some rocks until Pilar could reasonably be expected to have arrived at the *ejido*.

She got up, dusting off her jeans, and whistled to Estrella, who came to her side stepping daintily. Nicola caressed the soft nose. The relationship between horse and rider could be such a simple one, she thought, with trust and affection on both sides.

Her solitary rides had given her plenty of time to think about Luis and herself, and she knew now she had been all kinds of a fool to allow pride to get in her way. All she had achieved was to turn him back to Carlota Garcia. He was not a man to accept kindly a period of enforced celibacy when solace in his mistress's arms was only a comparatively short distance away.

And I, Nicola thought savagely, gave him up to her without even a struggle. I could have fought. I've novelty value for him, at least, and I'm younger than she is. And I can give him the child he wants. All I have to do is accept this marriage on his terms—go to him, tell him that I want him.

She sighed. Perhaps if they were close physically, then the emotional and spiritual rapport she craved might follow—one day.

Even though she had carefully checked out the route, it was further than she thought to the *ejido*, and she realised that she was not going to make it back to the *hacienda* for the midday meal. She moved her shoulders wearily. Well, probably she would not be greatly missed.

She reined in Estrella and looked down the slope at the small building, her eyes narrowing as she realised there was a wisp of smoke coming from the chimney. Either the authorities were incredibly obtuse, or Pilar and Miguel were suffering from an overdose of bravado, she thought.

She approached with caution, even though she couldn't see Pilar's horse tethered anywhere, or any other form of transport nearby either. She dismounted, and hung Estrella's reins over a convenient rail. Her boots clattered sharply on the rickety wooden verandah, but she could hear no sounds of movement or alarm inside the cabin itself, even when she knocked sharply at the door. There was no reply, so she pushed it open and went inside.

There were obvious signs that someone was in residence. The fire was lit, and the cooking pot hung over the modest flame, emitting steam and a savoury aroma which made Nicola's nose wrinkle appreciatively, reminding her how long it was since she had eaten her sweet rolls and coffee at breakfast.

The place was cleaner too, she thought incredulously. The floor had been swept, and the table scrubbed. She noticed crockery—even a bottle of wine—and the bed made up with pillows and blankets. Every modern convenience, she thought bleakly. Two glasses for the wine. Two pillows on the bed.

Oh, Pilar! What is your mother going to say about all this? she wondered silently.

The food, all the preparations seemed to suggest that Pilar and her lover would be using the cabin in the very near future. Well, she would stable Estrella in the ramshackle building at the rear and await their arrival.

She took off her hat and pitched it on to the bed, then sat down on one of the stools. The air in the cabin was warm and close, and she unfastened a couple of buttons on her shirt, fanning herself languidly with her gloves.

Just how long had this been going on? she asked herself, gazing curiously around her. She couldn't imagine Pilar working to clean up the cabin, but perhaps she had enjoyed playing house there. Nicola found it sad.

She looked at her watch, noting resignedly that it was now well past the lunch hour, and hoping no hue and cry had been started.

She got up, gave the food on the fire a quick stir to ensure that it wasn't sticking, then poured herself a glass of the wine.

'*Salud,*' she thought. 'To absent friends.'

All the same, she hoped they wouldn't be absent for much longer. The wine was pleasant, but it made the cabin seem warmer than ever, and after a few minutes she put her folded arms on the table and rested her head on them. She wouldn't go to sleep, she assured herself, although she could not deny she was drowsy. But she could close her eyes for a few moments. That would do no harm, because she would be sure to hear them when they arrived.

Eventually she sat up with a start, feeling slightly dazed. She had no idea what had roused her, but it certainly wasn't anyone's arrival. She was still alone, and the fire was nearly out.

Nicola got up, stretching cramped limbs. She would find some more wood, and see to poor Estrella, she thought guiltily. She opened the cabin door and went out on to the verandah, but there was no greeting whinny. The mare had gone.

For a moment Nicola stood motionless, telling herself that she was hallucinating, the result of her long ride in the sun. Then she whistled long and frantically, but without the slightest effect. She stared at the verandah rail where she had tied the mare, trying to collect her thoughts. The rail was still intact, so Estrella hadn't dragged herself free, which meant that somone had quite deliberately released her.

Pilar, she thought helplessly. Who else? She turned and went slowly back into the cabin. Could it be that all the time she had thought she was trailing Pilar, the other girl had been following her, just waiting for an opportunity to leave her stranded? After all, she had warned Nicola she would make her sorry, and Nicola supposed that Pilar had known perfectly well that she had been on her track for the last few days and had decided to teach her a lesson.

She groaned, although she supposed she should be thankful she hadn't fallen asleep earlier under her rock, otherwise Pilar might have taken the mare then, and she would be out in the open without food or water in the full heat of the day. As it was, if she had to be abandoned somewhere, at least here there was a modicum of comfort, she thought resignedly. It could have been so much worse.

But she was anxious about Estrella. Pilar could not take her back to her stable without giving herself away, and she hoped desperately that she wouldn't just turn the mare loose and leave her to fend for herself.

I'll be all right, she thought. Sooner or later someone will come looking for me, and if I'm careful with the food there should be enough for several days.

But surely even Pilar would not be that vindictive, she hoped without too much conviction. What did she hope to gain anyway, when she knew Nicola would be found eventually, and that there'd be hell to pay when she was? Yes, Luis would be angry when he found Nicola had disobeyed him by riding alone, even with the best of motives, but was that enough for Pilar? She couldn't believe it. The malice in Pilar's face that time had indicated a wish for revenge altogether deeper and darker than this rather childish trick.

The time dragged past. She was really hungry now, so she ate a little of the stew from the pot, and drank some more wine, thinking enviously of the cool dim *comedor* at the *hacienda*. Pilar would be at home by now, sitting with an innocent face, while the others wondered where she was, no doubt.

The room became hotter, and hotter. It was getting late now, she saw by her watch, and time for *siesta*, although she was too angry to be tired. But she had nothing else to do, so she took off her boots and lay down on the bed on top of the blankets, remembering the last time she had lain there with Luis' arm around her, holding her close to the curve of his body. She sighed, twisting restlessly on the pillow. So much for honour, she thought bitterly. If he had taken her that night, she would now be his slave, and she would have been saved an incredible amount of heartache, even if it was at the expense of her pride.

But pride didn't seem important whn you were jealous and lonely, and when you woke each night with your body crying out for fulfilment.

At last she managed to doze again for a while, and woke to find it was sunset. If she wasn't careful, it would be dark soon, and she needed to light the lamp and light the fire again. She sat up wearily, swinging her legs to the floor, then tensed as she thought she heard the sound of a horse's hooves. Imagination, she decided, as it had been all those other times she had heard the same thing during that interminable afternoon. And yet . . .

She bent her head, listening intently, her heart leaping with sudden hope. It was a horse. Someone was coming. Perhaps it was even Pilar who had relented and was bringing back Estrella. Maybe she wanted to do a deal for Nicola's silence about the Jurado man. She jumped up and took two quick steps towards the door.

It swung open with a crash, and Luis strode in.

Nicola halted, staring at him dazedly. He was the last person she had expected to see. He hadn't been expected before tomorrow at the earliest.

She said falteringly, noting how grim he looked, 'Luis? Did she tell you where I was? Please don't be angry. It—it was only a prank . . .'

'Yes,' he said softly, 'she told me. As to my anger, and whether or not this is a—prank, as you call it— well, I make no guarantees. Naturally you are surprised to see me.'

Nicola began, 'Well, yes . . .' but before she could say anything else, he had cut across her.

'No doubt you are also disappointed. You have had a long and tedious wait—and all for nothing. You must be asking yourself even now why I am here, and not Ramón, and I must tell you, *chica*, that my cousin has had the good fortune to sustain a broken collarbone, so he will not be able to join you. A fall from his horse this morning,' he added sardonically.

'Join me?' All her initial joy at seeing him was subsiding under the growing conviction that something was terribly wrong. 'I don't understand.'

'Neither did I—at first. I concluded my business in Sonora sooner than I had anticipated, so I came back to the *hacienda*—to see you, *amiga*, to try and put things right between us—isn't that amusing? I found the place in confusion. Ramón had had this accident, and the doctor had been sent for. Then one of the servants asked to speak to me. Earlier, before Ramón was brought home, she had cleaned his room, and found this——'

He extended his hand. The butterfly clip he had given her lay in his palm.

'But—but that's impossible!' Her brain was reeling. She hadn't worn the clip since their wedding night. She had put it away in the case with the rest of the jewellery he had given her.

'Is it, *querida*?' That dreadful quietness in his voice, and the setting sun filling the room with the colour of blood. 'I asked her where she had found it, and eventually, reluctantly she told me. In the bed of Señor Don Ramón.' He spoke these last words with a cold terrible precision.

Nicola said, 'She's lying.'

'She is a good, honest woman, who has served our family for many years. As she gave me this—thing——' he tossed it to the floor at Nicola's feet '—there were tears in her eyes.'

She said desperately, 'Luis, I swear to you that if this woman found my clip where she says she did, I don't know how it got there.'

'Don't you, my beautiful wife? Then you lack imagination, because a very obvious explanation occurs to me. But then you have so many other virtues, don't you—the domestic ones, for example. You have taken a miserable hovel and turned it into a love nest. I congratulate you.'

She exclaimed with a gasp, 'You can't think that I did all this! This was how it was when I arrived—the food, the wine—everything. I was looking for Pilar.'

'An amazing coincidence, *chica*, because she was also looking for you, but a long way from here. She found your horse wandering loose near the *hacienda* and took charge of her, afraid that something might have happened to you. Juan Hernandez and some of the men searched the immediate vicinity in case you had suffered the same fate as Ramón, but when there was no sign of you, Pilar confessed she might know where you had gone.'

The red sun was slipping away now below the horizon, and a web of darkness was slowly spinning round her.

'She told me she had kept silent before only because of her love for her brother, but that she had known for some time that you were meeting secretly here at the cabin. That she had heard him mention the place to you one morning—outside his bedroom,' he added silkily. 'Do you deny it?'

'Not the last bit, no, but we were talking about your friend Miguel Jurado—about the possibility that he might be seeing Pilar. Ask Ramón if you don't believe me.'

'I do not believe you,' he said. 'As for asking Ramón, the doctor has given him something to make him sleep. I said, did I not, that he was fortunate to break his collarbone, because if he had not, *querida*, I would most assuredly have broken his neck.'

There was a savagery in his voice which terrified her. She said, almost weeping, 'Luis—please—you can't believe all those lies! Pilar hates me, you know that. She would say anything . . .'

'That I considered.' His voice was meditative. 'Yet Juan Hernandez has no reason to hate you, and he told me in all innocence that several times this week you had left the *hacienda* alone, saying you were to meet Ramón.'

'Oh God—yes, I've said that, but it was just an excuse I invented, so that I could be alone.'

'Alone with your lover. So eager to be alone with him, *chica*, that you could not even tie up a valuable horse properly.' Luis began to take off his gloves, very slowly. 'Ramón must have succeeded most admirably with you. The next hour should prove—instructive.'

'What do you mean?' Nicola asked hoarsely.

He shrugged. 'Because an accident has robbed you of your lover, you need not be totally deprived of entertainment, *amada*. I've never followed in Ramón's footsteps before, so it will be interesting to learn what you've discovered in his arms about pleasing a man.'

She began to back away, but he followed her until the table blocked off any further retreat.

Her voice was desperate. 'Luis! I swear to you that Ramón isn't my lover. The only time I've been in his arms was at the wedding . . .' Her voice trailed away as she realised that it had probably been a mistake to remind him.

He said, 'I remember that only too well. Do you think I haven't seen you together—seen the way you look at him—smile at him, you bitch, as you've never smiled at me.' He took a handful of her hair, and jerked her head back, forcing her to meet his gaze. 'Smile at me now, *mi corazón*, and I may take the trouble to please you as well as myself when the time comes.'

His grip on her hair hurt, and she moaned in pain as well as fear as she begged, 'Luis—no—please . . .'

His fingers insolently probed her unfastened shirt, seeking the swell of her breast, then slid down to the waistband of her jeans, tugging at the zip. She began to struggle, and he bent his head and kissed her on the mouth. It was a hard bruising kiss, which held neither tenderness nor very much desire. It was merely an effective means of silencing further protest while he achieved his objective.

He picked her up, and dropped her on to the bed, joining her there immediately, almost casually unfastening his own clothes as he did so.

'Oh God—no!' Her voice broke. 'Not like this—please! Not like this.'

'You find my attentions lack finesse, *señora*? Luis asked with savage mockery. 'When you deny a starving man food, you must expect him to snatch at crumbs.'

His mouth burned on her uncovered breasts, and fear
and misery notwithstanding, she felt her body shiver
with pleasure. In spite of everything, he was who he
was, and her starved senses knew it, and hungered in
their turn.

'Show me what he has taught you.' His voice was
relentless. His hands moved on her mercilessly, exploring every inch. 'Does he do this to you—and this?'

'No,' she moaned. The excitement he was engendering
in her was almost intolerable in spite of his cruelty, and
her body twisted restlessly against his, arching involuntarily to meet him when the moment came.

She was transfixed by pain. She had never dreamed
anything could hurt so much, and a brief cry escaped
her before she sank her teeth into the softness of her
inner lip so deeply that she could taste blood in her
mouth. Her whole body tautened instinctively, rejecting
the starkness of the invasion she had been subjected to,
and a tear escaped her closed lids and trickled scaldingly
down the curve of her cheek.

Above her Luis was suddenly motionless, and she
could only be thankful, because if he moved, if he sought
to further his possession of her, she thought she might
faint.

She felt his hands cup her face, smoothing back the
dishevelled hair, and her eyes opened slowly and unwillingly. His face was only inches from hers, and in spite
of the dim light in the cabin, she could see the horrified
comprehension dawning in his eyes. Then with a long
shaken groan, he rolled away from her, and lay with
one arm flung across his face.

Nicola lay trembling, waiting for the ache in her body
to subside. At last she sat up slowly, pulling the edges
of her shirt across her breasts, and looking to see where
the rest of her clothing lay tumbled on the floor where
he had thrown it.

Luis said, 'Be still,' in a voice she barely recognised.

He lifted himself off the bed, re-fastening his own clothes with swift jerky movements. Then he fetched her clothes and brought them back to the bed. She put out a hand to take them from him, but he ignored it completely, dressing her as gently as if she had been a child. He fetched her discarded boots and fitted them on her feet, then wrapped her carefully in the blanket they had been lying on before he lifted her in his arms and carried her to the door.

Outside, the dark shape that was Malagueno lifted his head and whinnied softly.

Luis paused suddenly and looked down at her. He said hoarsely, '*Por Dios*, Nicola—speak to me—say something!'

She said quietly, 'Pilar told me she would make me sorry I was born. She has succeeded beyond her wildest dreams.'

Lights seemed to be blazing all round the *hacienda* as they approached. As Luis lifted her down, Nicola whispered, 'I can walk,' but again he ignored this, and carried her into the hall, which seemed to be full of people, all of them talking and exclaiming at once. Nicola turned her face into Luis's shirt, thankful for the sheltering blanket.

She heard Doña Isabella's voice, high and wailing. 'Luis, where have you been? Pilar has gone—run away—eloped with that scoundrel, that outlaw Miguel Jurado! You must follow her—you must bring her back at once. The shame—the disgrace—*ay de mi*!'

Luis paused, one foot on the bottom stair, and said something brief, succinct and obscene in Spanish. Doña Isabella gave a gasp, turned purple and sagged back against the uncertain support of her maid, a gaunt woman, while Luis continued up the stairs leaving a mystified silence behind him.

He took Nicola to her room, and put her gently down on the stool in front of her dressing table.

'Shall I fetch Maria to you?'

'No—please.' The blanket was slipping, and she could see bruises appearing on her shoulders under her loosened shirt, and knew there would be other marks on her breasts and thighs. She bruised relatively easily, and his handling of her had not been gentle.

After a brief hesitation, Luis went into the bathroom and she heard the sound of running water. She let the blanket drop to the floor with a little shudder, then stripped off the shirt. She looked into the mirror and saw that Luis had returned and was standing behind her, looking at the marks on her body with an expression of such bleak anguish that she wanted to weep— not for herself, but for him.

The bath was half full of warm scented water and she relaxed into it gratefully. Luis had not accompanied her into the bathroom. He had asked instead what she wanted him to do with the clothes and blanket she had left on the floor, and she had said, 'Get rid of them— please.'

When she got out of the bath, he reappeared and stood waiting with a towel. He enveloped her in it, then took her hand and led her back to the bedroom, and the wide bed with its turned-back covers. He lifted her into the bed, unwrapped the towel and removed it, then drew the covers up over her body. His face was taut and very contained, and there was no expression in his eyes.

He said very quietly, 'Sleep well,' and made to turn away. Nicole put out a hand and gripped his sleeve.

'Luis, stay with me, *por favor*.'

He hesitated for so long she thought for one terrible moment he was going to refuse, then he nodded curtly and sat down on the edge of the bed to remove his boots. Making no attempt to undress, he lay down beside her, but outside the covers, and his arm went round her, drawing her gently against him. She rested her head on his shoulder. There was no violence any more, she thought, no anger or fear, no high emotion, or even particularly man and woman. Just two tired, unhappy people drawing close for comfort.

And she thought, 'I'm safe,' before she fell asleep.

She still felt safe the next morning when she awoke, her hand reaching to touch Luis for reassurance even before she opened her eyes. But she was alone, and the space beside her was empty, and she was suddenly wide awake and sitting up in swift alarm.

Someone was watching her, and she turned and saw Carlota Garcia sitting beside the bed, looking soignée and beautiful in a black and white dress.

For a moment Nicola felt she must still be asleep and having another nightmare, then she realised it was all too real, and she dived at the covers, dragging them up to hide herself, her cheeks suddenly crimson.

Carlota Garcia smiled, her face pleasant and friendly. '*Buenos dias, señora*. Luis asked me to sit with you. He did not wish you to wake alone.'

Nicola said stiffly, 'That was—considerate of him.' She tried to anchor the slipping sheet more firmly round her breasts.

Señora Garcia rose. 'Would you be more comfortable in a nightgown? Tell me where they are kept and I will fetch one for you.'

Unwillingly, Nicola directed her, and Carlota Garcia came back with a drift of palest yellow over her arm. She dropped it deftly over Nicola's head and turned tactfully away while she did the rest. Nicola prayed she would go, but instead she resumed her seat beside the bed.

She said, 'Doña Nicola, I think someone has been repeating ancient gossip to you. I knew at the wedding that there was something wrong—you have honest eyes, *pequeña*—so perhaps I may speak frankly to you?'

Nicola looked down at her folded hands. 'If you wish.'

'I do wish it.' Carlota Garcia paused. 'A long time ago, I was lonely and very miserable. My husband had died, and I had loved him. I found that to be a widow did not stop me also being a woman. Luis had been my husband's friend, my family's friend and mine too.' She paused again. 'And for a brief time, it is true, we were more than—just friends. It was good, and I do not regret it. I said I would be frank with you. But it is over, and has been so for longer than I care to remember. I have a full and happy life again, and Luis, I hope, is still my friend, but no more than that.'

'But he still visits you, *señora*,' Nicola said in a low voice. 'Can you deny that?'

'No—but the visits he has made recently, the meetings we have attended together have had no personal motive. They have been prompted only by our mutual concern for my brother.'

'Your brother? I don't think I understand?'

Señora Garcia sighed. 'Did no one tell you, Doña Nicola, that Miguel Jurado is my brother? Luis has been using his influence to try and win him some kind of amnesty. The man he wounded has made a full recovery, praise God——' she crossed herself —'so that the charges he may face are not so severe as they might have been.' Her eyes were full of sudden tears. 'Forgive me, but this is a great sadness to me. I always believed that Miguel would be a great man—a great lawyer, and instead he has chosen to live his life outside the law.'

'And Luis has been trying to help him?'

'Luis does not forget their past friendship, although he cannot condone what Miguel has done. And now of course he has even more reason to be angry with him.'

'Oh,' Nicola said slowly. 'Pilar.'

'*Si*—that is why I am here.' Señora Garcia sighed again. 'They arrived at my house last night, demanding that I should help them, but of course I refused. Miguel cannot take the responsibility of a wife, with all that he has to face. I said at once that they must return here, and Pilar became very agitated, and said she would never come back. I questioned her, naturally, but it was

Miguel who finally obtained the truth from her. She admitted everything—her dislike of you, her jealousy, her wish to punish Luis, and the terrible means of revenge that she took. She knew that you suspected her, and decided to lay a trap for you at the *ejido*. She stole your butterfly and left it in Ramón's room in case anything went wrong with her original plan. She could not guess, of course, that Ramón would break his collarbone, but it was a blessing that he did so, otherwise the repercussions might have been truly dreadful.'

She leaned forward and took Nicola's hand. '*Señora*, I ask you to believe that if my brother had known anything of what she intended, he would have prevented it. He has been horrified by her conduct, but even so he does not think she is truly evil, just spoiled and misguided, and eaten with jealousy of anyone more happy than herself.'

Nicola winced inwardly. Did that really apply to her? Did she seem happy to others? Was it possible they didn't feel the inner tension in her?

She said, 'What are you suggesting, *señora*—that I should just overlook what she did?'

Carlota Garcia grimaced slightly. 'That is hardly possible. And Luis has declared that he will no longer harbour her under his roof—so I have invited her to stay with me. She can help with my correspondence and make herself useful in various ways. It will stop her thinking so much about herself, and later perhaps she can continue her education. This time, her mother's protests will go unheeded, I think.'

Nicola stared down at the butterflies on the coverlet. 'Was Luis—very angry with her?'

Señora Garcia shrugged. 'I would not have wished to face him. I do not know what he said to her, because they spoke in private, but afterwards she wept and wept. One could not see her without pitying her. And as for her mother, I do not think Doña Isabella will ever speak again,' she added with wry amusement. 'She is mortified to her soul by what Pilar has done.'

Nicola could only pity both mother and daughter. She had faced Luis' anger and contempt, and the memory hung over her like a shadow, in no way diminished by the almost austere consideration he had shown her on their return to La Mariposa. Her heart seemed to contract as she remembered it. He had performed the most intimate services for her, yet had displayed no more emotion than if she had been a—a piece of statuary he had been required to look after for a while. And this morning, she had not woken in his arms . . .

She became aware that Señora Garcia was staring at her, her face concerned and slightly questioning. She said quickly, 'Perhaps I'd better get dressed, and see what I can do to restore peace.'

'I think it would be better if you remained where you are,' Carlota Garcia smiled faintly. 'There is a truce—of sorts—and Pilar is packing the rest of her things. I will be leaving with her very soon now, and it would be kind of you, Doña Nicola, to permit her to leave without having to confront you in person.' She rose to her feet. 'And now I will go and tell Luis that you are awake.'

With another brief smile, she departed.

Nicola leaned back against her pillows, trying to assimilate everything she had been told. She should have been overjoyed by Carlota Garcia's assurances, but in the light of everything else that had happened, they seemed unimportant. The agony of jealousy she had experienced each time she had thought of them together was fading under the weight of this new uncertainty.

Her teeth worried her lower lip as she watched the door, waiting for it to open.

As he entered, she thought he looked as if he hadn't slept for a week, and an aching tenderness filled her. Last night he had comforted her, now she wanted to do the same for him—to open her arms to him, to offer her body as his pillow. As he came to stand by the bed, she looked up at him, her lips curving tentatively and shyly.

If he had returned her smile, she would have reached for him, but there was no answering warmth in his eyes or on his mouth. When he spoke, his voice was cool and formal.

'Are you well this morning? The doctor is visiting Ramón, and if you wish I can arrange for him to see you.'

Nicola flushed. 'I'm fine—really I am.'

'That is good. If you would like breakfast, Maria will bring you a tray.'

'Thank you.' Oh God, she thought wildly, what's going wrong? He was treating her as if she was a guest, a stranger under his roof, demanding the conventions of politeness.

He said, 'Later—when you have eaten—perhaps you would come to the study. There are things we must discuss.'

She said shyly, 'Can't we talk about them now?' Hold me, her heart cried out to him. Make love to me.

'I would prefer to speak to you in the study. I have people to see—calls to make—certain arrangements to finalise. I am sure you understand.'

'Arrangements about Pilar?'

'Yes.' She saw the muscle in his jaw clench. 'Among others. If you will excuse me.'

He made her a brief bow, and turned away. Nicola watched him go aware of a growing dread inside her.

She forced herself to eat some of the food which Maria brought her, then bathed and dressed with immense care, brushing a silken gloss back into her hair, banishing the pallor from her cheeks with subtly applied blusher, and accentuating the curve of her mouth with lipstick. She put on a simple dark green dress, with a skirt shaped like a bell, and a wide sash belt which drew attention to the slenderness of her waist.

She had planned to pin the silver butterfly into her hair, but remembered too late that it was still lying on the cabin floor where Luis had tossed it. Sudden tears rose in her eyes as she looked at herself in the mirror. Why had Pilar used that piece of jewellery out of all that Luis had given her? She had loved it so. But then, of course, that was precisely why it had been used, she thought bitterly. It was as if someone had deliberately destroyed a good luck talisman. And intuition was telling her that she was going to need all the luck she could get.

It took courage to go downstairs. Should she go straight to Luis' study, she wondered, or wait in the *salón* until he sent for her?

She was standing at the foot of the stairs, torn by indecision, when the loud clamorous peal of the doorbell almost made her jump out of her senses.

Carlos appeared, to answer the door, and Nicola turned towards the *salón*. If there were to be visitors, then her interview with Luis would have to be postponed, she thought with a kind of relief.

A voice, feminine and familiar, she realised with shaken disbelief, said, 'I wish to see the Señorita Nicola Tarrant. Is she here?'

It was Teresita. As Carlos stepped aside, she walked into the hall followed by Cliff. Nicola moved forward uncertainly, and Teresita ran to her, throwing her arms around her.

'Nicky—oh, Nicky, you are here! I could not believe your letter. Tell me it isn't true. Oh, Nicky—that man— what has he done to you?'

CHAPTER NINE

NICOLA returned the embrace, then looked at Carlos, who was looking frankly scandalised. She moistened her lips. 'That will be all, Carlos. Teresita, come into the *salón*. We can talk there.'

'We are not staying,' Teresita said firmly. 'We are leaving at once, and you are coming with us. This marriage must not happen. I will not allow it. The brute—the tyrant—he will not do this thing!'

Nicola saw Cliff look past her, and his face change as he dropped a warning hand on his wife's shoulder.

'Welcome to my house, Señorita Dominguez,' Luis said silkily. 'Or should I now call you by another name?'

Teresita gave him a defiant glance, and Cliff interposed hastily, 'Don Luis, you must wonder about this intrusion, but the fact is my wife had this letter from Nicky here, and it upset her so much she insisted we come here and get everything sorted out.'

'*Usted es muy amable.*' Luis' tone was ironic. 'Shall we go into the *salón*, and I will ask for refreshments to be brought.'

'We do not wish for refreshments,' said Teresita, but she went into the room he indicated. 'We have come for Nicky. She came here to save me, and I will not allow her to sacrifice herself in my place.'

Luis said icily, 'You are too late, *señora*. I regret to inform you that the sacrifice has already been made.'

Teresita gasped. 'Then we are too late? Nicky, you cannot be already married! It is not possible. How did he force you to do such a thing? *Madre de Dios,* I should never have allowed you to come here!'

'You can say that again,' Cliff muttered. '*Señor*, I don't

want to apportion blame here, but it seems we have one hell of a mess. Now, I want your assurance that you didn't use any element of coercion with Nicky here . . .'

Luis shrugged 'I can give no such assurance. I offered Nicola the choice between marriage, or dishonour and jail.'

Cliff's lips parted, then with a helpless gesture, he turned away in silence.

'*Tirano*—bully!' Teresita exclaimed. 'You should be made to suffer for the rest of your life for what you have done. Oh, my poor Nicky!'

Watching Luis, Nicola saw the firm lips tighten.

He said, 'Your "poor Nicky" is free to leave my house whenever she wishes. I regretted my conduct towards her a long time ago, and I intend to seek an annulment. Does that satisfy you?'

Nicola felt as if she had been turned to stone. She wanted to cry out, to utter some protest, but no words would come. She stared at Luis, her green eyes widening with shock and hurt, but he seemed oblivious to her gaze.

He was speaking to Cliff. 'Your arrival, *señor*, is in fact opportune. I presume you are willing to escort my—wife to wherever she wishes to go?'

'Sure—anything you say,' Cliff agreed, looking embarrassed to death. 'How—how soon can you be ready, honey?' He looked at Nicola.

She was still watching Luis and she saw the flicker of distaste that the casual endearment provoked.

She said shakily, 'Can you wait for a moment? I would like to speak to my husband in private.'

The pleading in her eyes met only coldness in his. For a moment she thought, panicking, that he was going to refuse. Then he gave a brief curt nod. She followed him out of the room, conscious that Cliff and Teresita were watching them in frank amazement. Once the door had closed behind them, she caught at his sleeve.

'Luis . . .'

'One moment.' He detached himself from her fingers. 'This hallway is hardly private. We had better go to my study.'

The shutters had been drawn and the room was dim and cool. He set a chair for her, and she sank into it, her eyes watching him with painful intensity.

She asked, 'Why are you sending me away?'

'You can ask me that after what has happened between us? This marriage I forced on you was madness, and it is time we regained our sanity before we harm each other further. Go away from here, Nicola, leave Mexico, and soon this brief time in your life will seem like a bad dream.'

'Another one.' She tried to smile, but her lips were trembling. 'Luis, you don't—you can't still think that I—that Ramón . . .'

'*Dios,* no!' She saw him flinch. 'No, every foul lie that bitch told is known to me. And besides,' his mouth twisted bitterly, 'had I not already proved your—innocence for myself? I behaved like an animal to you, treated you in a way I would not have treated a girl of the streets. The only way I can make amends is to give you your freedom.'

Freedom, she thought, when her love would be a chain to bind me to you for ever.

She tried to steady her voice, 'Then you don't want me any more?'

He turned a derisive look on her. 'Not want you, *chica*? You have a lovely face and an entrancing body. Who would not want you? But now I acknowledge it is hardly a sufficient basis for marriage.'

Nicola felt as cold as ice. She said, 'But you thought it was once.'

Luis gave a slight shrug, his face cynical. 'I thought I had explained that when we encountered each other, Nicola, I was bored with the prospect of the marriage which awaited me. For a time you were a—charming novelty, but now that time is past.'

She said almost inaudibly, 'You told—your family that you had fallen in love with me at first sight. Was it true—or was it just a story?'

He walked across the room and stood with his back to her, looking out through the shutters. He said quietly, 'It was just a story.'

Her breath escaped in a swift, painful sigh, then she stood up. He turned back, alerted by her movement. He said evenly, 'You will need money—and this.' He produced her passport from a drawer and slid it across the desk to her. 'When you have decided on a place of residence, perhaps you would let me know so that my lawyers can contact you.'

She said, 'As simple as that.' She picked up the passport and saw there was money inside it. She let it fall to the desk. 'I don't need your charity, Luis. I have friends, and I'm quite capable of earning my living, as I did before we met.'

He stiffened. 'Naturally, there will be a settlement . . .'

'Which I shall refuse.' She met his eyes steadily. 'I'll take the little I came with, and nothing else. Perhaps you would be good enough to say goodbye to Ramón for me.'

She went out of the room without a backward glance, and straight up to her bedroom. For a moment she stood there, looking around her almost wildly, as she tried to remember where Maria had put her shoulder bag. The girl had disapproved of its size and clumsiness and wanted to dispose of it altogether, but Nicola had refused, and she was thankful that she had done so. A brief search of one of the capacious cupboards revealed it, and she threw it on the bed and began packing things into it—her passport for a start, then a handful of underwear, and her cosmetics and toilet things. She would need a nightgown. She looked round for the yellow one she had worn earlier, but it had already been removed for laundering, and the first one she found in the chest of drawers was the exquisite confection Señora Mendez had created for her wedding night. She dropped it as hurriedly as if it had been one of the gowns of fable which scorched the unlucky wearer. Wherever she slept tonight, she would make do without one, and tomorrow she would borrow some cash from Teresita and do some essential shopping. She imagined they would take her to the Californian border, and if so she could make her way to Los Angeles, and find Elaine. There might even still be a job with Trans-Chem, and she would find herself somewhere to live, maybe beside the ocean. She liked the sea, although she hadn't seen that much of it in her life. Luis had a villa beside the ocean which she had never seen, and now she never would.

She stopped, closing her eyes, as pain tore through her. There was no profit in thinking of all the 'nevers' in her life, but how could she ban them from her mind? Never to touch him, never to kiss him, or feel the hard masculine weight of his body against hers again. Never to look up and meet his eyes across the dining table. Never to ride with him in the warm darkness under the stars. Never to feel his child stirring under her heart.

She stripped off the green dress, as if she was shedding a skin, and changed into the blue one she had worn when she first came here, tying her hair back at the nape of her neck with a wide navy ribbon.

Teresita and Cliff were waiting for her in the hall. Cliff's brows rose. 'Is this all you have?'

'No,' she said. 'But it's all I'm taking.'

'You really wish to leave like this?' Teresita put a hand on her arm. 'Surely he owes you something for treating you so callously . . .'

'He owes me nothing,' Nicola said steadily. 'Can you give me a moment while I say one last goodbye.' She walked into the dining room and looked up at the portrait of Doña Manuela. She looked at the rose, and the butterfly pinned into the dark hair, and let the pain have its way with her again. She thought, 'I really let the Mariposa legend get to me. I wanted to be like you. I wanted Luis to love me, as you were loved, but it was always impossible.'

A bewildered Carlos was standing outside as she emerged.

'You are going on a trip, *señora*?' He was clearly at a loss about her lack of luggage, and slightly disapproving too, as if he had a poor opinion of any young bride who went on a trip without her husband.

She nodded. 'Is—is Don Luis still in his study? I'd like another word with him.'

Carlos looked genuinely distressed. 'Ah, no, *señora*. The Señor has gone to the stables. He gave orders that Malagueno should be saddled for him. He could not have realised that you intended to depart so soon . . .'

'It's all right, Carlos,' she said gently. 'I've already said *adios*. I was just being foolish.'

He said, '*Vaya con Dios, senora,* and come back to us soon.'

Nicola smiled waveringly, and went out to the waiting car.

Teresita and Cliff were more than kind, although Nicola guessed they must both be burning with questions. She sat in the back of the big car, and stared out of the window as it ate up the miles between La Mariposa and their eventual destination. She was too listless even to enquire where that might be.

At last they pulled into a small town, and Cliff stopped the car.

'Time to eat,' he announced.

Nicola would have preferred to remain in the car. The thought of food nauseated her, but she didn't want to upset Cliff and Teresita, so she accompanied them to a small restaurant in the central square, with a terrace overlooking the bustling market. A smiling girl brought them drinks, and they ordered black bean soup, flavoured with *epazote*, to be followed with strips of grilled steak topped with cheese, and served with *enchiladas*, fried beans, onions and chilies.

Nicola's mind was running in circles, but she forced herself to sip her drink.

Cliff was watching her. 'You look awful pale, honey.'

'And what wonder is that?' Teresita demanded warmly. 'How she has been made to suffer!'

Nicola shook her head. 'Whatever happened, I deserved.'

'I hear what you're saying, but it doesn't make much sense,' said Cliff. 'The guy has done you dirt, then and now. Okay, so what, you tried to pull with him was one crazy stunt, but hell, he didn't have to react as strongly as that about it. You don't practically kidnap a girl and make her marry you.'

She said wearily, 'It was an impulse.'

'He seems to have a lot of them,' Cliff muttered. 'And now he gets another impulse and decides enough is enough.'

Nicola bent her head. 'It—it was never a real marriage. There's no reason for either of us to feel tied by it.'

'And what are these impulses?' Teresita demanded. 'Don Luis does not give way to such things. Whenever I met him, he was always so correct—so aloof, never ruffled.'

'Except once,' Nicola reminded her with a faint smile. 'When he tried to give you a ride on his horse.'

'Ay!' Teresita clapped a hand to her head. 'I had forgotten. Oh, my poor mother, how mortified she was!'

'Look,' said Cliff, 'can we postpone the reminiscences? Nicky has a problem here. We're driving towards California, and I don't know that we should be because back there is a guy who forced her into some kind of weirdo marriage. Now, Nicky, you have every justification for hating his guts, but that doesn't mean you should let him get away with it like this.'

'I don't hate him,' Nicola said simply.

Teresita put down her glass and stared at her. 'Nicky, what are you saying? You cannot be serious!'

Nicola moved her shoulders wearily. 'I was never more serious in my life.' She smiled bitterly. 'Yes, he did pressure me into marrying him at first, but he didn't need to. I—I wanted him before I even realised who he was.'

Teresita said shakily, '*Dios*, you are in love with him. Then why did you leave with us?'

'Because he doesn't love me, and I was afraid to show him how much I cared. It was all a disaster from the start,' Nicola confessed miserably, but the actual statement of the problem made her begin to feel better. Sitting in the car, she had gone over that final scene with Luis over and over again, trying to make sense of what had happened. He had behaved as if he was indifferent to her, but surely if that was the case he could not have been so angry, so jealous over her supposed affair with Ramón. Surely his violent reaction proved that he must care?

But she wouldn't think about caring. He had admitted he still wanted her and she could have built on that, even if that was all there would ever be in any relationship between them.

'*Ay de mi!*' Teresita put her hand on her husband's arm. 'Cliff, we must return to La Mariposa at once.'

'No,' Nicola protested. 'It—it's over. I can't go back.'

'Nothing is over,' Teresita said severely. 'You told us that it was not a real marriage, so how can it be over when it has not even begun? And if you go to California, it never will, because Don Luis will never follow you there. He is too proud.'

'Here comes the soup,' Cliff put in practically. 'I'll drive anywhere I'm told, but not on an empty stomach. And whether Nicky wants to go on to California, or back to the *hacienda*, she needs to eat, or she'll fall flat at Don Luis' feet in a faint, and that's not the idea at all.'

It was a long, leisurely meal, and Nicola sat, chafing

silently as she forced herself to swallow as little food as she could get away with. It was mid-afternoon before they began the return journey, and she sat quietly wondering what to say, how to make things right between them.

It would not be easy, there was more than his pride to conquer. There was the sense of shame that his treatment of her the previous night had engendered, and her own shyness.

She sighed inwardly. It would have been so much less complicated if she had simply woken in his arms this morning. She could have turned to him then, convinced him somehow that the harshness of his initial possession of her was unimportant, and that she wanted him as passionately as he desired her. Her own woman's instincts would have carried her through, making stammered explanations unnecessary. Whereas now . . .

She stopped herself short. That was defeatism, and it had no place in her plans. She loved Luis, and she wanted him, and everything would be all right because it had to be.

Nevertheless, she still had her fingers crossed superstitiously as they turned under the high arched gate and drove up the private road beyond the *hacienda*. It was almost dark, and she didn't know whether to be glad or sorry about that.

Cliff halted the car in front of the main entrance, and she rang the bell.

Carlos' jaw dropped when he saw her. '*Ay, señora!* You have returned to us. Don Luis will be a happy man.'

'I certainly hope so,' she said with a calmness she was far from feeling. 'Will you arrange for a room to be prepared for Señor and Señora Arnold in the guest wing, Carlos? They'll be staying the night.'

'It is my pleasure, *señora*.' He was already moving to greet them, to collect their luggage.

Nicola took a deep breath and went up the stairs. She

had plenty of time to change before dinner, and if she hurried, there might be a chance to talk to Luis first. He would probably be in his own room now, and she would try to catch him before he went down to the *salón*, although she still wasn't sure exactly what she was going to say to him.

Lost in thought, she went into her room and walked across to the bed to switch on the big lamp. As the light came on, she nearly jumped out of her skin.

Luis was there, lying face downwards across the bed, his face buried in her pillow. He was fully dressed except for his boots which were lying covered in dust in the middle of the bedroom floor where he had clearly thrown them. On the chest beside the bed was a bottle and a used glass. Nicola glanced at it, grimacing at the faint reek of spirits, and her heart sank. Had he drunk himself into insensibility? But a further look at the bottle provided reassurance. It was still more than two thirds full, and she guessed that if he had intended to drink himself to sleep, he had been overtaken by sheer exhaustion first.

One arm dangled limply over the edge of the bed, and on the floor below something glittered faintly which had obviously fallen there from his relaxed fingers. Nicola bent, and picked up her silver butterfly.

She cradled it in her hand, her happiness soaring. He must have ridden all the way to the *ejido* to fetch it, and that had to be a hopeful sign, because it had no great intrinsic value for him to pursue. She touched the butterfly to her lips, then placed it on the bedside chest beside the glass.

Luis, she addressed him silently, my handsome, desirable, beloved, stubborn husband, it's time you woke up. She bent and lightly kissed the dishevelled black hair. He stirred immediately, but by the time he had lifted himself on to one elbow and was looking around him, she was several feet away, standing on the edge of the circle of lamplight, and smiling at him.

She said, *'Buenas noches, señor.'*

For a long moment, he stared at her. His face was still grim and set, but there was a new uncertainty in his eyes.

At last he said quietly, 'If I am dreaming, then I hope I never wake.'

'I'm not a dream, *señor*. I'm flesh and blood, as I shall soon prove to you.' She kicked off her sandals and pivoted slowly on one bare foot. 'See—I'm real. All of me.'

'I see,' he said drily. 'Nicola, what are you doing here? Why have you come back—and how?'

'Teresita and Cliff brought me. They're in the guest wing. And I'm here because you cheated me, Don Luis. Before you married me, you promised me passion, and you've cheated me. And today, I realised why.' Again she did that long slow pivot, allowing her skirt to swing out around her.

'And of course you are going to tell me.' His voice was even.

'Of course. You married me because you didn't want a dull, conventional marriage. But our life together just hasn't had the sort of excitement you wanted. So——' she smiled at him again —'I have decided that I shall just have to be more entertaining in future. Starting now.'

She began to unzip her dress. When it was completely unfastened, she slipped it off her shoulders and let it fall to the floor, then kicked it away. She risked a glance at him under her lashes and saw with heart-stopping satisfaction that she had his whole and undivided attention. She unhooked the waistband of her lacy underskirt and let it float away. She was by no means as confident as she hoped she appeared. In fact, she could easily have cracked apart with nervousness. She lifted her hands as if to unclip her bra, then raised them further to pull loose the ribbon confining her hair instead. She shook the long tawny strands over her shoulders, and moisten-

ing suddenly dry lips, reached once more to undo her
bra.

She hadn't seen him move, but he was beside her, his
hands slipping round her body, pulling her against him.
His dark head bent over her in passionate acceptance
of the mute invitation of her parted lips.

When at last she could speak, she said huskily, 'Señor,
this is an outrage! The audience are forbidden to take
part in the floorshow.'

'Is that so, mi amada?' His voice held an edge of
laughter. 'Naturally, I know little of such things, but I
always understood that the show was over—once the
girl was naked.'

Nicola was going to say, 'But I'm not,' when she
realised in time what those sensuously caressing hands
had achieved while he was kissing her. She felt hot
colour invade her face.

'Blushing, querida?' He touched his lips to one flushed
cheek. 'I am sure no real showgirl would do so.'

'But I'm not a real showgirl,' she said in a low voice,
staring as if mesmerised at his shirt buttons. 'I'm not
even a real wife—but I love you, Luis, and I want you
so much that if you don't take me, I think I'll
break into little pieces,' she ended on a rush of words.

He slid a hand under her knees, swinging her up into
his arms. 'Then I am at your service, querida,' he said
softly. 'It would be a tragedy if harm should come to
anything so exquisite——' he bent his head and kissed
her body —'and so perfect through any neglect of
mine.'

There was no longer any room for doubt and misunderstanding, and certainly none for fear. He kissed
her as he lowered her gently on to the bed, and her
arms clung round his neck as at last he made to draw
away slightly.

'Querida, I'm not leaving you,' he whispered. 'I only
want to take off my clothes and then . . .'

'I'll help you.' She knelt up on the bed, tugging at the

buttons on his shirt, the speed of her shaking fingers not matching her eagerness, so that she tore the buttons from their fastenings, and when at last there were no further barriers between them, and for the first time she felt the warmth and strength of him totally against her own skin, she gave a little sigh of sheer sensual delight.

His hands and mouth caressed her, arousing such unhurried, delicious torment that the last remnants of her self-control fled, and she clung to him mindlessly, her body moving against his in fevered excitement while she whispered his name against his skin. There were no inhibitions left in her response. She kissed him as he was kissing her, touched him as she had yearned to do, her hands sliding without reservation along the lean, graceful length of his naked body, knowing a stinging joy when her caresses made him groan with pleasure.

His patience with her was endless, his generosity infinite, and although she was prepared for more pain, there was none—only a shattering pleasure as he took her with him into a vortex of sensual satisfaction bordering on agony.

Later, lying dreamily content in his arms, she said, 'I tore your beautiful shirt.'

'I have numerous shirts, *amada*. If it is to be the prelude to this kind of paradise, then you may rip each of them to shreds with my blessing.' His hand cupped her breast, his fingertips drawing tiny erotic spirals on her skin.

Nicola giggled, brushing her lips against the bronze column of his throat. 'What would the servants say?'

'Nothing, if they know what is good for them,' he returned lazily.

'Luis, can I ask you something? You won't be angry?'

'Ask anything you wish, *mi mujer*. And I am never less likely to be angry in the whole of our lives together than at this moment.'

She said shyly, 'You said—paradise, but it can't have

been like that for you. You—you've had other women, and it was really the first time for me—so . . .'

'So it was also the first time for me. The first time with you, *querida*, my wife, the woman I love. Yes, I admit there have been other women, although I have not spent my entire life in bed,' he added wryly. 'And now I will make an even more shocking confession, my liberated English rose. I would rather have my wife a willing pupil in my arms than my match in experience.'

She gasped. 'That's a double standard!'

'I know, my beloved, and I am deeply ashamed.'

'You are a liar, *señor*.' She bit him delicately on the shoulder, then kissed him, her mouth lingering softly on his. 'Has anyone ever told you that you're beautiful?'

'No,' he said gravely. 'So—another first time for me. *Muchas gracias, mi amada.* And has anyone ever told you how sweet you are, how smooth and soft and completely desirable? And that I love you more than life itself?'

'Then why did you try to send me away?'

He sighed. 'What else could I do? I told myself I had ruined everything, destroyed for ever any chance we had of happiness together. I was so cruel to you, *amiga*, so clumsy and brutal, and my only excuse was that I was crazy with wanting you, and crazy with jealousy of poor Ramón.'

'That was my fault.'

'A little, perhaps,' he said. 'But it doesn't matter. I told myself it was impossible you could forgive me after what I had done to you, that I would always be terrified that you would look at me as you did on our wedding night—as if I was some kind of satyr. I lay here last night, holding you, and realised I could not face that again. But having tasted your sweetness, however briefly, I knew also that I could not go back to leading the separate lives we had lived up to then. So it seemed best to send you away.'

Nicola said in a low voice, 'Luis, I never thought of

you as a satyr. It was myself I was frightened of then—
and later—and all the things I knew you could make me
feel. I knew that I loved you, and I was scared to show
it in case you laughed at me.'

'Laughed?' He sounded shaken. 'Nicola, I would have
thanked God on my knees for one kind word, one look
from you. Before all this happened with Pilar, I had
already decided that I had been wrong to try and start
our life together here, although you seemed to like La
Mariposa. I thought I would take you away—on that
trip to the south you had planned before we met. It
would be our honeymoon, I told myself, and I would
do anything in the world to make you fall in love with
me, and with me alone. Then today after you had gone,
I rode out to the cabin to find the butterfly I had given
you. I stayed there for hours, remembering how we met,
torturing myself, and I knew I could not let you go.
When I came back I phoned the airline and booked
myself a ticket to England. I thought you might go home
to your family, and that if you did I would be there
waiting for you, asking you to come back to me on my
knees if necessary.'

Nicola's heart lifted. Teresita had been wrong about
his pride. He had been ready to sacrifice even that because he loved her.

'But instead I came to you,' she said. 'And you got
what you wanted.'

He grinned lazily. 'Indeed, *señora*, in innumerable
ways. Which particular one were you thinking of?'

'You once said that you wanted to hear your name
and no one else's on my lips,' she reminded him. 'Luis,
can I tell you about Ewan?'

He shrugged slightly. 'If you wish, *querida*. He is
hardly important.'

'No, but I don't wany any question marks from the
past cropping up in the future,' she said, knowing that
the shadow of Carlota Garcia no longer lay between
them. Briefly she told him of the events which had led

up to her leaving Zurich. 'Those dreams I had were really of you, only I'd had this letter which my parents sent on to me. They didn't know who it was from, and neither did I until I opened it. I read it, just before you came to my room on our wedding night—and it was then I realised that I'd hardly loved him at all. That when I measured it against what I felt for you, it barely existed.' She swallowed. 'I realised too why I'd never tried to run away again, and I was frightened.'

'So that was it,' he said softly. 'I knew there was something, although at first I decided you were merely absorbed in the music I had arranged for you.'

'And so I was. That was a lovely thought, Luis.' She paused. 'Why didn't you let those others play for us at the motel that night?'

He grimaced. 'Because I was just beginning to realise that my plans for you went further than mere seduction, *querida*. The serenaders thought we were lovers, which was what I had intended, and then it occurred to me that I wanted serenades for you on all kinds of occasions, and not just as a means to get you into my bed.' He kissed her mouth. 'I have cursed myself for my scruples since, believe me.'

'Oh, I do,' she assured him, lifting a hand to stroke his cheek. 'Luis, I still have that letter. Do you want to read it?'

'Only if that is what you want, *mi corazón*.'

She slipped out of his arms and went across to the dressing table, retrieving the crumpled ball of paper from the back of the drawer. Very much at his ease, Luis watched her return to the bed.

'How lovely you are.' His hand stroked her body, as she settled once more into the curve of his arm. 'I shall have to invent errands for you all over the room, *querida*, so I can watch you.'

She pulled a mischievous face at him. 'Read the letter, or I'll get dressed!'

He kissed her, his mouth warm and searching. 'Don't

count on that. I may never let you leave this room again.'

'Oh.' Nicola suddenly thought of something. 'But Luis, I must—we must. Teresita and Cliff. It's long past dinner time. They'll be wondering where we are and . . .'

'I think they have sufficient imagination to know where we are, *amada*. We will see them tomorrow. Now let me read this letter.'

He smoothed out the sheet of paper, and began to read, frowning. When he had finished, he said, 'Poor creature.'

'Ewan?' She threw him a startled glance.

'No, his wife, may her soul rest in peace.' He tore the letter in half and dropped the pieces on the floor. 'So that is the end of him. You have been spared much unhappiness with this man, *amada*. But as you say, no more question marks.'

'And the whole future ahead of us.' She pressed close to him, joyously aware that his caressing hand was once more causing tendrils of pleasure to curl along her nerve-endings. 'How nice that it contains tonight.'

'How nice that it contains you, love of my heart,' he said, and smiled down into her eyes. It was the look she had longed to see, and it made her catch her breath.

She said softly, 'Oh Luis—oh, Luis, I love you so. I— I can't begin to tell you . . .'

'Yes, you can, *mi querida*.' He began to kiss her, softly at first, and then with deepening passion. 'Tell me—like this . . .'

PAGAN ADVERSARY

PAGAN
ADVERSARY

BY

SARA CRAVEN

MILLS & BOON LIMITED
Eton House, 18–24 Paradise Road
Richmond, Surrey TW9 1SR

*First published in Great Britain 1983
by Mills & Boon Limited*

© Sara Craven 1983

*Australian copyright 1983
Philippine copyright 1983
Reprinted 1983
This edition 1988*

ISBN 0 263 76069 3

*Set in Monophoto Times 10 pt
19–0288–60116*

*Printed and bound in Great Britain by
Cox & Wyman Ltd, Reading*

CHAPTER ONE

'WHAT you're saying is that there's nothing I can do—that I can't win.' By a superhuman effort Harriet Masters kept her voice steady.

The man sitting opposite her at the wide, polished desk gave a slight shrug. 'You are mistaken if you regard this as a battle, Thespinis Masters. But if you insist on doing so, then I must tell you it is one you will find impossible to win. My client is prepared to carry his claim for custody of his nephew to any court either in this country or internationally. It would be a costly process, but one that he could afford. Whereas you——' he glanced down at some papers in front of him— 'You, I see, are a secretary.'

'Nothing so important,' Harriet said defiantly. 'I'm a typist. I earn a reasonable salary, but I can't fight the Marcos millions—I admit that. But my claim to Nicky is on moral grounds.' She took a deep breath. 'My sister was my only living relative. When she and Kostas married—when they had Nicky, they let me become part of their family. I—I even had a room in their house, and I was actually looking after Nicky when—when. . . .' She paused, struggling for composure.

'I am aware of that, *thespinis*,' Mr Philippides looked at her with a trace of compassion. 'It was a great tragedy, a grievous shock for you. But surely you wish for the best for the boy.'

Harriet returned his glance coolly. 'Naturally. But I think we differ on how we would interpret what's best for him.'

Mr Philippides pursed his lips. 'Come, *thespinis*.' There was a trace of impatience in his voice. 'In his uncle's care, he will have every possible advantage.'

'I'd find that easier to believe if that same uncle had

taken the slightest interest in him when he was born, and during the time before Kostas and Becca were— killed,' Harriet retorted, and was glad to see Mr Philippides look uncomfortable. In a detached way, she could almost feel sorry for him. He had a wretched job to do, and one that was probably little to his taste. But on the other hand, she thought cynically, Alex Marcos was undoubtedly paying him well to persuade her to hand little Nicky over without a struggle.

When she had arrived at the imposing suite of offices which housed the London branch of the Marcos corporation, she had been frankly terrified in case she had to face Alex Marcos himself. She had never met him, but Kostas naturally had spoken of him often, and although Harriet acknowledged that his view was coloured by the fact that there was little love lost between the brothers, there was no doubt that he sounded a formidable figure.

She had found Mr Philippides with his grizzled hair and rotund person a distinct relief, although she did not underestimate him. Anyone Alex Marcos employed would have high professional skills, and would be expected to win any encounters they undertook on his behalf.

But not this one, Harriet thought, her nails digging painfully into the palms of her hands. Not this one. I can't let Nicky go. He's all I have.

She stole a swift glance at herself in the huge mirror which dominated one wall of the office, and was glad to see that apart from a telltale spot of colour in each cheek, she looked relatively calm. She was thankful that Mr Philippides could not know how near collapse she had been through sheer tension as the lift had borne her swiftly upwards to the penthouse.

Alex Marcos' arrogant claim to Nicky had come as a complete shock to her. He and Kostas had been on cool terms for several years, and relations between them had been totally severed when Kostas married Becca against his family's wishes. From that moment on there had been no contact, either by letter or telephone, and Kostas had declared savagely that he would never go back to Greece again. Harriet could only be glad he had never known how tragically his prophecy would be fulfilled. He and Becca had been killed instantly on their way home from a friend's house when a car driven by a drunk had careered into their own vehicle at some crossroads.

From that moment, life had become a nightmare for Harriet, but she had coped with the inquest and the funeral because there was no one else to do it. And no one else to look after Nicky. The firm she worked for had allowed her several weeks leave with pay while she made what arrangements she could. The house had to be sold. It was on a mortgage, and she could not afford the payments. It was as much as she could do to pay the rent on the large bedsitter she had found. It was an airy room, but she had to share the kitchen and bathroom, and when Nicky grew older she would have to find something larger.

But she had been prepared for that. Prepared for all the eventualities and sacrifices that would be necessary, because she loved Nicky.

She had got him a place with a registered child-minder, a girl only a few years older than herself with twins of Nicky's age, and a pleasantly untidy house and garden. Manda Lane was a serene, unruffled personality and Harriet had taken to her immediately, and, what was more important, so had Nicky, who although too young to fully comprehend the rapid change in his circumstances, was nevertheless disturbed by it, and inclined to cling.

Life wasn't easy, and money was tight, but she was coping.

And then had come the letter from Alex Marcos' solicitors, informing her that he was claiming custody of his brother's child, and offering her payment in compensation.

She had been stunned by the letter's cruelty and

insensitivity, and had dashed off an impetuous refusal of his terms by return of post.

The next communication had been couched in slightly more conciliatory terms, but with no alteration in the basic demand. Nicky was to leave England and take up residence in Greece in his uncle's charge, and she, Harriet, was to relinquish all claims to him. Her reply to this showed no lessening of her own determination. There had been a lengthy pause, and she had begun to hope, idiotically, that Alex Marcos had thought better of engaging in what the media called a 'tug of love' over a child who was a total stranger to him.

He didn't need Nicky, she had persuaded herself. He had so much else—wealth, property, business interests which took him all over the world, and if the gossip columns were to be believed, more female company than was decent.

'We were born the wrong way round,' Kostas had said once ruefully. 'Alex is a wild man, a rover, a true pagan. That is the role of the young brother, *ne*? Whereas I—I am the tame, domesticated man. Very dull.'

He had laughed and looked at Becca, and something in their eyes and intimate smiles had brought a lump to Harriet's throat. There was nothing dull about their lives together, she'd thought.

Led by her thoughts, aloud she said, 'Judging by what one reads in the papers, I'd have said Alex Marcos is the last man in the world to want to saddle himself with a small child. Won't it cramp his usual style?'

Mr Philippides almost gaped at her, and she saw with satisfaction that a faint film of perspiration had broken out on his swarthy forehead.

He said repressively, 'That is hardly a subject for discussion. You forget, *thespinis*, that the child Nicos is his heir.'

Harriet smiled. 'And he forgets that Nicky is my heir too.'

'Po, po, po,' Mr Philippides gestured impatiently. 'Let us speak seriously, Thespinis Masters, and practically too. What can you possibly hope to give the child in comparison to the Marcos family?'

'I can give him love,' Harriet said bravely. 'Nicky isn't a commodity, as Mr Marcos seems to think, judging by the insulting offer he made to me.'

Mr Philippides avoided her gaze 'That was perhaps—unfortunate.'

'That is putting it extremely mildly,' said Harriet.

Mr Philippides leaned forward. 'You must not mistake yourself, my dear young lady, that the child will not be cared for. As well as his uncle, his grandmother is also anxious to receive him.'

'What a pity they weren't equally anxious to receive my sister.' Harriet's tone held a note of steel.

She could remember Kostas' distress at the implacable silence which greeted his marriage. 'Mama and Alex!' he had raged. 'All my life I have taken their orders—obeyed them dutifully. But all that is forgotten now. In their eyes I have transgressed—and neither of them will forgive or forget.'

Harriet's heart muscles contracted at the thought of little Nicky growing up in such an atmosphere.

Mr Philippides sighed. 'It could hardly be expected they would welcome such a match,' he said, clearly making an effort to be placatory. 'You do not fully understand, dear young lady, that in our country such matters are often still arranged. A bride had already been chosen for the late Mr Marcos. His marriage to your sister caused great offence—deep embarrassment.'

'Then why didn't Alex marry her himself, if it was so important?' Harriet snapped. 'As for Nicky being his heir, that's a ridiculous argument. He's bound to marry and have children himself one day—if he can find any woman fool enough to tie herself up to him—and where will Nicky be then?' She thumped the desk with her clenched fist. 'He has—everything, Mr Philippides— and I only have Nicky. I won't give him up. If Mr Marcos wants him, he'll have to fight for him!'

'I hope that is not your final word, Thespinis Masters.' As Harriet rose to her feet, Mr Philippides stood up too.

'No,' said Harriet. 'My final word is—tyrant. A Greek word, I think. In England, we don't believe in them.'

She marched to the door without a backward glance.

Her bravado had faded slightly when she reached the street. In fact she was shaking so much, she had to pause for a few moments in the doorway until she had regained her self-control

The interview had not in fact taken as long as she had anticipated, and there was still nearly three-quarters of an hour left of her lunch break, although she had little appetite.

It was a fine sunny day, and several of the pubs she passed on her way back to her own office had awnings out, and tables on the pavement. Reasoning that she couldn't do a full afternoon's work on an empty stomach, no matter how churned-up that stomach might be, Harriet sat down at one of the outside tables, ordering a tomato juice and a cheese sandwich.

She might have promised Alex Marcos a fight, she thought sombrely, but Mr Philippides had been right when he said she could not win. He had everything going for him—money, power, resources. How could she hope to convince anyone, let alone a court of law, that she would be a more suitable guardian for a small child?

She sighed, and tossed the remains of a crust to a hopefully strutting pigeon.

Besides, couldn't it be argued that by attempting to keep Nicky, she was actually being selfish? She did want Nicky to have all the advantages that the Marcos family could provide, but she could not. Had she any real justification for depriving him of them?

She thought wistfully how lonely life would be

without Nicky. At just over two and a half, he was
beginning to talk quite fluently, and enjoy the nursery
rhymes and stories she read to him. The thought of
losing that close and loving relationship for ever—of
abandoning him to people who were strangers, who
even spoke an alien language—chilled her to the bone.

If the relationship between Kostas and his brother
had been a normal one, the situation could have been
so different, she thought sadly. But the Marcos family
had never even acknowledged Becca, and the feelings of
her younger sister would have no significance at all in
their reckonings. The fact that they had cynically
offered her a sum of money to induce her to part with
Nicky without a fuss proved how little they estimated
her.

Poor Kostas, she thought. He had always been
reticent on the exact nature of the quarrel which had
driven him to England, away from his family, but if it
was to escape an unwanted marriage with a comparative
stranger, then it was quite understandable.

When he and Becca had met, it had been several
months before he had even told her that he was related
to the Marcos family. In fact their romance had nearly
ended when Becca discovered the truth, because she felt
almost overwhelmed by it. She was a gentle girl, and the
jet-setting lifestyle of the man who was to be her
brother-in-law repelled and frightened her. It took all
the persuasion and all the assurances that Kostas was
capable of to convince her that his was a very different
personality.

Harriet suspected that the unconcealed hostility of
the Marcos family to the marriage had almost come as
a relief to Becca. Kostas was working as an accountant
and earning sufficient to provide for their needs, and
that was all she wanted.

Harriet sighed. If only Alex Marcos or his mother
had seen them together, she thought passionately, had
seen how much they loved each other, then they must
have relented. But at the same time, a small cold voice

deep inside her told her that she was being sentimental. A man as ruthlessly successful as Alex Marcos would regard any such change of heart as a sign of weakness.

She got up, brushing a few stray crumbs from her navy pleated skirt, and began to walk along the street, not hurrying, looking into the windows of shops she passed with unseeing eyes.

There was a danger, and she could see it, of making Nicky the centre of her world. She rarely went out now in the evenings. For one thing, baby-sitters cost money, but more importantly it seemed wrong not to spend as much time as possible with Nicky at the only time it was possible—after work. She had never grudged him one minute of her time, or felt deprived, but sometimes when she heard the other girls she worked with chatting animatedly about boy-friends and outings, she felt as if she occupied another world.

At twenty-one, she was hardly likely to be written off as a spinster, the archetypal maiden aunt, she knew. She wasn't conceited, but she was aware that her pale fair hair and wide grey eyes had an attraction all their own. But she also knew that Nicky's existence in her life was a drawback as far as men were concerned. Roy, for instance.

She flushed slightly as she remembered that she had actually been considering becoming engaged to Roy. Then the accident had happened, and her life had changed overnight, and somehow Roy wasn't there any more. She'd been bewildered, and more than a little hurt, because she had counted on his support. But he had been almost brutally frank.

'I'm sorry, love,' he'd said, 'but I didn't bargain for a ready-made family. I don't want to have to share your attention with a kid who isn't even my own.'

Harriet had told herself she was well rid of him, and knew that it was true, but the hurt still lingered, and made her chary of accepting such invitations that did come her way.

Claudia who occupied the adjoining desk at the office

pool was always trying to make dates for her, and urging her to go out more, insisting that she owed it to herself. But Harriet felt that it was Nicky who was owed—owed as settled and secure an environment as she could create for him, at least for the time being.

Claudia was waiting agog for her return. 'What happened?' she hissed.

Harriet shrugged. 'We talked. I lost my temper.'

Claudia grinned. 'It's amazing,' she said. 'You are the image of a cool blonde, and yet it's like an ice-cap over a volcano. Was it the great man himself?'

Harriet shook her head, and Claudia made a frustrated noise.

'Damn, there goes my last chance of finding out what a really sexy man is like! I expected you to come reeling back here with stars in your eyes and no buttons left on your blouse.'

'You're joking, of course.' Harriet was acid.

'Not really,' Claudia grinned. 'After all, he must have something. Look at the birds he pulls!'

Harriet smiled cynically as she wound papers and carbons into her typewriter. 'Oh, he's got something all right,' she agreed. 'Money.'

Claudia snorted. 'Bet it's more than that. Haven't you ever seen a photograph of him?'

Harriet shrugged. 'The odd newspaper one. But they don't tell you much except he hasn't got two heads. It's a pity he hasn't, really,' she added thoughtfully, 'then everyone would know what a monster he is.'

'Miss Masters!' The typing pool supervisor material-ised beside Harriet's desk, looking severe. 'Miss Greystoke has buzzed. You're wanted in the chairman's suite.'

Harriet's fingers stilled on the keys of her machine. She was a good efficient worker, and she had sometimes taken dictation for the managing director and the company secretary when their own girls were away, but the chairman was another kettle of fish altogether. None of the typing pool ever filled in for the remote

and efficient Miss Greystoke. And anyway, if Miss
Greystoke had buzzed, it was reasonable to suppose
that she was there, and not requiring a substitute.

'When you're quite ready, Miss Masters,' the
supervisor reminded her sarcastically.

The chairman's suite and the other executive offices
were one floor up, and Harriet walked up the stairs,
trying to tuck errant strands of hair back into the
smooth coil she wore on top of her head. What on earth
could Sir Michael want her for? she wondered in alarm.
In the two years she had been with the company, she
had never even spoken to him. When Kostas and Becca
had been killed, it had been the company secretary Mr
Crane who had dealt with her, and he had been
kindness himself. But perhaps Sir Michael didn't think
she was worth the time and the money she had been
allowed. But if so, was it likely he would summon her
to tell her so himself?

She was totally mystified by the time she reached
Miss Greystoke's office. Miss Greystoke was looking at
her watch ostentatiously when she knocked politely and
went in.

'At last,' she said coolly. 'You're to go straight in.'

'Yes.' Harriet hesitated. 'Do—do you know by any
chance what it's about?'

Miss Greystoke looked as if she was about to be
withering, then suddenly relented, perhaps noticing for
the first time Harriet's pallor.

'I haven't the slightest idea. There was a message
waiting when I got back from lunch.' She smiled. 'But
don't look so worried. He's not a bad old stick, you
know,' she added, lowering her voice.

Harriet returned the smile nervously. She walked
over to the door of the inner office, squared her
shoulders resolutely, pressed the handle down and went
in.

Unlike Miss Greystoke's office, which was arti-
ficially lit, the chairman's room had windows the
length of one wall, and the sudden glare of sunlight

almost dazzled Harriet as she stood hesitating, just
inside the door.

For a moment, all she was aware of was a man's
figure standing at one of the windows, and then as he
turned and came towards her, she realised in an odd
panic that whoever this was, it wasn't Sir Michael.

For one thing, this man was at least twenty years his
junior, black-haired with a dark, harshly attractive face.
He was tall too, and expensive tailoring did full justice
to the breadth of his shoulders and his lean hips and
long legs.

Harriet took a breath. 'I'm sorry—there's been some
mistake,' she began, backing towards the door.

He held up a swift authoritative hand, halting her.

'Oh, don't run away, Miss Masters.' His voice was as
harsh as his face, with a faint foreign intonation. 'You
were brave enough to my lawyer not so long ago. What
do you dare say to my face, I wonder?'

Oh God, Harriet thought in anguish. It can't be true!
It can't be him.

Trying to sound cool, she said, 'Am I supposed to
know who you are?'

'We'll dispense with the games, if you please,' he said.
'We're both well aware of each other's identity.'

Harriet swallowed. 'How—how did you know where
I work?'

'I know everything I need to know about you,' he
said cuttingly. 'Including the fact that you are not a fit
person to be in charge of my brother's child.'

Harriet gasped. 'You have no right to say that!'

'I have every right,' he said. 'Every word you said to
Philippides revealed your immaturity, your headstrong
foolishness. You destroyed any case you might have
had for retaining Nicos in your care with your own silly
tongue.'

'Mr Philippides didn't waste any time in making a
full report,' she said furiously. 'Did he use a tape
recorder?'

'No, Miss Masters. I saw and heard you myself.' He

paused. 'The mirror in that room has another function apart from allowing young girls to preen themselves in it.'

A two-way mirror. Harriet had only heard of such things.

She said, 'That's the most despicable thing I've ever heard!'

'But then your experience had been so limited.'

'No wonder your brother was glad to get away from you,' she said recklessly, and halted, appalled at the expression of molten rage on his face.

She said in a voice that didn't sound like her own. 'I—I didn't mean that.'

'I should hope not.' His face was grim.

Harriet made a little helpless movement with her hands. 'I don't think you understand how upset I've been—about Nicky. He's all I have in the world.'

'At present, perhaps,' he agreed. 'Apart from the fact that you have a tongue like a shrew, you shouldn't find it hard to attract a husband, particularly with the money I have offered you as a dowry.'

Harriet's newly acquired cool went up in smoke. 'I wouldn't touch a penny of your bloody money!'

'Your language is unbecoming,' he said icily. 'If you think to force me into making a higher offer by your intransigence, then forget it. You're not worth what I have already suggested, but I wish to have the matter settled quickly. The child's grandmother wishes to see him.'

'The child's grandmother could have had every opportunity of seeing him over the past two years.' Harriet's voice shook.

'Was that what your sister counted on?' he asked. 'That the birth of her child would give her the entrée into our family? How mistaken she was! Let me advise you not to fall into the same error, Miss Masters, of playing for stakes that are beyond you. You will only lose.'

She took two hasty steps forward, her hand swung up, and she slapped him hard across his face.

The sound was like a shot going off in the quiet room, and it was followed by a terrifying silence. Harriet stood in horror, watching the marks of her fingers appear across his swarthy cheek. She saw an almost murderous flare in his eyes and braced herself for some kind of retaliation, to be shaken perhaps, or slapped in her turn, but none came.

At last he said, 'Violent as well as insolent. What have you to say now?'

She said, 'If you're waiting for me to apologise, then you'll wait for ever! You can report me to Sir Michael if you want—I don't care. I suppose you must be a friend of his or he wouldn't have let you use this room. But whatever you do, I'm not prepared to hear you say things like that about Becca. You—you didn't know her, and that was your loss, but she wasn't interested in your family for the sort of mercenary motives that you think. There was nothing about the way you lived your lives that attracted her. She wanted Kostas and Nicky and they were enough. But she saw that the—estrangement between you hurt Kostas, so she was hurt too. That's all.'

'A very moving story,' he said cynically. 'Kostas would seem to have chosen a rare gem for his wife. Unfortunately my knowledge of him and his judgment makes that doubtful. However, I give you credit for believing what you say, and for having affection for your sister. But let us not forget that the real issue is Nicos.'

'Nicky isn't an—issue! He's a child, a little human being. He's my nephew as much as yours, and whatever you may think I'm quite capable of bringing him up. And that's what I intend to do,' she added in a little rush.

As she fumbled with the door handle she was afraid that he might come after her and stop her leaving, but he didn't move, and at last she got the door open and shot through it into the outer room under Miss Greystoke's startled gaze.

As she reached the corridor she was crying, and she made straight for the staff cloakroom on the ground floor. Fortunately it was unoccupied, and she sank down on the bench against the wall and let her emotions have their way with her. She was sick and trembling when the tears finally stopped, and the face which stared back at her from the mirror looked pale and ravaged. She bathed her eyes with cool water, and let the tap run over her wrists in an attempt to steady her racing pulses. Then she snatched her blazer from its peg and slung it round her shoulders.

Her thoughts weren't particularly coherent, but the necessity to get Nicky out of London predominated. She had no idea where to go, or how to find a hiding place which Alex Marcos' money would not disclose, but speed was of the essence.

She had a little money in her bag, and more at the flat, and some savings in a building society. If she went to one of the big stations in the rush hour, she thought feverishly, it was unlikely anyone would remember a girl with a young child. She would travel as far as she could afford, and pretend Nicky was hers—that she was an unmarried mother. She could disguise herself, she thought wildly, dye her hair, or buy a wig. If she could lie low for long enough, surely Alex Marcos would get tired of looking for them and return to Greece.

She bit her lip. There was no way she could make that sound convincing to herself. I said I'd fight him, so I'm damned if I'll just give in without a struggle, she thought.

She felt guilty about leaving the company without a word of explanation, or handing in her notice but she had no alternative. She didn't think anyone had seen her leaving the building, but she kept glancing behind her as she anxiously waited for a bus.

Manda looked surprised as she opened the door. 'You're early,' she exclaimed. 'I've just put him down for a nap.'

'Yes,' Harriet forced a smile. 'I'm sorry, Manda, but

I must take him with me. And he won't be coming tomorrow—or until further notice. In fact I don't know if—or when. . . .'

Manda gave her a searching look. 'The kettle's just boiled,' she said. 'Go and make yourself a cup of something while I get Nicky up and put his coat on. On your own head be it too,' she added as Harriet moved obediently towards the kitchen. 'He's hell if he's woken before he's ready.'

Nicky was plainly disgruntled when he appeared in Manda's arms, but still too sleepy to be real hell. He held his arms out imperatively to Harriet, who took him, her welcoming smile wavering as she felt his warm little body curling trustingly into her lap.

'Don't squeeze him to death,' advised Manda, refilling her own cup. 'What's the matter? Has the Wicked Uncle appeared and started putting pressure on?'

Harriet nodded, and Manda sighed. 'Well, I suppose it was inevitable.' She put out a hand and affectionately ruffled Nicky's thick dark hair. 'Goodbye, love. Our yard today—a millionaires' playground tomorrow. Can't be bad.'

'He's not having him!' Harriet's voice was fierce.

'I admire your spirit, but I don't think you're being very realistic.' Manda sounded almost matter-of-fact. 'Greeks are very patriarchal, you know, and Nicky has Marcos blood in his veins. And just suppose you did persuade his uncle to let you keep him—do you think Nicky would always be grateful? Unless he was superhuman, he might start reckoning up on some of the things he'd missed out on.'

'That's—horrible,' Harriet said slowly.

'Yes, isn't it?' Manda agreed. 'But being an orphan doesn't automatically confer sanctity as well, you know.'

'So you think I should just—give him up?' Harriet was astounded.

'No.' Manda frowned. 'Of course not. But surely you

should be able to do some kind of deal with the Marcos man—agree that Nicky should spend a certain amount of time with you each year.'

Harriet groaned. 'After what's happened today, I don't think he'd agree to Nicky even sending me a Christmas card!' She gave Manda a succinct account of the day's events, and her intentions, and Manda looked startled.

'For God's sake, Harriet, don't do anything hasty. If you grab Nicky and start dashing all over the country with him, you'll be giving Alex Marcos the gun to shoot you down with. He may be an arrogant swine, but you won't beat him by acting like a madwoman. You run away and you'll just be playing into his hands.'

'Whose side are you on?' Harriet joked weakly.

'Nicky's.' Manda gave her a gentle smile. 'Take him home if you want, but do some good, hard thinking once you get there. If you don't you could end by losing out completely, and that would be a bad thing for you both.'

Harriet's thoughts were sober as she walked along, pushing the baby buggy. Nicky was fast asleep, his dark lashes making half-moons on his pink cheeks. She looked down at him with tenderness. The thought of losing him was frankly intolerable, but Manda's words had hit home.

At first, as she turned into her road, she was barely aware of the car, and when she did notice it, it was with a kind of detached curiosity. There were plenty of cars in the road, especially at weekends, all the popular models and mostly with elderly registrations, but this was very different.

A Rolls-Royce, she thought incredulously, and her steps began to slow instinctively, her white-knuckled hands gripping the handle of the buggy.

There was a uniformed driver in the front seat, and his passenger was already getting out, tossing his half-smoked cigar into the gutter as he waited for her.

Alex Marcos said with a glittering smile, 'Welcome home, Miss Masters. So this is Nicos. Thank you for bringing him to me.'

CHAPTER TWO

HARRIET stood staring at him. Her lips moved almost helplessly, 'But—I didn't. . . .'

'Oh, I am quite sure you did not,' he said sardonically. 'Nevertheless, the boy is here, and I am here, which is what I wanted.'

Harriet looked down at the sleeping Nicky, and knew that Alex Marcos' gaze had followed her own.

'He is very much a Marcos,' he said after a pause, his voice expressionless.

'He has my sister's eyes.' Harriet's grip tightened almost defeatedly on the handle of the pushchair. She swallowed. 'Will you be taking him now—or do I have time to pack his things?'

'You speak as if I planned to kidnap the child.' He did not bother to disguise the note of irritation in his voice. 'I do not, I promise you. However, this is hardly the place to discuss the matter. Shall we go indoors before we begin to attract unwelcome attention?'

Harriet hesitated, but really she had very little choice, she thought angrily as she began to manoeuvre the pushchair up the rather overgrown path to the front door.

In the hall, she bent to release Nicky. Alex Marcos was at her side.

'Give him to me.' His voice was authoritative, and he took Nicky from her, not waiting for any sign of assent on her part, leaving her to fold the buggy and lead the way up the stairs.

As she unlocked her own door, she was thankful that the room was tidy and clean. She hated coming home at the end of a long day to any kind of mess, and she was glad now that she had made the usual effort to clear up before leaving that morning. She was thankful too that the small clothes-horse only held a selection of Nicky's garments, and none of her own.

'He has not woken,' Alex Marcos said from behind her. 'What shall I do with him?'

Harriet indicated the cot in the corner, shielded from the rest of the room by a small screen which she had re-covered herself in a collage of bright pictures cut from magazines.

'He'll sleep for a while,' she said with something of an effort. 'Until he realises it's teatime.'

She watched him put Nicky down in the cot, his movements deft and gentle. Unusually so, she thought, because he could not be a man who was used to children.

He straightened, and turned unsmilingly, the brilliant dark gaze going over the room in candid assessment. Harriet felt an absurd desire to apologise for it. The square of carpet had come from a saleroom, as had much of the furniture. The rest had been picked up from junk shops and lovingly repaired where necessary, and polished, but few of the pieces were beautiful, and none of them were valuable. And besides, there was something in Alex Marcos' sheer physical presence, she realised crossly, that made the surroundings seem far more cramped and shabby than they actually were.

No, she was damned if she would apologise that it was only a room and not a flat, or justify herself in any way. This was her home, and he could make whatever judgments he liked. At the same time, she was his hostess, however reluctant.

She said slowly, 'Can I offer you some refresh-ment?'—some imp of perversity making her continue, 'I've some sherry left over from Christmas, some instant coffee, or tea-bags.'

He inclined his head mockingly. 'You are most gracious. Perhaps—the coffee.'

She had hoped he would stay where he was, but he followed her along the passage to the first-floor communal kitchen. She could just imagine what he thought of that too, from the elderly gas cooker to the enormous peeling fridge. She opened the cupboard where she kept her provisions and crockery and extracted the coffee and a couple of pottery mugs, while the kettle was boiling.

Alex Marcos was lounging in the doorway, very much at his ease, but not missing a thing, Harriet thought.

She said, 'There's no point in waiting here. The kettle takes rather a long time.'

'I imagine that it might,' he said, smiling faintly.

'It must all be very different from what you're used to,' she said stiffly. 'You should have stayed in the West End, where you belong.'

His brows lifted. 'You have never visited Greece, it is clear, Miss Masters, or you would know that for many of our people such a kitchen would be the height of luxury.'

'But you're not among them.'

'That is true. But my own good fortune does not lead me to feel contempt for the way others lead their lives.'

That wasn't the picture Kostas had painted, Harriet thought, as they went back to the flat. He had spoken with feeling of unyielding pride and arrogance, of a total inability to make allowances for the weakness or feelings of others, or to forgive—and with good reason, considering the way he had been treated by his family. Not his marriage, not Nicky's birth, had done anything to heal whatever breach was between them. Harriet was aware that the Marcos family had been notified when Kostas was killed, but she had frankly never expected to hear from them again. Certainly there had been no flowers, no message of condolence at the funeral. For months there had been silence—and then the bombshell about Nicky had exploded.

Nicky still hadn't stirred when they got back, and Harriet moved round quietly taking his aired clothes from the clothes-horse and folding them, before putting them away in the small chest of drawers. She opened

the window a little too, letting some of the later
afternoon sunlight into the room, along with the distant
noise of traffic, and the overhead throb of a passing jet.

This was the time of day she usually looked forward
to—tea with Nicky, then playtime before she got him
ready for his bath and bed. But for how many more
times? she wondered desolately.

As she turned away from the window, she found Alex
Marcos was watching her, and there must have been
something about the droop of her shoulders which had
betrayed her, because his voice had softened a little as
he said, 'You cannot pretend that you wish to spend the
rest of your life in this way—looking after someone
else's child. You are young. You should be planning a
life of your own—children of your own.'

'I'm perfectly content as I am,' Harriet said
woodenly.

'You do not wish to marry?' His mouth curled
slightly in satirical amusement. 'That is hard to believe.
Are you afraid of men?'

Harriet gasped. 'Of course not! How dare you
imply. . . .' Her voice tailed away rather helplessly.

He shrugged. 'What else is one to think? You must be
aware that you do not lack—attraction.'

His eyes went over her in one swift, sexual assessment
which brought the colour roaring into her face.

She didn't know whether to be angrier with him for
looking at her like that, or herself for blushing so
stupidly. After all, she was reasonably used to being
looked over like that. You could hardly work in a large
office and avoid it, and Harriet supposed it was part of
the 'sexual harassment' that so many women complained of nowadays. But while it remained tacit, and at
a distance, she had never felt it was worth complaining
about.

But then, she thought furiously, she had never been
so frankly or so completely mentally undressed by any
man. He had a skin-tingling expertise which rocked her
on her heels and made her feel tremblingly vulnerable.

The sound of the kettle's piercing whistle rescued her, and she had to force herself to walk out of the room, not run, with at least a semblance of composure. In the kitchen, she fought for complete control, setting the mugs on a tray and pouring milk into a jug, and sugar into a basin, instead of serving them in their respective containers, as she felt inclined.

It was his constant, unnerving scrutiny which was getting to her, she told herself as she added boiling water to the coffee granules, and not just the sensual element which had intervened. She disliked the knowledge that every detail of her environment, every facet of her life, the way she dressed, moved, spoke and looked, was being continuously judged by a total stranger. If he was looking for faults, he wouldn't have to look far, she thought crossly.

As she carried the tray into the room, he came and took it from her, placing it on a small table in front of the studio couch. He declined both sugar and milk, so her efforts had been a waste of time as she took it black too.

He remained standing, obviously waiting for her to sit down beside him on the studio couch, which made sense as it was the only really comfortable form of seating in the room. She had two high-backed wooden dining chairs tucked back against the wall with her small drop-leaf table, and she wished she had the nerve to go and fetch one of them to establish some kind of independence, but something warned her that he would not interpret her action in that way, and that she might simply be exposing herself to more mocking comments about feminine fears. But she made a point of seating herself as far from him as the width of the couch would permit, and ignored the slightly derisive twist of his lips.

He said silkily, 'Let us return to the subject of Nicos. It is clear that this present situation cannot continue. As he becomes older and more active, these surroundings will become impossible.'

Harriet said coolly, 'I've already been considering

that.' And panicking about it, she thought, but he didn't have to know that.

'And what conclusions have you come to?'

She hedged. 'Well, clearly I'll need a bigger flat—a ground floor one, preferably—with a garden.' Or a castle in Spain, she added silently and hysterically.

Alex Marcos drank some of the coffee. 'You have somewhere in mind, perhaps?' He sounded politely interested, but Harriet was not deceived.

She said with a sigh, 'You know I haven't.'

He nodded. 'And even if such a haven were to present itself, the rent would be beyond your means—is it not so?'

'Yes.' Damn you, she thought. Damn you!

There was a silence. She had begun to shake again inside, and she gulped at the transient comfort the hot coffee gave her, although in terms of Dutch courage she might have done better to opt for the sherry, she thought.

He said at last, 'Miss Masters—if this unhappy business between us were to become a legal battle— what do you imagine a judge would say about the circumstances in which you are trying to raise my nephew?'

Harriet did not meet his gaze. 'I believe—I hope that he would say I was doing my best,' she said wearily.

'I do not doubt that for a moment. But is that what you truly want—a battle in the courts—to make Nicos the subject of gossip and speculation and lurid newspaper stories?'

'I'd have thought you would be used to such things.'

'But I am not the subject under discussion,' he said too softly. 'We are speaking of a two-year-old child, who may one day be embarrassed and emotionally torn by our past battles.'

She gave him an incredulous glance. 'That's blackmail!'

He shrugged. 'I would prefer to describe it as a valid

possibility. He is already old enough to sense conflict
and be disturbed by it.'

'And therefore I should just be prepared to hand him
over,' Harriet said bitterly. 'I think not, Mr Marcos.
Doesn't it occur to you that Nicky might one day wonder
why I let him go so easily, and be hurt by it? You're not
denying that you intend to separate us permanently?'

'No,' he said. 'That has always been my intention.'

'At least we understand each other,' she said huskily.
'I refuse to let Nicky go under such circumstances.'

'What are you hoping for?' His voice was suddenly
harsh. 'A place under my roof for yourself? A more
generous financial offer than the one already made? If
so, you will be disappointed.'

'I want nothing from you,' Harriet said vehemently.
'The fact that we've even met is your doing, not mine.'

He gave her a weary look. 'Why are you being so
stubborn? You are scarcely more than a child yourself.
You cannot wish to bear such a burden unaided for
perhaps twenty years longer.'

Put like that, it sounded daunting, but Harriet had
always faced up to what her responsibilities to Nicky
would entail.

'I might ask you the same thing,' she countered. 'All
this time you haven't displayed the slightest interest in
Nicky. We could both have starved or been homeless
for all you knew. Yet now you want him—why?'

'Because it is my duty to care for him,' he said.
'Kostas would have expected it, whatever the relations
were between us. The child is of my blood.'

'And mine.'

'Nevertheless,' he said, 'if Kostas had wished you to
have charge of the boy, he would have left a
document—a will, even a letter saying so. Yet he did
not—is it not so?'

Harriet finished her coffee and put the mug down.
'No, there was nothing,' she said after a pause. 'They
were so young—too young to be thinking about wills—
anything of that kind.'

Alex Marcos' mouth twisted. 'When one has responsibilities Thespinis Masters, one is never too young, and it is never too soon to make provision for the future. Kostas knew, in fact, that if the worst happened, I would take charge of Nicos. He was always happy to shelve his responsibilities.'

Harriet was uneasily aware that her own solicitor had deplored the absence of a will, but she had been too fond of her late brother-in-law to meekly hear him criticised.

'Kostas was too busy being happy and making my sister happy to worry about the worst happening. He was a warm, loving man, so what does it matter if he wasn't perhaps the greatest businessman in the world?'

'If he had stayed with the Marcos Corporation, then it might have mattered a great deal,' Alex Marcos said coldly. 'But we stray towards matters that do not concern you. You will do well to reflect, Miss Masters. At the moment, you claim that Nicky has your whole heart. That is—commendable. But with the money I have offered you, you could buy a new wardrobe—go perhaps for a cruise round the world—meet someone who would make you glad that you are young—and without encumbrances.'

'God, you're insulting!' Harriet muttered between her teeth.

The dark brows rose in exaggerated surprise. 'Why? Because I imply that if you had more time to yourself, you would have little difficulty in attracting a man? I am paying you a compliment.'

'Not as far as I'm concerned. Oddly enough, I quite like my life—and my present *wardrobe*. Marriage isn't the be-all and end-all in my life.'

He smiled. 'So I was right,' he said lazily. 'You are afraid of men.'

'That's ridiculous!'

'What is more,' he said slowly, his eyes never leaving her face, 'you are afraid of me.'

'Nonsense!' said Harriet with a robust conviction she was far from feeling.

His smile widened. His eyes travelled slowly downwards, over the soft swell of her breasts, rising and falling more quickly than she could control under the crisp blouse, then on down to the smooth line of her thighs outlined by the cling of the trim navy skirt, then back, swiftly, to her face where spots of outraged colour were now burning in each cheek.

He said very softly, 'And all this because I—look. What would you do if I touched?'

'Nothing at all,' said Harriet very quickly. 'I'm not afraid, Mr Marcos, just not interested. I expect in your own circle, you find that women are pushovers. Probably a lot of very wealthy men find the same thing. But I don't belong to your circle, I'm not bothered about your money—and frankly, Mr Marcos, you leave me cold.' She paused, aware that her breathing was constricted, and that there was an odd tightening in her throat.

She saw the amusement fade from his eyes, to be replaced by something deeper and more dangerous, saw a muscle jerk in his cheek, and wished desperately that she'd kept quiet. But it was too late to retract or even apologise. He was already reaching for her, his hands not gentle as they pulled her across his hard body.

He said something quietly in his own language, and then he bent his head, putting his mouth on hers with an almost soulless precision.

At first she fought, her lips clamped tight against any deeper invasion, but even then she was aware of other factors subtly undermining her instinctive resistance. Her hands were imprisoned helplessly between their bodies, her palms flat against the wall of his chest, deepening her consciousness of his warm muscularity. The scent of his skin was in her nostrils, emphasised by the faint muskiness of some cologne. If she opened her eyes he would fill her vision, and they seemed enveloped in a cone of silence broken only by their own uneven breathing. Harriet had been kissed before, but she had never before known a domination overpowering her every sense. Ultimately, she had always known she was in control.

Yet now. . . . Her lips parted on a little sigh of capitulation that had nothing to do with coercion suddenly, because she was as eager as he was, as greedy for the deeper intimacy he was already seeking, his teeth grazing the softness of her inner lip, his tongue delicately and erotically exploring all the soft moist contours of her mouth.

Gently his hand freed the blouse from her waistband, and his warm fingers moved caressingly on her back, tracing the length of her spine with a featherlight touch that had her arching against him in unspoken delight.

For the first time in her life, Harriet knew need, knew the simple and unequivocal ache for fulfilment. And knew how easy it would be to release the last hold on sanity and let herself drift inevitably on this warm tide of pleasure.

And then from the corner, behind the sheltering screen she heard a small whimpering cry, 'Harry!'

Nicky was awake, and suddenly so was she—jolted out of her dangerous dream and back in reality.

Alex Marcos had heard the child too. He was no longer holding her so tightly, and she was able to sit up and draw away from him, combing shaking fingers through her fair hair.

Her legs were trembling, but she made herself stand up, nervously ramming her disordered blouse back into the waist of her skirt. She stole a sidelong glance at him, biting her lip.

He was leaning back watching her. His tie was loosened, and the black hair was dishevelled. His dark eyes were brilliant, not with thwarted passion, but with stinging, cynical mockery.

He said softly, 'You were saying something about your immunity, I think.'

Hot colour flooded her face, and she lifted her hands,

pressing them almost helplessly to her burning cheeks.
Then, as Nicky's whimper threatened to develop into a
wail, she walked across the room and lifted him out of
his cot. Thumb in his mouth, still half asleep, he hitched
a chubby arm round her neck as she carried him
towards the centre of the room. Alex Marcos stood
waiting, hands on hips. Nicky lifted his head and stared
at him.

Harriet said gently, 'This is your uncle Alex, Nicky.
Say hello.'

He wasn't good with strangers. He didn't always
oblige. Perhaps in her secret heart, Harriet hoped this
would be one of those times, and that he would either
become silent and clinging or—which was more likely—
roar with temper.

But he did neither. He summoned a shy engaging
smile and said, ' 'Lo,' before burying his face in
Harriet's shoulder.

Alex spoke to him in Greek, and Harriet felt the little
body in her arms stiffen as if the soft words had
sparked off an association, an elusive memory he was
trying to recapture. Eventually a small muffled voice
said uncertainly, 'Papa?'

Harriet felt tears prick at her eyes.

'Did you have to do that?' she demanded.

'He is half Greek,' Alex said flatly. 'It is right he
should remember and learn to speak his father's
tongue.'

'You heard what he said. He thinks you're his father.'
Harriet spoke fiercely.

'As far as he is concerned, that is what I shall be.
Explanations can wait until he is old enough to
understand.'

'And the succession of surrogate "mothers" in his
life? How old will he be before you explain them?'

He said silkily, 'Guard your tongue, my little English
wasp, or you may have cause to regret it. Yes, I enjoy
the company of women, in bed and out of it. Why
should I deny it? Perhaps you have forgotten that if

Nicos had not woken when he did I might well have persuaded you to share some of that—enjoyment.'

Harriet's lips parted in impetuous denial—and closed again in silence.

Alex smiled faintly. 'Very wise,' he approved. 'I hope you behave with equal wisdom during the rest of our dealings together.'

Harriet stared at the floor. She said, 'I would prefer to deal with Mr Philippides.'

'I'm sure you would,' he said sardonically. 'Now, I wish to get to know my nephew, and preferably without your sheltering arms around him. Would it be convenient for him to spend the weekend with me?'

She glanced up. 'You have a house in London?'

'I have a hotel suite.'

'And you're going to look after him?' Harriet shook her head. 'He—he still wears nappies a lot of the time. . . .'

'I've brought a nursemaid with me from Greece,' he said impatiently. 'She will deal with such matters, not I.'

'I see.' She did see too. She saw his power, and the certainty and arrogance which that power bestowed, and she hated it. So sure of his ultimate victory that he'd even brought a nanny, she thought. 'And if I refuse?'

He lifted his brows. 'Are you sure that you can? You may resist my claim to total rights, but as his uncle surely I can demand rights that are equal to yours at least.' He paused. 'I give you my word I will not attempt to take the boy out of the country. Will that satisfy you?'

Harriet moved her shoulders wearily. 'I doubt if I could stop you, whatever you wanted to do,' she said. 'When would you want to collect him? Tomorrow afternoon? If you give me a time, I'll have his things ready.'

'Shall we say three o'clock? And I'll return him to you on Sunday evening.'

'Very well,' she agreed dully. It was the beginning of

the end, she knew. He wouldn't snatch Nicky away as she'd first thought, but detach the child from her by degrees. And there wasn't a thing she could do about it.

He said, 'Until tomorrow, then.' He put out a hand and ruffled Nicky's curls, then ran a finger down his cheek. For a shocked moment, Harriet wondered if he was going to try the same caress on her, because she wasn't at all confident that her reaction would have the necessary cool, but he made no attempt to touch her again.

He said, '*Herete*', and walked out of the room, closing the door behind him.

Harriet stood holding Nicky, her arms tightening round him until he wriggled in protest, demanding to be set down and given his tea. Toast, he wanted, and Marmite and 'ronge'.

'Yes, darling,' she promised penitently, because usually he'd been fed by now at Manda's. But she didn't put him down at once. She carried him over to the window and pulled back the shrouding net curtain, looking into the street below.

Alex Marcos was just about to get into the car. As she watched, he turned and looked up at the window, lifting a hand in mocking acknowledgment of her presence. Furious with herself, Harriet let the curtain fall hurriedly into place, and moved away, wishing that she'd been strong-minded enough to ignore his departure—and wondering why she had failed. . . .

Friday was a miserable day. Harriet had phoned the personnel officer at work first thing and received a sympathetic response when she gave family troubles as the reason for her hasty departure the previous day, and for her continued absence. Then she phoned Manda and told her what had happened, or at least an edited version.

She still found it hard to believe that she had behaved as she did. She had let a man who was almost a stranger, and certainly her enemy, kiss her and arouse feelings within her which had kept her awake and restless most of the night. The warm, airless atmosphere of the room hadn't helped either, and more than once Harriet had found herself wishing wryly for the cliché comfort of a cold shower. But it was only people with money and private bathrooms who could afford such luxuries, she thought regretfully. The bathroom she shared had nothing so sophisticated as a shower in any temperature, and the old-fashioned plumbing made such an infernal din that except in cases of emergency the residents tried to use it as little as possible at night.

Manda heard her explanation of why Nicky would not be spending the day with her without much comment. When Harriet had finished she merely asked, 'And what's he like—Alex Marcos?'

Even in her own ears, Harriet's laugh sounded artificial and she hoped fervently that Manda would assume it was some distortion on the line. 'Oh—just as you'd imagine, I suppose. The answer to the maiden's prayer.'

'Depending, of course,' Manda said gravely, 'on what the maiden happened to be praying for. See you, love. Take care now.'

As she replaced the receiver, Harriet pondered on the real note of warning in Manda's voice, and reflected rather despondently that it was no use trying to fool her, even at a distance.

She tidied and cleaned the flat again almost compulsively, then tucked Nicky into the buggy and took him to the nearby shops which he loved. The sun was shining, and the Italian greengrocer gave him an orange, and Harriet, in a moment of weakness, bought him some sweets. While she was in the newsagents' she treated herself to a daily paper, and some magazines, because she had a whole weekend to fill for once.

Of course she didn't have to stay in the flat, she told herself robustly. She had always promised herself that one day she would do the whole tourist bit—go to the British Museum, or the Zoo, or take a boat down to

Greenwich—but she had always put the idea to the back of her mind, telling herself it could wait till Nicky was older and could enjoy it with her. Well, there seemed little point in delaying any longer, she thought, with a kind of unhappy resolution.

She cooked Nicky's favourite food for lunch—fish fingers, baked beans and oven chips. Manda, who believed in wholefoods and a balanced diet, would have frowned a little, but Nicky was jubilant and ate every scrap, including the ice cream which followed.

Harriet tried to explain to him that he was going to have a little holiday with his uncle, but wasn't sure how much she'd got through to him, because he seemed far more interested in his toy cars than in the fact that she was packing his night things and the best of his clothes in a small case.

He's only a baby, she thought as she watched him play, quite oblivious to her own mental and emotional turmoil. He's too little to be taken from all the security he knows, and be made to speak Greek, and all the other things he'll have to learn.

Yet on the other hand there was the very real danger that out of love and inexperience she might keep him a baby too long, might try too hard to protect him from the world which he was as much a part of as she was herself. A man's influence in his life was probably essential, Harriet thought—but what would be the effect of someone like Alex Marcos, wealthy, cynical and amoral, on the mind of an impressionable child?

It was inevitable that when she sat down with the newspaper and a cup of coffee while Nicky played on the carpet at her feet, Alex's picture should be the first to leap out at her. And, again, inevitably, it was the gossip column, and he wasn't alone. He was sitting at a table in a restaurant or a night club—Harriet didn't recognise the name anyway—and the girl beside him, smiling radiantly at the camera had her arm through his and her head on his shoulder.

Her red head on his shoulder, Harriet discovered as

she read through the piece that accompanied the photograph. Alex, it said, was in London on business and lovely model Vicky Hanlon was just the girl to help him unwind from his busy schedule.

After an unctuous dwelling on Vicky Hanlon's physical attributes which would have had even the mildest Women's Libber spitting carpet tacks and reaching for the telephone, the columnist quoted her as saying, 'Poor Alex leads such a hectic life. I just want to help him relax as much as possible.'

'Yuck!' said Harriet violently, dropping the paper as if it had bitten her. She marched down the passage to the bathroom and washed her face and cleaned her teeth thoroughly which, while a relatively futile gesture, nevertheless made her feel better.

She was increasingly on edge as three o'clock approached. Nicky had grown tired of his toys and demanded a story, and she was just following The Little Gingerbread Man with the Three Billy Goats Gruff when she heard the sound of a car door slam in the street below.

Her voice hesitated and died away right in the middle of the troll's threat, and her whole body tensed. Nicky bounced plaintively and said, 'Troll.'

She hugged him fiercely. 'Another time, darling. Your—your uncle's come to fetch you, and you're going to have a wonderful time.'

She remembered what Alex had said the previous day about her sheltering arms and was careful to let Nicky walk beside her to the door as the buzzer sounded imperatively.

Her palms were damp, and her mouth was dry. She had brushed her hair until it shone, and the dress she was wearing, although simple and sleeveless, was the most becoming in her wardrobe, its cool blues and greens accentuating her fairness, and the very fact that she had chosen to wear it was evidence enough that she was on the verge of making a complete and utter fool of herself.

She made herself reach out and release the Yale knob and turn the handle.

There was a man outside, stockily built and swarthy in a chauffeur's uniform, his cap under one arm, and accompanied by a middle-aged woman with greying black hair who looked nervous.

It was the woman who spoke. 'Thespinis Masters—I am Yannina. I have come from Kyrios Marcos to fetch his nephew, the little Nicos.' Her anxious expression splintered into a broad smile as she spied Nicky, who had relapsed into instant shyness at the sight of strangers and who was peering at them from behind Harriet's skirt.

She crouched down, holding out her arms and murmuring encouragingly in Greek, and slowly Nicky edged towards her.

Harriet picked up his case and handed it to the chauffeur, who nodded respectfully to her.

'Kyrios Marcos wishes to assure you that the boy will be returned to you on Sunday evening, not later than six o'clock,' he said in careful heavily accented English.

'Thank you.' Harriet hesitated. 'I—I thought he would be coming to fetch Nicky himself.'

The chauffeur looked surprised. 'He is waiting below in the car, *thespinis*. If you have a message for him, I would be glad to convey it.'

Not, Harriet thought, the sort of message I have in mind. She forced a smile and shook her head, and stepped backward as Yannina took Nicky's hand and began to lead him away. He looked back once and grinned and waved, and Harriet felt a lump rise in her throat as she shut the door between them.

This time, wild horses weren't going to drag her to the window to watch them go.

So he'd decided to stay downstairs in the car, which was a delicate way of telling her not to read too much into a kiss. Had he sensed something in her untutored, unguarded response to what he would regard as quite a casual caress that had warned him it might be kinder to keep his distance?

The thought shamed her to the core. She felt sick and empty, and although she tried to blame this on Nicky's carefree departure, she knew she was fooling herself.

The unpalatable truth she had to face was that every nerve, every pulse beat in her body had been counting away the hours, the minutes, the seconds before she saw Alex Marcos again. She knew too that the ache beginning inside her now was deeper and more wounding than mere disappointment or injured pride, and she remembered Manda's warning, and was frightened.

CHAPTER THREE

HARRIET felt pleasantly tired as she walked back towards the house late on Saturday evening. She had done all the things she had promised herself to do, and had managed to fill her day too full for thought, even treating herself to the pure luxury of afternoon tea at a hotel.

When Becca had been carrying Nicky, she had once laughingly remarked that when you were pregnant, every second person you met seemed to be in the same condition. Paradoxically, Harriet thought, when you were alone, everyone else seemed to be in couples. But then London had always been a bad place in which to be solitary.

But she didn't have to be alone, she told herself. If and when Nicky went to Greece, she would find a flat to share with girls of her own age. There were plenty advertised.

She opened the front door and walked into the hall, to be pounced on by one of the downstairs tenants, looking severe. 'Three times!' she announced with a kind of annoyed triumph. 'That's how many times the phone has rung for you in the past hour and a half, Miss Masters, and you not here!'

'I'm sorry,' said Harriet in bewilderment. 'Was there a message?'

Mrs Robertson produced a slip of paper. 'You're to ring this number and ask for this extension. And now if I might get back to my television programme,' she added aggressively as if she suspected Harriet of being in league with the unknown caller to keep her from the last few minutes of 'Dynasty'.

Harriet dialled, and was answered from the switchboard of a famous London hotel. Faintly she gave the extension number, thinking frantically, 'Nicky—my God, something's happened to Nicky!'

Alex Marcos answered so promptly that he might have been waiting by the phone. Her heart gave the oddest bound when she heard his voice, and then she was aware of something else—background noises which were quite unmistakably Nicky screaming with temper.

She asked in swift alarm, 'Is he ill?'

'His health is perfect,' Alex Marcos said grimly. 'I wish I could say the same for his disposition. He seems to have been thoroughly spoilt. Last night, Yannina managed to get him to sleep with difficulty. This evening it has been quite impossible. Everything she has tried with him has failed. He merely screams all the louder and cries for you.'

'He's not at all spoilt,' Harriet said indignantly. 'I really don't know what else you expected. He's far too young to take such a complete change in his environment in his stride. He's in a strange room with strange faces round him, and he's frightened.'

'You have missed your vocation, Miss Masters. You should clearly have been a child psychologist,' he drawled. 'Did it occur to you to warn Yannina that he might react in this way?'

Harriet sighed. 'I honestly didn't know. He—he went with her willingly enough. And I tried to explain that it was a little holiday. . . .'

He said tightly, 'Very well, Miss Masters, you are absolved. He is, as you say, a very young child, and he is deeply distressed. If I send my car for you, will you come to him?'

Harriet swallowed. 'Of course.'

She heard his phone go down, and replaced her own receiver.

She went upstairs to the flat and stood looking round rather helplessly, wondering what she should do. She didn't know whether or not she should pack a bag with some overnight essentials. Nothing had been said about her staying the night with Nicky, and perhaps she would just be expected to get him calm and off to sleep before she was chauffeured back here again.

In the end, she compromised by tucking some clean undies and her toothbrush into the bottom of her biggest shoulder bag.

The car was at the door almost before it seemed possible. She would have preferred to sit in the front with the driver, but she was gravely ushered into the back, and even offered a rug to put round her, which she declined.

It had all happened so fast that she hadn't time to be nervous or consider the implications of what she was doing, or not until now. Sitting alone in the car's unaccustomed luxury, she tried to compose her thoughts and emotions, reminding herself over and over again that she was only seeing Alex Marcos again because Nicky needed her, and that her concern must be for him.

She even began to wonder whether Alex might be having second thoughts about taking Nicky to Greece, with the prospect of nightly scenes to contend with.

The suite Alex occupied was on the second floor of the hotel, and as soon as Harriet left the lift, she could hear Nicky roaring.

The chauffeur led her along the corridor and knocked deferentially. Alex opened the door himself. He was casually dressed in close-fitting dark slacks and a loose sweatshirt, and in spite of his ill-temper, he looked more attractive than ever, Harriet thought, her stomach tying itself in knots.

She said insanely, 'We should have called him Macbeth!'

He stared at her. 'What in the name of God are you talking about?'

'It's the play,' she said quickly. 'By Shakespeare. Macbeth murdered sleep in it, when he murdered Duncan.'

His mouth twisted. 'I imagine my unfortunate neighbours in the adjoining suites may well be contemplating the same solution. There have already been discreet enquiries from the management, you understand.' He shook her head. 'I never knew a child's lungs could have such power!'

There was a cot in Nicky's room and he was standing up in it, gripping the bars with small desperate fists, his face swollen and blubbered with weeping. Yannina sat on a chair facing him, her motherly face contorted with a kind of despair as she talked to him in a swift monotone. A congealing cup of milk on a side table, and various untouched fruit drinks, bore mute witness to her attempts to find some form of pacification. As she entered the room, Harriet's foot turned against something soft and she looked down to see Nicky's teddy bear. She bent and retrieved it. Hurling his beloved toy across the room was the ultimate in despairing gestures as far as Nicky was concerned.

He was quiet as Harriet approached the cot, his whole being indrawn, intent on producing the next explosion of anguish at the maximum volume. And then he saw her. He screamed again, but on a different note, and his arms reached for her imperatively.

As she lifted him, he clutched at her fiercely, clinging like a damp limpet.

'Thespinis Masters, I am sorry, so sorry.' Yannina was almost weeping herself. 'He wanted nothing and no one only you.'

Harriet gave her a reassuring smile and began walking up and down the room with Nicky, holding him tightly and crooning wordlessly to him, as Becca had done when he was teething. Slowly the convulsive sobs tearing at his body began to weaken until he was quiet, except for the occasional hiccup. Gradually one hand relinquished its painful hold on her neck, and she knew instinctively that his thumb had gone to his mouth. His weight had altered too. He seemed heavier because he had relaxed, and Harriet knew that he was probably more than half asleep.

Confirming this, Yannina whispered 'His eyes are

closing. *Thespinis*, may God be praised! Ah, the poor little one!' She moved to the cot and began straightening and smoothing the sheets and blankets and shaking up the single pillow.

Harriet turned and began another length of the room, slowing her pace deliberately. As she did so, she saw Alex standing in the doorway watching her, his brows drawn together in a thunderous frown. She bit her lip. Clearly her methods with Nicky did not have his approval, so why then had he sent for her? She ventured another glance at the doorway and saw that he had gone.

When she was sure that Nicky had slipped over the edge of drowsiness into actual slumber, she carried him to the cot and placed him gently in it, smoothing the covers with care over his small body. His face was still blotched with tears, she saw with a pang. She straightened with a sigh, and went to the door where Yannina was waiting for her, looking round first to make sure that Nicky hadn't stirred.

She had been too eager to get to his side to take much notice of her surroundings previously, but now she realised that she was in a large sitting room, off which the other rooms presumably opened.

A waiter had appeared with a trolley, and Harriet saw to her astonishment that covers were being whipped deftly off an assortment of delicious-looking sandwiches and other savouries, and that there was a bottle of champagne cooling on ice.

Alex was lounging on one of the thickly cushioned sofas, but he rose as she came rather uncertainly into the room. He had stopped frowning, she saw, but the rather formal smile he gave her did not reach his eyes.

'Champagne is the best pick-me-up in the world,' he said. 'I am sure you are as much in need of it as I am.'

Harriet thought wryly of the other two occasions in her life when she had drunk champagne—at Becca's wedding, and Nicky's christening. She had always regarded it as a form of luxurious celebration rather than a tonic, but she was willing to be convinced.

She chose a seat on the sofa facing the one which Alex was occupying, and pretended she did not see the expression of derision which flitted across his face.

He tipped the waiter and dismissed him with a nod.

'Please help yourself,' he told Harriet courteously. 'I hope you like smoked salmon.'

Harriet murmured something evasive. She was damned if she was going to admit she hadn't the faintest idea whether she liked it or not. And that bowl full of something black and glistening—surely that couldn't be caviare? There were vol-au-vents too, filled with chicken and mushroom in a creamy sauce. It was all a far cry from the scrambled eggs on toast she had planned for supper. And she was hungry too. Her tea seemed a very long time ago, but at the same time she knew that Alex's presence would have an inhibiting effect on her appetite.

She took the tall slender glass he unsmilingly handed her, and sipped some of the wine it contained, wishing for the first time in her life that she knew enough about wines to appreciate the vintage.

She tasted a little of everything on the trolley, aware all the time of the sombre scrutiny of the man who sat opposite. He ate nothing, she noticed, merely drinking his wine and refilling the glasses when it became necessary.

Alex broke the silence at last. 'I tried several times to telephone you this evening.' His brow lifted sardonically. 'I began to wonder if you had taken advantage of Nicky's absence to spend the night with your lover.'

Aware that she was being baited, Harriet smiled sweetly and confined her reply to, 'No.'

'Nevertheless my summons to you must have upset your plans in some way at least.'

Harriet thought without regret of the scrambled eggs. 'Only slightly.'

'You are fortunate. I had to postpone an appointment this evening.'

Another relaxation session with his beautiful redhead? Harriet wondered.

It was probably the champagne which made her say, 'Never mind, Mr Marcos. I'm sure she'll forgive you.'

A faint smile touched the corners of his mouth. 'Now what makes you think my appointment was with a woman? You should not believe everything you read in the papers.'

'I don't,' she denied with more haste than dignity. 'Read the papers, I mean—or at least read about you in them.'

'You surprise me. Judging by some of your remarks to Philippides, I imagined you had made a lifelong study of my way of life through their columns.' Narrowing his eyes, he held up his glass, studying with apparent fascination the bubbles rising to its rim.

'Eavesdroppers,' Harriet said sedately, taking another smoked salmon sandwich, 'rarely hear any good of themselves. How did you know my telephone number anyway?'

He sighed. 'I made a note of it as I was leaving yesterday—in case of just such an emergency as this.'

'Well, I hardly imagined it would be for any other reason,' Harriet snapped.

'Have some more champagne.' He refilled her glass. 'Perhaps it will sweeten your disposition.'

'I don't think so,' she said. 'Nicky gets his temper from my side of the family.'

'You alarm me. The Marcos temper is also supposed to be formidable.'

'Poor Nicky. He may never smile again,' Harriet said cheerfully.

'That is what I am afraid of,' he murmured. 'Will he sleep now until morning, do you suppose?'

'I think he will.' She looked round for her bag. 'I—I really ought to be going.'

'I think not,' said Alex. 'In my opinion it would be far better if you were here when the child awakes.'

Harriet didn't meet his gaze. 'You mean—you'd like me to come back first thing in the morning.'

'I mean nothing of the kind,' he said irritably. 'I am suggesting that you stay the night here.'

Harriet continued to stare at the carpet. 'I really think it would be better if I went home.'

'And I cannot formulate one good reason why you should do so.' The dark eyes glittered wickedly. 'Why so reluctant, Harriet *mou*? Are you perhaps afraid that the bed I'm offering you is my own?'

She decided prudently that she had had enough champagne and put the glass down.

She said, 'No, I'm not, but I admit that remarks like that aren't very reassuring.'

His mouth twisted. 'Is that what you want—reassurance?'

She said wearily, 'I don't want anything from you, Mr Marcos. I came here tonight because Nicky needs me, not to indulge in verbal or any other kind of battles with you. I think I'd better go home.'

'No, stay,' he said, and there was the authentic note of the autocrat in his voice. 'I admit it amuses me to make you blush, but I have no designs on your virtue. And if I was in the mood for a woman tonight, I would choose a willing partner, and not a frightened virgin,' he added, the dark eyes flicking cruelly over her.

Harriet hadn't the slightest wish to afford him any more amusement, but she could do nothing to prevent the betraying colour rising in her face. He made being a virgin sound like an insult, she thought fiercely, and knew a momentary impulse to categorically deny she was any such thing which she hastily subdued. He was in a strange mood tonight, and she already knew to her cost how unpredictable he could be.

Trying to sound composed, she said, 'Thank you. Do I share Nicky's room? I saw there was a bed in there and. . . .'

'No,' he said. 'Yannina sleeps there. Your room is

there.' He nodded at a door on the opposite side of the room.

Harriet was taken aback. 'But if Nicky wakes up. . . .' she began.

'Then Yannina will no doubt call you,' he said impatiently. 'Why make difficulties where there are none? Everything has been prepared for you in there.'

Harriet suppressed a sigh. 'Very well. Goodnight, Mr Marcos.'

He gave her a sardonic look. 'As we shall be sharing a bathroom, perhaps you had better call me Alex.' He laughed at her startled expression. 'Don't look so stricken,' he mocked. 'There is a bolt on the inside of the door which you may use. Do you make all this fuss at your house where every day you share a bathroom with half a dozen other people or more?'

That, Harriet thought, was a different matter entirely, and he knew it.

She said calmly, 'My only concern, Mr Marcos, is that I seem to be putting you to a great deal of inconvenience.'

'I am becoming accustomed to that.' As Harriet rose to her feet, he got up too. 'And I told you to call me Alex.'

'I see no need for that,' Harriet said quietly. 'After all, we—we are strangers—or comparatively so,' she added as she began to laugh again.

'Strangers?' he queried. 'You have a short memory, little one. Adversaries, perhaps, but hardly strangers.' For a moment the dark eyes rested almost speculatively on her mouth, and Harriet felt herself quiver inwardly.

'Yes, well,' she said idiotically, 'I think I'll go to bed.'

He grinned and moved forward, and Harriet made herself stand her ground. She was thankful she had done so, and not jumped away like a fool, because he was only reaching for more champagne, and not for her at all.

She gave him a meaningless smile and walked across to the door he had indicated, aware that he was watching her every step of the way. It was a relief to close the door between them.

It was a large room, luxuriously and efficiently furnished in shades of beige and chocolate, but anonymous just the same in the way that so many hotels rooms are. The bathroom wasn't much smaller, with a shower cubicle and a sunken bath hidden behind smoked glass doors, and basins sunk in a vanitory unit which ran the length of one wall, with mirrors above lit like a film star's dressing room. There was an abundance of towels, and in one of the cupboards of the unit, Harriet found tissues, shampoos, heated rollers and a hair-dryer.

She caught a glimpse of herself in one of the mirrors as she straightened, and bit her lip. She wasn't just slim, she was thin, and her face looked pale and strained. Her navy shirtwaister was clean and reasonably becoming, but it wouldn't knock anyone's eye out either.

There was a towelling bathrobe hanging on the door which presumably led to Alex's room, and a leather toilet case spilling its contents across one of the surfaces of the unit. There was a faint scent of cologne in the air which Harriet recognised instantly, as it assaulted her nostrils with an unbearable familiarity.

One kiss, she told herself with a kind of despair. That's all it was. No big deal, and certainly nothing to build the rest of your life around.

But for the first time she wished she was someone entirely different, someone wordly and experienced, who regarded sex as one of the many pleasures life had to bestow. Someone who would attract Alex Marcos, and who could signal without words that she was the kind of willing partner he desired.

But that's not me, she told herself forlornly. All I ever signal are my hang-ups.

As she went back into the bedroom, she suddenly found she was thinking of Kostas and Becca. It was incredible that Alex and Kostas were actually brothers. Apart from a passing physical likeness, there was hardly a point of resemblance between them.

Harriet remembered wistfully how much in love they had been. How strong Kostas had always been with her sister, how tender and protective. And when Nicky had been born, he had been hardly able to contain his pride in them both.

It was impossible to imagine Alex in similar circumstances. The role of besotted husband and father would sit oddly on his cynical shoulders. He took women, used them and let them go. She could remember Kostas saying so with a rueful shrug.

'I pity his wife, when he marries,' he had said. 'But no doubt Mama will find him a discreet Greek girl who will pretend not to mind that he is not faithful to her.'

'I'd mind,' Harriet thought violently. 'If he so much as looked at another woman, I'd mind like hell.' She paused, horrified at the tenor of her own thoughts.

She sat down on the edge of one of the beds, lacing her fingers tightly together in her lap. All this could so easily have been avoided, she thought. If only she hadn't lost her temper and sounded off to Mr Philippides, she might never have met Alex, or at least if she had it would simply have been for very formal discussions in lawyers' offices. Never alone, she thought painfully.

She gave herself a mental shake. She was depressed because she was tired after wandering round London all day long, and then the unexpected nervous hassle of coping with Nicky. And she wasn't used to champagne. That was why her thoughts were flying wildly in all sorts of unexpected and unwanted directions. Sleep, she decided, was what she needed.

She was momentarily diverted by finding a vast tentlike nightgown folded on the other bed. It was made of white cotton with insertions of lace, like something from another century, and had a high neck and long sleeves. For a moment, Harriet thought furiously it was a malicious gesture from Alex, and then she realised shamedly that it must belong to Yannina, whose well-meaning kindness was beyond reproach.

She wasn't sure whether she could cope with being swathed in so many yards of material in bed, but as a dressing gown, it would be superb. She undressed and put it on, smiling at the voluminous ripples of white falling round her bare feet. And then she remembered that she had left her bag with her toothbrush in it on the sofa in the sitting room. For a moment she contemplated getting dressed again, then she went over to the bedroom door and opened it a cautious crack.

The trolley and the champagne bucket had disappeared, and the room was empty, lit only by one lamp burning in the corner. There were no lights showing under any doors but her own, and Harriet guessed that Alex had gone off to keep his appointment, albeit belatedly.

She gathered up the folds of nightdress so that she wouldn't trip, and walked across to the sofa. As she picked up her bag, she heard the sound of a key in the main door of the suite, and turned frantically to run for cover. But even as she did so an escaping fold of nightgown caught on a small occasional table standing by the sofa and overturned it, together with the ashtray it supported.

Harriet muttered, 'Oh, hell!' and knelt resignedly to retrieve it. As she did so, she heard the door open and close and Alex's voice say, 'Holy Saints!'

She straightened slowly, and turned to face him. She was prepared for amusement, but he wasn't laughing. There was an odd, arrested startled look on his face which slowly gave way to a kind of anger, but he certainly wasn't laughing.

'I'm sorry.' For no reason she could fathom, Harriet felt she had to apologise. She held up her bag. 'I—I was looking for a toothbrush.'

He said nothing. His swift, impatient stride took him past her, through her room and into the bathroom beyond. As Harriet trailed awkwardly after him, he opened a cupboard and produced a handful of new

toothbrushes in cellophane wrappers which he tossed
on to the unit.

He looked at her with a kind of weary resignation, 'Is
there anything else you need—Miss Masters?'

She said huskily, 'No—yes, I mean—could you show
me how the shower operates?'

'It would be a pleasure,' he said with icy formality.

The floor tiles felt cold under her bare feet as she
stood and watched him demonstrate the various dials
and levers. At last he switched on the water and
adjusted the temperature.

'Are you going to use this thing?' he asked. 'Or would
you find the bath easier?'

'The shower will be fine,' she said hastily. 'Thank you
very much.' She put her bag down on the vanitory unit
and waited for him to go.

He stood watching her, his dark eyes cool and
speculative. She was totally covered from throat to
feet—Yannina's nightdress was probably the most totally
opaque garment in the history of the world—but she felt
as if she was naked. Her throat began to close up nervously.

Alex said softly, 'Why do you not take your shower?
Do you need more help?'

She wasn't capable of moving. She stood quite still as
he walked towards her. Almost detachedly he reached
out a hand and began to undo the long row of buttons
down the front of the nightdress. There seemed to be no
sound in the room other than the gentle splash of water
on to the tiles in the shower cubicle, and her own
ragged, tortuous breathing.

When he had unfastened the last button, Alex's hand
moved back to the prim neckline, pushing aside the
lace-trimmed collar as his fingers found the silky skin
beneath in a caress as soft as the brush of a butterfly's
wing. He stroked her throat, lingering momentarily on
the convulsive leap of the pulse at its base, then moved
his hand smoothly and gently along the supple line of
her bare shoulder, easing the nightgown away from her
body as he did so.

He said smoothly and cynically, 'Before I am carried away by the vision of your naked loveliness, my English rose, may I know from your own lips that this is what you want?'

Harriet stared at him, her eyes widening in shocked incredulity as he went on, 'It occurs to me that this is some ploy of yours to retain control of Nicos—either by taking me to the point of no return, and then coyly refusing, or by seeking to appeal to my generosity by the sweetness of your surrender.' He smiled coldly down into her paling face. 'I should warn you now, Harriet *mou*, that neither tactic will work. Besides, a girl's first time with a man is rarely comfortable or particularly rewarding, and I would hate to think you were making such a sacrifice for all the wrong reasons.'

She said in a choking voice, 'You're—vile!'

'Ah!' He grinned mockingly and stepped back, away from her. 'Do I take it that you have changed your mind about giving yourself to me?'

Harriet felt sick. 'I——I never intended. . . .'

'No?' Alex lifted his brows disbelievingly. 'Then it was all a coincidence that you just happened to be in the other room when I returned—that you happened to need a toothbrush—that you happened to want a shower? And this travesty of a garment with its frills and little buttons—was that too part of the plan? If so, my congratulations. Removing it would have been a great and lingering pleasure.'

'The nightdress belongs to Yannina—as you're probably well aware.' Harriet dragged the gaping edges at her throat together with a hand that shook. 'And none of your rotten insinuations are true. I'm here because you needed help with Nicky—not because I wanted to be. I never wanted to see you again—and as for lying in wait, hoping for an opportunity to—to seduce you—My God, that's the last thing I wanted!' She paused for breath. 'And as for the shower,' she added savagely, 'strange as it may seem to a—a conceited, arrogant—ape like you, I've never had one

before. I didn't know how it worked—and I didn't want
to be frozen or scalded. . . .'

'Then try it now,' he said between his teeth, his
face dark with temper. 'You should find it exactly
right.'

He picked her up, kicking and struggling, and
dumped her, nightdress and all, directly under the full
jet of water. Drenched and gasping, she slipped on the
wet tiles and sat down heavily, trapped in the clinging
yards of material, hearing dimly above the noise of the
water the slam of the bathroom door as he left.

Somehow she managed to reduce the flow, and then
switch it off completely. Shivering with rage, she
stripped off the soaking nightdress and hurled it, a
dripping bundle, into the corner, before snatching one
of the voluminous bath sheets provided by the hotel
and wrapping herself in it. She stormed back into her
room and kicked the door shut behind her. She was a
sorry sight, innumerable little rivulets from her wet hair
running down her back and shoulders. Ruefully she
dabbed her face dry, and wrung as much water from the
ends of her hair as she could, before rubbing it
vigorously with an end of the towel.

She was still shaking inside, and she felt close to
tears. She tried to tell herself that Alex's cynical
misinterpretation of her motives and behaviour was all
to the good. For those few moments, just his lightest
touch on her skin had had her dizzy with wanting him.
Right now, she might have been in bed with him, and
that would have been disastrous, because the last thing
she wanted was to be just another in a long line of
women. And what she did want from Alex was
something she didn't even dare to contemplate.

She wanted to fetch the hair-dryer she had noticed
earlier, but she didn't dare. Alex might hear her moving
about, opening cupboards, and she couldn't face
another confrontation.

In fact, if it hadn't been for Nicky waking the next
morning and perhaps calling out for her, she would

have dressed and gone home, even if she had to walk all the way.

She draped the bath sheet over the long radiator under the central window and crept into bed. It was a warm night, but it was a long time before she stopped shivering, and an hour after that before her chaotically whirling thoughts began to blur at the edges, and she slipped gradually into a restless sleep haunted by strange and disturbing images.

She dreamed she was alone, and that she was crying because she was alone, and there was no comfort anywhere. And then suddenly there were arms around her which were warm and strong, and held her closely, and she dreamed she turned to that strength, like a flower to the sun, whispering, 'Alex,' and smiling in her sleep.

CHAPTER FOUR

THE dream seemed so real that it was almost a shock when she opened reluctant eyes the next morning and found she was alone. She sat up slowly, pushing her hair back from her face, and wondering what had woken her, and then she heard the soft knock on the door and Yannina's voice, 'Thespinis Masters—the little one has woken and is asking for you.'

'I'll be there right away,' Harriet called, pushing back the bedclothes. She put on the clean undies she had brought with her and washed swiftly, a wary eye on the door which led to Alex's room, but there was no sound at all.

As soon as she was dressed, she went straight to Nicky's rom. A small table and chair had been installed, and he was sitting there in his pyjamas, watery-eyed but silent, dividing looks of acute suspicion between Yannina and the bowl of his favourite milky cereal before him.

'Good morning, scamp.' Harriet ruffled his hair teasing. 'Is breakfast no longer being eaten in these circles?'

Nicky's smile wavering at first lit up his whole face enchantingly. He picked up his spoon and began to eat with his usual gargantuan appetite, occasionally stealing glances at Harriet to make sure she had not gone away.

Yannina sighed. 'It is you that he needs, *thespinis*,' she said rather sadly. 'It was a blessing you were able to come to him so swiftly. I hope you slept in God's good health.'

'Yes.' Harriet hesitated. 'Yannina—I'm afraid I had a slight accident last night. I was trying to find how the shower worked, and it—it came on rather unexpectedly and your lovely nightdress got very wet.'

'*Po, po, po,*' Yannina shrugged, her rather anxious face softening warmly. 'It is nothing, *thespinis*. You are welcome to anything I have. A little water matters not at all. You must not concern yourself.'

She clearly thought the faint flush that had risen in Harriet's cheeks had been put there by guilt and remorse over the fate of the nightdress, and Harriet could only devoutly be thankful the good woman had no idea of the truth.

She lingered as long as possible, watching Nicky eat the rest of his breakfast, and then getting washed and dressed in his favourite tee-shirt and shorts. Yannina was already clearly his slave and he knew it, which wasn't altogether a good thing, thought Harriet wryly, but there was nothing she could say or do. Soon Nicky's character building and training would be out of her hands completely.

When Yannina had asked her for the third time with increasing astonishment if she herself was not hungry for her own breakfast, she realised that she could not hang round Nicky's room like a spare part all morning.

She had to nerve herself to go back in the sitting room Alex was sitting at a table which had been set in the window, deep in the financial pages of one of the Sunday papers. He rose politely as Harriet hesitated, and indicated that she should join him, his face unsmiling and enigmatic. He was wearing a dark suit this morning, she noticed. The jacket was tossed across a nearby chair, and he was tieless, with both his waistcoat and several buttons on his immaculate shirt left casually undone, so that the strong brown column of his throat and the beginnings of the curling mat of dark hair on his chest were visible.

She sat down, not looking at him, concentrating on shaking out the linen napkin and spreading it across her lap.

'Orange juice?' Alex asked. 'Croissants? Or would you prefer eggs and bacon?'

She shook her head, murmuring a faint negative,

because it seemed unlikely she would be able to force a crumb past her lips anyway. The orange juice was easy enough, freshly squeezed, slightly tart and totally delicious, and that, combined with the sun coming warmly and benignly through the window, made her spirits begin to rise a little.

A waiter appeared as if by magic with a pot of fresh coffee, and a basket crammed with rolls, still hot to the touch, and flaky croissants. The smell of warm, fresh bread was irresistible and Harriet succumbed, although she was still on edge, waiting for Alex to say something—anything. Fresh bread and tension, she thought ruefully. I shall probably die of indigestion.

He was being very civil, pouring her coffee and passing her butter and cherry jam almost before she was aware she wanted them, but apart from that his attention seemed wholly absorbed in his newspaper.

At last, when he folded it and put it aside, she decided she had better break the silence.

She said rather nervously, 'I'm sure Nicky will be fine now. I really ought to go home.'

'I wish I shared your optimism.' He gave her a long look. 'Did it take a long time for Nicos to adjust to you after my brother and his wife were killed?'

She hesitated. 'He was disturbed, naturally, but I—I'd always been there. I actually lived with them, so he was used to me. He used to ask for them both constantly, of course. He still does.'

'And what do you say?'

She shrugged. 'I'm afraid I evade the issue—distract him with something. I'm not a psychologist and I don't know how to handle it. He's too young to understand the truth.'

He nodded expressionlessly, and made no further comment, merely asking if she wanted more coffee.

'No, thanks.' Harriet put her crumpled napkin on the table. 'I really should be getting back.'

'Why?' he asked. 'You have some urgent appointment, perhaps?'

'Of course not. It's Sunday.'

'And what do you usually do on Sundays?' He drank the last of his coffee, watching her over the rim of the cup.

She shrugged. 'Tidy the flat—make lunch—take Nicky to a park if it's fine.'

'It sounds a reasonable plan,' he said. 'And it can be as easily carried out here as at your dismal room.'

'No,' said Harriet. Her hands were beginning to tremble again, and she wedged them together in her lap below the edge of the table. 'I—I do have a life of my own to lead, and I have things to do.'

He gave her a derisive look. 'You made me believe that Nicos was your whole life. Is it not so?'

'And you've made me believe that it's time I thought differently,' she said flatly. 'So that's what I'm going to do, starting now.'

'I wish it could be as simple as that. It must be obvious from Nicos' reaction last night, and to a lesser extent on the previous evening, that he will need a substantial—period of adjustment to his new circumstances.' He paused. 'I am going to need your help—Miss Masters.'

Harriet ignored the unmistakable note of mockery investing the last two words. 'My help? I thought you couldn't wait to remove Nicky from my sphere of influence altogether.'

'But then I was not aware of the extent of his dependence on you,' he said coldly. 'You have made yourself necessary to the child.'

'Oh, I'm so sorry,' said Harriet with immense sarcasm. 'Of course I see now I should have neglected and ill-treated him, just to make things easier for you. What a pity I didn't realise earlier that you were going to come marching into our lives like—like. . . .'

'Like a tyrant,' he supplied too softly. 'Or—a conceited, arrogant ape.'

'Yes,' she said defiantly. 'Exactly like that.'

'I wonder,' he said after another, longer pause,

'why no one has ever beaten you soundly, Harriet *mou.*'

She had never felt less like smiling, but in spite of herself the corners of her mouth turned up wryly. She said, 'Probably because I seem to—to get along with most people.'

'And I think, for Nicos' sake, you are going to have to make an effort to get along with me. Can we at least agree that his wellbeing is of paramount importance?'

'Yes,' she acknowledged dully. She knew what was coming—another reasoned argument why Nicky would be so much better living as a millionaire's heir in Greece, rather than surviving just above the breadline in London with her.

And the trouble was she couldn't think of a single riposte. All the steam, the anger, the defensiveness had drained out of her. Her protective shell had smashed, and she felt weary and vulnerable.

'Yes,' she said with a sigh, 'I think we can agree about that.'

'Progress at last,' he said mockingly. 'Shall I order some more champagne?'

She shook her head, looking down at her hands still clenched tightly in her lap.

'And you will stay today—for Nicky's sake.'

'Yes,' she said, 'I will—for Nicky's sake.'

They had lunch by the river, a very traditional affair of roast beef and Yorkshire pudding, with strawberries and cream to follow, and Nicky behaved impeccably by anyone's standards. He enjoyed eating, and he also enjoyed being the centre of approving and admiring attention. Harriet recognised rather bitterly that Alex had set out to win his nephew over, and was succeeding brilliantly. She was ashamed of the way she felt when Nicky stretched out imperative arms to his uncle to lift him down from his chair when the meal was over.

A lot of people at neighbouring tables had been watching them during lunch, which Harriet supposed was inevitable. Even if they couldn't all put a name to him, Alex was clearly a celebrity of some kind. But some of their fellow-lunchers had recognised him, Harriet discovered as she passed the bar on the way to the powder room.

'This place must be getting fashionable,' an over-weight man with grey hair and a moustache was proclaiming. 'That tycoon fellow Alex Marcos is out on the terrace with a floozy, and one of his few mistakes in life, by the look of it,' and he bellowed with laughter.

It would give Harriet immense pleasure to have emptied his vodka and tonic all over his opulently waistcoated stomach, but she passed by grimly on the other side.

The powder room was momentarily deserted, and she took a long rather weary look at herself. A floozy—and in particular Alex Marcos' floozy? If it wasn't so funny, it could also have been sad. Probably by now someone had enlightened the fat man that Alex Marcos' taste ran more to voluptuous redheads than to over-slim blondes in chain store dresses and very ordinary sandals. And that, of course, when she thought about it—and she'd done very little else all morning—was why Alex had turned her down last night.

Because that was what that scene in the bathroom had been all about—Alex being cruel to be kind, pretending the onus was on her whether their relationship proceeded to bed or not when, in fact, he could have said quite simply that she wasn't his type— that he didn't want her.

He was an experienced man. It wouldn't have taken him long to deduce the way she was beginning to feel about him, and that was the last thing he wanted, so he had decided to administer the death-blow.

It was shaming to think he had had to do it, she thought miserably. She must have been terribly obvious. But then she had given herself away that first evening when he had kissed her. She should have remembered that he hadn't been motivated by passion, but by a cynical compulsion to make a point. He had been determined to make her respond, and he had succeeded only too well, but now he was drawing the line, treating her with an aloof and slightly wary courtesy.

It could be worse, Harriet thought with a sigh, but she didn't see how. She took out her lipstick, contemplated it, then tossed it back in her bag. To hell with it, she thought. She was an outsider trying to compete in a race which was strictly an invitation event.

She left the hotel by the side entrance which led to the car park. At first she couldn't see Alex and Nicky, but eventually they came into sight, walking slowly from the direction of the gardens which sloped down to the river. Nicky was trotting at his uncle's side, holding his hand, occasionally giving a little hop of excitement, and as Alex looked down at the child his harshly attractive features were softened by a smile.

They were alike, Harriet admitted to herself with a pang as she stood beside the car, and watched them approach. With their thick dark hair and olive skins, it was little wonder that they had been taken for father and son.

'I'm sorry if we have kept you waiting,' Alex apologised formally as they joined her. 'Nicos wishes to give some bread to the swans.'

She made an effort to smile. 'Did he know what they were? Up to now he's only encountered ducks.'

'Then it is clearly time his horizons were broadened,' Alex remarked, and Harriet flushed at the implied criticism.

'By a trip to Greece, no doubt,' she said.

The driver had come round to open the rear door of the car and was lifting Nicky in. Alex's hand closed suddenly round her wrist with a grip that hurt.

'Are you still determined to fight me over this?' he demanded in an undertone.

Harriet looked away, unable to meet his arrogant dark gaze. 'I don't know,' she said after an unhappy pause. 'Please let go—you're hurting me,' she added urgently as his fingers tightened.

He muttered something in his own language and released her, walking round to the other side of the car. The return journey was accomplished in an uneasy silence which Nicky, sitting between them, filled with his own happy chatter about the 'Long ducks'. At any other time Harriet would have laughed and hugged him to her, but now it seemed unwise. He was going to be taken from her, she knew, and her best course was to start letting him go, in her mind at least.

As the car purred through the suburbs, she glanced at Alex. 'Would it be too much trouble to drop me at the flat? I—I'm sure you'll enjoy your afternoon with Nicky far better without me.'

His mouth twisted. 'Saint Harriet the Martyr,' he jibed. 'I think not, however. Nicos might decide to stage another demonstration of how indispensable you are to him.'

'I don't think so. He seems to be much more used to you now and. . . .'

Alex shook his head. 'The moment you are out of his sight he is looking for you, becoming anxious,' he said impatiently. 'He can be diverted, but only for a short time.'

She said colourlessly, 'He stays with Manda—the girl who looks after him while I work.'

'Ah yes,' he said. 'Because he knows that when work is over, you will come for him.'

'You speak as if I were to blame in some way. What was I supposed to do after—after. . . .' She paused, swallowing, recapturing her self-control. 'The authorities suggested I let him be fostered, but I didn't want that. I felt I'd be betraying Kostas and Becca if I let that happen. Are you telling me now I was wrong? How did I know that you were going to arrive, staking your claim?'

'You did not, of course, but you might have guessed,' he said. 'Did Kostas never warn you that what our family has, it holds—for ever?'

'You didn't hold him,' Harriet said unevenly.

Alex smiled cynically. 'He would have returned eventually,' he said. 'When he came to realise how much his little bid for independence had deprived him of, and once his infatuation for your sister had faded, as it surely would have done.'

Her lips were parting to call him a swine when she was aware of a tiny whimper from Nicky. He couldn't grasp the conversation, but he could pick up the vibrations and be upset by them, and Harriet, with a little gasp of compunction, turned away and stared out of the window, her eyes blinded with angry tears that she refused to shed.

Once back in Alex's suite, she excused herself in a small taut voice and went into the bathroom, bolting the door behind her. She bathed her stinging eyes with cool water, and let the tap splash over her wrists, calming her racing pulses. She found it impossible to understand why Alex was so bitter still about Kostas and Becca. Even if he felt, as he obviously did, that his brother had married beneath himself and his family, then surely it couldn't matter any longer.

Harriet sighed, wishing that Alex had met Becca just once. Her vibrant gaiety and charm must surely have captivated him as it had done Kostas.

When she was sure she was once more in control of her temper and emotions, she returned to the sitting room.

Alex was standing alone by the window, staring down into the street below. He turned as she entered, and gave her a long thoughtful look.

'Where's Nicky?' Harriet looked around her, puzzled by the hush which had fallen over the suite.

'Yannina has taken him for a walk,' he said coolly. 'It seemed to me it would be best if we continued our discussion in private.'

'There's nothing to discuss,' she said in a low voice. 'I—I can't win against you. I won't stop you taking Nicky, or make any kind of fuss. It would be selfish to try and deprive him of the kind of advantages you

could give him. I've always known that—I just didn't
want to admit it.' She swallowed. 'But you will be—
kind to him? You won't blame him because he's Becca's
child as well as your brother's?'

'Holy God,' he said slowly, 'what kind of a monster
do you think I am?' His voice was icily furious, and
Harriet shrank inwardly.

But she lifted her chin, and kept her voice steady.
'What does it matter what I think? It won't make the
slightest difference to—to what you intend to do. Will I
be allowed to write to him, when he's older—send
Christmas presents?'

He said something succinct and violent in his own
language and came over to her. 'Sit down,' he ordered,
and she obeyed, because she was afraid if she hesitated
he might make her do what he wanted, and the thought
of being touched by him again, even in anger, was an
unbearable one. She thought he might be going to sit
beside her, and her whole body tensed uncontrollably,
but he remained standing, looming over her, his dark
brows drawn together in a thunderous frown.

He said quietly and coldly, 'Yes, it was my intention
to take Nicos away—it would be pointless to deny it.
But I had not realised then how strong the child's
feeling was for you—how necessary you had become to
him. It would be an act of senseless cruelty to separate
you so absolutely.' He paused. 'So there must be a
compromise.'

She looked at him bewilderedly, trying to decide what
he meant. Was it possible that he was going to let Nicky
stay with her, but contribute to his support?

He said, 'When I take Nicos to Greece, you will have
to come with us.'

Harriet had been leaning back against the cushions,
but now she shot bolt upright, sending him a horrified
glance.

'No!' she almost choked. 'No, I won't. It—it's
impossible!'

'How is it so?'

Because I don't want to see you any more, she thought. Because I dare not spend any more time in your company than I have to.

She said, 'Because, as you once reminded me, I have my own life to lead. I have a home—a job. They've been good to me—the company I work for—very understanding, but they're not going to make allowances for ever. And jobs are hard to come by at the moment. And my flat—it may not seem much to you, but. . . .'

'These things—they mean more to you than Nicos?' he demanded coldly.

She gasped, 'Of course not!'

'Then you imagine that if you oblige me in this, I should leave you homeless and without employment?' he asked with contempt.

Harriet shook her head. 'I—I don't want charity.'

'And I do not offer it,' he returned impatiently. 'We shall reach a proper agreement before you leave. . . .'

This was going too fast. She said, 'I don't know yet that I'm leaving for anywhere.'

'Always this resistance!' Alex flung his hands up in a kind of angry resignation. 'When you thought I was prepared to take Nicos from you, you argued. Now I say that you can go with him, and you are still arguing!'

'Put like that, of course, it all sounds so simple,' Harriet said defiantly. 'You make the decisions, and I agree without a murmur. Has it never occurred to you that I might not want my life turned upside down?'

He shrugged. 'Are you saying that it is entirely to your satisfaction? That you have everything you want?' His eyes held hers mercilessly. 'Well?'

'Does anyone have that?' Harriet shifted nervously. 'But that doesn't mean I want to—to throw away everything I've worked for.' She sighed. 'But I can't expect you to understand. Compared with the Marcos Corporation, my efforts must seem totally pathetic. But they're important to me.'

'More important than the wellbeing of your nephew,' he said flatly.

'You know that isn't true!'

'Then there must be some other reason.' He paused. 'Is there, after all, some man you cannot bear to leave?'

'There's no one,' she said, and could have cursed herself for the hastiness of her reply. That was an excuse he might have accepted.

'Then I fail to understand what problem exists, except in your stubborn little mind,' he said. He was frowning again. 'You saw how Nicos was last night. It cannot be good for a small child to be so deeply disturbed.'

'And I can't see how my going to Greece with you would improve the situation.' Harriet stared down at her hands—slim but capable, the nails neatly manicured, a working girl's hands. 'Won't it make matters worse when Nicky and I do part eventually?'

'I do not think so.' Alex shrugged off his jacket, throwing it on the sofa behind him, and loosened his tie before lowering himself almost wearily on to the cushions. 'I shall take Nicos to my home on Corfu. My mother lives there, and her sister. You would stay there for a while and then, as Nicos began to settle, you could perhaps take a few trips—cruise round the other islands—visit the mainland. Gradually he will become used to his new surroundings, and to your absences.'

'Yes,' she said. 'That's—quite practical. And how would you pass me off to your family—as his English nanny? I can hardly suppose I'm going to be very welcome.'

'No.' His mouth twisted wryly. 'But there will be no pretence that you are anything but Nicos' aunt. Any other suggestion would be an insult.'

Harriet sighed again swiftly. 'And how long would you want me to stay?' she asked in a low voice.

If he was pleased at her capitulation, the enigmatic dark eyes gave no sign of it. 'For as long as it takes, Harriet *mou*. No more, no less. How soon can you be ready to leave?'

'I don't know. I'll need a passport. . . .' Her voice trailed away.

He looked at her, frowning incredulously. 'Then you have never been out of England?'

'Never,' she acknowledged. 'Even package tours cost money, Mr Marcos.'

'Alex,' he said autocratically. 'This continued formality of yours is absurd, and will stop now.'

'Yes, sir,' she muttered, and he laughed suddenly.

'You will be the most reluctant guest I have ever entertained! And yet I promise you that you will like Corfu. It has a beauty all its own.'

'So I've heard,' she said. 'Don't they say it's the island that Shakespeare wrote about in *The Tempest*?'

'I believe so.' His smile was slightly ironic. 'Does that increase its charm for you?'

'It doesn't have to charm me,' Harriet said stonily. 'I'm simply going there to do a job. It's Nicky you'll have to sell it to.'

The amusement died from his face. 'Of course.' He was silent for a moment. 'Nicos will need clothing— lighter than you would provide for an English summer, I think.'

'Yes,' she said. 'I won't bring him in rags.'

His mouth tightened in exasperation. 'Harriet *mou*, were you ever slapped as a child, because if you were not, it is a deficit I could gladly repay!'

She was going to say, 'You wouldn't dare,' but as their eyes met, she knew that wasn't true at all. He'd dare all that and more, and her heart lurched suddenly in panic and an odd excitement which stilled the defiant words on her lips.

She said stiffly, 'I'm sorry. I'll buy him whatever he needs, of course.'

'Yes, do that,' he said smoothly. 'I will have Philippides advance you sufficient money.'

She began, 'I can afford. . . .' then subsided, with a weary shrug of her shoulders. 'Just as you wish.'

'You mean that?' he said with soft mockery. 'Another

miracle?' He paused. 'Philippides will help with everything you need. Go to him with any problems that you have—understood?' She looked at him, her expression mutely questioning, and he shook his head. 'No, I shall not be here. You will be relieved to hear that I am returning to Athens tomorrow. But I shall try to get to Corfu in time for your arrival.'

'Yes,' she said. 'I think it would be important for Nicky to find you there.'

He smiled faintly. 'Of course.'

In the corner the telephone rang imperatively, and he sighed impatiently as he got to his feet to answer it, stretching a little as if he was dismissing some lingering tension now that the battle was over and he had won again.

'Only a minor battle,' Harriet thought, her eyes drawn involuntarily by his movement to the lean muscular length of his body. But even so his victory had to be complete. She shivered, watching him cross the room, moving as lightly and gracefully as some big cat. For a man who spent his life directing a huge corporation, he was in good physical shape, she acknowledged, doubting whether he was as much as an ounce overweight. Probably that restless, dynamic energy that seethed in him kept him slim, she thought. Certainly he made the executives in her own company look pale and flabby in contrast.

He said a brusque, 'Yes?' as he lifted the receiver, and then she saw his face change, begin to smile. His voice deepened to a husky drawl, '*Kougla mou*, how delightful of you to call me! No, of course I hadn't forgotten— how could I?' He listened, his smile widening, then said drily, 'You flatter me, my lovely one. As you say—until tonight.'

Harriet stared down at the carpet, listening with a pang to the note of lazy intimacy in his voice. Vicky Hanlon, she wondered wildly, or someone else. Where other men had little black books, Alex Marcos probably had a computer! she thought angrily.

She glanced up and found him looking down at her, his eyes amused as if he could read her thoughts. Her face burned.

She said hurriedly, 'Will Yannina be very long? I really ought to take Nicky home. He—he usually has a nap in the afternoon, and he'll be getting tired and cross.'

'He could rest here,' he suggested softly.

She shook her head. 'It would really be best if we left.' She looked away. 'You have other plans—we'll be in the way.'

'My—other plans are for much later,' he said. 'Why are you in such a hurry to run away, Harriet *mou*?'

'I'm not.' The denial sounded weak even in her own ears.

'There will be nowhere to run to on Corfu.' The dark eyes gleamed wickedly. 'It is a much smaller island than this one.'

'Yes, I know.' She bit her lip. 'You're determined not to make this easy for me, aren't you?'

His smile was grim suddenly. 'I am just preparing you, little one, because on the island it will not be easy at all—not for any of us. Neither my mother nor her sister Thia Zoe have ever forgiven Kostas for—his marriage. You must not expect to hear your sister's name mentioned, Harriet *mou*, and for yourself—I regret that you must anticipate resentment—perhaps even hostility. Are you prepared to suffer these things— for Nicos' sake?'

No, she thought, for yours. Because although it's insanity, and gall and wormwood to have to admit it, even to myself, I'd face a pit full of snakes if it meant seeing you again.

She said quietly, 'Yes—for Nicky's sake.'

And wished with a kind of agonised intensity that it could really be as simple as that.

CHAPTER FIVE

As the plane swooped over the lagoon towards touchdown, Harriet found she was clutching the armrest of her seat until her knuckles turned white. On her lap, Nicky whimpered fretfully, pressing a damp sticky face against her, and she hugged him reassuringly, wishing wryly that there was someone to hug her.

But she could hardly call on Mr Philippides for that, kind and helpful as he had been over the past few weeks. In her heart, she supposed she had hoped that some insuperable obstacle would be discovered that would keep Nicky and herself safely in London, but each minor snag had been smoothed away, almost before she was aware of them. Mr Philippides had been cautious at first, perhaps fearing a repeat performance of that first stormy interview, but gradually his manner had softened, and it was clear he found Nicky enchanting.

Harriet's mouth curved tenderly as she looked down at the small plaintive figure on her lap. He had been incredibly good during the flight, crying only during take-off and touchdown because of the pressure in his ears, but she had been warned to expect this. Apart from that, he had been in his element, and although Harriet had found her first flight frankly an ordeal, she had been careful to conceal this in the face of Nicky's wide-eyed excitement.

Although of course the flight was as nothing to the ordeal which awaited her once they actually landed, she thought ruefully. Mr Philippides in the past couple of days had mellowed sufficiently to drop a few very discreet hints about the kind of difficulties Harriet might be expected to encounter, and Harriet guessed that his guarded comments represented merely the tip of the iceberg.

He was clearly puzzled too about why Alex Marcos had changed his mind about separating Harriet from Nicky. Although he never actually said so directly, he obviously felt that Harriet would have done better to have accepted the generous financial settlement offered by Kyrios Alex, and resigned herself to the loss of the child.

Harriet was touched by the real concern in his eyes as he skirted delicately round the subject, but it did little to support her teetering morale.

She felt very much as if she was being sent into a cage of tigers without even the usual chair and whip to defend herself with.

All over the world, people were marrying other people that their parents neither liked nor approved of, but who were making the best of it, not reacting with the kind of senseless bigotry the Marcos family had displayed towards Kostas and Becca.

She had once tried to broach the subject openly with Mr Philippides.

'But if they feel like that, why do they want Nicky so badly?'

Mr Philippides had shifted papers on his desk in an embarrassed manner and muttered something about 'a male heir'.

'What a pity he wasn't a girl.' Harriet's eyes blazed suddenly. 'Then they might have left us in peace!'

Peace, she thought as the ground rushed up to meet them, routine, monotony. All the things people groaned at and dismissed as boring. She had done so herself, but now she was beginning to realise how precious they could be, how safe and secure.

With a slight thump, the plane was down, and in spite of the warnings to remain seated until it had come to a complete halt, people were already shifting, reaching for hand luggage, preparing themselves for disembarkation, and a fresh babble of chatter had broken out, now that the inevitable tension of the landing had dissipated.

Harriet fumbled in her bag for her sunglasses before she joined the file of people in the aisle. It had been a cool, grey day in London, and here at Corfu airport, the brilliance of the sunlight and the rush of heat once the aircraft doors were opened seemed disturbingly intense and alien.

It was a short walk across the tarmac to the Immigration buildings, and Nicky insisted on walking, giving small excited skips. Harriet wondered if they were being observed from the buildings ahead of them, and moistened dry lips with the tip of her tongue. She had to restrain Nicky from running on ahead, and he wriggled crossly, saying, 'Thio Alex,' as he looked up at her reproachfully.

She hoped he wouldn't be disappointed. Mr Philippides had come with them, she knew, to ease their arrival in case Alex Marcos was too involved in business matters elsewhere. Only the day before they left he had been talking worriedly of problems in New York and Rio de Janeiro.

Immigration could not have been simpler. It seemed to Harriet they were whisked through with just the briefest formalities. Retrieving their luggage took only a little longer.

Harriet was glad Manda had persuaded her to blow her savings on some new lightweight cases, and some new clothes with which to fill them. At least she wasn't arriving like the poor relation. But she had been scrupulous about spending the incredible sum of money which Alex had advanced her through Mr Philippides on Nicky alone, and she had managed to equip him fully without spending even a quarter of it.

Manda had gone shopping with her for her own things, and Harriet knew wryly that she would not have bought half the things folded in layers of tissue in her case without her prompting.

'Beach things,' Manda had decreed. 'And not those ghastly regulation things,' she had added in horror as Harriet had begun to look through a rack of one-pieces.

'You're going to Corfu, for God's sake, not entering for the school swimming gala! You need bikinis—and some of those lovely skirts and shirts to match.'

Harriet's protests that she wasn't going to Corfu for a holiday were brushed aside as irrelevant.

'Even if you're shut up in some nursery with Nicky all day long, there'll be these trips that were mentioned. You can't cruise round the isles of Greece in your office gear. You'll need shorts and tops—and some of those white cotton jeans,' Manda decreed inexorably.

However much she had demurred at the time, and whatever limits her bank balance had sunk to, Harriet was glad she had taken Manda's advice, and was not facing the prospect of confronting the formidable Marcos clan in last year's summer dresses. The outfit she had worn to travel was one of her favourites—a smoothly flared skirt in a cream-coloured silky fabric, with a matching sleeveless top with the low neckline and armholes bound in a contrasting blue. The same blue edged cuffs and collarless neck of the long-sleeved jacket which she had already discarded and was carrying over her arm. She hoped she looked cooler and more composed than she felt.

She heard Mr Philippides greet someone and turned slowly, her heart thumping, to find she was confronting the man who had driven Alex's car in London. He was grinning broadly and scooping their cases up as if they were stuffed with thistledown, as he led the way to the exit.

Nicky ran ahead with Mr Philippides, but Harriet hung back, panic chilling her, closing her throat. She tried to tell herself that it was natural that a car should have been sent for them, it was only common courtesy. It did not—would not mean that anyone else was waiting too.

But he was there. The area in front of the airport was a hive of activity, but she saw him at once through the moving, talking hordes of people. Her eyes sought him as if they were magnetised. He was wearing dark glasses so she couldn't be sure whether or not he was aware of her presence or not, but he couldn't be unaware of Nicky. People turned smiling indulgently as the child squealed and ran full tilt towards the tall man waiting by the car. Alex bent, lifting him, swinging him off his feet while Nicky squealed again with delight.

Harriet's feet felt like lead. She watched Mr Philippides reach them, observed them shake hands. Her own hand felt damp and clammy and she wiped it unobtrusively down the side of her skirt as she walked up to the little group.

'Welcome to Corfu, Harriet.' His voice was formal, and so was the smile which accompanied the words. Any expression in his eyes was hidden by his glasses. 'Did you have a good journey?'

She said faintly, 'Yes, thank you.'

'I hope the remainder of it will be as pleasant. We have to cross the island to reach my home.'

Harriet silently took her place in the back of the car, where Alex joined her with Nicky, and Mr Philippides sat in front with the driver. It wasn't the sort of limousine he had used in London, but a low-slung sports-type saloon. As they threaded their way through the traffic away from the airport, Harriet wondered if it ever got a chance to demonstrate its full power on the crowded island roads. Glancing around her as they drove, she thought she'd never seen as many mopeds and scooters in her life, most of them carrying two laughing if not very stable passengers. They were all so brown and apparently carefree, she thought rather wistfully, considering the pallor of her own skin, and she wished she was one of them, just another anonymous tourist with a hotel room and a budget.

She leaned back with a little sigh, stretching her legs out gratefully in front of her. The plane had been comfortable but confining, she thought, lifting a hand and rubbing the cramped muscles in her neck. Aware of a movement beside her, she turned her head slightly and realised Alex was looking at her, at the thrust of her breasts against the silky top which her own action had revealed. Embarrassed, she straightened almost violently tugging, as she did so, at her skirt which had ridden up slightly over her knees. Alex made no comment, but the lines beside his mouth deepened sardonically before he turned away, giving his attention once more to Nicky, who was bombarding him with not always intelligible questions and comments.

Harriet gazed determinedly out of her own window, struggling for control of her hurried breathing. Then gradually the sights and scents and sounds outside the car began to invade her consciousness like a healing balm, and she started to relax. She could understand now why some of the girls she worked with scrimped and saved all year for their few weeks in the sun. It was all so incredibly, exotically different. Heat, she had expected, and dust and rocks, but she hadn't bargained for the frantic beauty of the flowering shrubs, pouring over every garden wall and terrace.

Everywhere she looked there was colour, and even the sheltering greenery had a more vibrant glow. The car turned a corner, and she saw watermelons like great green globes, piled high at the side of the road. For a moment she imagined she could smell them, their clean fragrance invading the overriding smells of exhaust fumes and suntan oil which the faint breeze brought dizzyingly through the open window.

No one actually seemed to be doing any actual construction work, but there were half-built houses everywhere, sometimes only a single storey high, the exposed girders and rods giving them a vulnerable almost skeletal look.

Feeling pressure against her, she looked down and saw that Nicky was drooping wearily, struggling to keep his eyes open, and gently she adjusted his position so that he could slide down putting his head on her lap. She hoped he would sleep, if the car journey was going to be a long one as she suspected it might be. She didn't want his arrival at the Marcos' home to be marred by the kind of tantrum that tiredness and over-excitement often inspired at his age.

Alex and Philippides were conversing softly in Greek, and half her mind registered the unfamiliarity of the liquid cadences as she watched the passing landscape.

The car was climbing now, the tavernas and the souvenir shops left behind, and Harriet was looking at dark pools of olive groves in the sharp decline of the valley beside the road. The air was clearer as they got higher and the breeze held a hint of citrus. The road twisted and almost turned back on itself as it fought the bleak terrain of the hillside, and Harriet found herself trying not to care that the driver hadn't slackened his pace at all, and very much trying not to notice how stark the drop was becoming only a few inches from their wheels.

Alex said, 'Relax—Stavros knows this road well.'

She jumped slightly, because she hadn't realised her tension was so obvious.

She said stiffly, 'Well, let's hope anyone coming in the other direction is equally well acquainted,' and heard him laugh softly.

'Concentrate on the view,' he advised mockingly.

His advice was worth taking. The hills ahead were grey and purple against the unbroken blue of the sky, and deep shadows mottled the valleys. Among the groves, she saw scattered houses with patches of cultivations like wounds in the thrusting vegetation. Donkeys waited in the shade, and tethered goats nibbled voraciously, lifting restless inquisitive heads to stare as the car went by. The blare and bustle of Corfu town behind them seemed a million miles away.

'And not a tourist in sight,' Harriet said, half to herself.

'Oh, they come here,' he said. 'But generally they're just passing through to reach Paleo. This is one of the routes.' He saw her puzzled look and explained, 'Paleocastritsa—it's a holiday resort now, but it is still very beautiful. There is a monastery there too which people like to visit, with some famous icons.'

'Is it near your house?'

He shook his head. 'I live further along the coast—in a comparatively secluded area,' he added, slanting her an ironic smile.

'Naturally,' she returned with equal irony. 'Do you have your own beach as well?'

'Of a kind—not very large and rather rocky.' He paused. 'The descent to it through the gardens is very steep—a mixture of a path and steps. Nicos must not go down there alone, and I have already given orders that a gate must be fixed at the top and kept bolted all the time.'

'Does that mean he can never go down to the beach?' Harriet asked in slight dismay.

'Of course he may, if properly supervised, and the same rule must also apply to the swimming pool.' He shot her a lightning glance. 'Can you swim?'

'Of course.'

'Well enough to teach Nicos?'

'I think so,' she said. 'I had planned to take him to the local baths at home, anyway. They run mother and child classes. . . .' she paused, flushing abruptly as she met his sardonic look.

'At least you have been spared that,' he murmured.

The car was slowing and turning off on to a side road which seemed to Harriet barely wide enough to accommodate it. Citrus orchards pressed on both sides, and the silver glint of olive trees reached across the road in places. And ahead of her, suddenly, she could see the turquoise opalescent gleam of the sea, and she caught her breath. No matter what problems might confront her when she arrived at the house, nothing could detract from the lush appeal of the island's beauty.

The landscape was beginning to change too, cultivation giving way to rioting shrubs, blazing in pinks and crimsons and purples, and as the car wove its way down a steep and winding hill, Harriet saw the sun glinting off a wide expanse of green-tiled roof.

It was like an English garden, only in vivid Technicolor, she thought, looking at the enormous brilliantly green lawns, all with their sprinklers working energetically. The air was heavy suddenly with the scent of roses, and there were beds of them stretching as far as the eye could see, each bush and tree almost bowed down with blossom, the vibrant colours jostling for attention.

The villa itself was something of a surprise—not as palatial as Harriet had vaguely imagined, but lower-built and more rambling, its gleaming white walls hung with vines and creepers which wound their way also round the elaborate wrought-iron of the first floor balconies. In front of the big double doors, a fountain was playing—a stone nymph smiling in remote mystery as she allowed the water to cascade endlessly from the shell she held in her cupped hands.

Apart from the splash of the water, and the constant whirring of the unseen cicadas, it was very still, and the warmth of the sun seemed like a benison as it fell on Harriet's unprotected head.

She thought, 'How beautiful,' and tried to ignore the feeling of apprehension that assailed her at the thought of what might await her behind the cool privacy of those white walls.

She turned to get Nicky, but found Alex had forestalled her. He already had the sleepy child in his arms, and was smiling down at him as Nicky opened uncomprehending eyes and looked around.

The doors swung open, and Yannina appeared, beaming. 'Ah, *pedhi mou!*' Alex swung Nicky to the ground, and he ran towards Yannina with a chuckle of recognition.

Harriet tried to suppress the ignoble pang of jealousy deep within her. She tried to tell herself robustly that it was all for the good, and that the sooner Nicky settled in his new surroundings, the sooner she could be off to get on with her own life.

But what life? Her prospects seemed frankly bleak.

Mr Philippides had spoken of a job being found for her with the Marcos Corporation, but this was the last thing she wanted. Her only hope was to remove herself from Alex's aegis as promptly and completely as possible. The thought of working for him in some obscure section of his empire, of looking forward pitifully to some annual visit where he might or might not remember who she was, was an abhorrent prospect.

She almost started as his hand clasped her arm, urging her forward inexorably towards the open front door.

Inside the villa, she was conscious of space and a blessed coolness which her own rationality told her was air-conditioning. But the décor added something, she thought, as she trod across cool marble floors and looked round at vistas in airy pastels.

There were more double doors in front of her, and they were opening too, and as she hesitated, swallowing nervously, Nicky wriggled free from Yannina and ran back to her, sliding a confiding hand into hers. She gave his hand an encouraging squeeze as they walked forward.

It was a large room, but its focus was solely the two dark-clad figures waiting in the middle of it. Both Madame Marcos and her sister were wearing black, like so many of the peasant women she had spied from the car on the journey here, but their black had the sombre shimmer of silk, and there was a proud glitter of diamonds at throat and wrist. Their eyes glittered too, Harriet realised, with hostility. Two haughty, inimical faces turned towards her.

She felt Alex's fingers tighten on her arm. He said coolly and pleasantly, 'Mama—Thia Zoe, may I present Thespinis Masters, who has brought Nicos to us from England.'

Madame Marcos' firm lips stretched in a travesty of a smile. But her sister was not even prepared for that concession. She glared at Harriet and said something low-voiced and undoubtedly venomous in Greek.

Alex's voice became more pleasant than ever. 'Perhaps we could all remember that Harriet does not speak our language, and only talk in English when she is present.'

Madame Marcos said stonily in perfect English, 'Welcome to our house, *thespinis*.' She made it sound like an insult, but as her eyes settled on Nicky they softened perceptibly, and Harriet fancied she saw a sudden glint of tears, fiercely suppressed.

Nicky was hanging back, pressing himself against her leg. Fierce-looking women dressed in black were something outside his limited experience, and clearly that was where he preferred them. Harriet tried to give him a reassuring smile, but his mouth was already trembling.

Thia Zoe said, 'So this is Kostas' child.' Her accent was more strongly marked than her sister's, and her voice grated slightly. Nicky began to wail, and both the older women stared at him in a kind of dignified amazement.

Yannina pushed forward. 'Pardon, *kyria*, but he is so tired, the little one. *Po-po-po*—all that long journey in a plane! Why should he not cry?'

She picked Nicky up and hugged him.

'He had better go to his room,' said Madame Marcos. 'You also—Thespinis Masters. You have had a tiring journey. Alex, there have already been telephone calls—one from Athens, one from Paris. Perhaps you would deal with them.' The turn of her head away from Harriet was a dismissal in itself.

Yannina said, '*Thespinis,* I will take the little one.' She hesitated. 'I do not know which room you have been given, but Androula will show you.' She nodded towards the elderly woman who had just joined them, also wearing black but with a neat white apron denoting her inferior station.

Harriet turned almost thankfully back to the door. The room seemed to have shrunk to a few square inches, hostility closing round her like a vice.

Yannina's broad form was already disappearing up the stairs with Nicky clasped firmly in her arms. Androula motioned Harriet to follow with an expressionless, 'If you please, *thespinis*.'

The stairs were also made of marble with a wrought-iron balustrade. Harriet's heels clicked emptily as she mounted them. She felt empty too. Her tentative smile at Androula had been met with a total blank, the black eyes impassive as they met hers. There was no real enmity, but she wasn't going out of her way to be friendly either. Clearly she was taking her lead from the mistress of the house, Harriet thought wryly.

Androula led the way along the gallery which looked down on the entrance hall, and turned down a wide corridor, its smooth walls interrupted at intervals by illuminated niches containing exquisite antique pottery. Harriet would have liked to have lingered and examined some of them more closely, but she told herself there was plenty of time for that. Androula led her to a door at the very end of the corridor and threw it open with less than a flourish.

'This is your room, *thespinis*,' she remarked. 'Your baggage will be brought to you.' She gave a curt nod and whisked herself away, leaving Harriet alone to stare round her new accommodation.

For a moment she thought there had been a mistake, or that Androula had had a brainstorm and shown her into a cupboard, but a second glance revealed that there was a bed duly made up, and a chest of drawers and hooks behind the door for those of her clothes which needed to be hung up. There was also, she realised, her temper rising, one very small window up towards the ceiling height, and clearly it had not been felt necessary to extend the air-conditioning towards this particular room, because it was already like an oven.

If she hadn't felt so angry, she would have burst into tears.

She sat down limply on the edge of the bed. This, she supposed, was the equivalent of the servants' quarters, or possibly even a dressing room, because she now realised that her bed was standing against a door leading to the adjoining room. She tried it gingerly, but it was securely locked, and there was no key to be seen anywhere. She listened and thought she could hear, through the woodwork, Nicky's clear high tones, and Yannina's low-pitched cheerful laugh as she answered him, and guessed that she was next door to what passed for the nursery.

She tried to tell herself that this was the room they assumed she would have chosen, if she had been given a choice—the nearest one to Nicky's, but it didn't sound convincing. If this particular room had been at the opposite end of the villa entirely, it would still have been allocated to her because it was intended as a snub, to show her quite plainly how little she was wanted in this house, how little regarded.

The bed she was sitting on was hard and narrow, although she supposed if it had been much wider, she would have had difficulty opening any of the drawers in the chest, and the pillow, as she touched it tentatively, felt as if it was stuffed with sawdust instead of down.

She wondered drily whether she was supposed to protest, to rush downstairs thoroughly miffed and demand to be returned to Britain on the next available flight. She shook her head. She was here for Nicky's sake, not for her own, so she would accept whatever treatment was handed out without a murmur because at least she knew it wasn't for ever. This rejection, this insult of a room would make it all the easier to leave when the time came, she told herself resolutely.

She decided to go next door and see Nicky, and as she opened her door, she nearly fell headlong over her cases, which had been dumped there without a word. Harriet set her jaw and lugged them into the room. There was just enough room for the things she had brought, and she was glad she had remembered her own dress hangers. It would have been a minor defeat to have had to ask Androula for some.

She had a smile firmly pinned on when she went into the next room. Nicky, already in his pyjamas, was sitting at a special low table by the window eating his way through fruit and yoghurt, fondly observed by Yannina.

'*Yasoo*, Nicos.' Harriet knelt beside him, accepting the piece of fruit he judiciously held out to her.

'Ah!' Yannina sounded delighted. 'You learn our language, *thespinis*?'

Harriet grimaced. 'A few phrases only,' she returned guardedly. 'Some words, Yannina, from a book I bought in London.'

'You will soon learn,' the other woman prophesied.

I shan't be around long enough for that, Harriet thought.

At least Nicky's room was a proper size, and beautifully cool. The walls were washed in a clear blue, and painted with a frieze of toy animals, and safety gates had been placed firmly across the french windows leading to the balcony. There seemed to be numerous brand-new toys about, and Harriet was relieved to see Nicky's rather battered Paddington Bear leaning against the pillow in his cot. Stick around, she addressed it silently, you could take lessons in hard stares from the ladies I've just met!

While Nicky went on with his food, Yannina led her round, proudly showing her where all his clothes had been put away. There were more toys in a cupboard too, Harriet noticed. There was also a bathroom, tiled in blue and white, which Harriet presumed she was to share. She smiled brightly at Yannina and approved of everything with a heavy heart.

However tired he might be, Nicky was determined not to go down without a struggle. He turned sulkily away from Yannina, stretching demanding arms towards Harriet, saying tearfully that he wanted a story. It was half a dozen nursery rhymes and one and a half versions of the Three Bears later when he finally consented to fall asleep.

As she turned away from the cot, Yannina shook her head at her.

'Ah, *thespinis*, you are so good with him. Good as his own mother, may God rest her soul,' she added, crossing herself.

Harriet was suddenly close to tears again. It was the first time, she thought, that she'd heard Becca referred to with kindness by anyone even remotely connected with the Marcos family.

She said, 'Shall I stay with him for a while.'

'No, *kyria*.' Yannina showed her with pride the wall-mounted microphone which would transmit Nicky's slightest cry to her own quarters. 'It is the time of the evening meal. You will be awaited downstairs.'

Harriet doubted that, but as she emerged from the nursery, it was to see Alex striding down the corridor towards her.

She noticed that he was wearing a dinner jacket, and that he was frowning heavily.

'What have you been doing?' he demanded. 'Dinner is being held back for you. Did Androula not inform you?'

His eyes went over her impatiently, critically, assimilating her crumpled, travel worn appearance, and Harriet smothered a sigh.

'I must have misunderstood,' she hedged. 'Was I supposed to change? I—I've been settling Nicky for the night.'

The frown still lingered. 'Yannina was supposed to do that. It is, after all, your first evening among us. You must not make the child so dependent on you.'

'I'm sorry.' Harriet lifted her head defiantly. 'I thought I was merely doing what was expected of me. If I'm to leave Nicky solely to Yannina then there's very little point in my being here. Would you like me to leave?'

His scowl deepened. 'Believe it or not, Harriet *mou*, I was thinking of you. Perhaps I expressed myself badly. I only arrived back early this morning, and I am still suffering a little from jet lag. Is Nicos asleep now?'

She said, 'Yes.' Then, with an effort, 'His—his room is lovely. I suppose your mother. . . .'

'No,' he said with a faint smile. 'I was responsible for it. Does that surprise you?'

'A little,' she admitted.

'You thought perhaps that all I wanted was to win. That once I had control of Nicos, I would lose interest in him.' He shook his head slowly. 'How little you know of me!'

Perhapsk she thought, *but even that little is too much for my peace of mind.*

She tried to smile. 'Well, I'm sure he'll be happy here. I'd better wash my hands before dinner.'

Alex nodded abruptly. 'Come down as soon as you are ready,' he directed.

She watched him walk away, wondering for the first time if he had planned her room along with Nicky's. Could it be his own way of showing her how little she figured in his plans?

Harriet sighed defeatedly and went back into her room to retrieve her toilet bag which was still in her case, lying on top of the bed. The only remaining possession as yet unpacked was a cardboard folder into which she had placed all the relevant papers and keepsakes that Nicky might want—his parent's marriage certificate, his own birth certificate, some letters Kostas had written to Becca before their marriage, the huge card he had bought her to celebrate their son's birth, and some photographs. One of them, an actual wedding photograph, was in its own leather frame, and with a kind of defiance she stood it on her chest of drawers.

She didn't bother to change. Keeping the family waiting any longer for their meal would be just another black mark against her, she thought resignedly, and failing to change would simply mean they would think she knew no better. But she washed her face and hands, brushed her hair, and applied some moisturiser, along with a touch of eye-shadow and a discreet modicum of lipstick before she went downstairs.

Androula was waiting in the hall, looking boot-faced. As Harriet came down the stairs, she motioned her towards the same room she had been conducted to when she first arrived.

Her arrival interrupted a heated conversation in Greek which was switched off as abruptly as a radio set as soon as she appeared in the doorway.

Alex was holding a glass containing some pale cloudy liquid.

He said formally, 'Good evening, Harriet. Would you like a drink before dinner?'

She would have loved a drink. She would have leapt head first into a bottle if there'd been one handy, she was so desperate for some kind of courage, but neither of the Marcos ladies appeared to be drinking, so she refused politely.

She looked at Madame Marcos. 'I'm sorry if I've kept you waiting.'

Madame gave her a remote look, and her sister shrugged as if to say it was no more than expected.

Harriet didn't anticipate enjoying the meal. One of the girls who worked with her had warned her that Greek food was usually tepid and everything tasted of olive oil, but the dinner which followed bore no relation to anything Janet had described. It began with an iced avocado soup, and progressed through grilled mullet, to veal cutlets with a delicate wine sauce, and fresh fruit— peaches and melon—for dessert.

Harriet ate with a heartier appetite than she could ever have envisaged under the circumstances. Apart from a few remarks which Alex directed at her, and to which she responded briefly, the meal was conducted in virtual silence.

The atmosphere did not lighten either when they returned to the other room for the tiny cups of thick rather bitter coffee. Madame and her sister produced fine needlework and shared a sofa, sewing and

conversing in low voices. Alex had been called to the
telephone once again, so as soon as Harriet had finished
her coffee, she rose, wished both ladies a polite
goodnight which they acknowledged with a frigid nod
apiece, and left the room.

'Where are you going?'

Harriet paused on the stairs and looked down. Alex
had appeared in the hall below and was staring up at
her.

'To my room,' she returned rather defensively. 'I'm
very tired.'

'I see.' He sounded sceptical, and she flushed slightly.

'Perhaps—would it make things easier if from now
on I had my meals with Nicky?'

'No, it would not,' he said coldly. 'However, if you
were too tired to come down this evening and would
have preferred a tray in your room, then you should
have said so.'

Harriet was tempted to retort that she doubted if
there was enough room for a tray, but she kept silent;
any such comment could be construed as a complaint,
or a plea for better treatment, and she didn't want that.

She said merely, 'I'll remember that in future.
Goodnight, Mr Marcos.'

'Harriet *mou*,' he said softly, 'what do I have to do to
get you to call me by my given name? I must remind
you once more that you are my guest here.'

A strange sort of guest, thought Harriet, shoved into
a cupboard, and virtually ignored by everyone from the
housekeeper upwards.

She said unsmilingly, 'I'll try and remember that too.'

He was standing just below her, and before she
could move, he took her hand from where it was resting
on the balustrade and pressed it to his lips. For a
fraction of a second she felt his mouth, warm and
sensuous against her palm, her fingertips, then she was
released.

He said, 'Goodnight, little one. And pleasant
dreams.'

He turned away and went across the hall to the room she had just quitted. Harriet stood on the stairs and watched the doors close behind him.

She recommenced her ascent of the stairs wearily, torn between laughter and tears.

He'd wished her pleasant dreams, she thought with irony, when in the same breath almost he had guaranteed her a sleepless night. She paused for a moment, lifting the hand he had kissed and holding it for a moment, achingly, yearningly against her cheek. Then she ran on up the stairs to the cramped loneliness of her room.

CHAPTER SIX

SHE didn't sleep, but it wasn't simply thoughts of Alex that kept her awake. By dint of standing on her bed, she had managed to open her window to its fullest extent, but the little room was still close and airless. She crept into Nicky's darkened—and blessedly cool—room and checked that he was deeply and peacefully asleep before using his bathroom to take a shower, and change into her brief cotton nightdress.

Back in her own room, she stripped the covers from the bed and folded them neatly before lying down, but within minutes she was tossing uncomfortably, hardly able to breathe, her body already damp with perspiration. She considered lugging her mattress through to Nicky's room, but reluctantly decided against it. Yannina might take it into her head to check Nicky during the night, and if she found Harriet there on the floor it would simply result in embarrassment all round. In a hotel, you could complain about your room. In a private house, you had to grin and bear it, Harriet thought bitterly.

For nearly two hours she tried to bear it, although she didn't grin very much. She even tried the insomniac's remedy—to put the hours of wakefulness to good use by writing a letter to Manda. But what was there to say? 'I'm here. No one is friendly, and they've put me to sleep in a sauna.' She decided it would be best to wait until she had something more cheerful to report. Such as 'I'll be home on the next flight', she thought.

She got out one of the paperbacks she had brought and tried to read it. It was a best-selling thriller and in the 'will the world survive this threat of nuclear holocaust?' genre, but as it was set in the recent past and creation was still going about its lawful business instead of lying around in piles of radioactive ash, Harriet found its gut-wrenching propensities so glowingly described on the jacket strangely elusive.

She sat up cross-legged on the bed, lifting her face towards the window and the non-existent breeze, thinking regretfully about the yoga course she'd once planned to take. It would have been nice to have been able to summon up some mantra which would raise her consciousness above such mundane details as being hot and miserable and unable to sleep despite being bone-weary.

At last she swung her feet to the floor with a faint groan. She had to get some fresh air or she would choke. She slipped on the simple peignoir which matched her nightgown, tying the ribbons which fastened it at throat and waist. She didn't bother with the heelless sandals she had brought instead of slippers. The chill of the floor under her bare soles was bliss.

The villa was very quiet. No one besides herself seemed to be stirring, which was all to the good, Harriet thought, as she slipped silently downstairs. She opened the doors leading to the big *saloni*. The drapes had not been drawn over the french windows which comprised one wall, and moonlight flooded the room. Harriet slid her hands down the frame, finding the bolts and drawing them quietly. As she did so, it occurred to her that the house might be covered by a burglar alarm, and she quailed for a moment waiting for flashing lights and alarm bells, but there was only silence, and after a while she breathed again, and opened the window, leaving it slightly ajar.

Except for the lack of colour, the broad terrace and the garden beyond could have been in daylight. Harriet walked to the edge of the terrace and stood breathing deeply and gratefully. It was hard to believe that the cool fragrance surrounding her was the same air which oozed in through her little window.

The cicadas were still busy. The night shift must have come on, Harriet thought, smiling to herself. Just being

outside the villa made her feel happier, more relaxed.
She walked slowly down the terrace steps, and turned
right along a broad paved path. She had no idea where
she was going, only that she had no wish to return to
the house just yet.

The path led right round the villa, she soon realised,
but other smaller paths led off it, one of them to a
tennis court, she discovered. She hadn't played tennis
since she left school, she thought, viewing the court
wistfully, and wondering if she still remembered how.
She sighed. What a beautiful place this was! If only
circumstances had been different she could have been
looking forward to the holiday of a lifetime.

She wandered back to the main path and paused
irresolutely. Somewhere near at hand she could hear the
splash of water. The swimming pool, she wondered, or
another fountain? She followed the sound down a wide
flight of shallow stone steps bordered by rockeries, and
under a stone archway hung with wisteria.

It was the pool, and the arch she had just emerged
from was one of a whole series bordering it, while
directly opposite was a single-storey building with a
tiled roof, and shuttered windows. Changing-rooms,
Harriet surmised in the moment before it occurred to
her that on such a still night there was no reason for
that slight splashing noise. Unless, of course, the pool
was occupied. . . .

Almost incredulously she registered the lean dark
shape cleaving through the water. Noticed other things
as well—the discarded clothing on one of the padded
loungers at the poolside, the bottle and attendant glass
on the table.

Even as an interior voice was warning her that it was
time she was on her way, Alex's hands gripped the side
of the pool, pulling himself lithely out of the water.

Harriet froze, her mouth going dry as she watched
him walk across to the table, refill his glass, then almost
casually reach for a towel and begin to dry himself.

He had a magnificent body, she thought numbly. She

hadn't expected him to be totally naked, but then he probably hadn't expected an audience either. But that, she knew instantly, was being naïve. If Alex Marcos wished to swim nude, then he would do so no matter how many people happened to be watching.

But, of course, he still didn't know that she was there. Harriet turned to creep noiselessly away, only to be halted in her tracks by his cool voice.

'Won't you join me? The water's wonderful, and the brandy is French.'

Swallowing, she turned back to face him. The towel knotted loosely round him, he was standing, hands on hips, watching her in some amusement.

She said lamely, glad that her blush didn't show in the moonlight, 'I—I didn't expect anyone to be down here.'

'Nor I,' he returned levelly. 'For a minute I thought you might be walking in your sleep. What are you doing down here?'

'I came out for some air—I couldn't sleep. And the gardens look so fantastic in the moonlight. . . .' Harriet was aware she was beginning to babble, and stopped.

'Earlier you claimed to be so tired you could not wait to get to your room,' he said softly. 'What has kept you awake?'

She gave an awkward shrug. 'I'm just not used to the heat—and my room seemed stuffy.'

He drank some brandy, watching her over the top of the goblet. 'All the rooms are air-conditioned. Or is it something else that you do not know how to operate?'

The sardonic note was not lost on her, and she groaned inwardly.

'If it has been inadvertently switched off,' he went on, 'you need only have rung the bell for Androula or one of the maids. They would have rectified matters for you—although naturally it is flattering that once again you turn to me in your dilemma.'

'I have not turned to you,' said Harriet between her teeth. 'It never occurred to me that you would be down here, or anywhere except your own room, for that matter. I thought you were complaining of jet-lag,' she added.

Alex lifted a shoulder, still gleaming with moisture, in a shrug. 'So I was. I came down here with my brandy earlier and fell asleep. When I woke, I decided to take a swim before going back to the villa.' He gave her a cynical smile. 'Had I known I was to have such charming company I would have waited, Harriet *mou*, and we could have swum together.'

She was aware she was being baited, and her fingers clenched tensely in the concealing folds of her peignoir. She said steadily, 'I've tried to explain that I didn't mean to intrude. I think I'd better return to my room.'

'Perhaps you should,' he agreed mockingly. 'But stay and have some brandy with me first.' He poured some into another goblet and held it out to her compellingly, daring her to refuse.

Moving reluctantly, Harriet crossed the short distance from the archway to the table beside which Alex was standing, and accepted the goblet from him. As she took it, his fingers brushed hers and her whole body flinched from the slight contact.

She swallowed, struggling to control the leaping of her pulses. She was playing with fire, and she knew it. The villa no longer seemed an airless prison, but a sanctuary that she wished she had never left.

Alex lifted his glass in silent toast, his dark eyes brilliant with amusement as they slid over her. 'This scene has a certain familiarity,' he said. 'Surely you did not borrow this——' his hand tugged gently at a fold of the peignoir—'from Yannina?'

'Of course not!' Harriet's embarrassment increased with every second. The last thing she wanted to be reminded of was that confrontation in the bathroom in London, and she heard Alex laugh softly as if he could sense her uneasiness. Her fingers tightened round the stem of her glass, and she bent her head to take a hasty gulp of the brandy, letting her hair curtain her face as she did so.

'Gently!' Alex removed the glass from her grasp and replaced it on the table. 'Brandy should be treated with more respect, especially when you are not used to it.'

Harriet felt obscurely irritated by his assumption that five-star brandy was not her usual nightcap. She wished she could have denied it, she wished she could have claimed the sort of sophistication which could take in its stride a moonlit drink with a half-naked man in the caressing warmth of an Ionian night, but it was impossible. She was completely and totally out of her depth, and she knew that he knew it too.

'You—you have a very beautiful home,' she ventured, aiming for a casual tone.

'I am glad that it meets with your approval. Perhaps your stay here will not be such an ordeal after all.'

'Perhaps not.' Harriet's tone was wooden, and she refused to meet his gaze. 'I think I'll go in now.'

He laughed. 'Enough air—enough brandy, or simply enough of me? Harriet *mou*, which is it?'

'A little of each,' she said tautly, and made to turn away, but his hand reached out, his fingers fastening firmly on the soft flesh above her elbow, making her pause.

'What a little coward you are,' he said softly. 'You tried to make me believe you were mature enough to have sole charge of my nephew, but in reality you are little more than a scared child.'

'If that's the case, please let me return to my nursery.'

'Later.' His tone didn't alter. 'When you have learned to be less afraid.'

His skin was incredibly cool under her fainting fingertips as he drew her close.

She said, 'Please—no. . . .' but it was already too late. His mouth felt cool too, but his kiss burned like a brand, searingly possessive. She was trembling, her body pliable as melting wax in his arms, achingly defenceless in her response. Alex moulded her against the length of his body, making her shakingly aware of every inch of bone, sinew and muscle, her sensual consciousness heightened by his lack of clothing. Her lips parted helplessly beneath his demand, her head spinning, her pulses thudding at the sheer ruthlessness of his domination over her. A voice in her head was crying out in protest, even as her senses melted, urging her to accede to anything he might ask of her.

He tore his mouth from hers, muttering something harshly in his own language, then began to kiss her throat, his lips sensuous, caressing the soft skin as lightly as the brush of a feather, lingering with deliberation on her hammering pulse. His fingers tugged impatiently at the ribbon bow at her throat, loosening it, before pushing aside her peignoir and the strap of her nightdress, baring her shoulder to his kiss.

A little husky sigh escaped her as his mouth explored the curve of her shoulder. She felt his hand at her waist, unfastening the other bow, then sliding inside as the edges of the peignoir fell completely apart, down the slender length of her body to her hip. His fingers stroked its gentle swell, then glided inwards and down, discovering the sharp vulnerable line of bone.

Harriet's throat was dry, her whole body poised, almost convulsed with thick excitement. Alex's lips were travelling downwards too, his tongue curling seductively into the hollow between her breasts, making her shiver with pleasure. The voice in her head was silent now, entirely subjected to the need he had aroused in her. His mouth returned to hers in another long, drugging kiss, and she felt his arm glide down under her knees, lifting her off her feet and bodily into his arms. Then she was aware of the softness of cushions beneath her, and realised he had carried her over to one of the nearby loungers, and some semblance of sanity began to return.

He was lying beside her on the wide deeply padded seat, his breathing harsh, his dark face almost terrifyingly intent as he bent over her. Cool, practised fingers slid up her thigh brushing aside the hem of her nightgown.

And suddenly, her excitement was intermingled with panic. It was all too far and too fast—way beyond anything her previous all too limited experience had prepared her for. She snatched at his hand, gasping, 'No!'

Alex said softly, 'Don't be a little fool. You knew when you came down here tonight what you were inviting, so why pretend?'

His head lowered towards her. If he kissed her again, she would be lost, Harriet thought wildly, twisting away from him.

She said, 'I didn't follow you—I told you why I was here. Please let me go,' she added in a stifled undertone. 'Please—Alex!'

His smile was mirthless as he looked down at her. 'So—you use my name at last. I wondered what it would take for you to do so, and now I know. But perhaps I do not please. What then?'

Harriet shook her head miserably. 'I—I just don't know. I—I'm sorry.'

'Why? Nothing happened.' His tone was ironic, dismissive, as he turned away from her and sat up, swinging his long legs to the floor. 'Or is that why you are sorry?' he added bitingly.

Harriet's hands shook as she retied the ribbons on her peignoir into untidy bows. 'You know what I meant,' she muttered.

'Yes,' he agreed wearily, 'I know. Let me give you some good advice, Harriet *mou*. Don't create situations you are not prepared—or equipped—to handle.'

'I didn't.' She was close to tears suddenly, knocked off her centre of balance, her emotions in turmoil, and her body hungry for the fulfilment it had been denied. She got to her feet, glaring at him. 'Whether you believe me or not, I did not follow you down here. I came out for a walk because I couldn't sleep and. . . .'

'And you think either of us will sleep now?' he questioned harshly, and she flushed, her eyes sliding away from his sardonic gaze.

'I think I'd better go indoors,' she said in a low voice.

'I think so too—before I forget again why I brought you here.' There was more than a trace of grimness in his voice. He readjusted the towel he was wearing more firmly, then gestured Harriet to precede him through the archway. She hung back.

'I can find my own way,' she protested.

'I don't doubt it, but it happens that I have also had my fill of—fresh air,' he said mockingly.

'You've forgotten your clothes,' she pointed out in a small voice.

'No,' he laughed softly. 'I sleep as I swim, my little English prude. The clothes I took off will be collected, laundered and returned to me later.'

Harriet was fiercely, painfully aware of him as they made their way back to the house. They were the only ones awake, she was sure, but nevertheless it seemed that dozens of eyes were watching them from behind the dark, shuttered windows as they approached. They re-entered the house the way Harriet had left it, and she paused as Alex closed the window and applied the bolt.

'Well—goodnight,' she said awkwardly.

'Not so fast,' he said. 'Don't you want me to show you how the air-conditioning works, or do you intend to spend the rest of the night going for walks in the garden?'

Harriet groaned inwardly. The last thing she wanted was Alex coming to her room on any pretext whatever, but on the other hand she could hardly tell him that the lack of air no longer bothered her when she had made such a point of it.

'Thank you,' she said woodenly. He followed her silently up the stairs and along the gallery to the passage leading to her room.

As they passed Nicky's room, Alex detained her, a hand on her arm. 'Have you forgotten where you are sleeping?' he demanded in an undertone, frowning slightly as he looked at her.

'No.' Harriet shook her head. 'Mine's the next door.'

'The next one?' The frown deepened. 'But that's nothing but. . . .' He stopped as Harriet opened the door, and pushed past her, standing looking around him, hands on hips, in an ominous silence.

At last he said very softly, 'Who told you that you were to sleep here?'

Harriet shrugged. 'It's the room next to Nicky's. I—I was just shown here.'

'Then I must apologise to you. This is not, as you may have gathered, a guest-room. It is small wonder that you could not sleep—or even breathe.' He paused, then said bleakly, 'My orders must have been misunderstood. If you will come with me, I will see that you are accommodated more comfortably for the remainder of the night.'

'Oh, no.' Harriet hung back. 'It's all right, really. I don't mind. . . .'

'But I do,' Alex said inexorably. 'Be so good as to follow me.'

He turned and strode out without bothering to see if she was going to obey or not. For a moment, Harriet hesitated, then reluctantly she picked up her toilet bag and followed him.

She caught up with him, just as he was turning out of the corridor. 'I—I don't want to be too far from Nicky.'

'For tonight that cannot be helped,' he said. 'Tomorrow I will see that suitable arrangements are made for you.'

The room he took her to was on the other side of the villa, and it could not have presented a greater contrast to the one she had just left. It was quite enormous, dominated by a huge divan bed, made up with crisp fresh linen, its handwoven coverlet turned back neatly at the foot. Matching curtains in the same creamy shade hung at the windows, and luxurious fur rugs provided islands of comfort on the cool tiled floor. The bed was surmounted by an elaborate headboard in some dark antique wood, heavily carved and patterned, and flanked by two low tables, their borders and legs carved into an identical pattern. Tall terra-cotta lamps with cream shades stood on the tables, and above each of them, set into the wall, was a console with various knobs and switches, controlling the air-conditioning, the lights, a concealed radio, and even a bell to summon a servant.

'When you are ready for breakfast in the morning, just ring,' Alex directed casually. He glanced round. 'I hope you will be comfortable.'

'I'm sure I shall,' Harriet said rather shyly. 'Thank you, Alex.'

'You have nothing to thank me for,' he said curtly. 'I am only sorry that you should have been given such a poor impression of our hospitality. There will be no more such misunderstandings,' he added grimly, and she knew that he was not merely referring to the room she had been given.

A brief formal 'goodnight' and the door closed behind him. Harriet sank down on the edge of the bed, trying to catch her thoughts and bring them together into some kind of coherent pattern.

She was still shaking in the aftermath of that confrontation beside the swimming pool, her body tingling in expectation of a consummation which would not be realised. She closed her eyes, trying to shutter the memory of the way Alex's mouth had moved against her breasts, the expert feather-light caresses which had brought undreamed of needs into shattering life.

She shivered, running the tip of her tongue over suddenly dry lips. Alex had spoken of misunderstandings—had admitted he had believed she had deliberately followed him to the swimming pool, but could she really blame him for his cynical attempt to exploit the situation? Her denials had been feeble enough in all conscience—and what had she done to fight him off— to convince him that he was quite wrong in his assessment?

Nothing at all, she thought wearily. On the contrary, she had fallen with passionate eagerness into his arms, behaved without pride or self-control—and that was what he would finally remember—not her denials, but the shaming truth of her surrender.

And his own admission that he had momentarily forgotten the reason for her being here on Corfu brought her no comfort either.

Because when Alex touched her, when Alex kissed her, it was all too fatally easy to forget why she was here, to forget all the reasons she had to hate him.

But for her own safety, her own peace of mind, those were the things she had to remember.

Just for a moment, when she woke the next morning, she thought she was still dreaming, and that if she closed her eyes again these brilliantly alien surroundings would shrink and compress themselves into her bed-sitter in London.

But when she looked again, shafts of bright sunshine were still spilling across the tiled floor from between the shutters, and the huge bed still held her in its luxurious embrace.

Harriet sat up slowly, pushing the tumbled hair out of her eyes as the events of the previous night came scrambling back into her mind. An alarmed glance at her watch showed her that it was almost ten o'clock, and rather hesitantly, remembering Alex's instructions, she pressed the bell on the console which would order breakfast.

She climbed off the bed, and picking up her toilet bag wandered towards the bathroom, taking in with amazed appreciation the dark vivid blue of the tiles and appointments, the mirrored walls, and the deep sunken bath. Real colour supplement stuff, she thought, amused by the reflections of half a dozen Harriets all vigorously cleaning their teeth.

The notion of using a bath the size of a small swimming pool was an intriguing one too, and she smiled as she began to look in the cupboards for bath oil.

There were certainly plenty of toiletries to choose

from, she discovered, but all of them had a distinctly
masculine orientation. With growing puzzlement, she
searched through the remaining cupboards, finding
cologne, aftershave, brushes and razors. She slammed
the last door, and stood looking round her with a
sudden chill of awareness. Up to then, she hadn't
noticed the black silk robe hanging on the back of the
door, but she saw it now, and she stared at it
frowningly, her mind trying to reject the obvious
conclusion.

She dismissed the idea of having a bath and walked
back into the bedroom.

This was Alex's room, she thought. It had to be. It
was the only answer.

There was another door adjoining that of the
bathroom, and she opened it and looked in. It was a
dressing room, its walls lined with fitted closets. She
tugged open the nearest door, registering with almost
ludicrous dismay the row of expensive suits it
contained.

There was a brief knock at the bedroom door, and a
young maid entered carrying a tray. As she saw Harriet,
her eyes grew round, and her jaw dropped. It was
obvious she believed the breakfast she had brought was
for the master of the house, and not for some female
guest, and Harriet felt a wave of reluctant colour rise in
her face.

Her gaze primly averted, as if she was afraid that at
any moment Alex Marcos himself might appear and
confirm her worst suspicions, the girl carried the tray
across the room and set it down on a convenient table
for a moment while she unfastened the shutters and slid
back the big glass doors which gave access to the
balcony. Then she carried the tray through into the
sunlight and set it down somewhere out of sight.

Harriet knew a burning desire to beat a strategic
retreat into the bathroom in order to avoid the girl's
knowing look on her return journey, but a small
interior voice told her that she owed it to herself to

stand her ground. After all, it wasn't true, she thought defensively. Nothing had happened. And yet—and yet no one who had chanced to witness their encounter by the swimming pool would ever believe it, she realised with sudden embarrassment.

The maid reappeared, her eyes flickering momentarily to the tumbled width of the huge bed. Harriet's teeth sank into the soft inner flesh of her lower lip, but she managed with an effort to say, 'Thank you.'

'*Parakalo*,' the girl returned almost indifferently, and was gone. Harriet found herself wondering how many times Alex Marcos had been found with a female companion when his breakfast tray had been summoned. The maid had clearly been surprised at first, but the reason for that wasn't far to seek, Harriet decided ruefully as she glimpsed her reflection in a full-length mirror facing her. She looked ruffled and absurdly young, and not in the least like a *femme fatale* while her choice of nightwear, although quite pretty, was practical and discreet, rather than glamorous. For a moment, her brows met in a frown of unconscious dissatisfaction, and she lifted her heavy fall of hair on to the top of her head, twisting it into one of the casual knots which she so much admired on other girls but which never seemed to work with her. It didn't really work this time either, she thought with a little sigh. It made her look slightly older, but that was only an illusion. She would never possess the true sophistication that someone like Alex Marcos would look for in a woman.

For a moment she allowed fantasy to run riot, pretending that he was there with her, taking imaginary pins and combs from her hair, and letting it spill softly on her shoulders. She shivered involuntarily, remembering the way his hands had held her, his fingers subtly caressing, arousing, tantalising. . . .

Harriet took a deep uneven breath. That was something she could not afford to remember. To remind herself that Alex Marcos was an experienced man who knew exactly how to make a woman's body respond to him was to do herself a deliberate hurt.

She turned away from the mirror and walked out into the sunshine. The tiles were already warm under her feet as she made her way across to a thickly cushioned wicker chair. She wasn't particularly hungry, but the breakfast awaiting her looked delectable enough to tempt anyone, she thought with unwilling appreciation, eyeing the bread rolls still warm from the oven wrapped in a snowy napkin, with their accompanying curls of creamy butter and assortment of preserves. Freshly squeezed orange juice to begin with too, and to round the meal off, a small wicker basket of huge golden peaches.

Later, as she licked peach juice from her fingers, she realised that she had had more appetite than she thought. All her life, she decided, she would remember this first breakfast on Corfu. Alex's room was situated at the back of the villa and the balcony looked out over the gardens to the sea. The view was incredible. Somewhere there had to be a horizon, but it was impossible to tell where, she thought, as sky and sea blurred together in a distant fusion of exquisite misty blue, while, nearer, the short the gentle swell of the water formed an amalgam of colours from jade to azure, and from turquoise to amethyst.

Beneath the balcony, hidden in the riot of flowering shrubs and trees, the cicadas were already raspingly busy, and behind Harriet's head a bee worked with a kind of drowsy industry in the tangle of bougainvillea which clung to the bright wall and draped its brilliant blossom over the balcony rail. The air was full of scents—citrus, roses and warm earth vying with each other.

And this would be Nicky's home, Harriet thought with a pang that she was not ashamed to recognise as envy. This was the beauty which would surround him as he grew up. No more battles with the many uglinesses of city life for him!

And now could Kostas, who had presumably been brought up here himself, have abandoned it with such readiness, settling instead for the very ordinary suburban house he had shared with Becca, and the vicissitudes of the English climate?

Harriet found herself speculating once again on the nature of the rift which had separated her brother-in-law from his family, and left such an incomprehensible residue of bitterness, some of which was bound to spill over towards her. That of course was why she had been given that cupboard of a room. It was a deliberate slight designed to make it plain to her how little she was regarded or wanted. But she couldn't pretend that she had not been warned.

Harriet sighed. This corner of Corfu was paradise, but every paradise had its secret serpent, hiding in the grass, waiting for an opportunity to turn everything sour, to pervert and destroy.

Alex said, 'You look very serious, Harriet *mou*. What are you thinking?'

She twisted hastily on the cushions. He was lounging against the window opening, casually dressed this morning, she noticed, in pale linen slacks and a dark short-sleeved sports shirt unfastened almost to the waist.

He said smoothly, 'I came and helped myself to some clothes earlier. You were asleep, so I was unable to ask your permission. I hope you passed a comfortable night.'

'Oh, extremely comfortable.' Her tone was ironic. 'That of course was before I realised that I was sleeping in your bed.'

His mouth still smiled, but his eyes hardened. 'Are you afraid you have been contaminated in some way? Allow me to reassure you. The room may have been prepared for me, but I've only used it to shower and change my clothes.'

'That isn't what I meant,' she said hurriedly. 'I'm objecting to the fact that you gave the room to me. It wasn't necessary.'

'You think not? I am afraid I must disagree with you,' he said coolly.

'What I mean is—there must surely be other rooms. By putting me in here, you've placed me in a very difficult position. I—I don't know what your staff—your family will think.'

'They already know exactly what to think, because I have made the position more than clear to them.' His glance was almost contemptuous. 'And—yes, of course there are other rooms, but none of them were prepared last night as this was. Or did you wish me to wake Androula and the maids in the middle of the night to make an alternative ready for you? Finding us together at that hour, dressed—or rather undressed as we were—might have begun exactly the kind of speculation you seem so anxious to avoid.'

'Yes, I see that,' Harriet said reluctantly, beginning to wish she had said nothing.

'I hope you do,' Alex returned sardonically. 'If it will placate your fear of scandal, perhaps I should say that your new room should now be ready, and I will call Androula to conduct you there.'

He was making her sound like a prude and an idiot, she realised with exasperation. However real her embarrassment had seemed to her, it was clearly foolish to him. But it was impossible for her to try and explain the reasoning behind her objection in case unwittingly she gave too much away.

Avoiding his glance, she said stiltedly, 'I'm sorry—but the maid—she clearly thought . . . I mean, it was obvious it wasn't the first time. . . .' She halted in total confusion.

'Not the first time I have had a woman in my room—in my bed?' he finished for her with awful courtesy. 'I won't deny it. Why should I? But let me assure you that my—companions of the night have all been women and not immature children incapable of knowing their own minds—or their own bodies. Does that satisfy you?'

Harriet felt as if she had been slapped across her face.

In a thickened tone, she said, 'Perfectly. Now, if you would be good enough to call your housekeeper, I'd rather like to get dressed.'

The dark eyes swept her lightly covered body with casual lack of interest, then Alex lifted one shoulder in a shrug which told her quite explicitly, without any further words being needed, that it would make no difference to him if she were stark naked.

Then he turned, and she heard the sound of his stride taking him across the room, and the distant slam of the bedroom door.

Harriet sank back against the cushions, staring unseeingly in front of her as the glorious view dissolved into a thousand shimmering fragments. Convulsively she closed her eyes, refusing to let the painful tears fall.

Only a few moments ago she had thought she was in paradise. Now she knew to her cost just how bitter paradise could be.

CHAPTER SEVEN

By an almost superhuman effort, Harriet was still managing to control her unhappiness when a frankly sulky-looking Androula came to fetch her a few minutes later.

Hardly had they left Alex's room when the woman began to chatter in her own language. Harriet couldn't understand what was being said, but she could recognise recrimination and self-justification when she heard it. It was obvious Androula had received a tongue-lashing from the master of the house over the standard of the accommodation assigned to his guest, and Harriet guessed wryly that a rough translation of Androula's remarks would have amounted to the fact that she was only obeying orders.

The room she was taken to was only slightly smaller than the one she had just left, and lacking nothing in luxury. When Androula had taken her still-aggrieved departure, Harriet discovered that her clothes had already been brought and unpacked for her. It was such a contrast to the treatment she had received the previous day that she could almost have laughed out loud.

That is if she hadn't been feeling so miserable, she amended inwardly.

But she wouldn't have been natural if she hadn't experienced some lift of the heart brought about by her new surroundings. She took a long, warm, scented bath, then dressed in cool, simple clothes—a cotton wrap-round skirt featuring giant poppies on a navy background, and a navy cotton tee shirt, short-sleeved and scoop-necked.

She was stroking a brush through her hair when there was a knock at the door, and a beaming Yannina ushered Nicky into the room.

'Oh.' Harriet dropped the brush and held out her arms to him. 'I was just coming to find you.'

He scrambled on to her lap, burying his face in her shoulder. 'I find you,' he said in a muffled voice.

'He slept well, *thespinis*,' Yannina informed her. She shook her head. 'But he would eat no breakfast.'

'Oh, Nicky!' Harriet gently detached his clinging hands. 'You must eat your meals.'

The small face was mutinous. 'Don't want it,' he muttered. 'Too hot. Don't like it.'

'Just wait a day or two,' Harriet soothed him. 'It will seem as if you've been here all your life. We're going to have a wonderful holiday—a lovely time with Uncle Alex. You'll see.'

She had to resist the impulse to hug him to her fiercely. This was all part of the letting-go process she was committed to. It had to be. But it would be so easy to play the traitor—to encourage Nicky in his quibbles about his new surroundings, to re-establish herself as the indispensable factor in his life. It would be easy—and balm for the ache inside her. But in the end, what would she gain?

Yannina was intervening, smiling again. 'Come, little one. Kyrios Alexandros is waiting to see you. We must not keep him waiting.'

God forbid, Harriet thought savagely, picking up her brush and attacking her unfortunate hair as if it was a dirty carpet.

She said, 'I'll see you later, Nicky. Perhaps we'll have a swim in the pool, hm?'

Nicky assented cautiously, and went off hand in hand with Yannina.

As the door closed behind them, Harriet expelled her breath on a little sigh as the unnaturally bright smile faded from her lips. Oh God, the next few weeks were going to be so hard—worse than her most pessimistic imaginings. The gradual parting from Nicky would have been bad enough alone, without this foolish, ill-judged passion which Alex had engendered in her, and the overt hostility from the Marcos women.

She supposed reluctantly that as the morning was half over, it was more than time she presented herself downstairs. She rose and looked at herself critically in the mirror, fiddling with the sash tie of her skirt, and an errant tress of hair. But she was simply procrastinating, she knew, and there was no point in trying to present herself as some kind of fashion plate when, to the women downstairs, she would never be anything more than Nicky's poor relation.

She was able to take in more of her surroundings in the warm, golden light of day, and she found the cool, spacious layout of the villa very much to her taste, accented as it was towards simplicity, the walls washed in plain colours, and natural fibres used alongside stone and wood.

When she arrived in the hall, all the doors opening from it were shut, and the place seemed deserted apart from one maid sweeping the floor. When she saw Harriet, the girl propped her broom against the wall and gestured that Harriet should accompany her, leading the way towards the room where Madame Marcos had received her the previous evening. Harriet wiped the suddenly damp palms of her hands down her skirt, tension filling her at the prospect of another inimical encounter, but when the door swung open there was only Mr Philippides, putting down the newspaper he had been glancing through and rising to meet her with a broad smile.

'*Kalimera*, Thespinis Masters,' he greeted her. 'I am so glad to have this opportunity to say goodbye to you before I return to London.'

'You're going back?' Harriet was dismayed. Mr Philippides was the closest she had to an ally in the house, apart from Yannina, and she had hope he would be there to help her through the first awkward days.

'I must, *thespinis*.' Perhaps Mr Philippides sensed her disquiet, because he looked at her sympathetically. 'I have meetings planned—business to transact which has already had to be delayed.'

'I didn't realise you'd made a special journey to escort us here,' Harriet said slowly. 'I—I'm sorry to have put you to so much trouble.'

'No trouble, but my pleasure, Thespinis Masters. You and the little Nicky will be safe and happy here in the care of Kyrios Marcos. It is a beautiful house, *ne*?'

'Very beautiful,' Harriet acknowledged woodenly. 'But at the same time I think it was a mistake for me to come here. Would—would there be room on your flight for me, do you suppose?'

Mr Philippides gave her a shocked glance. 'You distress me, *thespinis*. It would be an insult to Kyrios Marcos to leave so soon.' He paused, and gave an almost furtive look round to ensure that they were not being overheard. 'If you are disturbed by the coolness of your reception by Madame Marcos and Madame Constantis—this I can understand. It is very difficult, but I am sure that if you are—patient, then the situation will improve.'

'Thanks for the reassurance,' Harriet said caustically. 'I'm glad you understand what's going on, because I certainly don't. And if his mother and his aunt have these sort of feelings, then perhaps Mr Marcos should think again about bringing Nicky up here.'

Mr Philippides sighed. 'You—and the child, Thespinis Masters—are a reminder of an unhappy time in their lives. It will take time, but the ladies' attitude will mellow, I am sure. Or at least towards the little Nicos,' he added with a slightly apologetic note in his voice.

And if it ever mellows towards me, it isn't too important, because my stay here is only temporary anyway, Harriet supplied wryly and silently.

Aloud she said, 'But why do they feel like this, Mr Philippides, do you know?'

He looked instantly embarrassed, moving his shoulders defensively, and murmuring something about a private family matter, but Harriet was unconvinced.

Their dealings in London had shown her that Mr Philippides enjoyed a high degree of Alex Marcos' confidence, and there wouldn't be many family secrets kept from him. But such trust implied an equal amount of discretion, Harriet realised with a little inward sigh. Whatever secret had poisoned Kostas' relationship with his family, and still shadowed his memory, it was a mystery from which she was excluded.

And yet for Becca's sake, and perhaps more importantly for Nicky's, she felt it was something which should be solved. Yet not, she thought regretfully, through the agency of Mr Philippides.

She thanked him colourlessly for all his help in escorting her to Corfu, and for his kindness to them both, and said a quick goodbye, escaping out through the patio doors because she could hear female voices approaching through the hall.

Coward, she apostrophised herself when she was safely out of sight of the villa. You should have stayed and faced them, and demanded an explanation. She smiled then ruefully, trying to imagine anyone demanding anything of the stately Madame Marcos. Oddly enough, she thought, it was the vindictive-seeming Madame Constantis who seemed the less formidable of the pair, perhaps because her hostility was so open. Under Madame Marcos' cool civility, Harriet had detected something implacable and chilling. Perhaps Alex hadn't inherited all his ruthlessness from his father.

She stopped and looked round her almost curiously, as if it had suddenly occurred to her just how alien this environment was from any experience she had ever had. She liked flowers. She had always kept plants in her room at home, but there wasn't one brilliant shrub thrusting its way out of the raw-coloured earth that she could have put a name to. It was all new and strange, and she was alone in the midst of it.

She felt the strength of the sun beating down on her, and suddenly shivered as if a cold wind had blown on her, or an unknown hand touched her shoulder.

Harriet reached for the bottle of oil and began to smooth another coating over her legs. Her tan was coming along nicely—even and golden brown, but that, she thought drily, was hardly surprising as she had little to do but work on it over the past two weeks.

For the first few days of their stay, Nicky had been querulous, shy of the new faces and unaccustomed attention, and fractious because of the heat and change of diet. Harriet had been able to feel that her presence at the villa was at least justified, but now she was not so sure. Nicky had begun to turn more and more to the devoted Yannina for his needs, and Harriet had realised ruefully that much of the time he was hardly aware if she herself was there or not. But she couldn't blame him if that was so, she kept reminding herself. That, after all, was the whole purpose of the exercise, and it seemed that Nicky's settling down process was going to be more painless than they could ever have hoped or anticipated.

But when she had suggested quite diffidently to Alex that this might be a good time to take her departure, she had received a brisk rebuff.

Nicky, his uncle thought, was merely charmed by the novelty of his surroundings and Yannina's uncritical solicitude. Sooner or later the novelty would wear off, and Harriet's presence would be necessary to him again.

Harriet had attempted to argue the point, spurred on by her own private reasons for not wishing to remain on Corfu a day longer than she had to, but Alex had only grown coldly angry.

'I thought that you were devoted to Nicos' well-being, or so you would have me believe when we met in London,' he said with icy sarcasm. 'Why are you now so ready to shirk your responsibilities?'

Harriet gasped. 'I'm not shirking anything,' she responded warmly. 'I simply don't feel I'm fulfilling any real purpose by remaining.'

'You will kindly allow me to be the judge of that.'

Alex gave her a bleak look. 'And it is my wish that you remain here—until the end of the month at least,' he added, forestalling the further protest which was already trembling on her lips. 'I have to go away on business tomorrow, so perhaps we could delay any further discussion until my return.'

She had assented reluctantly, unable to subdue a swift inward pang at the news that he was going to be absent, even for a short time. Her own feelings aside, Alex was very much a bulwark between herself and the unvarying hostility still evinced towards her by his mother and aunt. Even in his presence, family mealtimes were an ordeal where she was made to feel like an unwanted outsider. It was subtly done, of course. There had been no repetition of the tactics which had led to her being allocated a room which a servant might have occupied.

Harriet had guessed from the tension in the atmosphere during the first few days of her stay that Alex had made his views on that more than clear. She was more than happy with her new room, and thankful for it too, because the heat was such that she knew she would never have got a moment's sleep in the other room, but at the same time she wished Alex had never found out, because the resultant fuss had just given his family something extra to resent her for.

It was absurd to feel hurt or even disturbed about that, but she did. She liked people, and she always had. She had had plenty of friends at work, even if her social life had become rather curtailed because of Nicky. She had written a number of letters since she had been at the villa, all of them giving glowing accounts of her surroundings, making it all sound more fun than it actually was. Not even to Manda had she confessed how miserable she really was. Not that she thought for a moment that anyone at the villa would actually go to the lengths of steaming open her correspondence to see what she was saying, but because her unhappiness was somehow more bearable if she didn't think about it too much. Writing about it might crystallise it in her mind, and make her life here totally unbearable.

It was easier to keep up the pretence that she was having a wonderful holiday in the sun in a particularly beautiful corner of the world. A very restricted corner, she reminded herself wryly. All she had seen of Corfu, apart from the initial trip across the island, was the villa garden, and the small beach which she had made her ultimate refuge.

There was little wonder that Alex had placed an embargo on Nicky going down there, and reinforced it with a gate which had to be kept bolted at all times. The path leading down there was little better than a track, steep and stony with a few rock steps provided here and there to assist with the worst bits and a wooden handrail. Even so anyone using the path needed to be surefooted and have their wits about them, and Harriet usually went down there in the middle of the day, after lunch when Nicky was having his siesta.

There was a small jetty on the beach, and a boatshed containing a sleek, racy-looking speedboat, as well as a variety of water-skiing and windsurfing equipment. Harriet supposed that Alex used them, but she didn't know when. It was certainly never when she was down at the cove.

She really hadn't had to worry at all about avoiding him, because it was all being done for her. Until they had clashed over her proposed return to London, he had been unfailingly civil, but always aloof, making it tacitly but positively clear that there would be no more love-making even of the most casual kind.

Harriet tried to tell herself that she should be grateful for this, because if Alex had ever decided to amuse himself by pursuing her in real earnest, then she could be in more trouble than she had ever dreamed of. And he was a man in need of amusement, she could be in no doubt of that. The even tenor of life at the villa could not hold him for long. There were few visitors, and when they did come, they were mostly older couples, friends of Madame Marcos and her sister.

Alex went out a great deal in the evenings, and Harriet was unable to blame him. She was thankful she had brought a bag of paperback books with her to occupy her, usually retiring to her room immediately after coffee was served each evening. Sometimes she was woken, her room being at the front of the house, by returning headlights, and she knew without even consulting her watch that it was the early hours of the morning, and that Alex was home at last.

None of the defensive arguments against him that she had managed to marshal could still the ache of longing deep within her which assailed her every time she saw him. Watching him swimming in the pool, or lying relaxed in the sun with only the minimal covering on his bronzed body, or even catching an occasional breath of the cologne he used as he went past her—all these things had the power to stir her, to rouse passionately bitter-sweet memories.

If she'd belonged to him, if she'd known what it was like to make love with him, then sleep in his arms, she couldn't have been more physically conscious of him. The strength of her emotions, the force of her awareness bewildered her. She'd never felt like this before. She didn't know how to handle it, how to subdue her feelings.

She had thought about love, of course. She had had other boy-friends apart from Roy, and when she had seen how happy Kostas and Becca were together, she had looked forward from courtship to a marriage of her own, because even in these uncertain days it seemed that love and security were still possible and attainable.

It had been a calm, peaceful optimism about the future, but she knew now that with Alex, she wouldn't care that there could never be any future just as long as there was a 'now'. She was ashamed of feeling like that. She had discovered depths within herself she had never suspected, an ability to desire, to need which had shaken her totally. In this alien place, far from home, she seemed to have become a stranger to herself.

She capped the sun-oil bottle and lay back on the sun-lounger, deliberately making herself relax as the warmth of the sun caressed her limbs, listening to the somnolent whisper of the sea, only yards away.

It was difficult to keep troubled thoughts at bay at times like this when solitude pressed on her. No one had suggested that she might like to do any sightseeing while she was here. Well, she could hardly expect an offer from Alex to show her the island in the circumstances, but his wasn't the only car, and the driver who had brought them from the airport wasn't overworked. But she couldn't ask. Any offer would have to come from Madame Marcos, and would be as unlikely as a sudden snow shower, she thought ruefully. Madame clearly felt that sunbathing most of the day, and playing with a small child, was the most her unwanted visitor could ask for, and Harriet knew that for many people, a fortnight in these surroundings with nothing to do and all day to do it in would be a dream holiday.

But she wasn't one of them. She felt restless and on edge. She had thought Alex's absence would make things easier, but she was wrong. The tension of actually being in his orbit was more than equalled by the tension of wondering what he was doing and when he would return. I can't win, she thought, half-closing her eyes so that the sun was a golden shimmer through her lashes.

And now she had at least an hour to spend before she need rouse herself and go up to the villa to see Nicky. Who could ask for anything more? she thought with self-mockery, knowing already what the answer was. She wanted so very much more, and yet, if they were offered, she would settle for crumbs instead of the proverbial half-loaf.

She was dozing lightly when she heard the sound of footsteps coming down the path. Her eyelids flew apart, and she sat up, propping herself on one elbow. A man's step. It couldn't surely be Alex. She had no idea how long he was going to be away, but she had formed the impression that it could be measured in days rather than hours. And though there was Andonis who worked mainly at the beach, seeing to the boat and the gear, he wasn't usually around in the afternoon.

No, the newcomer was a stranger to her. Young, male, wearing a towelling beach jacket over brief trunks. He was shorter than Alex, and stockier, with an apparently ready smile which he was aiming directly at her. As he approached, Harriet felt ridiculously that her black bikini was too revealing and half-reached for the thin shirt she had adopted as a cover-up between the villa and the beach, then stopped, telling herself firmly that she was just being prudish.

He reached her side and stood looking down at her. 'Thespinis Masters?' His voice was more heavily accented than Alex's. 'I am Spiro Constantis. My mother told me that we had the pleasure of your company here for a few weeks. She did not warn me, however, that you used this beach in the afternoon. I hope I do not intrude.'

Then where do they imagine I get to each day— disappear back into the woodwork? Harriet managed to refrain from saying.

Aloud, she said 'Of course not. I suppose I should ask you the same thing, Kyrios Constantis.'

'Spiro, if you please.' He pulled up another lounger and sat down. 'And I will call you Harriet, *ne*? It is so?'

Harriet supposed it was. He seemed pleasant enough. Compared with his maternal relations, he seemed positively charming, but for a reason she found it difficult to analyse, she didn't want to seem too forthcoming.

Spiro discarded his jacket, squinting appreciatively at the sky.

'A beautiful day—and a beautiful companion to share it with. I am fortunate. Usually if there is female company at the villa, I have to compete with my cousin Alex, and that'—he shrugged with self-depreciation—'is no contest at all.'

Harriet smiled rather stiffly. She had no need to be reminded of the electrifying effect Alex had on women. She had seen it operate in London, seen the glances which often couldn't even bother to be discreet or sidelong as he went his arrogant way.

Collecting her thoughts hurriedly, she asked if Spiro worked for the Marcos Corporation.

'Indeed yes—in the Athens office, but I was owed a few days' leave, so I thought I would come here and meet my new little cousin.' He sighed. 'Poor Kostas' son. What a tragedy!'

Harriet looked away, towards the sparkle of the sea. 'I thought it was,' she said steadily. 'I loved Kostas, and my sister Becca was a super girl. They were very happy.'

'That is a good thing to know,' Spiro said softly. 'When he was younger, he caused my aunt many anxious hours.'

'Oh?' Harriet's brows lifted. Kostas might have had wild oats to sow in the days before she had known him, but she could have sworn he had never given Becca as much as an anxious moment. She paused, then said rather woodenly, 'Then it's a pity she never found out what a good effect his marriage had on him. I—I suppose if it hadn't been for the accident, they'd have eventually been reconciled.' She made it into a question, and Spiro's smile faded as he considered it.

'Perhaps,' he said at last. 'Kostas was her favourite son, even if he was not—a satisfactory one. But I do not think—forgive me—that my aunt would ever have received your sister. She felt—she still feels great bitterness. You must understand that she felt—betrayed, and that your sister contributed to that betrayal.'

Harriet gasped. 'In what way, for heaven's sake?' she demanded indignantly.

Spiro looked uncomfortable. 'You do not know? But

I thought—I was sure that you would have been in your sister's confidence. Pardon me, I should not have spoken.'

'No—please.' Harriet spoke urgently. 'If there's something I should know, something which would help me understand, then I would prefer to be told.'

He gave a slight shrug. 'Perhaps, but I do not feel it is my place to tell you. Alex is the head of the family, after all.'

'Don't we know it,' Harriet muttered, and his gaze sharpened.

'So there has been—friction between you. Ah, poor Harriet, but it was inevitable.' He paused, then said flatly, 'It might have been better if you had not come here.'

'I had very little choice,' Harriet said defensively. 'Your cousin wanted to make Nicky's transfer to his new life and surroundings as easy as possible, and so. . . .'

'I see.' Spiro looked at her sympathetically. 'He is not with you today, the little Nicos?'

'No.' Harriet shook her head. 'I don't bring him down here often. The path is too steep and dangerous, for one thing, and he finds the sea rather overwhelming after the shallow end of the pool.'

'But he can swim?'

Harriet smiled. 'After a fashion. He loves splashing about.'

'You are clearly very fond of him. He is a fortunate child. To have the devotion of so lovely a girl and then—one day—to own all this.' He waved his hand around him. 'Unless of course Alex grants his mother's dearest wish by marrying and having children of his own,' he added casually.

Harriet experienced a pang so sharp she nearly cried out. The thought of Alex with another woman, looking with pride and satisfaction at the son she had borne him, was frankly intolerable. And she would know about it. There was no escape from that. The marriage of Alex Marcos, the birth of an heir to the Marcos Corporation, were events which the gossip columns of the world would hardly fail to record. But at least she wouldn't have to be here to see it. She'd be a thousand miles away, making a life for herself, trying to expunge the bitter-sweetness of this Corfu summer from her mind, something she had to do if she was ever to have any peace again.

She said with an admirable attempt at coolness, 'He's hardly likely to remain single.'

Spiro grimaced. 'He has escaped so far, but my aunt, I think hopes that he will make amends to the Xandreou family by marrying Maria.'

'Why should he do any such thing?' Harriet asked with unguarded sharpness. She immediately tried to dissemble. 'I mean, it's a pretty drastic way of making amends.'

'Not,' Spiro said gently, 'to the girl whom Kostas jilted to marry your sister. Something else you did not know, *ne*?'

'I didn't know he was actually engaged.'

Spiro shrugged. 'There was an understanding—an arrangement between the families. It was as binding, or should have been, as a formal engagement. Kostas'—defection was a humiliation for both families.'

Harriet could feel sympathy with this unknown Maria, but at the same time she had never found it in her heart to blame Kostas for escaping while he could from such a cold-blooded arrangement. And no one who had seen him with Becca, who had experienced their happiness would have blamed him either, she thought.

Except here. Here there was resentment, and a deep-seated grudge which might have hung over their lives and cast a shadow over that happiness.

She said slowly, 'So now there's another—arrangement with Alex?'

'Of a kind. Alex has never been the marrying kind, but he has a keen sense of family honour, and Maria is his mother's godchild, so they are often in each other's company.' His mouth twisted slightly. 'She is coming to stay here tomorrow, so you will be able to judge for yourself.'

Wonderful, Harriet thought wretchedly. Just what I want.

Aloud, she said, 'It won't be much of a judgment unless I see them together—and Alex is away.'

Spiro laughed. 'That is true—but he will return. You will see, little English Harriet.'

She forced herself to smile in return, as if he had said something very amusing. 'If he's prepared to cut short a business trip, then he must be serious.'

Spiro was still laughing. 'A business trip? Well, it is an excellent excuse. A little family life here at the villa is enough for Alex. Sooner or later he becomes bored, restricted, and he takes off for brighter lights. He has a mistress in Athens, you understand.'

She was hurting again badly, which was ridiculous because a man like Alex would have women wherever and whenever he wanted them. She couldn't pretend the news came as any surprise, she thought, remembering that phone call at the hotel in London, and Vicky Hanlon's voluptuous charm.

She said brightly, 'I hope his future wife doesn't know.'

Spiro's mouth twisted. 'Maria is a sensible girl. She would consider turning a blind eye to Alex's other interests a small price to pay for becoming the new Madame Marcos—for marrying the Marcos millions.'

'Then they should be perfect for each other,' Harriet said grimly. A small price, she thought incredulously. If she were in Maria's place, even the slightest hint of infidelity on Alex's part would be like losing a piece of herself.

If he was opting for marriage, it was small wonder he had decided on an arrangement with a Greek girl who would be 'sensible'. The last thing he would want would be a wife who clung and complained, and demanded all his attention.

'You are very quiet,' Spiro commented. Harriet looked at him and saw him watching her, his eyes frankly assessing her body, its curves barely concealed by the scraps of bikini. She had a ridiculous impulse to cover herself with her hands, because she suddenly realised she didn't want Spiro looking at her. In fact it occurred to her that although he was good-looking and seemed friendly, she didn't really like Spiro very much, but that was probably because he had told her things she didn't want to hear. They had executed messengers who brought bad news in the old days, and, just at the moment, it seemed like a good system.

She said stiltedly, 'I'd better go back to the house. Nicky will be waking up.'

'And he likes you to be there. I cannot blame him.'

The words sounded fulsome, and she said, embarrassed, 'He's only a baby really. For a while, I was all he had.'

He laughed. 'Of course. I said he was a fortunate child.'

She smiled uncertainly, reaching for her shirt and pulling it on, even fastening a couple of the buttons. Her hands were steady enough, but she was shaking inside.

She needed to get to the house, to her room, so she could fall to bits in private.

Spiro said, 'I hope to see you later,' and she mumbled something in reply as she made for the path. Once on it, she made herself slow down, picking her way carefully because she didn't want to fall, and it was too hot for running anyway.

I can't run, she thought. There's no escape. No way out. I'm trapped here until Alex chooses to release me. And tomorrow she'll be here—this Maria—and he'll be here too, and I shall have to watch them together.

She wanted to lift her hands in despair to the sky, shout something savage at the sun, but she knew she could still be seen from the beach, knew without turning her head that Spiro was watching her departure, so she thrust her balled fists into the pockets of her shirt, and went on climbing, her head bent, and her eyes fixed with a kind of desperation on the rough stones beneath her feet.

CHAPTER EIGHT

'Run, run as fast as you can——' Harriet paused, waiting for Nicky to join her joyously in the second half of the couplet. '"You can't catch me—I'm the gingerbread man!"'

But there was no response and when she looked at him, Nicky's small face was unsmiling, his bottom lip pouting slightly.

Harriet sighed. 'I thought you liked this story.'

'Don't want a story,' he said rebelliously. 'Want swimming.'

Harriet closed the book, and put it to one side. She'd tried all his favourites—The Little Red Hen, Three Billy Goats Gruff—in turn, but all to no avail, yet usually he listened entranced.

She had decided against the swimming pool that day because Yannina had reported that Nicky had been coughing a little in the night, and she thought herself he looked a trifle flushed as if he might be developing a slight temperature. But Nicky had become accustomed to his daily splash in the pool, and had made it clear from the outset that staying indoors and being read to was no substitute at all.

He seemed perfectly all right again too, she thought, eyeing him, with not a trace of a cough or a sniffle. There really seemed no valid reason to deny him his wish, and keep him in the villa—except. . . .

This time her sigh was inward. Except that Maria would be down at the pool, she thought wryly, and that was an ideal motive for keeping as far away as possible.

She had made all kinds of resolutions before Maria's arrival, mentally rehearsing the way she should behave, the things she should say, but she had wasted her time. Because from the moment she had entered the villa a week earlier, Maria had made it quite clear that she shared the view of her hostess, and that Harriet, and to a lesser extent Nicky, was less than the dust beneath her chariot wheels.

They had been introduced—Spiro had seen to that— and Maria had looked her over briefly and frowningly, then turned away after a perfunctory greeting which fell little short of overt rudeness. After that she behaved for the most part as if Harriet did not exist.

But in that, Harriet admitted drily to herself, her behaviour was a little different from the remainder of the household. No one wanted her there, and in Alex's absence they took little trouble to conceal it. Conversation at mealtimes was conducted wholly in Greek, and the only time that English was spoken to any extent in her presence was during Nicky's daily sessions with his grandmother, from which Harriet excused herself as often as possible.

Watching Madame Marcos struggling to entertain the child formed a poignant contrast to Harriet's memories of her own mother. Rachel Masters would not have sat on a sofa, stitching tapestry and holding a stilted conversation with a largely uncomprehending Nicky as he played at her feet. She would have been down there with him, among the building blocks and wind-up toys, uncaring about her appearance or dignity, and Madame Marcos, Harriet thought, was someone who would be positively improved by a little tomboyish ruffling.

In many ways, it was sad, because at times she watched Nicky with real yearning in her eyes. But although she insisted that he should be brought to the *saloni* each day after his afternoon nap, she still held him at arms' length, and in his turn Nicky regarded this black-clad stranger with caution still.

But at least he did not show her the aversion he felt for Madame Constantis. He had called her a witch once, but fortunately only Harriet had heard, or at least understood him. Harriet wondered sometimes if

Madame Marcos could have relaxed more with the child if her sister had not constantly been present, inhibiting her. Madame Constantis made no secret of the fact that she did not approve of Nicky's presence in the household, and the reason was not hard to guess at, Harriet had realised with wry amusement. With Kostas gone, the doting mother had decided that her Spiro was the rightful heir if Alex persisted in remaining a bachelor, and she openly resented the small intruder who had upset her cherished plan.

She acquitted Spiro of sharing his mother's ambitions. He seemed half embarrassed, half amused by some of her pointed remarks, and he more than made up for her marked indifference to Nicky.

In fact, Harriet had found herself warming to him as the days went by. His simple, uncomplex personality was a much-needed palliative to all the other tensions and hostility in the villa, and she realised that her earlier reservations about him had only existed because she was unconsciously comparing him with his cousin, to his detriment.

But she had ended up liking him in his own right, particularly because of his unswerving friendliness in the face of his mother's disapproval. And it was amusing to watch Madame Constantis' unsubtle and unavailing attempts to get him to desert herself, and pay all his attention to Maria.

Madame Marcos might have decided that she would be the ideal bride for Alex, but it was clear that her sister thought the Xandreou heiress would suit her own son much better. And it was equally clear that Spiro wanted no part of it.

Maria was a pretty girl, Harriet fair-mindedly admitted, and she would have been even more attractive without the petulant expression which marred her features so often. She had a spectacular figure which she showed off to the best advantage in a series of minuscule bikinis, each with its matching wrap or *pareu*. Even her sandals, with their incredibly high gilded heels, matched, as did the soft kid bags in which she carried her cosmetics and sunglasses.

Maria Xandreou, in fact, Harriet decided, was not short of the good things in life, and liked the world to know it.

Each day she appeared at the pool, oiling herself lavishly in order to deepen an already immaculate tan, but she never went into the water. But that, Harriet thought maliciously, was probably just as well, because Maria was so loaded down with gold chains and bracelets—round her neck, her waist and her wrists and ankles—that she would have sunk like a stone.

The greatest exertion she seemed capable of was looking through glossy fashion magazines—probably seeing pictures of Vicky Hanlon, if she did but know it—and Harriet wondered why she didn't go out of her skull with boredom. But hers not to reason why, she decided, and meanwhile it was better for her to concentrate on keeping Nicky well out of Maria's way, because she made it obvious that the noise of his play and chatter irritated her.

Nicky tugged at her hand. 'Swimming, Harry,' he pleaded, and whooped with pleasure when she reluctantly nodded. As he ran ahead of her into the sunlight, Harriet followed slowly, wishing there was some alternative delight to tempt him with.

Maria was already ensconced on her lounger when they arrived, the flowered sun umbrella adjusted to the correct angle, and a tray with a tall jug of iced fruit juice placed conveniently to hand on one of the tables.

She sat up as they approached and removed her sunglasses.

All the better to glare at us, thought Harriet, giving the other girl a swift impersonal smile as if she hadn't noticed a thing. She peeled off the simple cotton shift she was wearing and draped it over the back of one of the cushioned chairs stationed near the shallow end of the pool. Nicky, dancing with excitement, allowed her to remove his tee-shirt, then darted towards the steps leading down into the water.

Harriet sat on the tiled edge, dangling her feet in the water, and watching indulgently as he threshed about energetically. When he got tired, there was a huge inflatable swan for him to ride on—another evidence of Alex's thought. Nicky adored it, and often insisted on bringing some bread down from the house so that they could ceremoniously pretend to feed it.

Eventually she joined Nicky in the water, encouraging him to float on his back, and then to swim with proper strokes, all the time aware that Maria was watching them, her face set in lines of annoyance.

As she lifted him out at last, and wrapped him in a towel, she was not altogether surprised to see Maria beckoning imperiously.

She gave Nicky a quick hug. 'Dry your hair,' she urged in an undertone, then picking up her own towel she walked to where Maria was lying.

The Greek girl's eyes looked her over from the pale damp strands of hair on her shoulders, to her bare feet, taking in the white towelling chainstore bikini on the way.

She said glacially, 'Who gives you permission to use the pool at this time?'

Harriet frowned. 'I don't understand you, *thespinis*.'

Maria's chin lifted in affront. 'I speak very good English. You do not want to understand. I say you should not use the pool, or bring the child down here, when there are guests of the family present. The boy is noisy. Take him back to the nursery now, *parakalo*,' she added offhandedly.

Harriet felt a blaze of temper rise within her, but her smile didn't waver. 'I'm afraid that it's you who does not understand, *thespinis*. I am not Nicky's nanny. I'm his aunt, and I'm also a guest here.'

She didn't believe for a moment that Maria wasn't perfectly well aware of the relationship, but if she

expected her to look discomfited, then she was
disappointed.

Maria's shrug was negligent. 'There is a beach,' she
said. 'There he could make as much noise as he wishes.
Why do you not take him there?'

Harriet held on to her patience. 'Because the path
down to it is dangerous for someone of his age. Alex
has had a gate fixed to the top to prevent him from
straying down there, as you may have noticed.'

She saw Maria's eyes narrow at the use of Alex's
name, and went on hurriedly, 'I'm sorry if Nicky
disturbs you, *thespinis*. Perhaps you aren't used to small
children and. . . .'

'I am perfectly accustomed to them,' Maria said icily.
'Many of my friends are married, but Greek children
are taught to behave properly, to play quietly. English
children seem to me spoiled, and allowed to become—
hooligans.' She pronounced the word with a kind of
triumph.

Harriet said quietly, 'Nicky's half Greek, if you
remember,' then wished she hadn't, as she saw a flash
of real hatred in Maria's dark eyes. Every time Maria
looked at Nicky she must be reminded of Kostas, and
the fact that he had jilted her, she realised, and there
was no way she could convince the other girl that her
last remark had not been a deliberate jibe. She
suppressed a sigh and said, 'But if you really find him
such a nuisance, I'll take him elsewhere.'

Maria gave a slight shrug, implying that Harriet could
take him to the ends of the earth with her goodwill.

At that moment Spiro came striding under the
archway. He was casually dressed in shorts and a leisure
shirt, with espadrilles on his bare feet, and was carrying
a camera.

He halted when he saw them. 'Ah, you have already
been bathing,' he said with evident dissatisfaction. 'I
came to see whether you and Nicos would like to go
with me to Paleocastritsa. Behave like tourists for a
day, *ne*?'

Harriet forbore to remind him that, as far as it went, that was really all she was. She couldn't prevent a surge of excitement at the invitation, remembering that Alex had described Paleocastritsa as one of Corfu's beauty spots, but to escape from the environs of the villa for a while, she felt she would have jumped at a chance to tour the local gasworks.

She said smilingly, 'That would be lovely. Nicky, we're going to the seaside in Thio Spiro's car! That is—it is the seaside, isn't it?' She turned to Spiro in sudden doubt.

He laughed. 'Indeed it is. A fine beach, although very crowded, and a bay with tall cliffs and many caves. You will like it there.'

Harriet scooped their belongings together and hustled Nicky towards the villa, promising to be as quick as possible. She was sure she would like Paleocastritsa, and the glimpse she had got of the look of baffled temper on Maria's face had added an extra dimension to her anticipated pleasure.

Maria, she was sure, had no intentions of swapping Alex for Spiro, in spite of his mother's machinations, but at the same time she clearly felt that any invitations which were going should be aimed at her, rather than a little English nobody.

It was ignoble to feel triumphant, but she did.

While Yannina attended to Nicky, Harriet showered rapidly, and changed into another bikini, topping it with a one-piece playsuit in a pale lemon stretch fabric, and pushing her feet into simple leather sandals.

Spiro's eyes lit up with admiration as she came downstairs, holding Nicky's hand.

'How beautiful you look,' he said. 'Let us go quickly.'

'Before anyone sees us?' Harriet supplied drily, and he gave her a quizzical glance, and a faintly embarrassed shrug.

'You are in an unfortunate position in this house, Harriet,' he said when they were in his car and on their way.

Harriet sighed. 'You don't have to remind me! But I still don't see why. Kostas wasn't the first man in the world to marry someone his family didn't approve of, and he won't be the last.'

'That is true,' Spiro acknowledged. 'But it was not only the marriage——' He stopped short, as if aware he might have said too much, and Harriet turned to him impulsively.

'Please go on—I think I have a right to know what's going on, as I'm the one who's principally affected by it.'

Spiro looked uncomfortable. 'Perhaps, but Alex would not be pleased, I think, if I were to discuss a close family matter with. . . .' he hesitated.

'An outsider,' Harriet suggested woodenly. 'Of course, I could always ask him—telling him that you'd whetted my curiosity.'

'I hope you will do no such thing!' Spiro looked horrified, then laughed. 'Oh, very well. As you say, you have a right. I have seen how my aunt behaves towards you, and it is not kind.'

Not to mention your own mother who, of course, has been charm itself, Harriet thought with irony.

Aloud she said, 'Forgive me, but does Madame Constantis know that you're taking us to Paleocastritsa?'

He nodded. 'It was partly her own idea. You must understand, Harriet, that it would have given me much pleasure to have taken you out before, only. . . .'

'Only it might have upset too many people,' she said quietly. 'Are you quite certain you didn't misunderstand what your mother said to you?'

'You do not believe me? Well, I suppose I cannot blame you. You must understand that my mother is a woman who feels very deeply, both love and hate. Since the death of my father, she has been living here with my aunt. As they are widows, it is a good arrangement for them, but since she has come here my mother has become too concerned with'—he looked embarrassed again—'certain aspects of our family relationship.'

'You mean she saw you as Alex's heir.' Harriet stared at the tall sombre lines of a group of cypresses.

Spiro groaned. 'It is so obvious? I feared so, and yet it is ridiculous. It is inevitable that Alex will marry and have a son. Even if the little Nicos did not exist, it would be so. My father, God knows, was not a poor man, but always my mother has had this envy of the Marcos family, and of her younger sister who made this brilliant marriage. It is sad, but it is part of her nature.'

'Didn't any of them know that Kostas had had a son?'

'Alex knew, but said nothing, until his brother's death made it necessary for him to act, of course.'

'Well, that's something we aren't likely to agree on,' Harriet said drily. 'But why did Kostas quarrel with his family.'

Spiro sighed. 'I spoke of my mother's envy. Well, it is something from which the Marcos family themselves are not immune. And poor Kostas envied his brother. Alex was the oldest—and from childhood he had this power—this charisma. Kostas was always in his shadow, and he resented it. Thus, when he joined the Corporation, he tried certain—innovations, tried to pursue a line independent from Alex, who at that time was already the Chairman. But he lacked Alex's flair, his aggression in business dealings, and he failed badly, as Alex had warned him he was likely to do. Alex was very angry, as you can imagine, and harsh things were said.' He sighed again. 'Kostas was given an ultimatum—in future he was to—toe the line, and as a first step he was to marry Maria as it was the wish of both families that he should do so.' He paused heavily. 'There was a terrible scene, and he walked out. Eventually he went to England, but to work independently of the Marcos Corporation. That must have been when he met your sister.'

'Yes, he had a job in an accountant's office.' Harriet smiled wryly. 'When he told Becca who he was, I don't think she believed him.'

'Ah,' Spiro said. 'Then perhaps he acted as he did to convince her.'

Glancing at him, Harriet saw that his goodnatured face was grave. Trying to speak lightly, she asked, 'Well, what did he do?'

Spiro paused for a long moment, then said heavily, 'He stole a ruby ring from his mother to give to her.'

Harriet's lips parted in a gasp of sheer amazement. She glanced round at Nicky, but he was absorbed in a picture book on the back seat, and probably would not have understood the trend of the conversation anyway.

She said flatly, 'I don't believe you.'

'It is unhappily most true.' Spiro sent her a sympathetic look. 'It distresses you, I see, and I can understand it. It was not an action worthy of him, and it hurt my aunt deeply. It was a long time before she could bring herself to speak his name. Again, it is a sad story, full of anger. Kostas came here to the villa to tell his family that he was going to marry your sister, and to ask his mother for the ring which she had promised him for his future wife. It was to be a gift, you understand, for the bride. But my aunt refused to give it to him, stating that your sister was not the wife she had chosen, and she would not recognise her as such, that his marriage was an insult to Maria Xandreou and her family—oh, many things were said, as you can imagine.'

Harriet shuddered. 'Yes.'

'Kostas also said many things, accusing his mother of cherishing Alex as her favourite, of always preferring him. He said that unless his family agreed to receive your sister as his wife, he would have nothing more to do with them, that he would leave the next day, taking with him only what he was entitled to. There were certain documents, a precious icon which had been a present from his own godfather, all in the safe in Alex's study—where his mother's jewellery also was.'

Harriet didn't think she wanted to hear any more, but she knew that, having started this, she had to.

Spiro went on, 'The following day after he had left, it was realised the ring had gone. Alex, I think, would have followed him to London, made him give it back, but this my aunt would not permit. But it was your sister that she blamed in her heart. She said many times afterwards that Kostas would never have done such a thing unless this woman had prompted him.'

Harriet shook her head wretchedly. 'But there was no ruby ring. I remember the icon, because Kostas sold it when Nicky was expected to pay for all the things that were needed. But Becca never had any jewellery except her wedding ring, and her watch. Oh—and a little gold pendant with a pearl in it that Kostas bought her for Christmas.'

Spiro shrugged. 'Then he must have sold it also. There can be no other explanation.'

'But what did he do with the money, if so?' Harriet demanded. 'They never had any extra cash. Becca was even glad of what I could pay as rent when I lodged with them.'

'I cannot answer these questions. Again and again I have asked myself what made Kostas do such a thing, but I have never found an answer which gave me satisfaction.' His mouth tightened. 'I thought I knew him too—we were of an age—and I would have sworn it was not in his character to do such a thing—to hurt his mother so much, no matter how deeply they might have quarrelled.' He gave her a sidelong look. 'Perhaps he was ashamed afterwards and kept the ring somewhere, never daring to show it. In a safe deposit, maybe?'

'I'm sure he didn't.' Harriet was vehement. 'He was upset about the quarrel with his family, but that was all. And the theft of a valuable ring from his mother of all people would have preyed on his mind—made him miserable. I know it would. And he wasn't miserable. They were both so happy.'

'You are a loyal and affectionate friend, little Harriet.' Spiro smiled a little. 'But the evidence is—overwhelming.'

'I don't give a damn about evidence,' Harriet said roundly. 'I know Kostas was no thief, that's all.'

'Well, you and I will not quarrel about it,' he said hastily. 'There has been too much sadness and too much anger in the past, and perhaps it is best that this part of it remains a mystery.'

Harriet didn't think it was best for a moment, but Spiro was her host, and when he determinedly changed the subject to the changes he had seen overtake the island since his boyhood, she went along with him. But the shine had gone out of the day for her.

She was shocked to the core by Spiro's account, because although she had not the slightest doubt of Kostas' innocence, it was nevertheless a fact that a very valuable piece of jewellery had vanished, and that someone must have taken it. And if further enquiries had been passed over, it followed that Alex and his mother must have had good reason for thinking Kostas was the culprit.

One of the servants? she wondered. It seemed unlikely. She had already learned from Yannina that all of them had been with the family for years, apart from a couple of the young maids who were recent arrivals— far too recent to be implicated.

She asked herself whether Kostas knew what he was suspected of, and remembering his bitterness and his reluctance to discuss the rift with his family, thought it was only too likely.

As Spiro had prophesied, Paleocastritsa was teeming with people when they arrived. They parked the car and walked along the road beside the beach, Nicky becoming the proud possessor of a toy windmill purchased at one of the roadside stalls.

It wasn't an enormous bay, the high brooding cliffs giving an enclosed effect, but its deep green waters were alive with wind-surfers, swimmers and water-skiers. There were little ramshackle wooden jetties too, extending out from the beach where larger boats plied for trade, offering trips round the sea caves. Harriet

would have loved to have gone on one of these, but
Spiro did not suggest it, and she suspected that such
unsophisticated entertainments were probably beneath
him. But he was a good companion, solicitous for their
comfort, insisting that when they reached the sea wall at
the end of the bay they should stop at one of the
tavernas there for cold drinks.

Nicky had an enormous glass of orange and
amused himself by trying to drown the ice cubes with
his straw. When he tired of that, he wandered to the
edge and sat gripping the railing, and watching some
children playing with buckets and spades in the sand
below.

Finally he announced gleefully, 'That lady's bare!'

Harriet turned quickly and found him pointing at an
impressively topless beauty sauntering along at the water's
edge. Spiro snorted with amusement, his gaze following
her with frank appreciation.

'They start early in your family,' Harriet muttered,
turning back to her drink.

'In these days it is unavoidable.' Spiro drank some
beer, still looking amused. 'You do not approve,
Harriet?'

She flushed a little. 'I—I just know that I would
never have the nerve to do it.'

'I am grieved to hear it,' Spiro said politely. 'You will
be surprised to hear that my cousin Alex shares your
disapproval, but for a very different reason. He believes
that a woman's breasts should only be uncovered for
the eyes of her lover, and that she loses much of her
mystery by exposing herself thus to the gaze of any
passer-by.'

'Oh, does he?' Harriet was crossly aware that the
colour in her face had become more pronounced and
that Spiro was observing this with interest. 'How very
old-fashioned of him!'

Spiro chuckled. 'Shall I tell him you said so—when
he returns?'

'He doesn't seem in any great hurry to do so.' Harriet

grasped a straw that might lead the conversation back to the general.

Spiro grimaced. 'I cannot find it in my heart to blame him. If it was my fate to marry Maria, I too would stay away as long as possible.'

'Nonsense,' Harriet said stonily. 'I'm sure she'll make him a very good wife. Come away from those railings, Nicky, you're going to bang your head.'

To Harriet's delight, they got their boat-trip after all, Spiro indulgently sharing their pleasure as the boatmen guided his craft between the gleaming pinnacles of rock, and in and out of the dark grottoes where sea-urchins and starfish were clearly visible in the crystal clarity of the blue water, and shoals of tiny fish darted in and out.

Afterwards they ate at a taverna on the hillside above the bay, sitting on a vine-covered terrace, sharing a messy but satisfying platter of shellfish while Nicky made his way solemnly through an omelette. Spiro introduced Harriet to *retsina*, a clear golden wine tasting of resin which, after the first few sips, she found curiously palatable. They finished the meal with coffee and bowls of dark purple grapes, while Nicky chased butterflies in the garden below, and tried to persuade a thin and suspicious kitten to play with him.

When the meal was ended, they joined the other sunbathers on the sand, Nicky relapsing without protest into sleep in the shade of a large sun-umbrella which Spiro fetched from the boot of the car. Harriet stretched out beside him and closed her eyes, but she couldn't sleep.

Her mind kept reverting to the things that Spiro had told her earlier. No matter how hard she tried, it was impossible to keep them at bay. They were there, like corrosive acid, eating into her contentment, her peace of mind. She felt as if the shadow of the accusation made against Kostas had touched her too through Becca, and through Nicky. How could he grow up in this place among people who were ready to believe that his father had been a thief?

Was this what invaded Madame Marcos' thoughts each day when Nicky was with her. Remembering how deeply she had been hurt by the father, did she hesitate to give unstinting affection to his child? It seemed an inevitable conclusion to draw, and if it was true then surely even Alex could be made to see that it was better for Nicky to return to England rather than be brought up in such a shadow.

Her eyelids flew up as Spiro leaned over her and gently tweaked her foot. 'You look sad, Harriet, and this is not a day for sadness.' He paused. 'Do not fret over things you cannot change. Let us swim.'

The water felt gloriously cool and silky against her skin, and it buoyed up her spirits as well as her body as she swam and turned and floated, as carefree suddenly as a dolphin while Nicky shrieked and splashed at the water's edge.

She was more resigned, if not wholly at peace, as they drove home in the later afternoon, Harriet sitting in the back of the car with Nicky, his salt-sticky curls reposing on her lap as he dozed.

As the car came to rest by the front door of the villa, Yannina appeared as if by magic, beaming. '*Kalispera, thespinis*. It has been a good day, *ne*?'

'Very good.' Harriet was smiling as she passed Nicky over to the older woman's waiting arms. 'Tea, and then bed, I think, Yannina.'

'I think so too, *thespinis*.' Yannina vanished into the shadowy interior of the house, and Harriet was about to follow when Spiro detained her, a hand on her arm.

'The day does not have to end here,' he urged. 'Have dinner with me tonight. We could drive to Nissaki— there is a taverna there overlooking the sea. Say you will come with me!'

Harriet hesitated, sensing danger. Spiro had established himself firmly in her good opinion during the day, but that was as far as it went, or ever could go. There was a note in his voice which warned her that his interest might be deepening beyond a mere desire for companionship, and this worried her.

On the other hand, she could not deny that yet
another fraught meal *en famille* had very little appeal,
particularly as, in spite of Spiro's assurance, she was
wondering how Madame Constantis might regard her
day out in his company.

She said slowly, 'It sounds marvellous, Spiro,
only. . . .'

'Only I must be sure not to get any wrong ideas,' he
finished for her, his face frankly rueful. 'So—who is the
fortunate man, because there must be one. Not, I hope,
my cousin Alex,' he added sharply.

Harriet was terrified that betraying blush would
confound her, but by some miracle it did not come, and
she was even able to manage a light laugh.

'Of course not! I'm not a complete fool. Casual
womanisers just aren't my scene. No—there's someone
in London. His name's Roy. I—I expect we'll be
married when I go home.'

Spiro sighed, lifting his shoulders in a little shrug.
'Nevertheless, Harriet, I would very much like to take
you to dinner. With no strings—if that is what you
wish.'

'In that case, I'd like to have dinner with you. Thank
you, Spiro.' On an impulse, she reached up and kissed
him, brushing his swarthy cheek swiftly with her lips.

He grinned teasingly. 'Is that the most I can hope
for?' He bent towards her, and found her mouth with
his. It wasn't a passionate embrace by any standards,
but she was still beginning to pull away—even before
Alex's voice said curtly from the doorway behind them,
'I obviously intrude, may I suggest you choose a less
public place for your lovemaking?'

Harriet whirled, gasping, her hands flying up to press
against her warm cheeks.

She said shakily and ridiculously, 'Oh, you're back.'

'How perceptive of you.' The harshness in his voice
didn't soften, and the nod he gave Spiro was glacial.
'You have wasted no time, I see, cousin.'

'Following your own example—*cousin*,' Spiro came back at him lightly.

Alex's mouth tautened, and he said something in Greek which brought a dull flush of angry colour to Spiro's face. He started forward impetuously, but Harriet intervened, appalled.

'Oh—please!' She clutched at Spiro's arm. 'Please don't spoil my day.'

He paused, then shrugged almost sulkily, muttering something about putting the car away. He walked round, slamming into the driver's seat, and shot off with a screech of tyres that lifted a cloud of dust from the drive.

Leaving Harriet alone with Alex.

It was a wide doorway. Three people could probably have passed in it quite comfortably, yet his lean body seemed to be a sudden impassable barrier.

She passed her tongue round dry lips and said, 'Would you—excuse me, please.'

He said with ominous quiet, 'I wish to talk to you.'

'About Nicky?' She stared at the ground. 'Oh, he's fine. We—we took him to Paleocastritsa for the day. You were quite right—it is beautiful there.' Aware that she was babbling, she allowed her voice to fade into silence.

'Does Nicos invariably accompany you on your sightseeing tours with my cousin?'

She was about to point out that this had been the one and only trip she had made in Spiro's company, when a sudden gust of anger shook her. After all, she was supposed to be a guest in this house, not a servant or a prisoner. And no one was going to put Alex through a similar inquisition about his activities in Athens, she told herself furiously.

She lifted her chin. 'Not always,' she said coolly. 'For instance, he won't be going with us this evening when Spiro takes me to dinner at Nissaki. Now, if you'll excuse me, I should be getting ready.'

She expected him to move out of the way, but she

was wrong. The dark head was flung back slightly, and his eyes glinted arrogantly at her.

He said, 'But I do not excuse you anything, Harriet *mou*. And as it seems you have become so prodigal with your kisses in my absence, then the least you can do is welcome me as I would wish.'

His hands descended on her shoulders, pulling her inexorably towards him, and his mouth ravaged hers with slow sensual expertise. She clung to him, her fingers clenched round the soft folds of his shirt. He needed a shave. His chin rasped against her skin and she shivered, feeling her body dissolve in longing against his. When he lifted his head, and that fiercely pagan sting of his fingers on her flesh relaxed, a whimper of yearning—of protest that she could not control, was torn from her tight throat.

He said softly, 'Now go to Spiro.'

She could not move. It was he who turned and went, leaving her alone on the threshold.

It seemed very quiet suddenly, the air hushed and heavy with the advent of evening, even the cicadas silent. All she could hear was the splash of the fountain behind her, and she turned and looked at the nymph, remote and smiling on her pedestal, and realised that she too knew what it was to be turned to stone. But instead of the nymph's distant, unearthly smile, on her face there would have been tears, frozen there for all eternity. . . .

CHAPTER NINE

THE heat was almost stifling, Harriet thought, lifting her hair away from the nape of her neck with a little sigh. The slight languid breeze from the sea only stirred the air without cooling it, and each day seemed more oppressive than the last.

But this, she supposed, was why most people came to Corfu for their holidays—for the promise of this kind of brilliant, cloudless weather. And if she herself were merely a holidaymaker, she would probably be loving it too, she thought.

She had no right and little reason to feel so miserable, she told herself over and over again. By anyone's standards, she could be said to be having a wonderful time. Spiro had seen to that. She had explored the island in his company, visited the town, seen the shrine of Saint Spiridion in his own church where his mummified body reposed in a silver coffin, driven round the streets in an open-air carriage trimmed with bells behind a horse in a straw hat, watched cricket being played on the dusty square on the Esplanade, and shopped for souvenirs in the narrow crowded streets to the strains of the ever-present *syrtaki* music.

They had picnicked in coves, accessible only by boat, and Harriet had had her first tentative lessons in water-skiing in the bay below the villa, a smiling Andonis manoeuvring the boat while Spiro shouted instructions from the stern.

Each night she went to her room healthily tired with sun, sea and exercise, and each night she tossed and turned, unable to sleep, because it was only when she was alone that she was able to think, and the thoughts which came were as dark and oppressive as the nights themselves.

Alex obsessed her. Since the evening of his return, she had gone to great lengths to avoid being alone with him, but she couldn't ban him from her waking dreams, and he was the reason she found sleep so disturbingly elusive.

Not that he was so difficult to avoid during the day, she thought bitterly. That sudden, wild blaze of passion might only have existed in her imagination. Sometimes when she responded to one of his coolly civil greetings, or met the indifferent arrogance in his dark eyes, she thought perhaps she had invented the whole thing out of her own hidden longings. And yet the bruises on her mouth which she had had to disguise with cosmetics had been no mental fabrication. They had been real enough, and she had been afraid Spiro would notice and ask embarrassing questions. But if he was aware of the swollen contours of her mouth, he neither commented nor teased, and she was able to relax and enjoy her dinner.

The taverna he had taken her to was built on a concrete platform which jutted out over the water, and coloured lights clustered in the sheltering olive trees around its perimeter. They had eaten anchovies, and tiny fritters of green pepper and aubergine, and chunks of lamb, roasted with herbs. Later, lingering over coffee and liqueurs, they had watched a string of lighted fishing boats making their way over the tranquil waters.

Under Spiro's guidance, Harriet had learned to appreciate fully the simplicities of Greek taverna food, and to enjoy being invited into the kitchens to see what was being prepared rather than merely consult a written menu.

'It's very different to the food at the villa,' she had commented once, and Spiro had laughed.

'Alex's chef was imported from France,' he had pointed out, and she had smiled back, reflecting ruefully that of course she should have known.

The villa always ran efficiently, but when Alex was there, there was an extra spark in the air, and standards

generally peaked past their already high level. He
stalked through his domain, never missing a detail, his
every wish obeyed instantly, although Harriet had never
heard him raise his voice. In every area of life, he
expected compliance, and probably got it, she
thought with a trace of bitterness. Even Androula
scuttled around with vinegary smiles when he was
around.

She had braced herself for the pain of seeing him with
Maria—of perhaps watching him wooing her, but at
least she had been spared that. He was no more
attentive to her than any host might have been expected
to be with a guest, and although Maria smiled and
pouted and beguiled whenever he was near, Harriet had
once or twice surprised a faintly chagrined expression
on the other girl's face.

Perhaps she had expected pretty speeches, but if a
marriage was being arranged between them it would be
on his terms and not hers, Harriet told herself with
unwonted cynicism.

Meanwhile all Alex's smiles, and any pretty speeches
that were going, were being devoted to Nicky. Since his
arrival at the villa, he had hardly allowed the child out
of his sight, playing with him, spoiling him, carrying him
off on his shoulders while Nicky shouted with
excitement.

He was deliberately setting out to win him over,
Harriet thought with a pang, and that meant her days
on Corfu were numbered.

There were no more formal playtimes with Madame
Marcos. Alex was there too, and the whole atmosphere
was happier, more relaxed. Without ceremony Alex
picked Nicky up, putting him on to his mother's lap,
into her arms, and Harriet turned away, blaming herself
for being over-emotional as she saw the older woman's
face soften tremulously into pleasure.

Even Maria had the good sense to keep her real
thoughts to herself, and cooed and gushed whenever
Nicky was in the vicinity.

Yet something told Harriet that Madame Constantis still had not accepted that Nicky was now part of the household. Her attitude left Harriet feeling both worried and bewildered in a way she could hardly define. On the surface all seemed well. She even treated Harriet herself with courtesy, if not actual enthusiasm, and raised no overt objections to her going out with Spiro.

Yet even this was wrong, Harriet felt intuitively. Madame Constantis was ambitious for her son, and Harriet was sure she hadn't totally abandoned her plans to match him with Maria Xandreou. So why didn't she exert her considerable authority to prevent him making dates with Harriet, and encourage him to flatter Maria with his attentions in the face of Alex's continued indifference? Why did she pretend she didn't mind, because Harriet was ready to swear that she minded like blazes, and she would have given a great deal to know what was going on behind the acid smiles and the blank shuttered eyes.

Particularly where Nicky was concerned. Harriet had never seen Madame Constantis address him directly, or even look at him unless she was obliged to, and her sister's softening towards the little boy had made no difference in her attitude. If anything Harriet sensed a hardening, and additional tension—but it was only a feeling, and when she herself was so much on edge, it was fatally easy to read too much into atmosphere.

Spiro had told her that his mother possessed an apartment in Athens and a large house in the Pelopponese, to which she could return whenever she wished, and Harriet could only hope for Nicky's sake that it would be soon.

She could understand that Madame Marcos and her sister should wish to cling to each other's companionship in their widowhood, but surely the advent of her only grandchild had altered the need for such a dependency? Perhaps Madame Constantis sensed this, and resented it, because there was resentment, and Harriet knew it, although she couldn't prove it.

Harriet sighed and changed her position slightly on her lounger, but not too much because she had cautiously undone the top of her bikini to allow her back to tan evenly. Alex and Spiro had gone fishing and Nicky had gone with his grandmother to visit some friends so she had the beach to herself.

She rested her cheek on her folded arms, feeling the drops of sweat trickling down her forehead, and in the cleft between her breasts. The sky seemed to be clamped over everything like a great brazen lid, and she wondered incuriously whether there was going to be a storm. The air seemed to have that brooding quality about it which a storm might clear. At least she hoped so.

Only hopes, she thought. No certainties—about anything.

She wondered what would happen when she got back to London. That was where she would go, of course. Alex probably wouldn't remember he had guaranteed her employment after she left Corfu, and she had no intention of reminding him. In fact it would be much better if he forgot all about her existence, and she tried to forget about his.

She sighed silently, thinking how much better even than that it would have been if she had never seen him. She was in for a period of great unhappiness, and there seemed no way she could avoid it. How many nights would it take before she could fall asleep without remembering that last merciless pressure of his mouth against hers, and without hungering for his arms to hold her again even if it was anger rather than passion which prompted him.

She pressed her fist against her mouth. It was never likely to be passion. 'Go to Spiro', he had said, and his attitude since had merely underlined his total indifference to her.

She could hear the sound of the boat's engine. They were coming back, and she didn't want to face anyone at the moment. She considered beating a hasty retreat up the path, then opted for pretending to be asleep, closing her eyes and steadying her constricted breathing to a quiet rhythm.

She heard the engine roar to a stop and men's voices speaking in Greek, some laughter. They were approaching, walking up the beach and she felt a mass of tensions, and had to make herself relax.

But when the first cool drops descended on her back, she could maintain the pretence no longer, her eyes flying open as she propped herself up slightly and looked over her shoulder.

She had assumed it was Spiro, perhaps with a handful of seawater, but it was Alex, and he was holding her bottle of sun lotion in his hand. As their eyes met, he crouched lithely beside her and again she felt that delicious coolness on her warm skin, and realised that he was using the lotion on her. She moved restively.

'Keep still,' he ordered. 'It's a fool's trick to fall asleep in the sun. You could have been badly burned.'

She was burning now. As his hand stroked across her flesh, tiny fires were igniting all over her. And as his fingers moved downwards and began to apply the lotion to her lower spine and the gentle curve of her hips above her line of her bikini briefs, she had to sink her teeth into the soft flesh inside her lower lip to prevent herself from crying out.

Oh God, what kind of a state was she in, that his lightest touch could produce such pleasure and such pain at the same time? she wondered wildly.

When he had finished and was re-capping the bottle, Harriet murmured an awkward 'Thank you,' avoiding his gaze, aware that her cheeks were hectically flushed. Aware too that Spiro was standing only a few yards away, brows raised as he assimilated what was going on.

Her blush deepened. She said inanely, 'Hello. Did you catch anything?'

'Enough, I think,' he said drily.

Alex had turned, dropping the bottle of lotion on to the sand beside her lounger, and moving away to speak to Andonis, who was unloading the fishing gear from the boat at the small jetty.

Spiro walked across to the lounger and looked down at her. 'So we'll eat at the villa tonight, *ne*?'

'Yes,' she agreed brightly, fixing her eyes on him, rejecting the impulse to look round for Alex.

Spiro grinned at her, and his hand snaked down towards her catching her completely off guard. She had lifted herself on to her elbows, and before she could stop him he had twitched the bra of her bikini away from under her body and walked away with it.

'Spiro!' She sat up, wrapping her arms round her half-naked body. 'Bring that back here at once!'

His grin widened. 'Come and get it, *kougla mou*.' With teasing precision, he hung the strip of material from the branch of a convenient olive tree.

Angry and embarrassed, she hesitated, measuring the distance, and wondering if Spiro intended to allow her to retrieve the bra or whether he would simply make off with it again, forcing her to follow. The thought of perhaps having to chase after him through the gardens with only her hands to cover her had no appeal whatsoever.

She said entreatingly, 'Spiro—please?' and heard him laugh tauntingly.

Alex's shadow fell over her. She glanced up at him, her heart thudding with sudden apprehension as she registered the cold rage in his face. He looked almost murderous as he glared at Spiro, snarling something at him in Greek.

For a moment Harriet thought Spiro was going to defy his cousin, and she tensed as Alex took one long stride towards him, then Spiro shrugged almost ruefully, unhooked her top from the branch, and tossed it to him.

Alex turned and almost flung it at her. 'Cover yourself!' he ordered furiously.

She wasn't uncovered. Her folded arms hid more than the few inches of top had ever done, but she sensed that now was not the time to argue, and she turned her back while she fumbled the bra back into place, and fastened its clip.

When she turned back, Alex had gone, but Spiro was still there, gazing up the path with an odd, reflective little smile playing round his mouth.

She said sharply, 'Are you out of your mind? What possessed you to do such a thing?'

'It was an experiment, that is all.' He laughed at the outrage in her face. 'Oh, my poor Harriet, don't look like that! There is no need for you to be angry. Alex has already been angry enough for both of you.'

'I thought he was going to kill you,' she said with a little shiver.

'So did I,' he admitted candidly, and she caught a glimpse of that odd smile again.

Harriet sighed. 'I suppose you know best, Spiro, but as you work for—for your cousin, perhaps it might be better not to—to upset him.'

'I promise not to make a habit of it.' His voice sounded almost lighthearted. 'But perhaps we would be wiser to go without the delicious fresh fish that Alex's chef will be serving tonight, and eat out after all. What do you say?'

She said, 'Yes.' She wasn't hungry. That little incident had deprived her of appetite, but she couldn't bear the thought of encountering Alex again in that mood, and letting Spiro take her to dinner would be the best way she knew of avoiding him.

He had no reason to look at her like that—with such a blaze of contempt in his eyes, she thought stormily, particularly when only minutes before he had been putting lotion on her back, and presumably quite well aware that she wasn't wearing her top.

He operates a hell of a double standard, she thought fuming, wondering how many girls he had seen not merely topless but totally nude. And what would he

have done if she'd been one of the confident beauties
she'd seen parading at Dassia and Sidari on some of her
trips with Spiro? Probably exactly the same, she
acknowledged with a sigh.

She collected her things together and went slowly up
to the villa. She found Nicky in his room, and he
welcomed her with an exuberant hug and a kiss sticky
with lemonade and honey, and she stayed with him
while he had his evening meal, unwinding as she
listened to his excited and not always intelligible
chatter. He was a bright child, and each day he seemed
to pick up more Greek words. By the time he went to
school, he would probably be bi-lingual, and farther
apart from her than any distance could ever achieve.
She had to treasure these moments when she was alone
with him, because his new family were beginning to
close him in with them, and there was no place for her
in that small tight circle of wealth and power.

She bathed Nicky herself that evening, and he
squealed and splashed with all the old delight as they
played once familiar games under Yannina's benevo-
lently smiling gaze. As she wrapped the bath sheet
round his small dripping body, Harriet held him very
close for a moment, aware of a terrible tightness in her
throat, as if she was already saying goodbye to him.
The moment he began to struggle a little, alarmed by
the confining pressure of her arms, she let him go,
tickling him through the folds of towel, and playing
'Round and round the garden' and 'This little piggy'
until he relapsed into his usual happy giggles.

She sat by his bed, waiting for him to fall asleep, and
only when his eyelids had finally drooped did she
relinquish her post and go to her own room to get ready
for her dinner with Spiro.

She had replenished her small wardrobe in Corfu
town, buying several of the inexpensive cotton dresses
falling in masses of pleats from a brief crocheted yoke,
but tonight she decided to wear one of the few dresses
she had bought that she hadn't put on before. It was a

favourite of hers, and she supposed she'd been saving it
for some special occasion. Well, tonight was probably
going to be about as special as she was likely to get, she
thought, throwing it across the bed. It was made from
fine floating Indian cotton in shades of blue and gold,
full-skirted and wide-sleeved. The bodice fitted closely,
and the deeply slashed neckline was fastened at the
throat and halfway to her breasts with delicate blue
cords, finished off with tiny gilded tassels.

It was a romantic dress, a dress for a girl with happy
dreams in her eyes—not the look of strain that she
could disguise behind dark glasses during the daytime,
but which made her totally vulnerable when evening
came.

She applied her make-up with a light hand—a
dusting of shadow for her eyelids, and the merest touch
of colour on her mouth. The natural glow which the
sun had bestowed on her skin needed no extra
embellishment.

She had intended to wear her hair up in a coil, or at
least tied back, but at the last minute she decided to
leave it loose on her shoulders.

She was spraying scent on to her throat and wrists
when there was an abrupt knock on the door and
Androula came in.

'I'm asked to say the car is at the door, *thespinis*.' Her
voice was as unfriendly as her face.

Harriet swallowed as the woman's gaze flickered
disapprovingly over her. 'Please tell the *kyrios* that I'll
be down right away.'

Androula nodded silently and vanished.

Harriet gave herself a last searching look, decided it
was all the best she could do, and started downstairs.
Halfway along the corridor she met Madame
Constantis. She was surprised to see her, as the older
woman's room was in a different part of the house, and
she had rarely encountered her on the upper floor.

She glanced at Zoe Constantis, expecting the acid
twitch of the lips which passed for a smile with her, but

not even that was forthcoming. The look which reached her from under the heavy lids was pure venom—no longer even a pretence at friendliness and acceptance, and Harriet almost recoiled physically as if an actual blow had been aimed at her. She glanced back over her shoulder as she reached the corner, watching the thin upright figure move out of sight, like some kind of ancient Fury in her black dress, and had to pause for a moment to try and recover her composure.

She had never been wholly convinced about Madame Constantis' apparent change of attitude towards her, but she hadn't expected to have her suspicions so blightingly confirmed either.

Not for the first time, she wondered how such a grim woman could ever have given birth to such a pleasant easy-going son as Spiro.

The car was parked just outside the circle of light which spilled from the villa's open doors, and as Harriet crossed towards it, she heard in the distance the first rumble of thunder. It seemed the storm she had predicted was on its way.

The passenger door was already open, and she slipped into her seat, tucking her skirt protectively away from the door before she closed it. The engine was already running, she realised, purring like some big cat. Spiro was in a hurry to be off. Perhaps he had also had an encounter with his mother, and wanted to escape.

She said with a little gasp as the car moved forward, 'I'm sorry I'm late. I've been putting Nicky to bed and . . .' Her voice stopped abruptly, as she turned and looked at her companion for the first time.

Alex smiled sardonically at the frank shock in her eyes. 'And as always, Harriet *mou*, you are worth waiting for.'

'What are you doing here?' she demanded heatedly. 'Where is Spiro?'

'On his way back to Athens. His holiday is over for a while.'

For a moment she was unable to speak, then she said,

'Was that really necessary? What happened on the beach was only a joke, after all.'

His laugh had a bite to it. 'You flatter yourself! Spiro's tasteless horseplay has no connection with his departure. A minor problem has developed in the Athens office which I hope he can deal with before it blows up into a minor crisis, that is all. I am sorry he did not have time to explain in person, or say goodbye to you in the manner you would wish.'

'There's no need for that.' Her voice was stiff. 'A simple message telling me that the evening was off would have been sufficient.'

'But you're my guest, Harriet *mou*,' he said silkily. 'And a good host would not allow you to be deprived of an evening's pleasure when it is in his power to fill the inevitable void which Spiro's departure must create.'

'That's very kind of you,' she said woodenly. 'But I'd really prefer to go back to the villa, if you don't mind.'

'But I do mind,' he retorted. The car seemed to leap forward and Harriet, who had been fumbling with the catch on her seatbelt for no very coherent reason, sank back in her seat with a gasp. 'Tonight you are having dinner with me.'

'And my wishes don't matter, I suppose.' She stared down at her hands clamped rigidly together in her lap.

'On this occasion, no. We have things to discuss, Harriet, and privacy at my home is not always easy to achieve.'

She smoothed a fold of her dress. 'I—see. I suppose you want to talk about Nicky—and when I'm going home.'

'Those are among the topics we shall be considering,' he said drily. 'Or did you imagine that life was going to pursue its present course indefinitely?'

'Of course not.' She kept her head bent. 'As a matter of fact, I think Nicky's settled down amazingly well. I'm quite ready to leave whenever you say the word. There's—just one thing.' She paused, biting her lip.

'You've spent a lot of time with him lately. I think he's going to feel rather bereft—when you're away such a great deal. He might find the periods of separation easier to take, if you didn't pay him quite so much attention.'

He said coldly, 'I have no intention of being separated from Nicky for long periods, at least until he is old enough to go to school.'

She was taken aback. 'But you can hardly trail him round the world in your wake with a nursemaid in tow,' she protested. 'What kind of security is that?'

His brows lifted. 'Nicos will be with my wife, and my wife will be with me. A child's true security does not lie within four walls as much as in the love and warmth of those who care for him. We shall be his home.'

Harriet wanted to ask bitterly, 'Have you discussed this with Maria, and established her point of view?' But it seemed safer to remain silent. His words suggested that he wasn't entering marriage quite as cynically as Spiro had indicated. In fact they created a curiously intimate picture, considering he didn't appear to be in love with Maria. But then, she thought, Alex had always taken his responsibilities to the Marcos Corporation very seriously. Why should she imagine he would adopt a different attitude to his eventual marriage? Even the most dedicated playboy must surely tire of that kind of existence in the end.

'You are very quiet,' he said. 'Does my explanation not satisfy you?'

'It's—perfectly satisfactory.' She swallowed painfully. 'I—I hope you'll be very happy.'

'Do you, Harriet?' He laughed. 'I had formed the impression you would rather see me boiled in oil.'

'Perhaps so,' she said. 'But that wouldn't be the best thing for Nicky.'

He said, 'His happiness is what matters most to you still, Harriet. Is that not so?'

No, she thought. God help me, it's you that matters most. You matter more to me than anything in my life.

She said quietly, 'That's right.' She hesitated. 'I'm glad that your mother is—well—beginning. . . .'

'You need not struggle for words. I know what you are trying to say, and I am also glad. I had begun to wonder if she would ever be able to reconcile her need for Nicos with the unhappy memories his arrival was bound to revive.'

She bit her lip. 'You don't have to hedge round the subject, Alex. Spiro told me what was supposed to have happened.'

There was a silence, then in a voice shaken with anger Alex said, 'He had no right. . . .'

'I persuaded him,' she interrupted. 'I made him tell me. I had to know—for Nicky's sake. You must see that.' She paused, then added, 'And I don't believe a word of it.'

He said evenly, 'You are hardly in a position to say that. You were not here at the time.'

'I didn't have to be. I knew Kostas too. I never knew him to do anything mean or despicable, and I can't understand why—as his brother—you should have been so ready to condemn him.'

Alex pulled on the wheel, swerving the car off the road on to the verge beneath some trees, and stopping the engine.

'Is that what you think, Harriet? How little you know! Condemning Kostas, as you put it, was the hardest decision I have ever made. Yes, it was out of character for him to do such a thing, but that night he was not himself. He was more angry than I had ever seen him. He had quarrelled with our mother most bitterly. He had demanded the ring from her, and when she refused——' he shrugged, 'I can only presume he decided to take the law into his own hands. When I found the safe it had been rifled—every box had been opened, but only the ring had gone. That and the documents which had provided him with an excuse for going to the safe in the first place,' he added grimly.

'I don't care.' Stubbornly Harriet shook her head. 'I

still won't believe it. If he felt he was entitled to this ring for Becca, then why didn't he give it to her?'

His glance was cynical. 'He did not?'

'No!' she almost exploded.

He shrugged. 'A belated sense of shame, perhaps. Perhaps he honoured your sister by believing she would not be ready to ally herself with someone who would stoop to steal from his own family. Or would she?' His tone sharpened.

'Of course not,' she said wretchedly. 'The very least idea, and Becca would have had a fit!'

'My mother, of course, believes that he stole the ring at her urging.'

'So Spiro said. And that isn't true either. Becca may not have been the heiress your mother wanted for her son, but she was no gold-digger.' She glared at him. 'But I see now why you were so ready to offer me money to give up Nicky. You thought that we were— tarred with the same brush.'

'What do you want of me?' Alex asked softly. 'An insincere denial? Or my assurance that it is some time since I have speculated in those terms about either you or your late sister?'

'I don't give a damn what you think,' she said shakily. 'But if that's how it was, then why the hell did you bring me here?'

He said, 'I think you know why.'

His hands reached for her, lifting her bodily towards him out of her seat with an irresistible force. He turned her harshly so that she lay across his body, helpless in the crook of his arm, her eyes dilating with mingled alarm and excitement as his head came down towards her. He began to kiss her, lightly at first, the merest brushing of his mouth against her cheekbones, her temples and her startled eyes. When at last his lips took hers, it was in a kind of agony, as if he was dying, and she was an elixir that could bring him to life. Her mouth parted of its own volition and blind instinct took over, prompting a response as fierce and pagan as his own demand of her. Her hands locked tightly behind his head, drawing him down to her, holding him close. The touch of him, the taste of him was a sensual enslavement, and her body arched towards him in a silent offering of utter completeness.

He began to caress her, his fingers stroking her hair, then moving down to her throat and the soft sensitive hollows beneath her ears. His fingers were gentle, but they brought every nerve-ending to raw, aching life.

She heard herself whimper against his lips, but it was with pleasure, not protest, as he tugged open the little blue cords, and his hand slid under the soft cling of her neckline in intimate exploration. Her whole body seemed to clench as his thumb stroked delicately across the budding rose of her nipple, sending shafts of white-hot sensation through the very core of her being.

Nothing seemed to exist in the world but the heat of his body enfolding her, the warm draining languor of his mouth, and the sheer scorch of pleasure that his slow expert caresses were creating for her.

Her breath shuddered in her throat as he lifted his mouth from hers at last, pressing featherlight kisses down the smooth flesh of her neck to the curve of her shoulder. His lips brushed the soft veil of material away from her breasts, and her body was convulsed in yearning as his mouth took possession of the aroused rosy peaks, the insistent flick of his tongue against her flesh increasing her excitement almost to the point of frenzy.

She was touching him in her turn, her hands sliding over his body without inhibition, discovering the warmth of his skin, the play of muscle beneath the elegant clothes.

She was hungry for him as if, starved all her life, she had suddenly been offered a banquet. She loved Alex, and wanted him, and the need to tell him so was slowly overwhelming her.

Her lips moved to speak his name, but instead she

cried out, frightened, because the whole world was suddenly enveloped in blue-white light, and as the darkness rolled back, an immense crack of thunder exploded around them. And with the thunder came rain, drumming on the roof and splashing the windscreen.

Alex lifted himself away from her with evident reluctance, to close the window at his side. Harriet huddled back into her own seat, thankful that the shadows concealed her burning face. The shock of the lightning had restored her to a kind of shamed sanity, and she fumbled with her dress fastenings as she struggled for composure.

She had let him hold her, kiss her, explore her body with his hands and mouth when only a short while before he had spoken openly about his forthcoming marriage. A sense of decency at least should have made her fight him, reject his caresses, she thought, feeling sick.

The window adjusted to his satisfaction, he turned to her, and she spoke in a small strained voice. 'Will you take me back to the villa, please.'

He said slowly, 'The storm will pass. And we are supposed to be having dinner.'

'I hate storms. I'm terrified of them.' She certainly sounded as if she was, she thought detachedly. Her voice was almost cracking. 'Nicky hates them too', and I want to make sure he's all right. And I don't want any dinner. I—I couldn't eat anything,' she ended on a little rush of words.

'Well, that at least may be true,' he said, his voice hardening with contempt. 'I seem to have lost my appetite—for food—myself. As for your fear of storms, Harriet *mou*,—you're not a physical coward, merely a moral one. Yet you need not have worried. Seducing inexperienced girls in cars is a callow trick which has never appealed to me.'

The car engine started with a roar, and he turned the vehicle with almost savage expertise, and sent them rocketing back the way they had come, while the thunder growled and rumbled above their heads.

As he drew up at the entrance, Alex said with scarcely controlled impatience, 'Do you wish to wait here while I fetch some covering—an umbrella, perhaps?'

'N-no,' Harriet stammered. 'I'll be fine, honestly.'

'Honestly?' he echoed. 'I doubt if you know the meaning of the word. You had better run, then.'

Run she did, head bent, not glancing behind to see if he was following. She took the stairs two at a time, and went straight to Nicky's room. It was quite true, he hated storms—when he was awake. But it was extremely doubtful if the thunder would have woken him.

His door was standing ajar, which surprised her. Perhaps he had woken after all, and Yannina was with him, she thought, as she stopped inside.

But there was no comforting figure at Nicky's bedside, and the bed itself was empty.

Harriet stood very still, lower lip caught in her teeth, while she registered this.

She walked over to the baby alarm above the bed, and saw it was switched off. She turned it on and said, 'Yannina—is Nicky with you?' Then she sank down on the bedside chair and waited, trying not to panic.

It seemed a long time later, but it was actually only seconds, that feet came flying down the passage and Yannina burst into the room, her startled gaze seeking the empty bed. The expression on her face told Harriet all she needed to know.

She said carefully, 'It's all right, Yannina. He probably woke and was frightened by the storm and went downstairs.'

Yannina's eyes were round. 'But the handle on the door, *thespinis*. It is too high, and too stiff for him to manage, as you yourself know well. How could he have left the room? You did not leave the door open.'

No, thought Harriet, and the alarm was switched on, because I checked it as I always do.

She tried to smile. 'Well, someone came in—perhaps his grandmother—and took him downstairs because he was frightened.'

Nicky had never been a wakeful child at nights, nor a wanderer, she told herself. He was probably downstairs at this moment being fed titbits in the dining room.

She said, 'I'll go and check.'

She ran out of the room full tilt into Alex. He caught her by the arms steadying her, his eyes sharpening.

'What is it?' he demanded. 'Are you ill?'

'No.' She tried to steady her breathing. 'Is—is Nicky downstairs? Have you seen him?'

'No to both questions.' His fingers tightened on her arms until she could have cried out. 'What are you saying?'

Her voice was toneless. 'He's not in his room, and Yannina hasn't seen him. His door was open and someone had switched off the alarm.'

There was a greyish tinge suddenly under the swarthy skin as he stared at her. He reached out and gripped the door jamb for a moment as if he needed support, and beneath his breath he whispered something that might have been a prayer or an oath in Greek.

He looked at her grimly. 'I'll get a search going. Look in his room again—look in the bathroom in case he's hiding. You say the door was open. What about the window?'

For a moment she felt sick, then she said, 'No—the shutters were fastened,' and saw the relief on his face.

She searched as he'd told her, but Nicky wasn't hiding. If he had been, he would have come out when he heard their voices, she knew, unless he was too frightened. . . .

Frightened of what? The storm? Or something else?

She stood in the middle of the room, listening to the rapid sounds of activity elsewhere in the villa. So many rooms, so many places where a little boy could be lost, a child whom she had left sleeping deeply and safely.

Her palms were damp suddenly, and she wiped them mechanically on her floating skirt. She didn't like a single one of the thoughts that were beginning to press on her mind, but they had to be faced somehow.

With a new purpose she went out of the room, and towards the stairs. Alex was in the hall, and he looked up as she came towards him, his face taut. 'Well?'

She shook her head. 'No sign. I'm going to look outside.'

'He won't have gone out there,' he said with conviction. 'It is still pouring with rain, and you said he was frightened of storms.'

'Perhaps the storm hadn't started when he was taken out there,' she said.

'Taken?' The look sharpened to a glare, and his brown cheeks flushed ominously. 'Are you suggesting that someone in this house would do such a thing? Why?'

'Probably because he's his father's son,' Harriet said levelly. 'Or hasn't it ever occurred to you that someone got rid of Kostas too?'

She went past him and out into the rain and the darkness.

CHAPTER TEN

SHE was drenched to the skin within minutes, the thin cotton clinging uncomfortably round her limbs. Rain had made the paths slippery and she walked fast, but with care, pausing every few minutes to call, 'Nicky!'

As she reached the swimming pool, all the lights around it went on as if Alex, from the house, had guessed the route she had taken. She had to make herself look into the water, but the pool was empty except for the toy swan floating rather forlornly in the shallow end. Harriet bit her lip and hurried on.

The gate down to the beach stood wide. The ground seemed to fall away in front of her like a descent into hell, and she wished she had brought a flashlight, but there was not time to fetch one now. She slipped off her sandals and began to make her way slowly and painfully down the path, catching at shrubs and the branches of trees to steady her progress.

In the end she nearly fell over him. He was lying in a little crumpled heap at the side of the path, and she fell on her knees, touching him frantically, terribly afraid. The path was awash, and children older than Nicky had drowned in puddles before this. The relief when she felt his shallow breathing under her hands, and heard the slight moan he gave as she turned him, was enormous. He was soaked and cold, however, and next door to unconscious with a sizeable bump on his forehead, she discovered, her fingertips tenderly exploring. He might have other injuries—perhaps she shouldn't move him.

Above her on the path she heard the slither of other footsteps, and she flung back her head and almost screamed Alex's name, because it could be anyone coming down towards them in the darkness.

Alex said, 'Hush, *agape mou*. I am here.' He lifted her

gently to her feet, and she clung to him, her hands fierce with panic, her breath sobbing harshly in her throat. There were other people behind him—Andonis, she saw, and Yannina, her face twisted with anxiety.

She felt Alex's mouth brush her wet hair. He said, 'We must get him to the house. Can you walk or shall I help you?'

She disengaged herself from him, embarrassment taking the place of relief in her emotions. She had flung herself at him as if he was her hope of salvation.

'I can manage,' she muttered, averting her face.

Madame Marcos was standing in the hall as they all trooped in, Andonis carrying Nicky cradled protectively against his broad chest. She looked terrible, the usually immaculate coiffure dishevelled as if she had been clawing at it. Her hands were tearing at a lace-edged handkerchief. She started forward with a little cry, her face agonised, and Alex put a swiftly protective arm round her, speaking soothingly in his own language.

There was something strange and dreamlike about the whole scene, Harriet thought dazedly. In the distance she could hear the last growls of thunder as the storm finally retreated, and closer at hand above the splash of the rain through the open door, came the sound of a woman wailing and distraught.

She knew who it was. The hall was full of people, concerned, chattering and staring. Even Maria was there, her eyes nearly popping out of her head. There was only one person missing—the woman whose ambition for her son had been so disastrously underestimated. By all of us, Harriet thought numbly, remembering her own secret amusement as she'd watched Zoe Constantis trying to push Spiro and Maria together. And yet in her heart, surely she had always known that the older woman was no laughing matter. . . .

Alex was beside her. He said, 'The doctor is on his way.'

Her voice sounded far away. She said, 'That's good.

That's very good,' and the world tilted and slid slowly away.

The doctor was young and stocky with a heavy black moustache. In perfect but accented English he assured Harriet that her fainting fit had been caused by stress after the unfortunate events of the evening, and that sleep would soon restore her. This was the conclusion she had already drawn herself, but it was reassuring to have it confirmed.

She felt a fraud anyway, because once she had regained consciousness, and got out of her wet clothes and into a warm bath, she had begun to feel better almost at once. The chicken broth that a very subdued, red-eyed Androula had brought her had helped too, because, quite apart from anything else, she realised, she'd been *hungry*.

The doctor had calmed some of her fears about Nicky too. He had suffered other bumps and contusions as a result of his fall, but there were no broken bones, and he was only slightly concussed. Pneumonia was always a danger, but with care he felt it could be averted. He spoke with a certain amount of constraint, and Harriet guessed he was also thinking about the other patient he had been called to that evening. Presumably he had administered some kind of sedative, because the dreadful, spine-chilling wailing had stopped now.

'He is a strong healthy child, *thespinis*.' The doctor rose to leave. 'But it is a fortunate thing that he was found no later.' He smiled at her kindly. 'Although he was not born on the island, already our saint has him in his care. No harm will come to him now.'

It was a consoling thought, Harriet found, as she lay back against her pillows, agreeing meekly that it would be better for her to remain where she was rather than take a turn at sitting up with Nicky.

He asked her if he should leave her some tablets to help her sleep, but she refused. She felt exhausted, waves of tiredness seemed to be beating at her. She would have no trouble in sleeping, she told herself.

Nor did she. The trouble came in her dreams, dark, swamping confusions where everyone seemed her enemy, and she ran endlessly down black tunnels with Nicky in her arms, trying to escape the hatred which stalked behind. She was saying a name, crying it hysterically because the darkness was clamping round her, and this time he would not rescue her in time. It was like another miracle when his arms closed round her, lifting her up into light and safety and a warmth that made her bones ache.

She opened dazed eyes. She was lying wrapped in Alex's arms, her face buried into the curve of his throat.

With a stifled gasp she pulled herself away, out of his embrace.

'What are you doing here?'

'I came to make sure you were all right.' His voice was husky. 'You seemed to be having a nightmare, and I tried to comfort you. I did not mean to wake you. I'm sorry.'

She stared at him, shaken and incredulous. He wasn't actually in bed with her, just lying on top of it next to her, and that was bad enough.

She said, 'I'd hardly be likely to go on sleeping in the circumstances.'

His mouth twisted slightly. 'No? You did that night in London.' After a long, taut pause while she endeavoured to make sense of what he had just said, he added, 'You called my name then, too?'

She remembered that night, those dreams, the odd sense of loss in the morning when she had woken alone. Her voice sounded strangled. 'You—slept with me?'

'*You* slept, *agape mou*.' Propped on one elbow, he looked at her wryly. 'I spent an uncomfortable night fighting my conscience—and losing. I have cursed myself for being a fool a hundred times since then.'

'Don't!' Harriet pressed her hands against her burning face.

'Little hypocrite,' he said, amused. 'Are you really trying to pretend you do not know that I want you? And if I tell you that I know you want me too, will you call me names again?'

There was little point in denying it, she thought, staring down at the scalloped edge of the sheet she was clutching as if it was her shield and defender. Was it really only a few hours earlier that Alex had stirred her to that frenzied response? It seemed like a lifetime ago.

He talks about wanting, she thought. Not about love.

She said dully, 'No, I won't call you names. And I was—having a nightmare. I didn't realise I was making a noise.'

'Why should you?' he asked coolly. 'And don't sound apologetic, Harriet *mou*. After what has transpired in this house, you are entitled to a nightmare or two.'

She said in a muffled voice, 'I'm so sorry. It's so awful. Do you know why . . .?'

'Oh, yes.' The amusement vanished. He sounded tired and a little defeated. 'She had decided a long time ago that Spiro should be my heir. After Kostas, he was my nearest male relative. Perhaps you guessed?' She nodded. He went on, 'From speaking to my mother earlier, I gather that—my aunt encouraged the original rift between them and that when Kostas returned, she seized the opportunity to do him more harm. When he visited the safe, he was in too much of a temper to secure it properly, and she waited until the room was empty and then took the ring herself. It has been with her ever since, at the bottom of the bag in which she keeps her tapestries and threads,' he added with a kind of groan. 'My poor mother is shattered, as you can imagine. She has always known that Thia Zoe was envious because she felt my mother made a better marriage, but that her own sister could behave in such a way—cause her such agony—is beyond belief. And of course if my mother ever showed signs of softening towards Kostas, Thia Zoe was there, reminding her of the "wrong" he had done her.' He said something short and savage in his own language.

After a pause, he went on, 'Before Nicos ever came here she tried to turn my mother against him, by hinting that he might not be Kostas' child. She cited the indiscreet behaviour that some girls from England and other parts of Europe are guilty of when they come to Corfu, and said that your sister would share the same easy morals. She tried every way to turn my mother against the boy—but you probably know this?'

'I think I sensed it,' Harriet said. 'But there was nothing tangible. I knew she disliked me too, yet she seemed quite amenable when Spiro began taking me out, even though. . . .' She stopped abruptly.

'Even though what?'

She was flushing again. 'Even though she was trying to get Spiro to pay attention to Maria.'

'She intended Spiro to seduce you,' he said in a matter-of-fact tone. 'If he had done so, she would have used this as an excuse to have you sent away. She wished you to be sent back to England, because you were too close to Nicos, too protective. She has admitted this. She had convinced herself that I would never marry—and that with Nicos gone, that her son, or at least her grandson, would inherit the Marcos Corporation.' He paused, then said flatly, 'She knows better now.'

He meant that he was going to be married, she thought. She felt sick and dead inside, but she forced her voice to be as casual as his had been.

'Then why did she choose tonight . . .?'

'She is a sick woman. The news that Spiro had been sent to Athens—servants' gossip that it was because of you that he had been sent away must have finally unbalanced her. Androula had told her that we were out together, so she would have assumed that she was safe for several hours. Only—we came back.'

Harriet said, 'Yes.' Then, 'What are you going to do?'

'She cannot remain here. But to initiate any official intervention would cause a scandal, hurting many people. Instead I have decided it will be best if she returns to her house in the Peloponnese and remains there. Spiro of course will have to be told.' His mouth tightened. 'A task I do not relish.'

There were tears on her face suddenly. 'Poor Spiro!'

'Lucky Spiro,' he said grimly. 'When he has you to weep for him.'

He pulled her into his arms, his mouth hard on hers, and Harriet responded, her lips parting achingly, feverishly beneath the onslaught of his. Her body clung to his as if she had been magnetised, her arms winding round his neck in passionate abandon. All the doubts, the barriers she had imposed melted and dissolved as his kiss deepened. Alex turned her in his arms, his warm weight pressing her down into the softness of the mattress while his urgent mouth plundered kisses from her throat and shoulders.

His fingers slid aside the straps of her nightgown. He said gently, 'You do not need this, *agape mou*. Tonight you will wear only my kisses.'

She did not have time to feel shy. He had already unfastened the two decorous buttons that closed the bodice, and the gentle slide of his hands down her body as he uncovered her was a bewitchment in itself. But when it was done, and she was naked in his arms, she closed her eyes, a little afraid of the hunger she saw as he looked at her.

He said softly, 'Scared of me, *matia mou*! There is no need. If you want no more of me than this, I will hold you until you fall asleep.' He paused. 'Tell me which it is to be, my beautiful one, sleep or love.'

She couldn't say the word. It meant too much to her, while to him it was only a physical act. Instead she reached up, drawing him down to her, his mouth to hers, his hands to her breasts, and heard his hoarse sigh of pleasure against her lips.

The hunger was controlled like a leashed tiger as he aroused her gently, but with passionate skill. Loving him as she did, her compliance to his desire was ensured, but she soon learned he wanted more than that. Under his tender, sensuous tutelage she became mindless, rapturously acceptant as each new intimacy was unfolded to her, until at last there were no more secrets left.

Her body moved with his in a rhythm which bordered on savagery, the first confusion of pain and delight receding until only the pleasure was left, and she moaned aloud, her head falling back on the pillow as waves of sensation broke over her.

Alex kissed her, stroking the softness of her parted lips, and murmured to her in his own language. Harriet lay in his arms, dazed and trembling with joy. She pressed her mouth against the warmth of his shoulder, and stroked his face with her fingertips. She was lost for words, but that didn't seem to matter when touching and kissing seemed to say so much more.

Later they showered together, and she stood in the protective circle of his arms as the cool water cascaded over them.

She thought, 'It's not true, none of it can be true, and soon the door will open and someone will bring in breakfast and it will all have been a dream.'

Alex switched off the water. He said, 'You sigh, *agape mou*. Have I made you sad?'

She shook her head. 'I didn't know I could be so happy,' she confessed.

'Nor I.' His voice was quiet, almost reflective.

He wrapped her in one of the bath-sheets and carried her back to bed, his mouth warm and urgent against her body.

A long time later, a lifetime later, she opened her eyes. Alex was standing by the window, wearing his robe. As she stirred and sat up, he turned and smiled at her.

'*Kalimera*,' he said softly. 'Do you know how beautiful you are?'

Her face warmed, but with pleasure, not embarrassment. She was no longer shy when his dark arrogant gaze explored her body, instead she gloried in it.

She put out a hand to him. She said softly, 'It's lonely here.'

Alex groaned. 'You must not tempt me, my lovely one. It is almost light, and the servants will be moving around soon. You would not wish me to be found in your room.'

'I shouldn't mind.'

'Well, I should,' he said, the dark face suddenly austere. 'You must know as well as I do, Harriet, that this should not have happened.'

She felt cold suddenly, and hitched the sheet closer round her body. She said huskily, 'You're sorry that it did?'

'No.' His voice was impatient. 'How could I regret anything so—perfect, yet I did not intend. . . .' He paused, pushing a hand through his dark hair in a weary, slightly irritable gesture. 'I have to leave you now, Harriet, but later we must talk. You realise that?'

He came over to the bed and bending down kissed her mouth briefly and not too gently. She put her arms round his neck, wanting to draw him down to her, to hold him, to recapture even for a few minutes the passion and the tenderness they had shared, but Alex disengaged himself firmly.

'No,' he grated, and left her.

She was so cold now, she was shaking with it, huddling back against the pillows. With daylight, reality had come indeed, and it frightened her. She shivered. Last night had been the most precious experience of her life, but she had to face the fact that for Alex it could not have been the same, that for him she might simply have been one more girl in one more bed.

Oh no! she thought, pressing her fist against her trembling mouth. Alex was a sexual expert, he knew everything there was to know about women's bodies, how to gauge every kiss, every caress and intimacy in order to gain the response he wanted. And she had been no different. He had known she was a virgin, and the gentleness, the almost superhuman control he had shown while he was arousing her need not have been because he cared about her, but simply a means to an end, because he knew that in the end his restraint would reap its own reward.

As it had, she told herself numbly. She had never dreamed she was capable of such fevered, agonised passion, or that such heights of pleasure existed, let alone could be scaled.

Naïvely, she had seen Alex's possession of her as a beginning, but it could well be the opposite. All the old-fashioned laws about self-respect, about holding a man at arms' length in order to keep his interest, were coming back to haunt her. She had given Alex her body without reticence, loved him without holding back, presented him, in fact, with everything he wanted from her without ever questioning if it might be all he wanted.

In those dark hours of rapture, he had never once spoken of love, she realised unhappily. Loving had been her own connotation. His might be very different—no more than the gratification of a need.

Hurt clenched inside her. If Alex had stayed with her, she thought frantically, if she had woken up in his arms, warmed by his kisses she wouldn't be thinking like this. Yet he couldn't wait to get out of her room.

She turned over on to her stomach, convulsively burying her face in the pillow, trying to hold pain at bay. He had said that they would talk later, and perhaps then she would receive the reassurance she craved.

After a while she fell asleep, and when she next opened her eyes, the room was alive with sunlight, and Androula had brought in her breakfast. Harriet thanked her quietly, feeling selfconscious when the woman bent and retrieved her nightgown, still lying in a little crumpled heap on the floor where Alex had tossed it, and placed it expressionlessly on the bed.

She showered and dressed after she had drunk some

coffee, and left her room, intending to visit Nicky. But Androula was waiting for her in the corridor.

'Kyria Marcos wishes to speak to you, *thespinis*. She is waiting for you in the study.'

Harriet paused, frankly surprised, although she had expected there would be some sort of interview with Nicky's grandmother some time during the day.

She said slowly, 'But I was going to see Nicos. . . .'

'The doctor is with him, *thespinis*. And Kyria Marcos is waiting for you—now.' Androula was practically barring her way, and short of using force, Harriet couldn't see any way of getting past her. She wasn't looking forward to seeing Madame Marcos. It was going to be deeply embarrassing and difficult to discuss what had happened to Nicky when the person who had tried to harm him—who had inflicted such damage in the past—was Madame's own sister. Harriet would have to choose her words carefully.

Androula went with her, accompanying her to the study door, and even knocking and opening it for her. It was almost like being in custody Harriet thought with a slight inner grimace.

The room was shuttered and dim, and Madame was seated behind a large polished desk. She was very still, her hands folded in her lap, and her face, although ravaged, looked calm.

She said, 'I have to thank you, Miss Masters. I understand it was because of you that my grandson's peril was so quickly discovered.'

She spoke of thanks, but there was little evident gratitude in her face as she looked at Harriet, no warmth in the dark eyes. But then Harriet thought wryly, wasn't that just what she'd expected in the circumstances?

She said, 'You don't need to say any more, Madame. I love Nicky.'

'Yes, I am sure that you do.' Madame Marcos made a sudden restless movement. 'However, I am also sure that when you first came here, it was made clear that it could not be a permanent arrangement.'

Harriet felt herself tense into rigidity. She said, 'Yes—quite clear. Are—are you asking me to leave?'

'I think it is time that you did. Now that you are my son's mistress, you are hardly an appropriate companion for Nicos. You imagined I did not know?' she added harshly, as Harriet gasped and colour flared in her face. 'Do not attempt to deny it. I saw Alex with my own eyes going back to his own room this morning. I spoke with him before he left and he admitted he had spent the night with you.'

'Before—he left?' Harriet repeated, the words stinging her brain. 'You mean he isn't here?'

Madame Marcos said heavily, 'He is—escorting his aunt to her house in the Peloponnese.' Her tone sharpened. 'You look ill, Miss Masters. Perhaps you had better sit down. Clearly you have been cherishing some illusions about Alex's intentions towards you. Perhaps you even hoped to emulate your sister and contract a marriage within our family.' She shook her head. 'If so, you made a grave mistake. Alex will marry Maria Xandreou in the New Year.' She paused, studying Harriet gravely. 'He has been at fault in his behaviour towards you, *thespinis*, but——' she shrugged, 'he is very much a man, and you are an attractive girl. Alex has always taken and enjoyed whatever life has had to offer. But you must understand that your presence in this house, for Maria's sake, and for other reasons as well, is now an embarrassment, and it would be best for all of us if you were to leave.'

She hesitated again, then said levelly, 'If your—arrangement with my son had been a long-term one he would no doubt have made some financial provision for you. He is not ungenerous in such matters. As it is, I am to give you this.' She produced a long flat case, and pushed it across the desk towards Harriet.

A piece of jewellery, Harriet thought, staring at it numbly. The ultimate insult. She wanted to say something, but she could not make her voice work.

Madame Marcos was continuing. A seat had been

obtained for her on a plane to Athens, and another booking made from Athens to London. A maid would be sent to assist with her packing.

At last she found words. 'Am I—am I going to be allowed to say goodbye to Nicky?'

Madame Marcos' mouth tightened. 'Of course. We are not inhuman, Miss Masters, and you, I think are not a fool. You must have known that this—indelicate situation could not continue.'

Harriet sank her teeth into her lower lip. 'Yes,' she said tonelessly.

'I was certain you would be sensible.' Madame Marcos touched the box. 'You have forgotten your bracelet.'

'Is that what it is?' Harriet threw her head back. 'I haven't forgotten it. I just don't share your family's obsession with jewellery—the giving of it, or the withholding of it. Keep the bracelet for the next lady. After all, Alex is hardly likely to remain celibate until the New Year.' She sent the box sliding contemptuously back towards the older woman across the polished surface of the desk, and walked out.

She paused for a moment in the hall outside, struggling to maintain her composure, while a voice whispered crazily in her head, 'So that's it. Over. Finished.'

She wanted to cry and scream, but that was impossible. She didn't know how Alex's discarded women usually behaved, but she needed to salvage some rags of dignity, if she could.

One day, some day, perhaps she would be glad that he didn't know the truth, that she hadn't blurted out her love for him, but not yet. All she was aware of now was an emptiness as big as the world as she walked very slowly up the stairs to Nicky's room.

CHAPTER ELEVEN

HARRIET felt dispirited as she made her way back to Manda's house. The temporary job she had had since her return to London had ended that day, and the agency had nothing else for her at the moment. She felt ridiculously disappointed, because she had had every reason to believe that the temp job had been about to become a permanency. Roger Clayton who ran the office had spoken enthusiastically about her work, and a possible vacancy, but today he had simply shaken hands with her and muttered something about her efficiency.

At least she now had some money, she thought, and she could pay Manda and Bill something for allowing her to stay with them. They had been endlessly kind since she had arrived pale and hollow-eyed on their doorstep, insisting that she could stay as long as she needed to.

Harriet had been determined that it should only be a short stay. She had to pick up her life and go on. Her job with her old company had gone, of course, but the personnel department had taken her address and telephone number and promised they would be in touch if a new opportunity came up. So far, she had heard nothing, and she had begun to doubt if she ever would, so it wasn't yet feasible to start searching for a bed-sitter of her own again without a steady job to pay for it.

The children Manda was minding had all gone home, and Manda was sitting at the kitchen table with a freshly brewed pot of coffee in front of her as Harriet let herself in at the back door.

Manda smiled across at her. 'Well?'

Harriet shook her head. 'Ill,' she returned with an

effort at lightness. 'It's the dole next week, I'm afraid. Which reminds me——' She delved into her bag and produced her wage envelope.

'Keep it,' said Manda. 'You're airing the spare room for us, after all, and God knows, you don't eat enough to keep a fly alive.'

Harriet flushed slightly. Manda was a good cook, and it must have gone hard with her to sit opposite a guest who sat picking at her dinner most evenings. She had told Manda just enough to convince her that it would have been impossible for her to have stayed at the villa, without going into details over her involvement with Alex, and hoped they would interpret her general wanness and lack of appetite as pining for Nicky. But she had often intercepted a shrewd look from Manda and thought helplessly that her friend wasn't deceived for a minute, although she asked no embarrassing questions.

She said quietly, 'I'd rather pay my way—while I can.'

'Jobs with liveable wages are hard to come by,' Manda agreed. She poured coffee into a cup and pushed it across the table to Harriet. She went on reflectively, 'Of course you could always contact the Marcos Corporation and remind them that you only went to Corfu on the promise of a job when you returned.'

Harriet's flush deepened. She said, 'I'd rather die.'

'I thought so somehow,' Manda murmured, smiling into her own cup.

Harriet sighed abruptly. 'What do you want to know?' It might even be a relief to confide in someone, she thought.

Manda shrugged. 'What do I need to know?' she countered. 'You don't eat, and you don't sleep. Half the time you walk round in a dream. Nicky's a lovely child, but I can't believe he's had this profound effect.'

'No, he hasn't.' Harriet bit her lip. 'Although I miss him terribly. I—I worry about him too. He was still half-asleep when I saw him, and he started telling me something about "the witch". He could have nightmares for years about it all—or he could be ill.'

'I doubt it.' Manda patted her arm reassuringly, as Harriet's voice shook. 'Children are resilient little beasts, and everything that happened that night will probably just seem like a bad dream to him soon. It was hardly the psychological moment to get you to leave, though,' she added, her brow creased.

Harriet forced a smile. 'Oh, I don't know. I've had time to think since, and I believe in some ways Madame Marcos almost blamed me for what happened. I think she felt it was my presence which had pushed Madame Constantis to do as she did.'

'In other words, she'd rather have gone on sharing her home with a nut-case than learn the truth?' Manda questioned. She shook her head. 'I'll accept that you might have reminded her of things she'd rather pretend never happened, but so will Nicky, for heaven's sake, and she kept him. Drink your coffee,' she added prosaically.

Harriet obeyed shakily. After a pause, she said, 'You're right, of course. That was only part of it. She wanted to be rid of me because I was involved with— Alex.' She still found it hard to say his name.

Manda said carefully, 'When you say involved. . . .'

Harriet stared concentratedly into her cup as if she was trying to analyse the contents. 'That's exactly what I mean.'

'That's what I was afraid of,' Manda muttered, and gave an exasperated sigh.

'All right.' Harriet spread her hands defensively. 'Tell me what a fool I've been.'

Manda's mouth curved humorously. 'I'd say you know that already. Isn't that what you've been telling yourself night after night, walking up and down in your room? No, I haven't been listening at the door,' she added with a slight grimace. 'But I had to get up for the twins one night, and I saw your light on. I was afraid you might be ill.' She paused and said with unmistakable emphasis, 'You're not, are you?'

'No,' Harriet said tautly. 'No—I don't even have that.' It was something that had occurred to her once the first agony of her departure was over, that a new life could have been created from that one glorious night in Alex's arms. But she knew now that it was not to be.

'Don't talk like that,' Manda reproached. 'You know quite well from Nicky that bringing up a child singlehanded is no picnic. Even when the father is alive and well able to provide the financial support,' she added.

Harriet bent her head unhappily. 'I know. I know all that, but I still hoped. That's the sort of fool I've been.'

'Hell's bells,' Manda said helplessly. There was a long silence, then she said gently, 'Does he know how you feel?'

Harriet shook her head, and Manda's lips tightened. 'Well, he must be an insensitive bastard.'

'No.' Harriet was instantly defensive. 'I was careful never to let him guess.'

'While you were having a full-blooded affair?' Manda demanded sceptically. 'What did you do—tell him it was just your little hobby?'

'Hardly,' Harriet sighed. 'I don't think he'd have believed me. And it was a very short-lived affair,' she added with wry bitterness. 'One night, to be exact. Hardly a basis for declarations of undying love.'

'And certainly nothing to ruin the rest of your life for,' Manda told her.

She was right, and Harriet knew it. Those last few hours on Corfu had been full of forlorn hopes—that Alex would return by some miracle and prevent her from leaving, even that he'd snatch her off the plane before it could take off. But by the time she had waited at Athens for her connection, and endured the flight to London, a sober, more realistic train of thought had intervened. Alex wanted her to leave. His mother had only been carrying out his wishes. Her only hope of salvation was to forget him, to put everything that had happened out of her mind, no matter how long it took.

And if it meant cutting herself off from Nicky, then she
would have to do that too, however much it hurt.

She'd heard a saying once, 'Love makes time pass.
Time makes love pass.' Well, when time had done its
work, perhaps one day she could make contact again,
all passion spent. He would be married, of course. She
might even be married too, although nothing seemed
less likely.

She spent the weekend studying newspapers for
possible jobs, and writing endless letters of application
for anything that seemed of interest, not just in the
capital, but all over the country. A change of scene
might be what she needed, she thought.

On Monday it rained, and she spent a depressing day
going the rounds of more temp agencies, getting her
name on their books. Everywhere there seemed to be
retrenchment, and she wasn't offered much, apart from
a week's audio typing in ten days' time. It was late
afternoon by the time she made her way back to
Manda's feeling a little footsore, and wondering rather
fatalistically if she would ever have a regular job
again. . . .

She was walking up the path, when the door opened
and Manda leapt out at her, a child in her arms and
two more clinging to her long skirt.

'Thank heavens you're back!' she exclaimed. 'That
Greek's been on the telephone. Oh, honey, not him,' she
added woefully, as she took in Harriet's sudden
tautness. 'The other one—Mr Philippides.'

'But how did he know where I was?' Harriet
demanded.

'Search me. But he wants you to go to his office as
soon as possible. It's something about Nicky.' Manda's
eyes looked compassionately at Harriet's paling cheeks.
'He said it was pretty urgent, but he wouldn't go into
details.'

Harriet's mouth trembled. 'There was a chance—just
a chance of pneumonia. Oh, Manda, do you think . . .?'

'I don't know what to think, except that you'd better

do as he asks and get over there right away. He's left his number, so that I can phone and tell him you're on your way.'

Harriet lingered. 'Perhaps if I phoned he'd tell me. . . .'

'Go on!' Manda gave her a little push. 'If by any remote chance it is an emergency, he may want you to go with him somewhere. What about your passport? Have you got that?'

'It's in my bag.' Harriet felt sick. Nicky, she thought, ill—or worse. Nicky calling for her. It might already be too late. 'I'll go at once.'

'I'd come with you,' said Manda, 'only——' she gestured expressively at her small hangers-on. 'Will you let me know—whatever the news?'

'Of course I will.' Tiredness forgotten, Harriet began to run back the way she had come.

The journey seemed endless. She began to wonder what time Mr Philippides' office closed, and whether she would arrive in time. It would be torture if it was all shut up, and she had to go back to Manda's and wait on tenterhooks until the following day. She splurged on a taxi for the last few miles, and sat on the edge of her seat nervously watching the traffic, silently cursing every hold-up. Her destination reached, she thrust some money into the driver's hand after a cursory glance at the meter, and ran breathlessly up the steps. The commissionaire swung the door open, and by some miracle there was a lift waiting at the ground floor.

Outside the door to Mr Philippides' suite of offices, she paused and took one or two steadying breaths.

He stood up as she was shown into his room, with a welcoming smile that she did not feel capable of returning.

She said hoarsely, 'Nicky—what's happened to him?'

'Miss Masters—*thespinis*—sit down. Let me order my secretary to bring you some coffee.'

She moistened her dry mouth with the tip of her tongue. 'I don't want coffee, I just want to know about

Nicky. Please—I've come all this way. You must tell me!'

His face was compassionate as he looked at her. 'All in good time, dear young lady. But first that coffee.'

He went past her into the outer room, and Harriet buried her face in her hands with a little groan. If he really felt so strongly that she would need a stimulant, it had to be bad news.

She heard the door re-open, and looked up, summoning all her courage.

Alex stood watching her, his dark face set in grim, accusing lines.

Her lips parted in a soundless gasp. Then she whispered pleadingly, 'Nicky?'

'Apart from missing you, he is perfectly well,' he said harshly.

'Then—why the message?' It was so hard to speak, she felt as if she was using someone else's voice.

His mouth twisted sardonically. 'If I had said it was myself who wished to see you, would you have come?' He saw her flinch, and the dark brows drew together. 'I thought not.'

'You used Nicky,' she accused. 'How could you?'

He gestured impatiently. 'Nicky is at my hotel at this very moment. I assumed you would wish to see him. Was I wrong?'

Harriet shook her head.

'Then you shall,' he said almost conversationally. 'For a price.'

She lifted her head and stared at him, her face revealing her sense of shock. Her mouth moved slowly. 'What price?'

Alex gave a short angry laugh. 'Not what you seem to think. Just a talk—the one you cheated me of when you left Corfu so precipitately.'

She looked away. 'I think everything has been said already.'

'Well, I do not. Show me your hands, Harriet *mou*.'

She hesitated. 'I don't understand—why . . .?'

'Don't argue with me.' His voice softened dangerously. 'Just show me your hands.'

Mutely she extended them, palms upwards. He took
them in his, his fingers closing in a painful grip, turning
them over, his eyes flicking over the slim, ringless
fingers.

He said, 'So you are not engaged, or married yet.'

She pulled her hands away, hating the deep aching
need that his lightest touch could engender. 'No, of
course not.'

'Then what has gone wrong? Is it possible you
confessed something to your lover which has made
him have second thoughts? Perhaps a dowry might
sweeten him?' He reached in his pocket and drew out
a flat jeweller's case. Harriet recognised it at once. He
flicked it open and tossed it into her lap. The
sapphires and diamonds in the bracelet glittered
coldly at her. He said smoothly, 'I hope this will
compensate your fiancé for the loss of his—virgin
bride.'

She shivered, pushing at the box with unsteady hands
so that it slid off her lap on to the carpeted floor. 'I
don't want it.'

'Ah,' he said, bitterly mocking. 'You wanted
something better, perhaps. My mother's ruby ring, for
example.'

'Manda was right,' she said unevenly. 'You are an
insensitive bastard, Alex.'

'I advise you not to call me names. Since you left me,
I have had time and leisure to think of a few for you,'
he said bleakly.

'I don't want to hear them.' Harriet stood up. 'If the
talk you spoke of was just to give you another
opportunity to insult me with this——' she touched the
bracelet with the toe of her shoe—'then I'd rather not
hear any more of that, either.'

'Perhaps you had better consult your future husband
before you reject such a valuable gift.'

'I have no future husband,' she said stormily. 'Yes,

I'd like to see Nicky, but if it means I have to be tormented by you, Alex, then I'll go home instead.'

He stared at her. 'Spiro told me there was a man in England. He said he had it from your own lips even though you had denied it to me. When you ran out on me, I told myself it could only be to return to him.'

'Yes, I told Spiro something of the sort,' she admitted wearily. 'But only to stop him getting any ideas.'

'You were afraid he might make love to you.' He shook his head. 'He would not have done so.'

'What makes you so sure?'

He bit his lip. 'Because he knew that I wanted you for myself.'

'And nothing must stand in the way of what you want. That's right, isn't it, Alex? And nothing did, because you had me. Or have you forgotten?'

'No,' Alex said softly. 'I have forgotten nothing.'

The look in his eyes brought her to her feet. Harriet said hoarsely, 'Don't come near me! Don't touch me, or I'll scream the place down!'

He sighed impatiently. 'Harriet *mou*. You are in the London offices of the Marcos Corporation. You might scream your head off, but no one would come to your assistance, even if I were to rape you here on the carpet.' He paused. 'Except that we both know it would not be rape.'

She turned towards the door, aware that her pulses were hammering tumultuously and afraid that by some sensual perception he would know it too. She said quietly, 'I would like to go now, please. Give—give Nicky my love when you see him.'

Before she could reach the door he was at her side, his hand closing round her arm with a grip that hurt. 'You may give him your message yourself,' said Alex with a smile which did not reach his eyes.

'Let go of me!' she panted.

'Struggle or make a scene, and I will carry you down to the car,' he warned, and he was totally serious, she knew.

The place seemed deserted, but Harriet knew that was only an illusion. There were dozens of pairs of eyes watching them all the way to the lift, then across the foyer to the door and the car beyond. Alex's grip on her arm didn't relax by so much as an iota as he steered her down the steps and into the car.

She said huskily, 'This is an outrage!'

'You think so? Wait until you discover my plans for the remainder of the evening.'

He was actually laughing at her, she thought furiously, not deigning him a reply or even a glance, as she sat rigidly staring out of the window.

It was no real surprise to find the hotel suite empty, but she felt panic rising within her just the same.

She said, 'You lied to me.'

'I told you the truth. Nicky is in fact in the adjoining suite with my mother. We shall be joining her for dinner later. You may see him then.'

She drew a sharp breath. 'Dinner with your mother? Are you insane?'

He gave her a faint smile. 'I don't think so, Harriet *mou*. You are thinking perhaps of the last time you spoke to my mother. But then, you see, she was suffering from a misapprehension—several of them, in fact.'

She said faintly, 'I don't understand.'

Alex waved her to one of the sofas. 'Sit down and I will explain. My mother has a godchild to whom she feels a strong sense of duty. A few years ago she tried to arrange a marriage between the girl and my brother Kostas, and you know what became of that. So instead my mother got it fixed in her head that Maria and I would make each other happy. It has taken me a long time to convince her that the man capable of enduring Maria and her tantrums probably does not exist on this planet, but at last she believes me.'

It was very quiet in the suite. Harriet's hands were clasped together so tightly that the knuckles showed white.

'Her second misapprehension concerned you, *agape mou*. As you know, I did not want the servants to see me leaving your bedroom. What I did not bargain for was that Mama had been sitting up with Nicos and was on her way back to her own room to rest. She saw me. She was very angry, as you can imagine. She has few illusions about me, but I have never made a habit of seducing girls under the roof she shares with me. When she confronted me that morning there was little I could say in my defence. Besides, she was in a highly charged emotional state over—Thia Zoe. It seemed wiser to say as little as possible. But I did let her know that you were not merely a casual sexual fling.'

He sighed, then said flatly, 'This worried her. She had lost Kostas to your sister. She was afraid that she would lose me to you, so she decided to send you away, and use the bracelet she knew I had bought you from Athens as some kind of—kiss-off payment.' He paused. 'When I found you'd gone, and she admitted what she had done, I could not believe it. You see, *agape mou*, I had convinced myself that you were in love with me, and it seemed impossible that you should have given credence to what she had told you and just—left. I thought that you would have contacted me somehow, if not from the villa then at least when you changed planes at Athens, and asked for an explanation, or told me where you were going—an address—something. If Philippides had not happened to call the firm you used to work for, who told him where you were staying, it might have been weeks before I found you.'

Harriet stared down at a minute fleck on one of her nails as if mesmerised by it. She could not speak.

Alex went on, 'And then Spiro told me reluctantly about this man you had mentioned, and it seemed to explain why there had been no message—not even a word of goodbye. I felt sick to my stomach, so I took myself to Athens and got very drunk.'

She found her voice. 'And your mistress in Athens? What about her?'

'Spiro again,' he said savagely. 'No, Harriet, I did not visit Penelope. I had already said goodbye to her on a previous occasion. She knew from the start of our relationship that it would end as soon as I met the woman I intended to marry.'

'Poor Penelope! Did you get her a bracelet too?'

He swore. 'No, I did not! I bought your bracelet, not as a farewell, but to fasten round your wrist when I asked you to marry me, you little fool!'

She said slowly, 'You—wanted to marry me?'

'Why do you speak as if it is in the past?' he asked impatiently. 'Yes, I want to marry you. Why else should I be here? I told myself that this man could not mean anything to you, that if he had, you could not have surrendered to me as you did, my sweet one.'

He took a step towards her, and she shrank back against the cushions. 'Don't come near me!'

For a moment he stared at her, then he gave a slight shrug and sat down at the other end of the sofa. Perversely, Harriet was disappointed. She needed to keep a clear head, and if he touched her again, she would melt, she would die, but on the other hand she desperately needed him to take her in his arms and kiss away all the doubts, unhappiness and sheer panic which were making her wretched.

He had said he was not going to marry Maria, that he intended to marry her, and she could have been dazzled by that—except that there still had been no word of love.

That was what she had to remember. And that he had said he thought she loved him, which meant he was probably convinced she would fall into his arms without question.

She asked steadily, 'Why do you want to marry me? For—Nicky's sake?'

He smiled. 'It would solve many problems, as I am sure you agree.'

She bit her lip. 'And that's all?' she asked tautly.

The smile widened, and his dark eyes moved

lingeringly over her body. 'Why, no,' he said softly.
'Perhaps—also—to give my child a name.'

'I'm not pregnant,' she snapped, and he threw back
his head and laughed.

'But then you still have not heard my plans for the
remainder of the evening, *agape mou*.'

'And I'm not going to bed with you either.' She was
back on the defensive again.

He lifted his brows. 'No? Then it will prove a very
frustrating marriage for us both.'

Harriet snatched up her bag and got to her feet, her
heart thudding painfully. 'There'll be no marriage,' she
said. 'You—you've had the talk you wanted, so please
may I go now.'

Alex was beside her as she reached the door. He
twisted the strap of her bag from her fingers and tossed
it aside, then picked her up in his arms and carried her
effortlessly across the room to a door that could only
lead to a bedroom. Harriet kicked and squirmed
furiously, but he didn't even seem to notice. He stopped
suddenly, and his mouth came down on hers in a fierce
relentless kiss that seemed to go on for ever. Then he
dropped her, winded and breathless, in the very centre
of the kingsize bed.

Harriet lay, looking up at him, her eyes enormous as
he shrugged out of his elegant jacket and tugged off his
tie. As he began to unbutton his shirt, she rolled away
from him across the bed, but he was too quick for her,
dragging her back ruthlessly, and kneeling astride her,
pinioning her between his thighs to control her angry
struggles.

'If you touch me, you'll be sorry!' she spat at him.

'If I do not touch you, we shall both be sorry.' He
pulled off his shirt and tossed it on to the floor, and his
hand was caressing her, tracing the curve of her face, the
line of her jaw and throat, until her body seemed one
silent scream of pain and longing.

She tried to hit him, and he took both her wrists in
one hand and held them above her head while he

started to undress her. His mouth sought hers, but she turned her head away sharply in rejection, so he began to kiss her body instead, the warm seduction of his lips and tongue on her skin arousing a fever in her blood which was soon raging out of control.

She could fight him at a distance, but when she was lying in his arms like this, his lips and fingers moving over her in an exploration of heart-stopping intimacy, then she was fighting herself, all her deepest and most secret needs and cravings.

He released her wrists and her hands cradled his head, her fingers tangling in the thickness of his dark hair, her palms sliding smoothly over the planes and angles of his face.

Alex lifted himself away from her, staring down at her, his dark eyes hungry and intent. 'Now tell me you don't want me,' he said between his teeth.

Pain was like a stone in her throat. She said, 'But wanting isn't love, Alex. And it takes love to make a marriage.'

He was silent and very still for a moment, and then he sighed, a deep shuddering breath that seemed to shake his whole body.

He said in a dry, bleak voice, 'Was I wrong, then? But if this——' his hand touched her bare breast like a kiss '—and this—is all there is, then it is enough for a beginning, Harriet *mou*. Oh, my sweet one, I can teach you to need me in all the other ways, to trust me. Don't leave me again, my precious heart. Stay with me. I can make you love me.'

Hope was unfurling deep inside her like the petals of some strange, exotic flower.

On a whisper, she said, 'You—love me?'

He said huskily, 'Almost from the first, *agape mou*. How could you not know?'

'How could I?' she protested. That inner radiance was spreading, glowing in her face and eyes, curving her mouth. 'Why didn't you tell me?'

'Did it need words? And at first, I admit, I tried to

fight it. There had been Kostas—and it seemed there would always be too many obstacles, too many barriers between us. But you were in my heart, *matia mou*, almost before I knew it.'

He bent and kissed her, his mouth tender almost reverent.

Harriet said shyly, 'But you were so cold to me. . . .'

He sighed. 'I thought it was Spiro that you wanted. I came back from Athens half crazy for you. I'd intended to suggest that you take that cruise I mentioned—but with me instead of alone, and then I saw you with Spiro and it was like a knife in the guts.'

She stroked his cheek. 'He was only being kind. I think he knew I needed a friend.'

'I did not always appreciate his brand of friendship,' he said grimly. 'That day on the beach, for example, I was ready to kill him. I gave myself away completely. His first words to me afterwards were, "So you have been caught at last, cousin".'

'You did rather overreact.' She smiled at him. 'Poor Spiro! He's had a very rough time lately. We must be kind to him.'

'But not too kind,' Alex threatened mockingly, then sobered. 'Yes, he has been shocked and grieved beyond words, but he recognises now that his mother is a sick woman.' He paused. 'And I have made sure there is extra work, extra responsibility to keep his mind occupied.'

'And your mother?' she asked quietly. 'How have you managed to reconcile her?'

'I will not pretend it has been easy, but she is a determined woman, *agape mou*, not a heartless one. But for Thia Zoe's intervention I think she would eventually have forgiven Kostas and welcomed your sister. Now she has learned a lesson. She is not prepared to make the same mistake with me, and that is why she came to London with me—to make amends to you, to prove she is prepared to accept you as my wife.' He looked into her eyes. 'Tell me that you will marry me, Harriet, my dear love.'

Her hands stroked the strength of his naked shoulders, and moved provocatively down his back. A laugh quivered in her voice. 'It isn't exactly a conventional proposal, but I think I could be persuaded—Alex *mou*.'

He said huskily, 'Then I shall lose no time in persuading you.'

His lips took hers in warm possession, and her arms closed round him, her body yielding and eager, accepting love, accepting all life had to offer in her share of paradise with Alex.

The Perfect Gift.

Four new exciting novels from Mills and Boon:

SOME SORT OF SPELL – by Frances Roding
– An enchantment that couldn't last or could it?

MISTRESS OF PILLATORO – by Emma Darcy
– The spectacular setting for an unexpected romance.

STRICTLY BUSINESS – by Leigh Michaels
– highlights the shifting relationship between friends.

A GENTLE AWAKENING – by Betty Neels
– demonstrates the truth of the old adage 'the way to a man's heart…'

Make Mother's Day special with this perfect gift.
Available February 1988. Price: £4.80

From: Boots, Martins, John Menzies, W H Smith,
Woolworths and other paperback stockists.

TAKE 2 MILLS & BOON
BEST SELLER ROMANCES
ABSOLUTELY FREE

Having just enjoyed a Best Seller Romance from Mills & Boon, here is a special introductory offer that is guaranteed to appeal to you. Two top-selling Best Sellers **absolutely free** – plus a unique Mills & Boon tote bag with our compliments. It's our way of introducing you without commitment to our regular reader service. All we ask is that you take your 2 free Best Sellers (the most successful Romances republished by popular demand) and tote bag. Then, if you enjoy them (as we're sure you will) take out a regular subscription. Now turn the page and see the other benefits a subscription brings you...

▶▶▶

As a regular subscriber you'll enjoy

★ **FOUR WONDERFUL NEW BOOKS** – every two months, reserved at the printers and delivered direct to your door by Mills & Boon.

★ **NO COMMITMENT** – you are under no obligation and may cancel your subscription at any time.

★ **FREE POSTAGE AND PACKING** – unlike many other book clubs we pay all the extras.

★ **FREE REGULAR NEWSLETTER** – packed with exciting competitions, horoscopes, recipes, and handicrafts... plus information on top Mills & Boon authors.

★ **SPECIAL OFFERS** – specially selected books and offers, created exclusively for Reader Service subscribers.

★ **HELPFUL, FRIENDLY SERVICE** – from the ladies at Mills & Boon. You can call us any time on 01- 684 2141.

With personal service like this, and wonderful stories like the one you've just read, is it really any wonder that Mills & Boon is the most popular publisher of romantic fiction in the world?

This attractive white canvas tote bag, emblazoned with the Mills & Boon rose, is yours absolutely FREE!

Just fill in the coupon today and post to:
MILLS & BOON READER SERVICE, FREEPOST,
PO BOX 236, CROYDON, SURREY CR9 9EL.

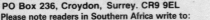